STORY OF
HARRY SINGH &
SOPHIE KAUR

STORY OF HARRY SINGH & SOPHIE KAUR

Madan Das

PARTRIDGE

A Penguin Random House Company

ISBN: Hardcover   978-1-4828-2136-9
            Softcover   978-1-4828-2135-2
            eBook   978-1-4828-2134-5

To order additional copies of this book, contact
Partridge India
000 800 10062 62
orders.india@partridgepublishing.com

www.partridgepublishing.com/india

CONTENTS

THE PARADE

The parade commander brought the parade to a perfect halt on the reviewing line, after the march past in column, in front of the reviewing officer Lieutenant General Eric Hodson, Advisor to His Excellency Viscount Mountbatten, Viceroy of India. Lieutenant General Hodson had never married and had spent his entire life in India, in the service of the crown, like his distant grand-uncle William Hodson. While his illustrious ancestor had laid down his life while suppressing the Indian Mutiny in 1858 on the battle field in Lucknow, his descendant standing on the saluting dais today was providing his services to the Empire sitting behind a desk, in non-military appointments, trouble-shooting for the British Government. This Hodson had been an officer on special duty with a number of governors at Madras and the British Government in New Delhi and was considered an expert on India. It was said that if he didn't know something about India then it wasn't worth knowing. So much so, that even the India office in London always took his view before taking any major decision concerning, Britain's "jewel in the crown". Hence, it came as no surprise when Lord Mountbatten on assuming his Vice-Regal duties in India on 21 February, 1947, took him in his secretariat as Advisor.

He had been sent to Wellington by the viceroy himself to give away the medals for gallantry, on behalf of His Majesty King George VI, to the awardees of the Madras Regiment who had shown courage beyond the call of duty in combat, against the enemy in battles, during World War-II. And that's how Hodson found himself on the saluting dais this 4th day of May 1947, as the reviewing officer of the parade.

1

It wasn't every day that such a high ranking and well-connected dignitary schedules a visit to a relatively small army establishment and hence the parade commander, Colonel JRH Tweed wanted the parade to conclude on a winning note, given that his beloved Madras Regiment had also attained glory on the conquest of Srirangapatnam on this very day, 148 years ago in 1799. So far it had gone off quite well. Tweed made much of himself, in his mind, when he heard the combined thunder of 279 pairs of army boots banging into the gravel of the 10,000 square yard parade ground of the Madras Regimental Centre, Wellington, like one, with, what the British Indian Army called josh, as the parade came to a flawless halt.

A commission into the British Indian Army was every cadet's dream at Sandhurst during training and Tweed was no different. Getting into it was however, another matter. The British Indian Army which Tweed and his ilk at Sandhurst, were so keen to join was based on pure one class regiments. These classes were ethnic or religious or regional groups, which meant that a regiment consisted of personnel from either one religion or one region or a caste or a single community. This system had been put in place by the East India Company two hundred years back, more out of convenience than strategic planning. The British soon become aware of the inherent advantages of this arrangement in view of the fact that a village or community elder was generally an NCO in the unit, who kept the recruits in line and also took care of their minor problems. Inculcating Army obedience into the recruits was also easy because Indian family and village or community already had a set of strict rules which were followed in day to day rural life and hence military discipline was effortlessly accepted by the draftees. The one class unit not only ensured discipline within the unit but also ensured that no one showed cowardice in the face of the enemy for fear of being shamed within their class or community. Accordingly a slew of one class regiments—Madras, Sikh, Maratha Light Infantry and so forth, were raised and each one of these had a history of unparalleled valour.

This structure instituted by the East India Company turned out to be so good that it has been in vogue ever since its inception, except that a multiple class configuration was imposed on some regiments because of their questionable conduct in the Indian Mutiny of 1857 against the crown. The Madras Regiment where the parade was now ongoing was not touched by this policy since the Madrasis had sided with the British during the mutiny. Thus from modest commencements, the British Indian Army had come a long way and honed itself into an exceptional fighting institution attracting British Cadets and Officers who had to vie with each other to be a part of this elite organization.

Colonel Tweed, now a battle hardened soldier considered him-self lucky to have been commissioned into the British Indian Army after passing out. He had worked his arse out while training at the academy to attain a superior grade to enable him to be positioned high in the final merit list. His hard work had paid off. His name at passing out was in the top dozen gentlemen cadets of his batch and his good ranking in the Order of Merit had assured the then young Tweed, a berth in the British Indian Army. Young Tweed had made one wish while training at the Royal Military Academy Sandhurst; to be commissioned into the British Indian Army and that had been fulfilled. He had made yet another wish while serving as a young subaltern with The Madras Regiment, this second wish was to command a battalion in real battle, this second wish too had been more than fulfilled; he had commanded a battalion belonging to the oldest regiment of the British Indian Army and that too during war on the Indo-Burma Border. It was here that a King's Commissioned Indian native officer, Captain RS Noronha, belonging to the Regiment had been awarded the Military Cross for bravery during the famous and decisive Battle of Tamu. He considered himself lucky to have been selected by Captain Sir Arthur Hope KCIE, MC, the out-going Colonel-in-Chief and General Archibald Nye, GCIE, KCB, KBE, MC the present Colonel-in-Chief of the Regiment, to take over as The Centre Commandant. Colonel Tweed shook himself out of his reverie; the parade was far from over. He took a deep breath before bellowing out the next word of command.

'Parr..rraade, Will Advance, L..l.e.f..ft, Turn.'

The British Army Drill uses Fronts & Flanks style of words of command and their Drill Manual accordingly splits the word of command into four parts. The initial part of the word of command is the "Identifier" i.e. "Parade", this is followed by the "Precautionary" part, in this case "Will Advance", to enable the parading troops to get ready to face the parade commander, then comes the "Cautionary" part which is given in a prolonged manner i.e. "Left". It is, however, the last or executive part of the word of command, which has to be crisp and precise; Col Tweed had correctly, done that, just as laid down in the drill manual when he snapped the word "Turn", at which, 276 officers, Viceroy Commissioned Officers and Other Ranks of the Madras Regiment marshalled in four companies of 21 files each, in three rows and their company & platoon commanders, turned 90 degrees left and the colour party comprising the ensign for the colour and the two escorts to the colour turned only 45 degrees, as one, pivoting on the ball of their right foot and heel of the left, the right foot heel raised and left foot flat on the ground both legs locked at the thighs and braced. There-after a distinct pause for a couple of seconds and then with lightning speed the right foot raised in such a way that the right thigh became parallel to the ground and the leg below the knee perpendicular to it, making a perfect inverted 'L' of the right leg. Then bringing the right foot crashing down, flat, so that the Dress Regulations, mandated 13 metallic hob-nails, set in four rows in the configuration 2-3-4-4 at the toe-end and the metallic horse-shoe at the heel-end of the sole of their shining black ankle boots struck the drill square asphalt simultaneously creating a thunderous clap which reverberated in the enclosed confines of the 87 year old, architectural master piece called Wellington Barracks.

The colour party now executed a "Spin-wheel" by pivoting on its centre in which the ensign marked-time, the outer escort marched forward but the inner escort marched back-wards, so that the entire colour party faced the saluting base and was in line with the centre row of the parade, in front of the band. The spin-wheel manoeuvre is not mentioned in any drill manual but yet has been carried out by the British Army since decades during ceremonial parades and its complex nature continues to be a discussion point within military circles.

Col Tweed next commanded the parade to "Order Arms" followed by an "Open Order March" which resulted in the colour party coming in line with the front row. He subsequently ordered the parade for an "Inward Dress" at which the front row troops turned their necks and faced inwards towards the centre of the parade and shuffled to come into a straight alignment with the colour party. This manoeuvre was done to straighten any kinks in the parade formation which may have resulted as a consequence of the march past, around the drill square. This tidying up movement resulted in disposing the parade into a perfect geometrical array. Afterwards he brought the parade to "Stand at Ease" which was the signal to the Reviewing Officer to commence his address.

General Hodson the Reviewing Officer glanced towards the spectator area while waiting for the lectern and microphone of the public address system to be positioned on the saluting base in front of him. He noticed that, as always, the enclosures nearest to the saluting dais were occupied by British and Anglo-Indian invitees and native army officers and their families and these were chock-a-block. He was aware that there were a few British families living in Conoor and nearby Ooty, British name for the native Ootacamund. The British owned the tea estates spread on the rolling slopes of the Nilgiri Hills around these two small and scenic hill stations. General Hodson reckoned that a good number of the British spectators must be tourists, from the sweltering coastal belt & blistering plains of South India, spending this hot summer month of May of 1947, in the salubrious Nilgiris which literally translates to Blue-Mountains, so named because these hills have a natural Indigo hue.

The Anglo-Indians in the stands were descendants of inter-racial unions between Indians & Europeans. This multiracial amalgamation was first spawned during the violent era preceding the brutal native mutiny of 1857. This epoch had witnessed the Dutch, the French & the Portuguese, vying for space to exploit and dominate the spice trade & colonise Southern Indian states to the chagrin of the local Indian Principalities. This had led to constant battles between the contenders. At the end of it all, British superiority, with dominant support of Madrasi troops ably led by a Major Stringer and competently assisted by a young Robert Clive, had prevailed and except for a couple of small French & Portuguese Enclaves, countries of continental Europe had, by and large, been ousted. While peace had been made with local principalities by the Brits, it did not last long, due to wrong policies of the British, especially Lord Dalhousie's "doctrine of lapse" which in essence meant that if a male heir was not born to an Indian state ruler, his kingdom would lapse to the British.

This unjust canon and a few minor issues sparked off a bloody mutiny in 1857, which was smothered with an iron hand by the British. This resulted in the British Government assuming direct control over the dominion from the East India Company. The first step initiated by the British Crown on taking over direct governance of India in 1858 in the aftermath of the mutiny, was to punish the active mutineers who had gone underground and therefore escaped being put to sword or hanged during the suppression of the rebellion. Such partakers were caught & tried. They were then sentenced to be either hanged or banished or put in dungeons as punishment by the English rulers. The few army regiments blamed for participating in the mutiny too had to be penalized to send the message home; therefore as punishment, these guilty regiments were reduced in numbers or were cleverly reorganized into a multiclass configuration to avoid a repetition of the 1857 uprising. The change to multiple class composition, in such faulted regiments was however not an upheaval, since one class uniqueness at company level was still retained in these reorganized regiments. Consequently, such regiments may comprise four different classes in their new avatar but each of its four companies continued to have just one class constitution; thus retaining the advantages of a single class structure in their innovative incarnation. The communities who had remained loyal to the crown were, naturally, gifted with more quotas in the army. While handsome reparations were obtained from the guilty chieftains and kings, the British on their side repealed the unfair doctrine of lapse. This put an end, once and for all, to the defiance, plotting and stratagem of the smaller Indian kingdoms and principalities to oust the English. The British were now firmly in the saddle.

In this period of turbulence, upheaval & chaos, several Dutch, Portuguese and French runaways, stragglers, deserters and idlers had taken Indian wives & concubines and settled in India. Later some home sick and lonesome British soldiers stationed in Indian garrisons and their equally forlorn British subjects working with the ever expanding Indian Railways had also taken Indian wives or mistresses, either due to sexual necessity or out-right love. The progeny of these dalliances was obviously of mixed blood. In the West, in the Americas or the Caribbean, descendants of white masters and their Negro slaves were known as Mulattos or Creoles depending on the nationality of the white parent, however no such terms were applied to the children of white fathers and coloured Indian mothers in India and the new hybrid race, so set off, colloquially came to be known as Anglo-Indians and their numbers swelled with passage of time. These Anglo-Indians, some of whom were sitting in the stands today, were now prominently employed with the Indian Railways, the tea gardens and the Indian Army, as officers.

Hodson's eyes continued to scour the stands in an outwardly casual manner but in reality he was trying to ferret out some one and at last his wandering eyes came to rest on her. She was seated on a sofa in the front row of the VIP enclosure wearing a low cut scarlet dress, red high heel court-shoes and a floral hat. Eric Hodson's heart beat accelerated as soon as he had set his eyes upon her. He got the impression that she was not looking at him but rather through him at some point beyond the dais, when suddenly she uncrossed her legs and opened them ever so slightly. Her seductive signal sent a rush of adrenaline into his blood stream which kick-started a stirring in his loins. Sophie's presence and her sexually inviting gestures always did this to him.

In his younger days Eric had been wild and libidinous and on many occasions mixed business with pleasure but now he was older in years and holding a respectable position, which had, subdued him. Though the site of his flame, Sophie, had made him horny, he could not possibly let his thoughts race towards the erotica especially now when he was standing on the saluting dais being watched by hundreds of spectators, press reporters and photographers diligently clicking away at

7

appropriate and interesting subjects; a bulge in the gabardine trousers of his ceremonial service dress at this juncture would become a spectacle of historic proportions. He had more important official business to attend-to and business came first. Pleasure would come later, at the appropriate time, for which he had deliberately asked Tweed not to programme any official engagement for him after the parade for the remainder of the day. So he and Sophie not only had the remaining day but also the whole night to themselves, except of course, for a couple of hours when he would have to leave her to attend the formal dinner night programmed in his honour by the regiment. With great effort Hodson willed himself to tear away his eyes from her as he attempted to banish her from his thoughts. Hodson glanced in the direction towards which Sophie's gaze continued to remain focussed to try and ascertain her point of interest on the parade ground but all he could see was the geometrically arrayed parade standing at ease. He mentally made a note to ask her on whom or on what her look was focused so intently when she came to him after the parade.

———◄o►———

SOPHIE

Hodson had met Sophie in 1932 at the Christmas dance held at the Railway Institute, Madras, where he had been invited by her husband Tim Blair, an old acquaintance from England. Tim had been an engineer with Vulcan Foundry, located at Lancashire which manufactured steam locomotives and had supplied a number of locomotives to the Indian Railways. He had been sent to India in 1929 for maintenance support to the railways and was stationed at Madras where he had met Miss Sophie D'Souza and fallen madly in love with her. After a whirl-wind round of dating and tempestuous romance Tim and Sophie had decided to get married.

They had selected the oldest Anglican Church in Madras, the St Mary's, as the venue for their nuptial. This historic church had been the place where Robert Clive, "of India" fame had been joined in wedlock with Margaret Maskelyne in 1753. Governor Elihu Yale, of Yale University eminence, too had been married at this very church in 1680, with Catherine Hymmer, widow of his predecessor. His notoriety for keeping a bevy of mistresses, brazen misuse of his official position for personal financial gains and his dishonourable role in child slavery during his gubernatorial stints was all but over looked by historians. Very few people knew that his association with an esteemed academic institution was by a stroke of luck. It so happened that he had donated six bales of goods worth 560 pounds sterling to Collegiate School in USA in 1718 and the grateful school reciprocated by changing its name to Yale College, in a thanks-giving gesture to their first benefactor and in the hope of receiving such largess in the future from the "illustrious & benevolent Governor Yale" and the rest as they say is history. Tim and Sophie were joined in matrimony at this famous church on 20th June 1931 and Hodson had been the best man at their wedding. After a brief honeymoon, Tim and Sophie moved into the railway quarters at Madras, where they continued to drool over and lap up each other and make unabated love.

Sophie was of mixed blood. She claimed that her great grand-father was a French noble and her great grand-mother was a princess from an unpronounceable South Indian state. The two had married in 1861 when India, was in a state of flux. Her great granny had been deprived of her kingdom by an English chap called Dalhousie and her great grandpa had to forsake all his French estate in France as a precondition to enable him to, marry a coloured Indian, even though she was blue-blooded royalty.

Her claim to her ancestry was only partially correct. The first white blood to enter her lineage was indeed through her French great grand-father who had married an Indian out of love in 1861 but that's where the accuracy ended. The exact status of the great grand-parents was in complete contrast to her held belief. The precise position being that, four years after the Indian mutiny against British rule, a French Naval deserter named Pierre Lefevre appeared on the water front in Madras. Lefevre who was from the province of Lyons had become a drifter while still in his teens and could not hold on to a job for long. His decades of wandering had taken him to all corners of France where he had worked as carpenter, locksmith, laundryman, tailor, plumber and handyman in various trades but he never could hold on to a job permanently anywhere. His roaming had finally taken him to Le Havre in Western France where he worked in a bakery for a few years and then one day he suddenly signed up and joined a merchant naval ship, M V *Helena*, where he was assigned duties as a cook in the ship's galley. He had sailed practically all around the world but his compulsion for change was so strong that he jumped ship after clearing one of the ship's safes of all its cash in silver coins at Madras, when the Captain and most of the crew were ashore on liberty, humping away native prostitutes in their brothels in the red light area of the Madras Marina, on their last night in harbor, before setting sail for Ceylon the next morning.

The exhausted yet languorously happy Captain and crew had moseyed on to M V *Helena* in the wee hours the next morning. On coming aboard Captain de Gaul gave 'prepare to sail' orders and ambled to his cabin. He shut the cabin door and by force of habit, reached out to pick the sailing charts & maps from their shelf when he sensed that something was amiss. Captain de Gaul's perceptive eyes promptly took in the cabin view and he realized that one of the safes, the smaller one, kept under his bunk had been rifled. Cash in silver coins, which he used during voyages, for trade, ration & fresh water provisioning, minor ship and sail repairs and other administrative expenses at ports of call, amounting to 3500 francs, a king's ransom in 1861, stowed in it had been stolen. The skipper was hard as nails, hence his paralysis on discovery of the theft was only momentary and he came charging out of his cabin, hollering, whip in hand, his languid and happy countenance of a moment ago now replaced by fury and odium. He ordered his first officer to take a head count & have every centimeter of M V *Helena* searched 'from bow to stern, from port to starboard and from crow's nest to the hold'.

While the search did not unearth any stolen silver, it did uncover 200 grams of opium which had been cleverly hidden in the crew's quarters and the muster confirmed that a cook named Lefevre was missing along with his duffel bag. The skipper confiscated the opium and in his mind realized that this must have been pilfered by the crew from the large opium consignment unloaded at Shanghai. He then quickly re-entered his cabin where he concealed the just impounded contraband and fished out the 'Personnel Data File' of the crew. He rummaged, through it till he found Lefevre's page. He rapidly ran his index finger down the long list of the earlier jobs done by the rascal under the heading 'Previous Experience/Duration' and this is what he saw:—

Anterieur Experience/Duree

1. *XXXXXXXXXXXXXXXXX*
2. *Boulanger/3 annees*
3. *Charpentier/2 annees*
4. *Plombier/1 annees*
5. **Serrurier/2 annees**
6. *Tailleur/3 annees*
7. *XXXXXXXXXXXXXX*
8. *XXXXXXXXXXXXXX*

There it was, Serial 5)—"Smith-Lock/2 years", sandwiched between 4)—"Plumber/1 year" and 6)—"Tailor/3 years". He jabbed his index finger at the item and swore in a growling voice, as only angered old seafarers could. The discovery made Captain De Gaul figure-out, and rightly so, that the heist had been executed by Lefevre using his past experience as lock smith to pick the lock of the safe and pry it open. That took the wind out of him; he felt as if, he had been bludgeoned in his solar plexus with a ton of ballast. The irony of the situation sadly dawned on the Captain; that while he was fornicating with the two 18 year olds, claiming to be twin-sisters, in a three-some in their ramshackle brothel ashore last night; it was he, Captain De Gaul the skipper of M.V. *Helena* who was being had by the scoundrel Lefevre aboard his ship, in his own cabin at the same time. He had been badly had. And it hurt, really hurt.

De Gaul wanted retribution. He stood on a lashing container to gain height, faced the mustered ship's crew and barked, 'Ahoy, mateys! Scoundrel Lefavre has cleared the till and jumped ship. Hear ye men, when I catch up with the thieving bastard, I'm going to flagellate 'im till the skin of his back falls off.' To make his point, he snaked the whip above head level in front of him and yanked it back making a heart rending high octave cracking sound of the whip which sent shivers down the spines of the assembled crew. He continued, 'and then I'm going to walk 'im the plank on the shark infested high seas, and then vengeance will be mine. Yes, siree, I'm going to walk 'im the plank and feed him to the sharks.' He must have appeared a figure as intimidating to the assembled French crew of MV *Helena,* as his British counterpart, Captain Bligh standing on the deck of H M S *Bounty*, must have been, 76 years earlier on that 28th day of April 1790, berating his crew and thus triggering the infamous Mutiny on the *Bounty.* Continuing his tirade De Gaul postponed sailing of his clipper MV *Helena* and ordered a shore search for the deserter.

'I want the blackguard dead or alive but I want him,' he fumed. So saying he ordered that all six swords in the armoury of the ship be issued to the fencing experts in the crew, to be taken ashore and put to use in case the venal rat Lefevre offered resistance.

'I know where thieving vermin go to squander ill-gotten money. They go whoring 'n they go drinking. They go gambling 'n they go opium doping," he pontificated. And then wheedled, 'so go and search all the whore-houses, all the seedy hotels, all the gambling joints, all the boozing taverns and all the opium dens on the water front and bring back the villain to me. Mates, leave no stone unturned on the seafront. Just get him.'

'Aye, Aye, Cap'n,' replied the assembled sailors in unison in a full throated retort.

A second boat was lowered and 16 sailors from MV *Helena* armed with half a dozen foils mounted an assault in two boats on the Madras Marina led by their skipper. As he disembarked from the row boat, Captain De Gaul's foot got struck in the shallows and he had to be assisted up-to the shore line. He considered this mishap, at the commencement of a "do or die" mission, ill-omened. He felt as if he was engulfed by a menacing dark cloud, even as, the search party, on beaching, split into two groups and commenced the combing operation, the sailors cautiously proceeding inland to execute the task at hand. In the meantime, he himself made a bee-line to the twin sisters' bordello, on the pretext of searching it, whereas, he was actually looking forward to the delights awaiting him in that house of pleasure where he had attained complete bliss the previous night. Soon, he was sprawled on the large sized bed inside their bordello and as the two little harlots began to caress, kiss and stroke him, he started to truly believe that the menacing dark cloud engulfing him, indeed had a silver lining.

At the commencement of the hunt the skipper had been hopeful of nabbing the deserter and was heart-broken when the search did not bring him in, even after 48 hours. Two days and that many nights had been wasted; in more ways than one. Firstly, he had fallen behind the sailing schedule, second, neither the runaway cook had been apprehended nor the filched silver recovered and thirdly, his endeavours in the duo's parlour had been unfulfilling. De Gaul mused over his earlier visit, during which he had attained endless pleasure when the two under age tarts had taken him to cloud nine. While that stopover had been an enjoyable dream, the present sojourn was a nightmare because he had been haunted by the apparition of that bastard

Lefevre the whole time. A number of times the harlot duo had taken him towards Eden, and when he thought he was on the door-step of seventh heaven, that arse-hole, Lefevre would suddenly pop up in his mind's eye and take the wind out of his sails or rather erection out of his penis. They had tried again and again but nirvana eluded him; Lefevre's ghost would make his appearance just when he was on the threshold of paradise. He felt physically jaded and psychologically defeated. So the young pair adopted the next best course, they made De Gaul smoke opium in a *chillum*, the Indian cone shaped smoking clay pipe, and that seemed to help; next the teen age twosome had given him an oil bath therapy as per the Indian Medical System, the *Ayurveda* and that too appeared to rejuvenate him. As a result, by the end of the failed hunt, the two young *prostituee* had relieved, the done-in, captain, of his physical weariness, his mental tension and three of his silver pieces; a treasure, which was adequate to take-care of all the needs of the whore-house; madam, harlots, pimps and all, for a whole year, if not more.

The captain was aware that he had perishable cargo and bags of express mail in the hold of MV *Helena*. More over a large consignment of tea, cinnamon & other spices had to be picked up from Ceylon promptly. For these reasons, any further delay in setting out, especially after cook Lefevre episode, would draw wrath of the owners. It was under these circumstances that the hapless captain, perforce, had to take the excruciatingly painful decision to abort the search.

The captain was sad. Felon Lefevre had simply vanished, or maybe he had gone down while absconding, De Gaul speculated wishfully! Oh how he wished that his macabre conjecture was true. A dejected skipper watched his crew doing their pre-sailing chores as he entered his cabin, wishing landlubber Lefevre, death by scurvy. Once inside his cabin, he nicked a pinch of opium from the confiscated package he had stashed. He put a little tobacco in the palm of his left hand and added the opium pinch to it. He then pulverized this mixture with a to and fro movement of his right thumb over the tobacco in his left palm, exactly as the two nymphs had taught him. One learns every day or rather every night, he ruminated. After that he packed his pipe with this prepared heady mix and set it alight. As he pulled a long drag on the pipe the opium laced acrid smoke filled his lungs giving him a high and for the moment he forgot his blues and bitterness and made peace with the world. It is a historic reality that this intoxicating mélange had been smoked jointly by the warring "pale face" European immigrants and the indigenous "red injuns", far away, across two oceans and beyond two continents, on the other side of the world, in North America, to make peace. Their combined smoking ritual had indeed ended the hostilities between these two fighting groups and thus was coined the phrase "smoking the peace pipe". If pipe smoking had brought amity in far-away America in the distant past, it had presently, also brought peace of mind to a troubled naval skipper on board his ship in Madras.

Now completely relaxed, thanks to the opium, the captain picked up the ink pot and quill to write the ship's log and fudge the account books; whilst his clipper MV *Helena* cruised South South-West into the Bay of Bengal, towards Ceylon, at full sail, sans its cook and minus one pot of its silver; its acres of canvas billowing in the Indian Easterly, *Poorvia,* wind.

<o>

As soon as MV *Helena* disappeared over the horizon a starving and thirsty Lefevre made his appearance on the Madras water front. He had jumped ship at mid night two days back with the help of a local fishing boat. Though he had pilfered adequate food from the ship's galley, he had run out of food by evening of the first day since he had to, unavoidably, give a lion's share of his food supplies as payment, in kind, to the accomplice native fishermen who had rowed him ashore. Thus he had remained without food and water for more than 36 hours while in hiding as the, crew of MV *Helena* scoured the area. He was famished not having had even a single morsel of food for one and a half days and went straight to a food stall, commonly known as a *Dhaba,* being managed by a young Indian lassie.

She was vending palm sized, *idlis,* rice and lentil, steamed cakes and he quickly gobbled down half a dozen *idlis*, with its piping hot spiced *Sambhar,* pigeon-pea gravy, accompaniment served to him on a banana leaf. His tongue was on fire due to the

15

chili content of the gravy. He was looking for a drink of water to douse the inferno in his mouth when the graceful female hand of the young attendant offered him a green coconut scythed open at one end. He grabbed the proffered fruit and drank fresh coconut water, straight from the coconut. He was about to discard the empty shell of the fruit but was restrained by the same graceful hand which took possession of the shell and he saw her slice the shell into two equal halves, expertly, with one stroke of a hooked machete. She placed the two halves containing tender coconut flesh, in front of Lefavre, who tried to spoon the jelly like white nut with his fingers into his mouth but the semisolid nut kept slipping through his fingers back into the shell. Seeing his unsuccessful attempt to spoon the slippery jelly with his fingers brought a little subdued laughter from the native girl. The laughter did not offend him, on the contrary, it sounded like musical chimes to his ears. Her hand again appeared in his vision and offered him a rectangular piece of banana leaf about ten centimeters long which she folded and made into a scoop. He looked up inquiringly at her and the native lass by sign language conveyed to the French man to use the banana leaf to scoop out the runny coconut fruit from the shell. Lefavre took the improvised spoon from her and commenced eating the coconut jelly with it. After a few awkward moves he got the hang of using the ad hoc spoon and thereafter he handled the make-shift cutlery as if he had been using it all his life and each mouthful of the sweet coconut flesh subdued the chili spice ignited fire in his mouth.

He ordered another coconut in sign language and drank its clear sherbet in large gulps and then dug into its fruit as soon as the nut had been split open by native girl behind the counter. Sight of a white man digging into the nut ravenously brought another spell of laughter from the siren, wafting into his ears. Lefavre was undecided as to which of the two was sweeter, her laughter drifting into his ears or the coconut fruit he was savouring?

Breakfast over, he surveyed his surroundings. He was on a beach and could see the fishing boats coming-in, laden with their heavy cargo of fish netted during the night, far out in the ocean. The boats were met by the fisher women folk who collected the catch and laid it out on the beach while the men folk haggled with fishmongers for the correct price for their catch. Inland he could see the built up area of Madras and ramparts of a fort were prominent in the midst of the town-ship with one of its thick walls facing the sea. From the fort rose a high flag mast, like a phoenix, on which fluttered the flag of England. He again came back to his immediate surroundings and for the first time took a closer look at the young woman managing the stall whose peals of laughter had chimed into his ears during breakfast. She was dark complexioned, neither plump nor skinny. She had firm round breasts and a slim waist. She must be about 165 centimeters tall, guessed Lefevre. All in all, a radiant Indian beauty he judged. When she saw him staring at her, she blushed and then gave him a full bloom smile, exposing a set of the prettiest pearl like white teeth he had ever seen. His eyes remained riveted on this girl and he wanted to continue to feast on her dusky beauty ceaselessly and was not inclined to leave her presence. It was only the inescapable necessity of arranging a lodging which compelled Lefevre to wrench himself away from her company.

However, pulling away from her was easier said than done because of an unforeseen hurdle. There was difficulty in clearing his bill. Lefavre offered one silver piece to the girl but she was scared to accept it knowing fully-well that its value far exceeded his tab and she could not take an over payment and he on the other hand could not walk off without paying. They were in a catch-22 situation when her father appeared on the scene carrying a sack full of fish. He solved the problem pronto by accepting the silver piece but insisted that Lefavre eat at their stall regularly so that the balance could be adjusted for his future dining visits; all in sign language. As soon as the problem was resolved Lefavre tore his eyes away from the girl, with some effort and trudged inland to arrange for suitable quarters. He took a room in Hotel Majestic near the fort, where he parked his duffel bag and he also rented a safe deposit locker in which he locked his silver consignment and returned to the beach to feast his eyes on his pretty *jeune*. By dinner time the sailor knew that he had been lured by this dark skinned siren with sing-song

17

laughter and he had fallen, head over heels, in love with her, for the first time ever, in his 45 year life.

Lefevre became a regular visitor to the market on the sea front, ostensibly to eat or purchase fish or to angle and made it a point to greet the dark skinned Indian girl, who he thought, had a smile which could sink a thousand ships. He greeted her with a bowed head while voicing a soft *bonjour mademoiselle* before ordering his meal in sign language. Though she did not under-stand the white man's language, she knew that something nice was being said by him. She started to look forward to the smart white skinned gentleman's visits and it flattered her no end when he generously praised her cooking.

He soon came to know that she was a low caste Indian born on the 1st day of the Indian month of *Vaisak* in the year 1893 of the Indian *Vikrami* calendar, which corresponded to the 13th day of the month of April 1836 of the Western Calendar, into a fishing folks' family. She had been, accordingly given the name Vaisakhi. Her family had converted to Christianity and as a result her surname was now Masih, taken from Issa Masih, the Indian name for Lord Jesus Christ. She had lost her mother when she was still a toddler. Her father had remarried within a year of her demise and had sired six more children within the next one decade from his new mate. She had grown up on the sea front doing bidding of her cruel step-mother, looking after her step siblings and keeping clean the squalid shanty in which the family resided. Her body was taut and supple due to the strenuous chores she had to perform all day and her hands were hard and nails broken, a result of heaving and hauling of heavy fishing nets and cooking meals at her father's makeshift *Dhaba* restaurant on the beach; her bare feet had never had the luxury of slipping into any footwear all her life and the only clothing she possessed was a *saree* wrap, made from coarse cotton cloth. Although she wasn't a beauty while in her teens, she had started to bloom on entering her twenties, a bit late perhaps, but by the time she turned 25 she had fully blossomed and turned into an attractive maiden. Of course this poor Madras girl also had a couple of additional captivating qualities which had bewitched Lefevre off his feet.

As his visits became more regular, longer & greetings louder, her heart told her that the French gentleman was wooing her. Soon he had paid a princely sum of three hundred rupees as dowry to Vaisakhi's father for her hand in marriage. Lefevre presented a gold ring on their engagement and he purchased a spacious double storey house the same day in the up-market outer circle around Fort St George, Madras. He changed her name to 'Avril', French for April, the month of her birth in the Western calendar matching the Indian month of Vaisakh, from which her name Vaisakhi had been derived, ab-initio, at birth. Her new name may now be Avril but its Indian equivalent was still Vaisakhi. 'So, *monsieur*, why change a name; if the old and the new, both mean the same?' had been Vaisakhi's father's unanswered query.

Monsieur Pierre Lefevre and *Mademoiselle* Avril Masih were married on 30 November 1861 in the church at St. Thomas' Mount Madras. During her wedding on that last day of November, a bejewelled Avril, heavily made up like a chichi, dressed in a white voile trousseau, her feet adorned in matching white leather high heels was very happy indeed. The little nervousness she felt, stemmed from her apprehension of tumbling over because of her high heeled footwear, she therefore went through the ceremony, clutching on to Pierre's arm to prevent such a mishap. Their wedding was attended by the entire fishing community of Madras.

The raucous fishing folk commenced the wedding celebrations at the beach soon after the ceremony at the church was over. The revelry continued late into the night, by when most fisher men and a sizable number of the women folk were overwhelmed by the copious amount of alcohol consumed and passed out on the beach. It is needless, to mention that the fishing-community, did not venture out to sea for the daily fish catch that day, a rarest of rare phenomenon, in the life of fishermen. It was an acknowledged fact that the brave fisher folk cancelled sailing only when it was perilous to do so, due to stormy weather conditions. This perhaps was the only exception, when the fishing community of Madras did not venture out to sea, without any commandment from the weather Gods but due to a man-made tempest. When the fish merchants appeared on the seashore the next morning to purchase fish, they found empty fishing boats bobbing in the shallows and the entire fishing community literally beached, nursing a collective hang-over. Obviously, there were no fish hauls that morning and citizens of Madras went without their daily fish gravies and the British garrison inside the fort, ate their chips with tartar sauce dip but without the fish accompaniment.

The French groom and his Indian bride clutching his arm had broken away from the celebrations at the seaside, early and driven home in a horse drawn carriage, where the groom had carried his bride in his arms across the thresh-hold and into the bedroom of his palatial new house. The poor deprived waif who had been bullied and mistreated by a cruel step mother and had done back breaking menial chores, walked barefoot and worn tatters for clothes and lived in a broken down shanty all her 25 year life; had caught the fancy of this 45 year old aristocrat, who having sailed across many seas and oceans on his voyages around the world like Sinbad, had arrived in Madras and sought her hand in marriage. This rich Noble Prince had dressed her in lace lingerie, decked her in the finest silk gowns, put her feet in top quality sandals, all custom made on order exclusively for her. Prince Pierre Lefevre had married his Princess Avril and then taken her in a horse drawn carriage into his well-appointed spacious double storey Palace; where they would live happily ever after. Quite like the Cinderella fable, eh! Only this one was a true "happily ever after story" and not a fairy tale.

Sophie, who was watching the investiture parade at Wellington on that 4th day of May 1947 and who claimed descent from royalty because of her naïve belief that her great-grand-parents had been a blue blooded French Noble & a Royal Indian Princess; could perhaps be pardoned for her guileless belief, on account of the similarities between the replicated version of the story of her late great-grandparents to that of the Cinderella legend.

Pierre started *"Pastrie"*, a French Bakery on the ground floor of his capacious house and Avril ably assisted him in his work. Soon they added additional items on their menu the first addition being 'Fish & Chips' to cater to an insatiable demand of the British Tommy billeted inside the fort.

On 30 May 1862, six months after she had walked the aisle with Lefavre, a bonny baby girl was born to Avril. She was christened Jean. Birth of a healthy child six months after wedlock implied that the French deserter's pre-marital visits to the water front with a fishing-rod were not just to fish or loiter or to dine at her *Dhaba* eatery. He had obviously been busy, firstly in deflowering and then harpooning his mermaid Vaisakhi, or should we say Avril, on the beach regularly after Sun-set. And mind you, this was done under the stars, with the back-drop sound of rollers breaking when the surf hit the rocky out crop on the beach and with the warm sea eddies lapping at their feet as they lapped up each other, for at least three months, if not more, prior to wedlock. Cook Lefevre was, indeed, as hot blooded a French bloke, as De Gaul, his ex-captain but that's where their shared uniqueness ended. There was, not so subtle, a difference, between their sexual bents; the Captain did it for lust, whereas, the Cook did it for love. That in a nutshell was the story of "Captain 'n Cook".

Jean Lefevre had inherited her father's good looks and her mother's smile but not her dark skin. The moment Lefevre held his child, his own flesh and blood, he was exhilarated and experienced a warm affection towards the little beauty and he vowed to be always near her. He returned the baby to Avril and as soon as she put the baby's mouth on to her breast, the baby located the teat and started to feed on it hungrily. What a pretty picture they made. A euphoric Pierre watched mother and child for a moment and then knelt beside their bed and took the other teat in his mouth and replicated the baby's sucking. Avril did not push him away but instead took his head in the crook of her arm as he climbed on to the bed and lay on Avril's vacant side, without, even momentarily, releasing the nipple from his mouth. She was the happiest wife and mother as the pair drank away greedily from her breasts. The gurgling sounds father and daughter made individually were in bass and treble, but together, in concert, they sounded like a duet to her ears. She could see only the heads of the suckling two, from her supine position, whereas her desire was to view them from top to toe. She was aware that their entire four poster double bed could be observed in the large, framed, mirror of her dressing table. Pierre had placed it against the wall, facing the foot side of their bed and had been occasionally watching their sexual performance in it during copulation in the past. She was also cognizant of the fact that he had optimized its use for self voyeurism of their coupling in recent months; from the time she had become heavy with child and he had been compelled to cohabit with her in the doggie position, which made the viewing, of their live performance in the mirror, a lot more, easier. If Pierre could make use of the reflector for erotic purposes, what was stopping her from using it for watching the feeding duo leeched on to her lactating boobs? So she craned her neck to be able to view them all in the mirror. The moment she raised her neck she felt Pierre inserting a bolster below her raised head without letting go of her teat. With the cylindrical pillow supporting her raised head she could behold her entire family, in the mirror straight away. She now, not only had her whole world, literally, in her arms but could see it too. A happy Avril ran her fingers through Pierre's blond hair and immediately felt his hand on her crotch. She wondered how, Pierre would ever be able to take a sabbatical from love making for the mandatory forty days suggested by Indian midwife?

Jean started attending the local English school run by Christian missionaries, when she was six years old and as Lefevre escorted her to school he become conscious of the fact that his stay at Madras had been the longest at any one place given that he had been a rolling stone, for over three decades. More importantly, his yearning for moving on had simply died out. Home, hearth and family bliss had unwittingly pulled off a coup; it had converted a vagrant into a resident.

Jean was the apple of her father's eye and grew up to become a very attractive beauty. Since, Jean attended the local English school only in the mornings she helped her parents in their bakery and restaurant business in the afternoons. When she was 25 years of age she met Johannes van der Coot. The two became friendly and the thirty year old handsome Dutch became a regular customer at the "*Pastrie*".

Johannes van der Coot was scion of a rich Dutch family who were in the business of Import & Export of diamonds and some other commercial ventures. He had come to India to visit his grand-father's grave. The senior van der Coot had travelled to India in 1797 on a business trip, never to return to his beloved Amsterdam, having been consumed by a severe attack of malaria. He was laid to rest in a European cemetery in Madras and Johannes had been sent by the family to locate the elder van der Coot's grave and get it done up to a level commensurate with their family background.

While the elder van der Coot's voyage to India had been around South Africa via the Cape of Good Hope, in a sail ship pushed by the wind, Johannes' journey had been via Egypt through the Suez Canal, excavated not long ago, in a steam ship propelled by steam power. He arrived in Madras on 20th June 1887 and moved into the Marina Hotel. He hired a local guide and got to work. He wanted to finish the work on the double and get out, of the abominable heat and humidity, as soon as possible. He was also apprehensive of coming down with malaria and meeting the elder van der Coot's fate. Despite his intention of getting the job done promptly, it took him three weeks just to locate his grand-father's grave and that too after umpteen visits to the office of Registrar of European Births and Deaths and examination of their archives. He then visited the grave and found it in a deplorable condition. Ninety years of exposure to the elements, without any meaningful upkeep had reduced it to a derelict. The undertaking contractor, promised to bring it to a pristine condition and after a survey, assessed that it would take at least one month to do so. Johannes had no choice but to wait. He ordered the restoration of the grave and went straight to "Rails & Sails" his travel agents and told them to make arrangements for his return journey any time after 20th of August. Having time on his hands, he went sight-seeing.

While wandering around Fort St George, pangs of hunger brought him to the *Pastrie,* where he sat down at a table and started browsing through the menu card. He had decided on his order, by the time he sensed a waiter's presence next to his table. He looked up and came face to face with what he thought was an angel, a mulatto angel. He came out of his trance only after the smiling angel like waitress nudged him by delicately clearing her throat. After taking his order, the waitress promptly returned with his order and had a tankard of beer and a plate of fish and chips, in front of him. She then sat down at his table to make conversation. Johannes was flustered by this fetching maiden and he blundered as they made banter. By the time he had drained half his beer mug and finished half his fish fillet, he had made a decision to postpone his departure by another month and consolidate his new found friendship with the gorgeous Jean. He paid another visit to his travel agents the next day and instructed them accordingly.

Johannes became a regular visitor to the *Pastrie* and by and by she began to call him Hans, the Dutch short form for Johannes. He would always visit the bakery in the afternoon when the employees were taking a break and Jean's parents were taking their afternoon siesta and the *Pastrie* was being managed by Jean, all by herself. She would take him into the rear room where she would load the wood fired oven with biscuits, cookies, cakes, éclairs and buns for baking. The warm aroma of the baking process would fill their nostrils as Jean retrieved the baked product from the oven with Hans's help and they would taste her handiwork. It was not long before the two started tasting each other and their deep throated kisses went to the next level and soon Johannes was baking his salami in her oven; and he had made yet another visit to 'Rails & Sails', this time to cancel his return passage indefinitely and to wire home for more funds.

Jean educated him in the basics of the bakery business. She demonstrated the finer points of baking and gave him hands-on training in use of icing guns and icing bags and explained many other facets of the trade. He in turn taught her many naughty tricks, he had learned on the *Rossebuurt,* Red Light, District of Amsterdam, which she enjoyed learning. The large table adjoining the oven, now had a dual purpose, it was used for kneading dough and it was also used for making love. Johannes also made multiple uses of the icing cones. He would ice Jean's nipples and aureoles and other parts of her anatomy with cream and honey and then lick it away, slowly. While Hans and Jean were relishing each other in their own Garden of Eden, Lefevre fore-head was creased in consternation every time he examined the rising dairy and honey bill at the end of the month. He just could not fathom the reason for the increment in the bill when there was no matching boost in production of items using cream and honey. Jean knowingly smirked at his predicament. God, if he only knew that the unaccounted provisions were not vanishing but being utilized in preparation of their new creation, appropriately labelled by Jean as, 'Spiced Honey Cream Delight', which was now Han's favourite post lunch dessert. He loved to wolf it down and she just loved to serve it to him, on her dish.

Hans and Jean were married a year after they first met and Johannes moved in with the Lefevres. Their daughter Johanna, nicked named Jo, was born on 15th September 1890 two years and two months later. Sired by a white father from a mulatto mother, Jo was technically a Quadroon. Her proud French grand-father Lefevre put her weight at birth as three kilograms and 100 grams, the British nurse from the local missionary hospital recorded it as six pounds and 10 ounces in her records and the native Indian mid-wife who was assistant at child birth, noted the weight as three and a quarter seers. Lucky child; weight recorded in three different values. She was a healthy child, the three quarters white and one quarter coloured blood in her veins enhanced her beauty, exponentially.

Pierre accompanied Hans and Jean when she was admitted into the same school her mother had attended and Lefevre was delighted to see a number of old faces of the school staff still there. He reminisced, his first visit to the school 28 years ago when he had brought the six year old, toddler, Jean for enrolment. It was unlikely that he would be fortunate enough to repeat this trip with Johanna's child, he ruminated. Pierre's contemplation turned out to be right; he died in his sleep a week later. He was laid to rest in the European cemetery only a few yards away from the refurbished grave of the elder van der Coot. Avril was distraught but she helped Jean and Hans in keeping the *Pastrie* going.

Jo graduated from school at sixteen, after completion of her Senior Cambridge examination and joined the Presidency College, opting for graduation in arts. Jo was even prettier than her mother and grew up breaking many hearts on the way. She was a decent student at academics at the school but her forte was in extra-curricular—activities and the same held true in college as well. She liked fine arts, loved to travel and generally regarded outdoor programmes highly. Her love for travel had brought her to Goa, a Portuguese enclave on the Western coast of India along with her college excursion when she was eighteen. Here she had been swept off her feet by young D'Souza, the only son of an affluent Portuguese family from Lisbon, holidaying in Goa. She brought him to Madras to meet her family. Their decision to get married was approved reluctantly by the aristocratic D'Souza patriarch. But in the end he travelled to Madras from Lisbon to attend his son's wedding and his earlier opposition to the match evaporated the moment he set his eyes on Johanna. Johanna van der Coot and Melville D'Souza were married on 20th of March 1909 when she was just eighteen years and six months old. She accompanied her husband and her father-in-law to Lisbon and was not destined to return to her beloved India again.

Even as the whole world was ushering in the New Year, at mid-night of 31st December 1909, Johanna was laboriously ushering in a new life. A daughter was born to her at mid-night, as the gongs of clock towers struck twelve, on New Year's Day of 1910 at Lisbon, Portugal; the time in India at the *Pastrie* House at the child's birth would be 5.30 am. While the world was celebrating the arrival of the New Year, the D'Souza family was additionally rejoicing the arrival of a baby daughter in their family. The pretty baby, procreated by the union of a white father and a quadroon mother was technically a Mustee. This child was fairer than the fairest even though she would have inherited some coloured blood from her quadroon mother. She was christened Sophie by her proud father.

Melville D'Souza's business trip to New York, USA was long overdue and Jo had also been insisting on a visit to Amsterdam to meet the van der Coot family. Therefore Melville decided to kill two birds with one stone. He elected to take Jo and little Sophie along on his trip to New York. They could visit Jo's paternal family in Amsterdam, then take a short tour of Europe and thereafter make the transatlantic crossing to USA. He accordingly made an itinerary whereby they would reach Cherbourg, France by 9th April 1912 after their trip to Amsterdam and other selected places of tourist interest and board the unsinkable ship Titanic on her maiden voyage to New York. They looked forward to taking the cruise, in the much advertised luxury liner Titanic, the largest and the safest passenger vessel ever made. They travelled as planned and reached Cherbourg and boarded RMS Titanic once it came across the English Channel from Southampton, thirty minutes behind schedule, on 10th April 1912.

The ship stopped at Queenstown, Ireland to pick up some passengers the next day and then commenced its journey to New York. Each night of the journey aboard the splendid liner was memorable. There was partying, dancing with a live band playing golden tunes of the day, champagne flowed freely and the dining tables were laden with sumptuous exotic meals. There were extra marital affairs, as passengers let their hair down without inhibition. There was a carnival like atmosphere, that is, until it was hit by an iceberg. The collision, which took place about twenty minutes before midnight, when the ship was into the fourth day of its journey, ripped open a very large gash on the starboard side of the Titanic.

As the mighty ship started to sink, there came to fore many heroic deeds, selfless sacrifices and produced many heroes. Though, death stared everyone in the face, yet "women and children first" protocol to shift to lifeboats was enforced by the ship's crew with discipline. In one of the lifeboats being lowered, a young mother gave her cradled baby girl to her co-passenger, sitting beside her and jumped out of the life boat to be on her husband's side on the deck of the Titanic. Despite her husband's repeated entreaties to her, to return to the lifeboat and save herself, she stood steadfast at his side, all his pleas falling on deaf ears. Melville and Jo would go down together holding hands, with a prayer on their lips for the safety of their only child given in care to an unknown stranger in a life boat. The ship's band which had entertained the passengers on the dance floor these four nights, heroically played "Nearer, My God, to Thee" while the great steamer was sinking, it's Captain on the bridge and over 1500 people still entombed within her confines. In the last few seconds of her life, as its bows dipped inexorably into the ocean, the ship's stern came out of the sea pointing upwards and three giant propellers of this large vessel lay exposed, like entrails of a wounded behemoth. She went speeding down, bow first, into a dive towards the bottom of this icy cold ocean at 0230 hours on 15th April 1912. While all nights aboard the ship had been memorable for gaiety, it was this last night which was a night to remember, forever, for its un-paralleled tragedy.

Among the survivors picked up by the vessel Carpathia at day break, was the two year old girl child, left in someone else's arms by the brave adamant lady and ferried to New York. White Star Line, the owners of the ill-fated ship, made arrangements to bring back the survivors to England and when a black nurse disembarked with Sophie delicately cuddled in her arms at the quay at Southampton 20 days later, Johannes and Jean were on the pier, waiting. They had never seen the young Sophie but immediately recognised her, not from the Jo's locket which the child adorned on a chain around her neck or from Jo's hand writing on the note pinned on the inner-lining of the child's thick warm jacket but from her face; the child was an exact replica of her mother and for a moment Hans and Jean thought that they had journeyed back in time and were looking at a fairer version of their baby daughter, Johanna. They took the child to Lisbon to meet the senior D'Souza who had suffered a stroke on getting the devastating news and who was now under medical care and then they returned to Madras with the child.

Sophie grew up at Madras studying in the same school attended formerly by her mother and grand-mother and supervised work at the *Pastrie* the family bakery and restaurant business just as her ancestors had done before her. She married Tim Blair when she was 22 years old. After Sophie's marriage, Johannes and Jean closed down the bakery and restaurant business since Avril had already expired in 1915 and went to live in Amsterdam.

However, misfortune continued to plague Sophie. Her married bliss had not lasted for long. Tim died in a rail accident in the summer of 1937. Colonel Eric Hodson had attended the funeral and extended a helping hand to Sophie in her hour of need. Sophie had visited Hodson in his office at the fort a month later and requested for his guidance and help in re-opening the *Pastrie* and Hodson had willingly obliged. There was a large crowd invited for the reopening of the now modernized and refurbished restaurant six months later. Even the title board above the entrance had been smartened up, it was now bigger and advanced, the title *"Pastrie"* had been suffixed with its year of inception, *"Since 1861"*, in echelon, all in neon. After the function Sophie had profoundly thanked Eric for his help and support and invited him upstairs to see her residential quarters. There, they had exchanged their first kiss and passionate love making resulted in the days that followed and mutual obsession had not diminished in these ten years thought Hodson even though he had heard rumours that Sophie was now taking on young lovers from the garrison with consistent regularity.

She had by now been bequeathed with two inheritances, one at Portugal from the De Souza family and another at Amsterdam from the Dutch van der Coot family of her late maternal grand-father. This wind fall had enabled her to spend the summer months at her newly acquired villa in the Nilgiris at Ooty. She could have chosen to settle in Europe but instead continued to live in India and a vain Hodson believed that her continued stay here was because of her love for him since this very rich heiress had continued to accept him as a lover whenever he came to South India on visits. Her presence at the parade today had puffed up his ego further and gave credence to the notion that she was available to him as always. He thus put the tittle-tattle of her yen for young men, as gossip and nothing more. It never occurred to Hodson that her continued residence in India and her being there at the parade may be due to another reason.

————◄O►————

THE PARADE

*H*odson could sense that a microphone was being unobtrusively placed on his left flank adjacent to the saluting base, behind the left stick orderly. He knew that a similar contraption would soon be positioned in front of him as well. He was looking at the formed men on parade to determine the point of Sophie's interest but to no avail.

The British Officers of the Madras Regiment standing at ease, in front of their men on the drill square evoked another memory of the previous era in Hodson. This recollection pertained to the star officer of the Madras Regiment, Robert Clive. Clive too must have been quite like these youngsters as a lieutenant of this regiment. Who could have possibly imagined that in later life, the young Clive who had turned into a juvenile delinquent and had set up a protection racket and extorted money from Market Drayton's shopkeepers, where he was born, would become Clive of India one day. He thought that the course of world history would not have been what it was if Robert was as obedient as his one dozen siblings and therefore, would not have been shunted out to India by his frustrated father or if the gun with which he attempted suicide in India as a young clerk in the East India Company had not misfired, giving him a lease of life. For that matter if Major Stringer had not noticed his leadership qualities during the battle of Arcot he would have continued to remain a non-entity. But Lawrence Stringer had noticed him and Clive was given an ensign's commission. And the rest, as they say is History.

He established the military and political supremacy of the East India Company thereby securing India and the wealth that followed, for the British Crown. Robert Clive, 1st Baron of Plassey, rose to the rank of Major General in the British Indian Army and was appointed Governor General of India. The Mughals gave him title of Dewan of Bengal and the world gave him the handle *"Clive of India"*, not bad for a school drop-out. The people of Market Dreydon, Shropshire, who had celebrated, discreetly, behind closed-doors, the departure of young Clive, to India in 1743, were caused to celebrate again; openly, when Clive, *"one of their own"*, finally returned from India. The British Government honoured him with Order of the Bath and he was appointed Lord Lieutenant of Shropshire; the place where he had carried out his tormenting activities as a young gangster.

While his attempted suicide with a pistol as a young man, had providentially failed, his second endeavour had been successful; Clive committed suicide at his home in London by stabbing himself on 22 November 1774, leaving behind Margret, his wife of 21 years, his six children and a place in history, for himself. Few Great men have changed the world in the way Robert Clive had done, concluded Hodson. According to him there was no parallel to the story of Robert Clive in history. His life story therefore never failed to amaze Hodson. A suggestion of a mischievous smile flitted across his face in nostalgia as he completed reminiscing, his hero, Clive and turned, ever so slightly, continuing his scanning activity unobtrusively while awaiting further proceedings to continue.

Doraiswamy the short and stout, dark skinned Tamil interpreter had made his noise-less appearance next to the microphone placed recently on the reviewing officers left flank. Mr. Doraiswamy who was nick-named Sammy by his well-wishers as well his tormentors had been in service of the British Crown as interpreter and translator for two decades. He had served under, six Governors at Fort Saint George, Madras. His translation into the vernacular, Tamil and Urdu, from English and vice-versa was impeccable. He was never at a loss for words, either English or Tamil or Urdu & was known to interpret not only conversations but also translate extempore speeches of his bosses spontaneously. Sammy had changed during his one-score years of service under the crown in some ways. He had discarded his Madras clothing of Lungi, kurta and chappals and now dressed in Western attire and the reason ascribed to this change also went back one score years to the day of his appointment in His Majesty's service.

31

Today, he was wearing a dark brown lounge suite and if he wasn't festooning a tilak, the mark of the high caste Brahmin, on his forehead and if he was not adorning a turban on his head he would have surely passed off as an oriental gentleman. While Sammy had changed in his clothing habits, he could not get rid of his heavy South Indian accent while conversing in English, in spite of his best effort. He remembered with some personal embarrassment his final interview at selection time twenty years ago. He had answered all questions put to him by the distinguished interviewing board to their entire satisfaction and when he thought that the interview was over, the young board member with blonde hair, who had so far been a mute spectator to the selection proceedings came suddenly to life and said, 'Mr. Doraiswamy'.

'Sir'

'Spell the word "MINIMUM".'

Doraiswamy hid his feeling of glee, albeit, with some effort, on hearing such an easy question put to him by this smart blond aleck. With a poker face, Doraiswamy nattered out the spellings, pronouncing the letters as "YUM (that's M) YAEE (i.e. I) YEN (that one is N) YAEE YUM U YUM" in one breath.

The "Ya" sound prefix, was indigenous to the pronunciation of most South Indians. Other Indian groups too had their own unique way of articulating the English language. While such varied accents were a subject of great amusement for the English rulers, they also made it easier for them to assign the place of origin and sometimes the social background of the speaker. That day, the fair-haired examiner had deliberately asked the spellings of a word, he knew, would elicit the "Ya" sound prefix while the alliteration and assonance effect of its closely repeated alphabets would enhance the heavily accented reply of the South Indian Doraiswamy. His strategy had paid off. The entire interviewing board was rolling in loud uncontrolled laughter, the loudest coming from the blonde when Doraiswamy reply spilled forth. Their seemingly vulgar, raucous laughter continued for, what seemed a millennium to a miffed Doraiswamy. He had vowed then and there, not only to improve his English accent but also to become as British as the Brits themselves so that he would not become a butt of their humour in future. He had indeed achieved this to a substantial measure if one was to go by his Western attire but accent problems continued to plague him.

Sammy adjusted the height of the microphone in front of him while all the time his eyes remained riveted on Lieutenant General Hodson, the Reviewing Officer standing on the dais to his right. Having failed to find the subject of Sophie's eyes on the parade ground Hodson had reminisced Robert Clive and he now moved his gaze towards the other side and started to glance towards the stands on his left as if he wanted to take in the whole scene. His eyes momentarily came to pass over Sammy the interpreter, and Sammy seized the moment with alacrity, he bowed down with folded hands doing an elaborate Namaskar, the Indian Greeting, which was acknowledged with a curt nod by the Sahib while his eyes continued to scour the VIP stands, as well as the other enclosures. These were all filled up by the men of the Madras Regiment in their uniforms and local Tamil natives in their colourful dresses.

General Hodson noticed that in one of the native enclosure sat three Sikh spectators in Indian Army uniform. He had a special affinity to Sikhs given that the horse cavalry regiment raised by his ancestor William Hodson during the Indian Mutiny in the previous century had these gallant warriors in its rank and file. Though at some distance, he could faintly discern the round shape of a quoit in the badges pinned on the olive green turbans of the trio, which meant that they were not from the cavalry but most probably either from the Sikh or the newly raised and recently renamed Sikh Light Infantry Regiment. The pigment of their skin suggested the latter. Hodson concluded that these Sikh soldiers were perhaps guests of one of the four recipients who were to be anointed by him with their well-deserved medals for gallantry on behalf of His Majesty King George VI, during the investiture ceremony which was to be the denouement of today's parade.

Hodson was aware that the war had brought many geographically disparate units together on the front lines where many lasting friendships were born under fire, in sweat and blood. He assumed that the spectator Sikh soldiers were bonded with their Madrasi compatriot in one such friendship. Hodson's assumption was only partially correct, the Sikh spectators were *indeed friends of one of the gallantry award winners but their friendship was not inculcated on the battle field but went further back in time and was forged under very peculiar circumstances, even more trying than the field of battle.*

———◄o►———

HARRY SINGH

It was on 1000 Hours on 15 January 1942 that the duty bugler of the day sounded the bugle call summoning the Company Havildar Majors (CHMs), same as CSMs in the British Army. The bugle was sounded on command of the Battalion Havildar Major or BHM for short, of the newly raised 1st Battalion Mazhabi and Ramdasia Sikh Regiment located at Jullundur Cantonment, in the Punjab Province of North India. There were two buglers on duty in the unit. While one of them remained stationed in the quarter guard and sounded routine calls commencing from reveille at day break, through retreat at sundown, to lights out at night, the other accompanied the BHM, corresponding to the British RSM, for such unforeseen duties. On hearing the bugle call the CHMs of the subunits came on the double to receive the instructions. Orders for deputing an escort of three men to Station Headquarters, Fort St George, Madras, in South India, to collect an army deserter and bring him back to Jullundur was given to D Company by the BHM. The order had been received in the unit that morning in the *dak*, mail, from Station Headquarters Jullundur. Accordingly, the Adjutant had apprised the Commanding Officer and the orders were relayed down to the BHM through the chain of command with the adjutant's direction to depute an escort from one of the four rifle companies and he in turn had passed it to "Dog" or D Company for execution via the CHMs.

Naik or Corporal Harinder Singh nicknamed Harry, a high school dropout, of D Company, who had previous experience in this field, was deputed as the escort commander. There were different stories about the origins of his nickname, one was that it rhymed with Hari, the first four letters of his name Harinder; another was that because he was abnormally hairy his friends had named him so and with a little twist in the spellings he had become Harry instead of Hairy and another one suggested

35

that one of his ancestors who had served in the Sikh Pioneers had functioned under a British Officer named Harry and consequently he had doled out the nickname Harry at birth to the child. Be that as it may, the fact of the matter was that the five foot eight inch tall muscular Harinder was now called Harry, and he liked it. He put forward names of two sepoys or privates from his own village, Machiwara about three miles East of Ludhiana town of Punjab, to be part of the escort. His subjective selection was struck down by Subedar Major Jiwan Singh the senior most VCO of the battalion.

The British had created a middle rank, unique to the British Indian Army between its British officers and the native rank and file. This rank was termed as Viceroy Commissioned Officers or VCOs, for short. The VCOs were graded at three levels of rank; Jemedar stood at the lowest rung, the middle being Subedar and the highest was Subedar Major. The VCOs, were English speaking and had power over the rank and file but came under the British officers. They were of immense help in communicating between the officers and men and competently assisted them in command and control and in administration.

Subedar Major Jiwan Singh told the company VCO, to change the selection and accordingly two other men were selected to be part of the escort. He earmarked Sepoy Ram Singh nick named Matric because he had passed the high school or matric examination, even though it was in the third division and in his fourth attempt and that too with some outside help from the invigilator who happened to be friendly with his sister. Matric was a five foot seven inch tall slim athletic soldier who was English savvy. He hailed from village Shahdra, District Lahore. The other one picked up by the company VCO was Sepoy Laxman Singh nick named Lachu, who was five foot eight inch tall and his powerfully built body suggested that he was either a wrestler or a boxer, or a *kabadi* player or member of a tug-of-war team, as its "end of the tug rope, anchor man". He came from Patiala, a princely state of Punjab and had been an active wrestler before enlisting into the Army. He boasted to have been trained in wrestling by the legendary wrestler, Gama Pehelwan of Patiala. Selection made by the company Subedar was done to include one sprinter and one with strength.

His escort selection was to ensure that in case their prisoner attempted an escape the sprinter could catch him and the brawny one could then overpower and subdue him. The VCO was of the firm belief that there should always be a right person at the right place to cover unforeseen contingencies. Since the three were not from the same village they were unlikely to try and take some un-authorised break en-route, in alliance with one another. This selection was approved by the Subedar Major and their particulars were conveyed to the Adjutant's office for preparation of the Movement Order and to the Quartermaster for issue of necessary railway warrant for the to and fro journey and for making the train reservations to Madras.

Harinder made out a demand list comprising, Handcuffs—1 set, Blanket—2(for the prisoner for the return journey), *Chagal* or canvas water bag ½ gallon—2 (for storing drinking water during the journey), Anti-mosquito oil—1 bottle, Soap Washing—2 pieces, Petty Cash—Rupees 30/- and a pay advance of Rs 25/- for each of the party members from the Imprest Account. According to him these additional items and finance would be required by him for the given task. His demand was approved by the adjutant with some additional notations on the demand note; the Adjutant had directed that the escort should carry an additional rain cape for the prisoner since rain squalls are common in the Southern coastal plains; they should also be issued a wrist watch, a torch, a whistle and the chain attached with the irons should be at least six feet in length. Cash should be handed out, only on the day of the journey. The available stores were issued to the escort party commander, accordingly. Harry then ordered each member of his party to carry a mufti set, civil clothing, in addition beddings and kit as per unit standing orders. He also directed Lachu to carry Brass polish for the whole party and ordered Matric to take shoe polish and shoe brushes for them.

After that he distributed the stores drawn by him from the unit-stores, between his two subordinates equitably, keeping the wrist watch for himself. He would have also kept the whistle but it was marked "NA", not available, by the Quartermaster, for this reason it could not be issued. At that point he had the kit laid-out and inspected the same. Having buttoned up all loose ends, he then proceeded to add a few items to his baggage. He added a piece of chalk, a safety match box, a deck of cards and a miniature *kirpan* or sword to his baggage. And because he also enjoyed an odd drink during long train travels, he decanted rum from a rum bottle into his army issue, olive green metallic water bottle and carefully put this also in his journey gear.

On 17th January 1942 the escort party commander was provided with Rs 30/-, the Movement Order and an authority letter authorising him to collect the prisoner from Madras. They picked up the packed dinner from their *langar,* cook-house and were ferried to Jullundur Cantonment Railway Station in a ramshackle civil bus since the unit still did not have its own dedicated army transport. They exchanged the railway warrant for a check soldier ticket and waited for the Madras Express, which arrived one hour late, from Lahore. Indian Railways had three classes for travelling passengers; top of line was first class, next came, second class also called the intermediate or inter class and lastly the third class. Being a Non Commissioned Officer or NCO leading an escort, Naik Harinder Singh a k a, Harry and his party were entitled travel in Inter Class as per British Indian Army Travel Regulations and they, accordingly, boarded their reserved, Inter Class compartment for their forty hour journey to South India. Harry quickly scribbled 'Reserved—Military Escort' with chalk on the outside of their compartment as they were entraining, to ensure an undisturbed travel up to Madras.

The escort was travelling in a spacious inter class compartment which had four berths and an attached toilet. The seats were wide and cabin roomy, an outcome of the 5 feet 6 inches broad gauge of the Indian Railways. Matric earmarked a lower berth for Harry and quickly spread his bedding on it and switched off the two ceiling fans which were whirring unnecessarily in the empty compartment in this cold month of January. It was important that the boss remained in complete comfort and thus in good mood during the journey. Lachu had filled the two canvas *chagals* with water and he tied them securely to a window hook where evaporation caused by the wind rushing past the speeding train could cool them.

An hour later, when the train halted at Ludhiana, Harry sadly thought that he was just a stone's throw from his beloved village, Machiwara and in his view, his situation, was a classic case of being so near and yet so far. If that hawk, Subedar Major Jiwan Singh had not vetoed his suggestion to take his village cronies along as escort, they all would have surely visited the village to meet their families; and when full blooded soldiers pay a flying-visit to their wives there is always a chance of a poke. It was said nothing escaped Jiwan Singh's hawk like eyes and his computer like mind. It was rumoured that the man could count the pubic feathers of a flying bird. No wonder that he had seen through Harry's ploy to take his village cronies along, in no time. Maybe, he could devise some stratagem for a junket on the return journey to visit the village for a quick-fire pelvic thrust or two with his wife Jagtar Kaur whom he affectionately called Jagtaro. The train conductor's arrival at that juncture interrupted his thoughts. The train conductor was an Anglo-Indian who greeted the trio affably and inquired if there was any shortcoming in their cabin. The troika had noticed none. He advised them to latch their doors and pull the window shutters closed since a gang of thieves belonging to the *Sansi* tribe was operating in this belt.

The Indian subcontinent had a number of tribes or groups who were hereditary criminals. The most organized and ruthless amongst these were the thugs who had robbed and assassinated nearly a million travellers across India for several hundred years. Though the scourge of *thugee*, acts of thugs, had been successfully eradicated by the efforts of William Bentinck, and his chief Captain William Henry Sleeman, in mid nineteenth century; some ethnic or social communities still continued to remain hereditary professional offenders. These tribes were defined as "addicted to the systematic commission of non bail-able offences" and were registered under the Criminal Tribes Act enacted by the Brits. The *sansi* caste was one of the more prominent tribes on that list. Since they were described as habitual criminals, restrictions on their movements were imposed and adult male members were ordered to report weekly to the local police but they still managed to carry on thieving with impunity.

The railway guard on noticing one of the canvas water *chagals* sticking outside the window told them, to pull it inside. He apprised them that the *sansi* gang had formulated a unique way of robbing passengers. They had been using thorny *Kikar*, Mesquite Prosopis tree branches, to hook loose clothing of passengers through the open windows of moving trains. He informed them that the *sansi* placed or held *kikar* branches next to the railway tracks and brushed them against trains as they sped by. Any exposed or loose clothing exposed in the train windows got entangled in the *kikar* barbs and was pulled away by the offenders. There had been cases where loose clothing like turbans, *chunnis*, ladies' wraps, had got hooked onto the thorns of the *kikar* and yanked away by the *sansi* crooks. Only yesterday two turbans and three *chunnis* had been lost by the commuters of the Ambala-Amritsar Passenger. Having cautioned them not to expose any loose clothing in the open windows, he shook hands with them and after wishing them a comfortable journey he was away to the next coach. These Anglos were really polished and mannered guys, who did their job honourably, contemplated Harry, as he clambered aboard on hearing the whistle of the train's locomotive.

He looked out as the train sped South-ward and observed that it was getting dark. Soon it would be dinner time. He took out his mug and poured a shot of rum from his tin water bottle and without being beckoned Lachu untied one canvas *chagal* from its window anchor and poured the now quite cold water into the mug. Harry took a good swig and then he looked at the watch on his wrist. This was the first time he had worn a watch in his life. It seemed quite large and thick. He read the small sized print written in black on the white dial of the watch which told him that the watch had been manufactured by West End Watch Company Limited, London and was water and shock proof and had a radium dial. He had a faint idea of the meaning of these terms. Good stuff, he adjudicated. These English chaps procure only the best gear for their army, no wonder they rule the world. By his second shot of rum Harry knew that the handcuffs were manufactured by Chub and as two more ounces of rum glugged out of the tin bottle into his mug for his third slug, he was ready for dinner. When the train halted at Rajpura,

Matric darted out and procured three *Dona,* leaf bowls, of spicy *Kabuli chana,* chickpeas in sour gravy, from a vendor on the railway platform. Lachu simultaneously retrieved the packed dinner packets from their haversacks and served the same in their mess tins. Each packet had one *nafri,* or unit, comprising seven *chapatis,* Indian wheat flour tortillas, with cooked lentils and mixed vegetables. They ate their entire packed meal augmented by the hot chickpea gravy garnished with onion rings and chilies just bought from a vendor at the previous train halt. This was chased by a drink of cold water and followed by a fresh banana, dessert. The banana skins along with the empty *Dona,* leaf bowls, were discarded into the night through the open windows of the compartment.

Thereafter, they rinsed their mouths by noisily swirling water in their mouths and simultaneously inserting the index finger between the lips and running it over their teeth in a brushing movement. Some more rinsing and then they squirted the water forcefully from their mouths into the night through the open windows on either side of their moving cubicle. The problem of spewing liquid from a speeding train is, that it is pushed right back, by the train's slip stream, into the same compartment, through the same window, in the form of spray, right into the face of the errant. However, if it is jettisoned forcefully enough, then the returning spurt makes its re-entry through the windows of the trailing cabin. The loud expletives emanating from the adjoining back section, at the moment of their vigorous spout, was ample indication that our soldiers had shot into night with sufficient amount of power, drenching unsuspecting window seated selection of passengers, in the trailing cubicle.

Lachu rinsed his mouth once again and was jettisoning the water into the night through a window when the *sansi* struck. His protruding turban was hooked on the thorns of a fleeting *kikar* scrub and plucked from his head. And out it went, unravelling, into the night, through the window of the speeding train, unfurled like a flag, on its barbed mast. Lachu's attempt to retrieve the six yard long piece of cloth, being towed out of the window at 60 miles an hour and jerk it back was aborted when his endeavouring hand and jutting-out arm, was whacked, by another spiky branch with great momentum. The whole episode happened in a jiffy. Harry and Matric were oblivious to the mishap till they heard Lachu hollering in pain on being struck by the prickly timber. Alarmed at his howl they looked up and saw a turban-less Lachu in pain. The left sleeve of Lachu's jersey which had taken the impact was full of thorns and resembled the back of a porcupine. A small piece of a broken thorn was still embedded in the skin of his hand. Matric assisted the wrestler in removing the thorn from his hand and a cussing Lachu sucked at the wound and then compressed it with the thumb of his other hand to stop the bleeding.

Harry got up and examined Lachu's wound and told him to bandage it with his clean handkerchief. He then inspected his jersey and said, 'I think the jersey saved you from serious harm Lachu. Your hand wound is minor and will heal in a day or so.'

'The hand wound may heal in a day but what about my wounded ego, my humiliation?' retorted a seething Lachu. 'Boss, my turban was dislodged from my head and I am not going to forget that in a hurry.' A Sikh's turban is considered a symbol of pride and its forced removal by an adversary is considered to be shameful and degrading.

'The turban was removed by cunning by an unseen thug. You can't help if someone stabs you in the back without warning; and that too without rhyme or reason, can you? Even so, you did your best to retrieve the turban. Didn't you?' said Harry encouragingly.

Ustad was right he had been taken unawares and he indeed had made an effort to repossess the turban. Harry's soothing words had worked like salve on Lachu's hurt ego. Harry indeed had a way ease tensions and assuage one's hurt feelings.

'Yes I did make an effort to get hold of my flying turban. But I am feeling bad about the whole incident,' replied Lachu.

'Time is a great healer Lachu. You will soon put this mishap behind you and move on,' said Harry.

'You know boss, we should have taken the railway guard's advice, of caution, more seriously,' said Matric.

'Yeah and also carried a first aid kit,' responded Harry.

'*Ustad*, how will I make up for the loss of the turban?' said Lachu as he painstakingly commenced removing the countless quills implanted in his jersey pullover.

'You will be issued a new one after necessary inquiry. If the inquiry finds that the loss was due to negligence then you will have to pay for the new one. However if the inquiry feels that the loss occurred without any fault of yours then you will get a new one free of cost. I am confident that no blame or negligence could possibly be apportioned on you for this loss. So, don't worry.'

'Worry! Boss I have to worry. Don't you see? If there is an inquiry, the battalion is bound to learn that the turban was stolen, from my head, even as I was wearing it. Once the men get to know that, I will surely become the laughing stock of the battalion. I will turn into a subject of ridicule for having lost my turban to a thieving *sansi*. I don't want to undergo an inquiry. Please find a way out for me *ustad*,' implored Lachu.

'Well let me give it a thought. Meanwhile use the second turban you brought along,' said Harry.

They then shuttered the windows to keep the cold and the foraging *sansi*, out. Lachu was thereafter assisted in mopping up the shards from his jersey. Soon they had his pullover cleaned up. They changed into pyjamas, vests and jerseys for the night, applied anti-mosquito oil to their bodies and Harry declared 'Lights-out'.

As soon as his eyes adapted to the darkness, Harry removed the watch from his wrist and peered closely at its dial. He could see the two hands of the watch and all the twelve numerals on the dial, in green hue of the radium. He was excited, he had seen the time in the watch in total darkness; a radium dial watch would be a most useful appliance for use in his village, which like all Indian villages, was sans electric power. Whenever, he acquired a watch, it was going to be with a radium dial, he decided. He squinted at the watch again, the short hand of the watch was pointing towards X and the longer one was pointing to XII, so the time by his watch, he figured, was 10 o'clock. He was still admiring the contraption when sleep overwhelmed him and he started snoring, the watch slipping from his hand and falling on the floor with a clink, which went unheard by the sleeping soldiers. The train continued its noisy journey into the night.

They awoke just as the day was breaking and noticed that the train was at halt in the country-side, perhaps waiting for a green signal to proceed ahead. The time should be about six or seven in the morning guessed Harry, when he remembered that he had a wrist watch and could now state the exact time instead of a guesstimate. Accordingly, he brought his watch bearing left wrist in front of him with exaggerated flair to view the time but become disconcerted on seeing a bereft wrist. He went into a tizzy. The *sansi* had ripped off Lachu's turban from his head last evening, but they could not have possibly pinched the watch from his wrist. The windows were still shuttered and the doors latched. His flap ended only when he recalled last night's research of the radium-dial. The watch must have dropped on the bed when sleep had swamped him. He started to rummage through his bed with the other two lending a helping hand, when Matric yelled, 'Bingo', pointing to the watch lying on the floor next to Harry's sleeping berth. Harry quickly retrieved the watch and put it to his ear, lo and behold, the device was still working, it's ticking sound was music to Harry's ear. The watch was indeed shock proof, concluded Harry as he commenced winding it with a curling motion of his thumb and index finger on its knob. He then inquired about Lachu's hand wound. The wrestler extended his hand in Harry's direction for his inspection. The wound seemed to be healing well. In the meantime, Matric had detrained and broken a couple of thin young branches from a nearby *neem* tree. He brought them back into the train, where he cut them up into toothbrush size segments and distributed the same amongst the three of them. *Neem* is indigenous to India and is considered to have antiseptic qualities. It is considered good for oral care and its young stems called *Datuns* are popularly used for brushing teeth. The *neem* shoots now distributed by Matric, would be accordingly used as toothbrushes by them, by first softening one of its ends by chewing on it and after that utilizing the softened end as a toothbrush. The *datun* is discarded after its one time use.

The train reached Delhi railway station at 8 am, two hours behind schedule, by when the escort party had completed their ablutions and were dressed in their proper uniforms. The duration of the halt at Delhi was two hours; adequate time available for a visit to the historic Gurdwara Sis Ganj. During the times of the early Gurus, Sikh places of worship were referred to as Dharamsalas, where Sikhs could gather to hear the Guru speak. However Guru Hargobind the sixth guru, introduced the word Gurdwara, meaning the gateway through which the Guru could be reached and from then on all Sikh places of worship came to be known as Gurdwaras. Gurdwara Sis Ganj was so named because the "Sis", head, of the venerated ninth Sikh Guru, Guru Teg Bahadur, was barbarously severed by the ruling mughals at the site where the gurdwara now stood; half-a-mile from Delhi Railway Station at Chandni Chowk.

Since, Gurdwara Sis Ganj at Chandni Chowk was walking distance from the railway station, Harry and Matric set off on foot to pay obeisance at the shrine leaving Lachu to guard their belongings in the train. They crossed the road through the chaotic traffic of, *tongas & ekkas*, the Indian two wheeled horse carriages, bullock carts, hand carts, cycles, pedestrians, coolies, trams, buses, trucks, rickshaws and cars. They then cut across the well laid out and well maintained public-park, situated between the railway station and Chandni Chowk. They emerged at the clock tower square in front of the town hall in Chandni Chowk and veered left towards their destination, Harry having quickly compared the time by his watch with the time on the clock tower and found it in sync. They were impressed by the wide boulevard, which was as straight as an arrow leading towards the Red Fort. Long ago, there existed an octagonal pool where the clock tower now stood and from this pool emanated a canal which bisected the wide avenue throughout its entire length. It is said that light of the moon was reflected in the octagonal pool and the water channel giving an aura of glow. The Mughal Princess Jehanara, eldest daughter of Shah Jehan, the fifth Mughal Emperor, of the mighty mughal empire, who had conceived and supervised the project had accordingly christened it Chandni Chowk, which literally means Moonlit Square.

The origins of the Mughal Imperial family can be traced directly to two of the world's greatest conquerors; Genghis Khan, founder of the largest contiguous empire in the history of the world; and Amir Taimurlang, Taimur the lame, also called Tamerlane. Due to descent from Genghis Khan, who was a Mongol, the family was called Mughal, or Mogul, Persian for Mongol. Their influence and power were so, all pervading, that the English word "mogul", meaning influential, powerful, etcetera, was coined as a consequence of this dynasty and included in the English vocabulary. The mighty Mughal Empire remained in power for 300 years. Although the first six emperors saw the empire ascend, the later kings were weak, resulting in the mighty empire dwindling away and finally concluding, three centuries after its inception.

Each of the first half a dozen emperors could be ascribed a descriptive sobriquet. The first, Babur was the "Conqueror" having conquered India albeit in his fifth attempt and that too with some inside help; his son Humayun was the "Unlucky" having been dethroned by Sher Shah Suri the Afghan for a number of years and then having died of a fatal fall from a flight of stairs just after regaining his dominion. The next emperor arrogated the title Akbar, "the Great" on himself but he also full-filled the title in an exemplary way, everything about him was great, his conquests, his patronage of fine arts, his, attempt to create a new religion, so much so that even the size of his harem of 5000 women was great. This great ruler was followed by Jehangir the "Romantic" who lovingly laid out beautiful gardens and his only fixation being to have a larger harem than his famous father's and who drank himself to death like his two siblings while his beautiful wife Nur Jehan, ruled the empire; the fifth Mogul Emperor Shah Jehan, was the "Builder", having constructed the Taj Mahal, one of the Seven Wonders of the world and many other land mark buildings and forts, and whose daughter Jehanara had created the beautiful Chandni Chowk; he was succeeded by Aurangzeb the religious "Bigot", on whose orders the revered ninth Sikh Guru, Guru Tegh Bahadur was beheaded in Chandni Chowk for refusing to convert to Islam.

When Aurangzeb died, the Mughal Empire was at its zenith spanning three time-zones and covering nearly thirty degrees of the Northern Hemisphere astride the tropic of cancer. But after his demise the empire started to crumble, as governors of peripheral areas declared independence and a number of succession related conflicts ensued. These discords eroded the credibility of the empire and two foreign raiders took advantage of the weakening mughals. The first raider was Nadir Shah, a Timur descendent, who had usurped the throne in Persia and the second raider was Abdali an Afghan pillager. Their raids commenced in March 1939 and ended in 1761 and that too only when the Sikhs in Punjab gave resistence to the forces of Abdali. In the rout of Abdali one great Sikh fighter named Bhagel Singh came in to prominence.

The incompetent Mughal Monarchs of the time were less concerned about their dominion and more concerned about the vilification campaign by the populace, for their military weakness and rumoured non-performance in the harem. It was bad enough to have been proven militarily impotent by the raiders but the slander questioning their man-hood doing the rounds in the streets of Chandni Chowk was even worse. These rumours would have become a reality but for the prolonged and dedicated oral persuasions and the skilled hand ministrations with *sande-ka-tel*, sand lizard oil, by their faithful eunuchs and *laundis,* nautch girls.

The British took advantage of this state of affairs and started to move in-land from their coastal strongholds, the most decisive engagement being the Battle of Plassey which took place on 23 June 1757, where forces of the East India Company under Robert Clive defeated the army of Siraj-ud-Daulah, the Nawab of Bengal. Opinions on the conduct of the battle are divided. While Indian historians' point of view is that the battle was won by Clive by subterfuge, on the other hand the British perceive that the battle was won by superior tactics and deem it as the climax to Robert Clive's career. Be that as it may, the age old adage that everything is fair in love and war also applies to Plassey and the fact of the matter is that, this period is conventionally described as the beginning of British Rule of India. Clive, who in his early life seemed more likely to be heading for the hangman's noose than fame and fortune, got the British Sovereignty over India off the ground and himself became famous as "Clive of India".

In this state of affairs, Bhagel Singh, who having tasted victory in routing Abdali in the plains of Punjab entered Delhi on 11 March 1783. The Sikh leader was able to easily obtain a settlement from the ineffective Mughal Emperor Shah Alam II, under which he was permitted to construct gurdwaras on Sikh historical sites in the city and get a share of the city's revenue as well. Sis Ganj was one of the seven shrines built by him, from April to November 1783. Nonetheless, no sooner had Bhagel turned his back on Delhi, the site was re-occupied by the mughals. It finally came into Sikh hands during the British Rule.

The proverbial last nail in the coffin of the Mughal Empire was the failed native mutiny of 1857. While the Persian tyrant, Nadir Shah had taken the jewel studded Peacock Throne from the Mughals over a hundred years earlier, he had not fiddled with their realm. The Mughal Emperors had thus continued to be enthroned in Delhi and rule over India. On the other hand the British had captured and dethroned the last ruling emperor Bahadur Shah Zafar for his participation in the Indian Rebellion of 1857, depriving him of his throne and empire. He was exiled to Rangoon, Burma where he died in 1862; not in glory or fame but in obscurity, not as a king but as a commoner in pecuniary, writing beautiful but sad poetry filled with nostalgia which continues to be set to music and sung by the best Indian singers and wallowed by his admirers even today. Hence this last mughal monarch could also be awarded an epithet like his six illustrious ancestors; Zafar the "Poet". Mughal dynasty thus officially came to an end and the baton passed into the hands of the English.

———◄o►———

As Harry and Matric marched in step through Princess Jehanara's Chandni Chowk, the pool and the water canal created by her three centuries back were long gone. The British had added tramways on either side of the road and trams now hummed and clanged as they moved, up and down the length of Chandni Chowk, sending vibrations to the surrounding buildings and all but drowning the loud calls of *Aao, Aao* emanating from the rooftops of some houses where *Kabootar Baazi* addicts attempted to control their pigeon flocks in flight. *Kabootar,* meaning pigeon, *Baazi,* meaning game, is a sport played with pigeons. In this sport a flock of domesticated and trained pigeons is released by their trainers or *Baaz,* from their pigeon holes and these droves fly away, but not far, in near rectangle formation and respond to the calls of its trainer and return to their perch after some time. If a flock is able to pluck away a pigeon or two from a contending flight and bring these weaned pigeons with them to their own perch, without losing any of their birds, to a rival flock; then the flock is considered to be a victor. So a flock of, say, ten pigeons may return with its strength increased to twelve and conversely another assemblage may return with depleted numbers. If a complete flight is successfully lured away, it is like scoring a home run. This sport is considered an obsession and the hooked spend not only their money but also their life time on *Kabootar Baazi.*

Harry and Matric soon reached Gurdwara Sis Ganj. The two discarded their boots washed their hands and feet and entered the Gurdwara to pay obeisance. They first stood with folded hands and murmured a prayer and then, after kneeling down, they bowed and touched their fore-heads on the floor in front of Guru Granth Sahib, the Holy Book, kept on the *Takht,* Throne, as per Sikh *Maryada,* tradition. Next, they sat down to savour the *Shabad Kirtan,* religious hymns, for a few moments.

The sacrifice of the revered Guru Tegh Bahadur had roused the subjugated Hindus giving them pride and self-respect and earned the enduring title of *Hind-di-Chadar* or the Shield of India for the Guru. The Gurdwara was constructed one hundred and eight years later by Bhagel Singh. The present structure under which Harry and Matric now sat cross legged relishing *Shabad Kirtan* was of more recent vintage, having been constructed in 1930 during the British Raj. The trunk of the tree under which the revered Guru was martyred and the well from which he drew water for bathing during his incarceration, were left in-tact during the construction.

Harry and Matric were served dollops of *Krah Parsad,* religious offering made of wheat flour, sugar and *ghee,* clarified butter and stir-cooked over slow fire. The *parsad* is placed before the Guru Granth Sahib as offering and gets transubstantiated into some thing sacred and this is then distributed amongst the *sangat* or devotees in all the Gurdwaras.They consumed the holy *Parsad* and then wiped their ghee smeared hands on their beards and then twirled their moustaches. Their request for one additional helping for their colleague stuck at the railway station was immediately met. The two then moved to the *langar* or community kitchen where they did the traditional *Kar Seva*, voluntary work, by washing used utensils. They were then to be served with the *langar* meal but since they had to board the train immediately, the *sewadar* or assistant in the *langar* gave them the *langar* meal consisting of black lentils, cauliflower, potatoes, mango-pickles and *chapatis* carefully packed in *lifafas*, paper bags, so that they could eat the holy meal in the train.

The two hurried back towards the railway station. On the way Harry purchased an antiseptic plaster from a chemist and an army turban from a trader retailing army surplus gear, for Lachu. The park which had appeared so tidy during their morning crossing was now quite full with an assortment of people plying their trades. There were barbers, head and body masseurs with their array of coloured and fragrant oils, photographers with their tripod mounted large box cameras promising photograph prints within ten minutes. There were ear wax removers with their ear probes struck in the folds of their turbans, there were astrologers, there were conmen selling sex enhancing drugs and *Sande-ka-Tel,* Sand Lizard oil for penile massage and other magical aphrodisiacs, there were quack dentists claiming painless tooth extraction and quack eye specialists selling eye sight enhancing black kohl powder and a horde of other similar merchants and mendicants. It was more of a scene from Arabian Nights than British India. Harry and Matric successfully criss-crossed through this milieu, reaching their train compartment well in time and firstly gave the Holy *Parsad* to Lachu who accepted it in both hands with head bowed, in the traditional way. After eating it he too wiped his *ghee* laden hands on his beard and moustache just as the other two had done at the gurdwara. Harry then applied the medicated plaster on Lachu's wound and also handed over the turban to him. He told Lachu to reimburse one *taka* or two pice which was the cost of the turban.

Ordering Matric to arrange for breakfast Harry moved towards the locomotive of the train. As a child his maternal uncle, a fire man had shown him one from close quarters and since then he had been fascinated by rail engines. The engine which had just been coupled to the train had a large five pointed star painted in front and written on its side was 4-6-2. This was preceded by the letters XC and followed by a four digit number. Harry rightly guessed that it was the famous Pacific model manufactured by Vulcan Foundry of England for the Indian Railways. The locomotive belonged to the latest 'X' series and the 'C' meant that it was for hauling heavy passenger trains on trunk routes. The three hyphenated numerals gave out the wheel configuration; four small wheels in front, followed by six teamed large wheels connected to the steam piston to provide traction power and at the rear end were two small wheels to support the coal tender. The last four numerals were the registration no of behemoth. Harry observed that the Anglo-Indian driver was carrying out last minute checks and the fireman was shoveling coal into the boiler furnace while steam hissed out from the safety release valve; as if the loco was neighing and informing the driver that it was ready and raring to go. On hearing the guard's whistle followed by his full throated 'All aboard', announcement, Harry sped back to his carriage and his hurried entry into his compartment at 10.00 am by his watch, was heralded by a shrill whistle of the engine and then a jerky start of the train.

The train movement smoothened as it picked up speed and the escort sat down to breakfast of hot *poories*, deep fried *chapatis*, with potatoes in spiced gravy, served on *patal*, leaf platters and *donas* leaf bowls and sweet *lassi*, churned yogurt, dished up in *kulars*, terracotta tumblers. Breakfast over, a round of burping and then the used leaf platters, bowls and terracotta tumblers were disposed of in the normal manner, through the open windows of the moving train. Since Harry was of the view that, one must mind one's manners, at least during the day light hours, the rinsing of mouths and washing of hands was done in the toilet wash basin, by turns. One-time-use, leaf crockery thus taken care of and hand cutlery, fingers, nails, cuticles, palms and all, washed clean and dried, they wanted to attend to important work before commencing their day dreaming and personal administration. A happy Lachu gave Harry a one *taka* coin to cover the cost of his headgear. His loss having been made up, he would not be subjected to an inquiry now. Matric took out his pocket diary and miniature pencil to write the expenditure being incurred during this Madras Duty. He opened a fresh page and laboriously wrote as follows:—

MADRAS-DOUTY—JAN 1942
3 Dinnrs, 17/1 = 3 paise.
3 Brakefast, 18/1 = 1 anna, 2 paise.

He showed the entries to the boss who nodded his approval before closing the note book and putting it back into his pocket. Meanwhile Lachu had done 20 sit-ups as part of his daily fitness routine.

Presently Harry took out the movement order from his breast pocket and commenced reading it aloud to his captive audience. He started by first reading out the heading, 'MOVEMENT ORDER, and this, chaps, is in capitals,' and he continued, 'No 44XXXXX Naik Harinder Singh and a party of two Other Ranks, namely No 44XXXXX Sepoy Ram Singh and No 44XXXXX Sepoy Laxman Singh, will proceed on temporary duty to Station HQ, Madras for the purpose of collecting a deserter in custody of station HQ Madras and escort him to Jullundur.' He felt great to see his name on the order as in-charge of the escort. 'The party will take anti-malaria precaution and maintain discipline of a high order,' Harry made a note of this point to ensure its implementation and read on 'they will ensure security of all the equipment and stores on their charge. During the return journey they will also ensure security and well-being of the prisoner in their custody. In case of difficulty, they will report to the Movement Control Organization (MCO) for assistance.'

Mention of the prisoner in the document got Harry thinking. As per his knowledge, *thambis,* a generic term for all South Indian men, were by and large docile. However if this prisoner turned out to be a troublesome character, I will keep him in chains and even let wrestler Lachu work on him a bit, planned Harry. He continued reading the Movement Order, 'while travelling in the train, member(s) of the party will not, repeat, not drink alco—mmmm mm mmm,' he switched into a mumbling indiscernible mode mid-way into the sentence. Lord, he had nearly damned himself there. Just managed, in the nick of time, to cleverly commence mumbling incoherently to disguise the damaging part of the sentence thereby, hopefully, managing to fool his audience. 'Why disclose an aspect which is of no concern to his subordinates?' argued Harry, in his mind.

'Now, here is some-thing of interest to us,' he declared with gusto, as he re-commenced reciting the document, 'the party has been struck off ration strength (SORS) with effect from 18 January 1942 and is granted travel journey ration allowance (TJRA) for the journey period'. He stopped reading and said, 'boys, this means that we will get a ration allowance in addition to the travelling allowance. The implication being, that we will get money, a lot of money. Our pockets will be bulging when this job is done'. He again did a bit of muttering while browsing through the remainder part of the movement order, 'the remainder points are all routine and inconsequential', he declared as he folded the paper and inserted it back into his breast pocket.

They polished their boots, mended their scuffed clothing checked the buttons on their uniforms, washed and dried their inner garments, snoozed a bit, chit-chatted and played cards. At lunch time the trio did an *ardas,* prayer, with folded hands before digging into the holy langar meal given to them at the gurdwara in Delhi. They otherwise spent the day staring vacantly into the passing country side. Evening tea was purchased from a stall at a station en-route. As the Western sky turned dark from crimson Harry poured a sun-downer into his enamel mug from his army bottle and Lachu topped it with cold water from the canvas *chagal.* He also gave a shot each to his juniors. Alcohol always helps in keeping subordinates, in good humour and also ensures that any inappropriate incident occurring during the duty period was kept under wraps. The evening routine followed was like yesterday's, the only change being that the post dinner mouth cleaning, was done in the washbasin in the toilet and not through the windows. Harry saw the hour one last time on his radium dial watch after declaring lights out and then he dozed off. They all woke up during the night a couple of times. The first time was to discard their blanket covers and remove their jerseys because the weather was turning warmer with each mile of their Southward train journey. The second time was to switch on the fans in the compartment.

The time shown by Harry's watch was 11 am as the train came to a jerky halt at Madras. By then, Lachu had done his physical routine and book-keeper Matric had made three more expense related entries in the pocket size account ledger and the wrist watch had been wound up by Harry; their baggage was neatly packed and they themselves smartly turned-out in their summer uniforms. Since the weather in South India was hot and humid, they had adorned their uniforms without the jerseys. They got-off the train and Harry scanned the compartment one last time to re-check if any baggage had been inadvertently left behind. Satisfied by his survey he moved the escort with their tidily packed baggage to the MCO's office. The NCO on duty perused their papers and called for transport from Station HQ. Soon a snub nosed 15 cwt army truck arrived and ferried them to Fort St George and they were made to dismount in a unit of the Royal Gurkha Rifles. The unit BHM took their Movement Order and escorted them to the transient's barracks in the Administrative Platoon of the HQ Company and allotted them three cots. They unpacked and made their beds. They removed their mess tins, spoons and mugs from their haversacks and then neatly stacked their remainder baggage in the cupboard adjacent to their beds. The escort party was ignorant of the fact that they were lodged in historic quarters; it was the same barrack which had been inhabited by the first unit of the British Indian Army, over two centuries ago.

The activity in the barracks increased as the Gurkha Johnny returned from the training area. A Gurkha guide took them to the company dining hall where they were ladled out their lunch, consisting of boiled rice, lentils and vegetables, straight from the cooking pots into their mess tins by dining hall in-charge, at the food dispensing counter. A banana for dessert and their lunch was complete. They joined the unit soldiers at games in the afternoon followed by tea. They then took their uniforms to the unit *dhobi,* laundry-man, who ironed them with a heavy charcoal heated iron, followed by polishing of boots and they were prepared for the next day. After a bath and a change they attended the roll call fall-in, where next day's schedule was communicated to them by the CHM. Their intake parade was to be held in the morning and they were to attend a *Barakhana,* unit banquet, in the evening the next day. Soon thereafter the, evening meal was announced. Harry, unnoticeably, knocked back a shot from his water bottle before proceeding to the dining hall for dinner. On return to the barrack they draped their mosquito nets over their beds, hooking them in the stays provided in the walls on one side and the wire running along the entire length of the barrack on the other side. This would keep the mosquitoes at bay. Tooth brushing and a piss later they crawled into their beds for the night. They had had a long day and bid good night to one another, while the last note of the bugle sounding the "Last Post", signalling "Lights-out", resonated into their ears. Harry checked his watch it was 10 o'clock as they shut their eyes.

Up at 5 o'clock on the high timbre of the bugle sounding reveille, the trio attended one period of PT, Physical Training, with the unit personnel, where Lachu had showed off his physical prowess to the Gurkhas, followed by a hearty breakfast. They then changed, into their crisp uniforms, shining boots and perfectly tied turbans and were ready, half an hour before the appointed time, for the CO's "intake parade", by when Harry had wound up his wrist watch.

The CHM marched them off to the unit HQ fifteen minutes before arrival of the CO by when Jemedar Adjutant, Subedar-Major and the Adjutant, the in-chain officials had interviewed them. The CO arrived on the dot at eight and he shook hands with each one of them while the Subedar-Major and Adjutant explained the purpose of their duty. A wave of the hand and he was gone. The escort was thereafter assigned a guide, a smart Gurkha Rifleman or Private, wearing his army uniform of shirt, shorts, hose-stockings, neatly folded, one inch below the knee cap. His black boots were shining and the web anklets had shining buckles. His resplendent Gurkha hat was worn slightly askew and a *khukri*, the curved Gurkha knife, cased in a scabbard looped through his belt, dangled on his right buttock, all as per Dress Regulations. The *khukri* bounced on the right buttock at every alternate footstep of the guide, as he quick marched at 140 paces per minute, leading them to the quarter guard, for an audience with the subject of their duty to Madras.

They were taken to the cells where the prisoner was interned. There they met No XXXXXXXX Pioneer N Devar for the first time, in his cell. Devar had been a part of four Young Pioneers who on completion of their basic training, were being chaperoned by a Pioneer Corps NCO to their Pioneer unit. Their unit was deployed on construction of a railway track in the North West Frontier and when their train halted at Jullundur on a scheduled stop Pioneer Devar had run away. The NCO in charge had accordingly reported the matter to the MCO at Jullundur Cantonment Railway Station and proceeded ahead with the remainder party. Station HQ, Jullundur had issued necessary desertion papers and were accordingly dealing with the case for the last one year.

Harry's escort was now in Madras meeting the escapee to size him up since they were responsible to escort him back to Jullundur. Devar the South Indian *thambi*, was about 5 feet 8 inches tall, medium built, he was in clean clothing, shaved, close cut hair and as the escort would later recall, he was not dark but unexpectedly fair for a *thambi*. Harry informed him that they had been deputed to take him to Jullundur, the station from where he had absconded.

'So, Devar ready for your second trip to Jullundur?' said Harry. In his view, it was always good to communicate and put fear of God into your quarry, especially if the character had a history of slipping away, from trains, during journeys.

'Yes, saar,' replied the prisoner. South Indians tend to pronounce the word 'sir' as 'saar'.

'No hanky-panky, this time?'

'No hanky-panky, saar. I already regret I make mistake by running away earlier.'

'Good. Keep it that way. If you try any tricks with me, then you know what I'll do? I will put red chili powder in your backside and shove it in, right up to your throat and you will wish that you were never born. Am I clear?'

'Loud and clear, saar, loud and clear, I give you no trouble. I swear to God no trouble to your Highnesses.'

On a gesture from Harry, Lachu stepped forward and extended his hand towards the prisoner by way of introduction. The felon quickly grasped it and thus began an agonizing handshake for the unsuspecting *thambi*, who felt as if he had inserted his hand into a vice as the wrestler squeezed his hand. The hand was released only when he hollered with pain. 'That was a friendly handshake, buddy. So don't cross us till you are in our charge. If you do, then I will crush your balls.' said Lachu. He turned around towards Harry and continued, 'boss I think he understands us.' Looking back again, he said 'Right thambi?'

'Right, saar. I am a pious Catholic and I swear on my honour that I will not give you any trouble,' replied Devar as he put his bruised right hand into his left arm pit to relieve the pain.

'Excellent.'

The escort party was then taken to the JA who briefed them on the circumstances under which the runaway had been apprehended. The subject had got into a fracas with a local goon at a nearby liquor vend, called Diamond Bar, being operated illegally but obviously with police patronage. Wherever locally brewed moonshine is sold and consumed, fist fights are bound to take place; for this reason scuffles were common at this joint, but police never intervened, since they were paid patrons of the establishment. Given that the police never got involved in the unlawful goings-on at the pub and looked the other way, a local gangster had elbowed his way in and started collecting a weekly purse from the bar owner as protection money. The bar owner was also forced by the hoodlum to extend courtesy of providing copious amount of free hooch to him and his sidekicks. The owner was fed up paying two entities, the police and the goon. A trap was thus laid in collusion with the police, wherein the police agreed to pick up the hood if he ever got into a fight at the liquor vend. So no sooner had the palaver commenced between the thug and Devar, a regular at the bar, than the police appeared on the scene and arrested the feuding parties. The police while searching through the baggage of the inebriated customer came across an Army Pay Book and realized that the subject was a soldier without any leave certificate or any other legitimate absence document. They had immediately informed the Military Police, their counterparts in the army. That's how Devar landed up in the army cell as a prisoner.

After filling them with the circumstances leading to the prisoner's apprehension, the JA gave them an out pass to enable them to visit places of interest and told them to be back before the *Barakhana*. And out they went. They admired the high walls of Fort St George and guessed their height to be about 20 feet. The soldier in them immediately assessed that it was virtually impossible to over-run this place. They were awe struck by the wooden flag pole on which fluttered the English flag. This was the tallest flag pole they had ever seen. It was 150 feet high and made of teak wood. It is said that it was the middle sail mast of a sunken ship and had been salvaged from the ship wreck and erected here by the British. They visited the museum and the imposing church. Then they went out of the fort and loitered about in the area where they noticed a diner whose name "Pastry" had been mis-spelt as *"Pastrie"*. The owner must be a Punjabi rustic they had concluded. Who else would muddle up spellings of such an elegant eating place? They peeped inside to locate the illiterate Punjabi owner but were taken aback when they saw the prettiest *mem sahib,* English lady, managing the restaurant. It was only the worry of making a large reduction in their limited monetary resources, which stopped them from entering the diner.

'Boss, why is it that these *mem* sahibs are so pretty and also unabashed while our women are not so?' queried Matric.

'I don't know. It is perhaps the weather in those cold countries. Their boldness perhaps stems from their way of life.' replied Harry.

'Do you have any knowledge on *mem* sahibs Lachu?' said Matric

'Well, a distant relative of mine had participated in the Great War and was in a country called France,' commenced Lachu. Continuing he said, 'he is now quite old but his eyes still sparkle when he reminisces about his encounters with white women during his stay in France. He says that they are like angels. Their hair is flaxen and soft to the touch, bodies supple and smelling of flowers. Their breath is sweet-smelling and refreshing.'

'By Joe, your kin indeed was a lucky guy.'

Lachu regaled the others with the escapades of his ancestor in France as the three loitered around. Slowly but surely Harry learnt that Matric was still a virgin but both he and Lachu were in love with girls from their villages and would not mind a short visit to their homes.

'Cut-out this smutty talk. Stop your day dreaming and get back to the barracks, while I run an important errand,' interjected Harry. He had so far remained silent, listening to their heart-to-heart conversation, the content of which had again aroused a longing in him to visit his wife at his village. An idea was germinating in his mind, maybe just maybe, he could come up with a plan to break journey for a short while on the way back. He continued his order, 'and fetch, my lunch from the dining hall and keep it in my cupboard since I may get delayed. Also get a fresh set of *mufti,* civil clothing ready for the *Barakhana,* big feast banquet, being organized by the Gurkhas this evening.'

He then went to the Military Police and spoke with the NCO who had been deputed to collect the inebriated *thambi* from police custody and his next port of call was the Diamond Bar. It was at the drinking joint that he learnt that Devar had been a regular customer at the Diamond. The proprietor recalled that Devar had a friendly countenance and was fond of his drinks. His parents had expired and his only attachment was to a local girl, who, the owner recollected, had also been the reason for his desertion from the army. This affection too had been severed because the girl had emigrated and gone to Ceylon along with her family last month. The family planned to set up house in Ceylon and work on the tea plantations situated in the Central Highlands of the Island nation, where a large number of Indian Tamils were already settled.

At this juncture Harry decided to have another chat with *thambi* in his cell. He spent nearly half an hour with the prisoner. He was able to elicit corroboration of the information he had acquired from the seedy Diamond Bar. Additionally, he realized that *thambi* was mortally scared of the goon with whom he had had a brawl a few days back. Harry thus reasoned that since Devar's female accessory had moved out of Madras, to a far-away land and there was always going to be a lurking danger of a retaliatory attack on him by the goon in Madras; it was likely that *thambi* would feel safer in the army than in Madras. It was also a far-fetched notion that *thambi* would return to Madras only for a drink of hooch at his favourite, though sleazy, watering hole when his rum rations in the army were adequate to slake his thirst. Accordingly, Harry mentally made a case that there was only one course available to *thambi*, which was also the best course i.e. to stay in the army. In consequence he ruled out an escape attempt by the prisoner on their return journey.

By the time he returned to the barracks his lunch was waiting and his freshly ironed mufti was carefully laid out on his bed for the evening *Barakhana*. *Barakhana* is a banquet organized on special occasions like a raising-day, battle honour day, victory day, a holy day in an army unit. The Royal Gurkha unit, were celebrating a battle honour day this evening and the escort from Jullundur were invited to attend as guests.

Since there are nearly 800 men in an infantry battalion, a banquet for the entire unit can only be held outdoors in an open area. The Gurkhas had rightly chosen to hold it in their football field where tents had been erected for this purpose. The British Indian Army units are authorized assorted types of tents. Of these, Tent 180 pound GS is most versatile. It has two flies and when pitched in the normal manner in the inverted "V" configuration it is designed to accommodate one section of ten men. However, due to its flexibility it can be turned into an awning by simply using only its' outer fly and erecting it in an inverted "L" shape. This is achieved by raising one side of the fly and inserting two additional vertical poles under it and tightly tethering them to a couple of pickets.

Such tent outer fly canopies had been erected, in pairs, around the unit football field, which was doubling up as the venue for the *Barakhana*. These awnings were arrayed geometrically on three sides of the field in a hollow square arrangement, with military precision. The open side of these inverted "L" shaped shelters faced inwards towards the middle of the field where a raised platform had been constructed which was to be used as a stage for the entertainment programme. There was one pair of such awnings for each Rifle-Company, and two pairs for the HQ Company making a total of six pairs made from twelve tent outer flies. Each company had displayed its company coloured buntings on the open side of its shelter. Dining-tables and benches had been positioned under these awnings where the unit personnel now sat with their empty mess tins and unfilled enamel mugs. In addition, one additional tent per company had been pitched, out of view, behind these shelters, and used as pantries where cooked food in cauldrons and other cooking pots and pans had been stored. Water tanks filled with drinking water were parked next to the pantries. Further to the rear temporary urinals had been fabricated. A large marquee, store tent had been pitched, on the fourth side of the field for the officers and was furnished with sofas and reclining chairs facing the stage, behind which was a large dining table with dining chairs. A temporary fire point with adequate firefighting equipment had been put in place, nearby, as a safety measure.

Dressed in mufti, Harry and his escort party had made it to the venue of the *Barakhana* with their mess tins, plates and spoons well before the given time. The trio, were shepherded to one of the HQ company canopies. They sat down at their allotted sitting places facing the stage and took-in the view of the banquet arrangements and awaited arrival of the CO. The CO's arrival was heralded by the buglers playing the fanfare followed by a loud explosion detonated by the pioneer personnel of the unit and Harry looked at his watch, it was 7 o'clock. Lt Col Savage the CO got down from his jeep and was received by the second-in-command and commenced his round to various companies as the unit Pipe Band struck 'Hundred Pipers' the regimental march past. The banquet had commenced. He was escorted first towards "A" or "Able" Company where he was served a shot of rum in a mug. When he raised a toast to "A" Company, the whole company stood up, rum filled mugs in hand and gulped down the fiery liquid in one swig. He ate vegetable *pakoras,* deep fried fritters made from vegetables dipped in spiced chickpea batter which were served to him. He spoke to nearly every Gurkha Rifleman in Gurkhali language and he seemed to be-knowing each one of them personally. Visit to "A" Company over, he moved to the next company which was "B" or "Baker" Company and followed the same routine, only the snacks served were varied.

Watching from their enclosure, the Sikh trio were amazed to see that CO of the unit not only recognised all his men but also knew their names, but it was Lachu who voiced his astonishment, when he said, 'I say, these Gurkhas look all the same to me. How in heaven can the CO differentiate one from the other?' His observation brought chuckles of quiet laughter from the non Gurkhas sitting around him.

By the time the CO reached HQ Company, Harry and his team, were on their fourth snack and had been replenished with their second drink. Lt Colonel Savage came straight to the table where attached personnel were seated. Apart from the three Sikhs, there were two men from the Maratha Light Infantry, three from the Madras Regiment, one from the Ordnance corps. He inquired if their stay was comfortable and drank to their health. He also ordered another round of drinks for the attached men and requested the Sikh trio to demonstrate their Punjabi *Bhangra* dance at the end of the entertainment programme. A request made by a CO was more than a command so Harry and his side-kicks had no choice but to say *'theekh hai,* ok, sahib.'

No sooner had the CO reached the officers' enclosure after his round than the entertainment commenced. The performance began with an assortment of songs and skits followed by a *Khukri* dance by the unit dance troupe. *Khukri* is a mildly curved knife of Nepalese origin. It has an inwardly curved edge and is used as a knife, a tool and as a weapon. It is a symbolic weapon of all Gurkha Regiments and they had seen a sheathed one bobbing on the buttocks of their guide, on their way to the quarterguard that morning. It has a holding grip on one end and its blade gradually becomes wider, up to its curvature. Past the bend, it flares out rapidly and its widened broad blade also becomes heavy. Beyond its widest spot it commences to taper off, ending in a sharp point. It is said that when a mirror like polished *khukri* is brandished by the Gurkha, it temporarily blinds the enemy and once the nerve-racking battle cry "*Aayo-Gurkhali,* here cometh the Gurkha," falls on the bedazzled adversary's ears, most opponents prefer to scoot than fight. A live performance of the decapitating capacity of the *Khukri* can be witnessed in some Gurkha Regiments, on the religious day of Dussehra which falls on the tenth day of the Indian month of *Ashwin,* corresponding to October in the Western Calendar, when, as per a Gurkha custom, a buffalo is beheaded with one stroke of the *khukri.*

Today's *Barakhana* was part of the celebrations, marking the Battle Honour awarded to the unit, on its victory in the frontier province. On this very day over half a century ago this Gorkha unit had overcome a formidable enemy in a hard fought battle. Therefore, the grand finale of today's show was a Son-et Lu-mi-ere, portraying that hard fought battle. The light and sound show replicated the hand-to-hand fight between the defending Gurkhas and the attacking tribesmen. At its culmination it showed the Gurkhas, who having run out of ammunition, jumping out of their trenches, unsheathing their *khukris* and slaying the foe, with these curved knives, forcing him to abort the attack and retreat. All portrayed under the ethereal lighting of 2 inch mortar, parachute flares. The departure of the last surviving enemy brought a thunderous applause from the audience including the Sikh trio.

However, the entertainment was extended due to the direction given by CO to the Sikh trio during his round and a *Bhangra* Dance demonstration was added at the end as a valedictory performance. As soon as Harry and his boys commenced the *Bhangra,* four more Sikhs who were on the clerical and other support staff of the Gurkha unit also joined them. The beat of this earthy dance is so catchy that soon the whole unit was tapping its feet as the drummer frenziedly crashed his drum sticks on the *dholak,* drum. The clapping by the audience continued long after the drummer's crescendo.

Then began the banquet for which Harry invited the four *Bhangra* enthusiasts to their table. By the time the sumptuous *Barakhana* was over a thick friendship had developed between the *Bhangra* participants since three of them were from the Doab region of Punjab, not far from Harry's village.

The tipsy but happy unit returned to the barracks just as the last post was being sounded by the unit bugler. Lights out was delayed this evening and it was nearly 2300 hours by Harry's wrist watch when they finally shut their eyes and went to sleep, without opening out their mosquito nets and without brushing their teeth.

Next morning after PT, Harry was ordered to report to the Quartermaster office at 1000 hours. Harry wound-up his watch and reached the office area an hour and thirty minutes before the appointed time. Instead of going to the Quartermaster's office he went to the Adjutant's office and ferreted out last night's Bhangra buff who was a clerk there. After a warm handshake and a little black slapping, Harry invited his new found friend for a cup of tea in the unit canteen. Over a cup of tea and pastry Harry laid bare his request; to be given the movement order a day earlier than the day of departure so that he could visit his family en-route. The clerk said that on week days he could only give the movement order twelve hours in advance. He however suggested a way out. He advised that the journey should commence on a Monday morning in which case their out-take formalities would perforce have to be done on Saturday and that too before lunch because after that the officers would be on their week-end excursions till Monday morning. The clerk from the Doaba region of Punjab assured Harry that he would be able to hand over the movement order and other connected documents to him after lunch on Saturday if the journey was to commence early on a Monday. Harry cleared the two paisa bill and they headed back to the office area. A plan was already forming in his mind.

Harry reached the Quartermaster's office on time and was then given a railway warrant for the prisoner's travel and told to make reservations for the return journey for the party. He was assigned a motor cycle dispatch rider who took him to the railway station. Harry made the return journey reservations for the early morning train leaving Madras on Monday the 26th of January. Since the train's departure was at 0500 hours on a Monday therefore their out take parade would have to be done on Saturday. If his clerk friend kept his promise, Harry would get hold of the travel documents from him on Saturday the 24th of Jan and then they could catch an earlier train and have anything upwards of 24 hours of free time at their disposal, enough to enable them to visit their families on the return journey. While riding pillion on the motorcycle on the return trip, he continued to refine his plan in his mind and was so engrossed that the dispatch rider had to nudge him, to make him dismount from the pillion, on reaching the unit. Harry confirmed to his clerk friend in the adjutant's office that the return journey departure time was 0500 hours on Monday the 26th of January and he picked three foolscap white and two carbon papers from his table on his way out. He then informed the JA to plan their out-take parade on Saturday accordingly. A word with the Quartermaster's staff confirming the railway reservation and he was done with the officialdom. Now he had to take the other two on-board for the success of the planned shenanigan.

It was during lunch time that he broached the subject. 'Hey, you guys listen. Won't it be nice if you fellows could pay a visit home?'

'Wishful thinking,' retorted Matric.

'It would be nice,' responded Lachu, 'and you know my home town Patiala is just an hour's journey from Rajpura which is on our route. I could flit across and be back within four to five hours if we stop for that long at Rajpura.' One down and one to go thought Harry.

'You are thinking just about yourself because you want to meet your girl friend in Patiala. What about me? My place is beyond our destination, nearly three hours beyond Jullundur. How can I even think of bunking even if we take a four hour stop along the journey route?' piped in Matric. Wants but not sure how it can be pulled off, assessed Harry.

'You have a one track mind. I am not thinking of my girl fiend. I want to visit Patiala because wrestling matches are scheduled in last week of March in Patiala and wrestlers have been invited to enroll early for the same. The king's herald has been going from street to street, making this announcement. I just want register now so that I can participate in the wrestling bouts. Rumour has it that our *Maharani*, Queen is expecting a child in the coming months and astrologers have predicted that she will be blessed with a son. Arrival of a male child, an heir to the throne is always a time for festivities and dishing out of cash gifts from His Highness. If I perform well, in the wrestling matches, I may even win a cash prize. And a cash prize from his highness means a lot of money.'

'Don't make excuses. If you want to visit your girl, say so. Don't drag in big names to impress us.'

'You are a doubting Thomas, Mr. Matric. The purpose of my visit to Patiala is solely to sign up for the wrestling tournament. If a meeting with the girl does materialize it will be merely incidental.'

'I still don't believe you. How can you even think of a visit when you know that I don't stand a chance of visiting my place at Lahore?'

Time to butt in. 'Matric is right,' said Harry, 'if Lachu visits Patiala then Matric also visits Lahore and that too for a longer duration. For that I will devise a plan. I know that Lachu is keen for a visit but are you also interested Matric.'

'Sure, boss, I am interested. I am sceptical only because my home town is on the other side of our destination Jullundur. Other-wise I am all for it.'

All aboard, thought a delighted Harry. Even the mightiest succumb to lure of a visit to their sweethearts. These were mere mortals. 'Right, then a visit is on the cards,' said Harry with finality, 'but I must swear you to total secrecy. You will not divulge this clandestine excursion to any one.'

'Yes, boss.'

'We will assemble for a final briefing tomorrow in the unit Information Room at 1100 hours, when the Gurkhas will still be on their training and we can have the room to ourselves without fear of any eaves-dropper,' said Harry as he got up from the dining table after finishing his lunch.

On return to barracks he assigned them the task of taking over the prisoner's kit as per the inventory prepared by the unit. Thereafter they were to remind the BHM to have the prisoner examined by the medical officer and certified as "fit for travel". Harry sat down on his bed deep in thought. There were still a couple of hurdles to be resolved. While the travel documents would be in his possession on Saturday he must also ensure that the HQ Company *Havildar Major,* Sergeant Major did not oppose their move to the railway station a day in advance and its *Quartermaster Havildar*, Quartermaster Sergeant, gave orders to the cookhouse to provide them with a packed meal or two. He knew that on the way back they would be able obtain their meals from the railway caterers on payment but why spend money when you could obtain wholesome meals free of cost. There was also the question of taking over the prisoner from the guard commander at the quarter guard who would require a nod of approval from the Battalion *Havildar* Major for handing over the prisoner and his documents to them.

Harry racked his brains to come up with an answer and then suddenly he had a way out. He decided to tackle the Gurkha NCOs over a drink. The Gurkha and the Sikh have been classified by anthropologists as belonging to different races. Their physical appearance is entirely different from each other. The Sikhs are Caucasian Aryans and are characterized by a light skin colour ranging from white to dusky dark, straight black hair, prominent eyes, pronounced and well-shaped aquiline noses and sharp features, medium to well built muscular bodies and hail from the horizon touching plains of Punjab, the land of five rivers. The Gurkhas, on the other hand belong to the Mongoloid race and are characterized by yellowish or light skin, very less hair growth on their bodies, small almond-shaped eyes, short in height and very lean and well-developed muscles. They have a pug nose and mongoloid facial features and they come from the Himalayan region of Nepal, in the North North-East of India. Their habits too are different due to their way of life and habitat. While the Sikh prefers a game of Hockey and a wrestling bout, the Gurkha is a Soccer addict and is more into boxing, one is hairy the other is practically hairless, the Sikh is a loud mouthed extrovert whereas the Gurkha is a quiet introvert, staple diet of the Sikh is wheat based *chapati* bread, the Gurkha survives on rice. While the Gurkha woos a female with patience and showers her with gifts, the Sikh is more direct and abrupt and is quite capable of squeezing a free lunch from the fairer sex. They are practically two different peoples contrasting in most aspects but yet have a few common traits. They are both equally brave, they are both partial to alcohol and they are generous in friendship. It was these common qualities that Harry decided to exploit. He accordingly decided to invite the NCO power bloc of the unit to a return party in reciprocation to the *barakhana*. This would of course, require some planning and administrative support.

The first step in executing his plan was to cater for alcohol and to extend invitations to his guests. To begin with he would have to arrange for adequate booze for the planned party. He firstly took stock of his rum holding. He calculated that he had taken three slugs on each of the two nights in the train and his two associates had consumed one each on the train on one night. He had taken one shot on the first night of arrival at Madras that made seven shots for himself and two shots for his associates, a total of nine pegs had been poured out from his olive green tin carafe. So there should be at the most three or four pegs available. After making a physical check by shaking his water bottle and by determining its weight he assessed that the obtainable rum was about four to six fluid ounces. Certainly not enough for a party and a two thousand mile return journey especially when he knew that his guests could consume copious amounts of the fiery fluid. If his three guests and he himself consumed three pegs each, he would require one additional bottle of liquor at the very least and if the party prolonged then an additional bottle may well be necessary. Without waste of time Harry met his clerk friend who obtained sanction for issue of two bottles of XXX Rum on payment from the canteen. He collected the two bottles by paying ten annas the cost of the bottles. He knew that Mr. Hemvati Agarwal, the canteen contractor had over charged him by at least two annas since he had been purchasing rum at Jullundur at a lesser rate. He felt that the services of the canteen should be taken over and handled by the units themselves. His anger at the canteen contractor subsided as he stowed the dark liquid bottles alongside his army water bottle in his gear. His cache now became two full bottles and six fluid ounces of XXX Rum. His first task stood completed.

He then invited CHM Amar Bahadur Gurung and the CQMH Nar Bahadur Thapa for a drink at seven that evening and they both accepted without much persuasion. He then approached BHM Tej Bahadur who also accepted without any reservations. Invitations to the power brokers, whose writ ran in the barracks, too had been successfully extended. Having done with both responsibilities, he ordered his two subordinates to make an enclosure on one side of the barrack by draping blankets on the mosquito net wire in the barrack and make suitable other arrangements for the success of the party.

In the evening Harry visited the quarter guard and again spent some moments with the prisoner. He then met the guard commander and told him that he would be collecting the prisoner in a day or two for conducting him to Jullundur. The guard commander was already aware of the purpose of Harry and party's sojourn to Madras and assured Harry that prisoner had been medically examined and declared fit for travel and would be delivered over to the escort party on production of the return journey movement order with a suitable endorsement concerning the prisoner. He then showed Harry, the prisoner register wherein Harry would have to sign in his capacity as the recipient of the prisoner. On the way back he ordered snacks at the unit cafeteria to be delivered at the transients' barrack at 7.00 pm.

The NCOs started to arrive at 1900 hours and the last to come in was the BHM. Harry's two sidekicks served the drinks and the snacks and the party commenced in the temporary enclosure created and furnished with two benches and a table by Harry's boys. The *Langar* Commander, catering in-charge, had got wind of the get-together when furniture and crockery were requested from him, by the organizing duo. When the NCO Quartermaster attends a function of this nature it is traditional to serve him and his associates with the best possible buffet and soon the party goers were inundated by a variety of sumptuous and mouth-watering snacks prepared in the cookhouse and served by Gurkha men doubling up as waiters under the watchful eye of the *Langar* Commander. Harry had diplomatically broached his request to the guests after their third drink and by the time the party got over, repeated assurances of 'no problem in meeting your requests *sardarji*', "*sardarji*" is a respectful title given to a Sikh, 'no problem at all', were given individually and chorused collectively by the three powerful guests. The happy invitees bear-hugged the great *sardarji* and thanked him profusely for the bash, and then bidding goodnight they proceeded to their quarters.

One complete bottle of alcohol and half of the other had been consumed and Harry mentally graded the party a success as he decanted the left over booze into his water bottle. He was sure that it would be sufficient for the return journey. They razed the temporary enclosure as soon as the party got over, returned the borrowed items and Harry checked his watch it was nine thirty, they, were still thirty minutes away from lights out. He took out his note book and started making notes in it and continued to do so till lights out. He shut his notebook as the last post was sounded by the unit bugler. He then shut his eyes and went into a dreamless slumber.

The following morning, after breakfast Harry wound up his watch, sharpened his pencil, put the note book and the sharpened pencil in his breast pocket and marched towards the unit Information Room, armed with the three foolscap papers and the two carbons he had appropriated from his clerk friend's table the day before. The Information Room had a number of newspapers neatly displayed on desks. There was a carom board and a Chinese-checkers board arrayed on two tables. On the wall opposite to the entrance was a photograph of the British Monarch His Majesty King George VI and below that was the photograph of Victor Alexander Tim Hope, 2nd Marques of Linlithgow KG, KT, GCSI, GCIE, OBE, PC, Viceroy of India. Lower down were the stern faces of the Commander-in-chief of India and Colonel of the Regiment of the Royal Gurkhas, looking out from their bust sized photographs, their names followed by their string of decorations neatly written underneath. Lower down were the photographs of Gallantry Award winners of the regiment. On another wall was displayed other motivational material. There was a map of the British Empire prominently displayed. All this did not interest Harry.

He pulled out a chair and sat down at a table and removed a pin from his turban and used it to staple the three blank papers together. He then inserted the two carbon papers between the three white blank papers alternately, so that he could obtain two carbon copies of his handiwork. He spread this pinned booklet of blank and carbon papers in front of him, took out his pencil, tested its point on the tip of his finger and got to work.

Standing next to the train at Ludhiana Railway Station during the outward journey, five days back on Sunday the 17th of January, Harry had yearned to visit his wife in village Machiwara adjoining Ludhiana. He had been unable to fructify his desire into reality because of the motley profile of his group, who he feared, were likely to divulge his illegal jaunt to the unit on return. However, in these five days the members of the variegated group had come closer to each other and he had successfully taken them on-board his planned adventure by promising them a visit to their homes, Patiala for Lachu and Lahore for Matric. As a matter of fact he had not only got an enthusiastic response from the other two but also a vow to secrecy when he had put his proposal to them; after all an additional visit home, even if it was a flying visit was most welcome. With each one colluding in the plot, chances of any one letting the cat out of the bag were remote; after all, there is always honour amongst thieves or shall we say amongst participating cohorts. Accordingly Harry made an audacious plan under which they all could visit their homes on the return journey, on French leave for up to a day each, without any one becoming the wiser. Harry was now confident of the success of the plan and hoped that *thambi* the prisoner did not give them any trouble during the journey.

He was ready and had mentally rehearsed his briefing by the time his two associates joined him. He removed the pin fastener from the sketch he had just prepared and inserted it back into his turban. The three sat down at the carom table and Harry placed the original copy of the sketch, he had prepared so painstakingly, on the table and distributed its carbon copies to each of his other two associates. He folded the used carbon papers neatly and then carefully inserted the same into the folds of his pay book for future use. The pay book and the sharpened pencil went into his breast pocket next. He then commenced the briefing.

'Right fellows pay attention,' commenced Harry, 'I will brief you on Exercise "Visit Home". If you have any doubts you can ask me during the briefing or alternatively ask me at the end, right?'

'Right *Ustad*,' replied his two subordinates in unison. *Ustad* is a respectful form of speech generally used by other ranks in the Indian Army, to address a senior or boss or instructor.

He produced *a Killi,* a blunt wooden nail, approximately four inches long used by Sikhs to push any disheveled hair which may give an untidy appearance, back into place under their turbans or beard nets, as the case may be, to make their appearance neat and well-groomed. In this case the *Killi* was used as an aid, in lieu of a pointer to indicate various places on the sketch during the briefing.

'Let me first introduce the sketch which covers the area of our surreptitious operation. The North of the sketch is as indicated by the arrow,' he began, pointing to the arrow mark on the sketch with his *Killi* pointer, 'and the sketch is not to scale.' He produced a notebook from his pocket on which he had jotted down his briefing last night and referred to it.

'Landmarks,' he began, using the *Killi* to point at the various landmarks, 'Up North is Amritsar, 60 miles to its South, is Jullundur and another 40 miles further South is Ludhiana and four miles to its East is Machiwara. Another 40 miles towards Delhi is Rajpura and 20 miles to its South is Ambala. Now as we move back up North, we come to Patiala 20 miles West of Rajpura,' he continued pointing to the landmarks on the sketch in the laid down clock-wise direction, as he went on, 'and further North is Lahore, 20 miles West of Amritsar,' and he moved his *Killi* pointer towards Lahore and Amritsar, in synch with his monologue; 'and back to Amritsar.' He repeated the landmarks once more as laid down in the training manuals, again in a clock-wise direction.

EXERCISE VISIT HOME

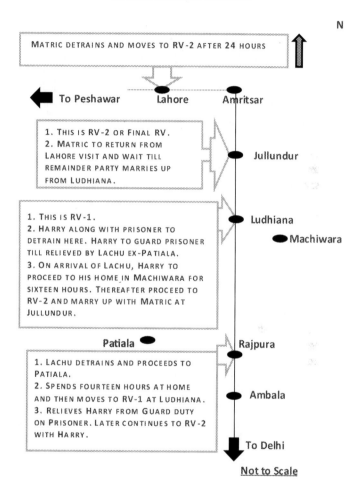

N

MATRIC DETRAINS AND MOVES TO RV-2 AFTER 24 HOURS

To Peshawar   Lahore   Amritsar

1. THIS IS RV-2 OR FINAL RV.
2. MATRIC TO RETURN FROM LAHORE VISIT AND WAIT TILL REMAINDER PARTY MARRIES UP FROM LUDHIANA.

Jullundur

1. THIS IS RV-1.
2. HARRY ALONG WITH PRISONER TO DETRAIN HERE. HARRY TO GUARD PRISONER TILL RELIEVED BY LACHU EX-PATIALA.
3. ON ARRIVAL OF LACHU, HARRY TO PROCEED TO HIS HOME IN MACHIWARA FOR SIXTEEN HOURS. THEREAFTER PROCEED TO RV-2 AND MARRY UP WITH MATRIC AT JULLUNDUR.

Ludhiana

Machiwara

Patiala

Rajpura

1. LACHU DETRAINS AND PROCEEDS TO PATIALA.
2. SPENDS FOURTEEN HOURS AT HOME AND THEN MOVES TO RV-1 AT LUDHIANA.
3. RELIEVES HARRY FROM GUARD DUTY ON PRISONER. LATER CONTINUES TO RV-2 WITH HARRY.

Ambala

To Delhi

Not to Scale

Landmarks done he moved to the next heading.

'Information: The information about our prisoner, Devar or *thambi* is that he understands English but he also understands us. I have ascertained from the Diamond Bar, the Hooch joint from where he was arrested by the police, that our subject is fond of his drinks and was a regular customer at the Diamond.

He also had a girl-friend tucked away in a nearby village but she had recently moved to Ceylon with her parents. He, therefore, has no alluring interest in Madras any more. He also knows we mean business and is unlikely to attempt an escape but since he has a history of slipping away, we will have to remain alert and thwart any evil design, he may still hold.' He resumed with own information, 'as far as our information is concerned, I have stage managed to obtain our travel documents 36 hours prior to our official time of departure which means we can comfortably visit our homes on our way back.' Hearing the last sentence their happy faces became more cheerful.

'Task: Our task is to visit our homes in Lahore, Patiala and Machiwara individually in a fixed time frame'. He repeated the task again as laid down in the training manuals.

He referred to his notes, 'now comes the Method,' he announced, 'we will conduct the exercise in four phases as follows:—

'Phase1: Visit by Lachu to his home in Patiala.
'Phase2: Visit by Matric to his home in Lahore.
'Phase3: My visit to my home in Machiwara.
'Phase4: Coordinated arrival and rendezvous of all members at Jullundur.

'Phase1. In this phase Lachu will detrain at Rajpura at V Hour on J plus 2 day, where J is the day of commencement of journey from Madras, and proceed to Patiala where he can remain for fourteen hours up-to V plus 14. The remainder party will continue its journey up to Ludhiana. Self along with the prisoner, *Thambi* will disembark at Ludhiana not before V plus 1 hour and establish RV-1. However Matric will continue his journey towards Lahore. I will remain guarding the prisoner at RV-1, till V plus 14 hours by when Lachu will come and relieve me after his home visit.

'Phase2. In this phase Matric will detrain at Lahore not before V plus 4 hours. He will proceed to his home at Shahdra, Lahore and can stay there for 24 hours up to V plus 28. After the visit he will move to RV-2 at Jullundur and marry up with the entire party.

'Phase3. In this phase I will proceed to my home not before V plus 14, leaving *Thambi* under guard of Lachu at RV-1. I will return to RV-1 by V plus 30 hours and resume command from Lachu.

'Phase4. This is the final rendezvous phase. In this Self, Lachu and *Thambi* will board the Madras Express train coming from Madras on J plus 3 Day at Ludhiana not before V plus 30 and disembark at Jullundur, our RV-2, an hour later, as if we have travelled in the train all the way from Madras. Matric coming from the opposite direction will lie incognito till our arrival and will marry up with us in-conspicuously. On the other hand if we land up at Jullundur before Matric then we will wait till he marries up with us. We will then proceed to the unit as one disciplined escort party with our prisoner.

'Miscellaneous

'RV1: Ludhiana Railway Station, Platform No1, adjacent to the Railway Police Post.
'RV-2: Jullundur Cantonment Railway Station Platform No 1.

'Entraining-station: Madras.

'Entraining/Journey Day: J Day.

'J Day: That is the day journey commences—Saturday, 24 January 1942 (AN).

'V Hour: The Time of arrival of the train at Rajpura.

'Security of prisoner: The prisoner will be hand cuffed during entire halt at RV-1. Hand cuffs may be removed when train is in motion. Lachu will ensure that all compartment doors are latched during the night. In the unlikely event of the prisoner attempting an escape or escaping the emergency chain of the train will be pulled and train halted. The prisoner will be chased and re-apprehended and properly secured.

'Contingency Planning: There can be innumerable contingencies but the main thing is that if there is an emergency situation I will call off the exercise. On the other hand in case opportunity presents itself to extend our domestic sojourn we will grasp it. Just keep alert and follow my bidding.

'Code word: Code word to abort the exercise is "Khatam".

'Administration

'Rations: Each one of us will take one cooked meal in our haversacks from the unit cook house for the journey. The remaining meals will be purchased en-route from railway hawkers.

'Accounts: Expenditure will continue to be incurred and noted by Matric.

'Well, that's it. I have already given to you a self-explanatory annotated diagram of the plan in out-line but if you still have any doubts you may now shoot your questions,' he concluded.

Matric raised his hand and on getting a nod of approval from the superior commander, said, 'boss the plan you have drawn out is audacious and yet flawless. Even the white sahibs can't make such a sound plan. In our eyes you are officer material and we wish you early and quick promotions.'

'Flattery will not get you any additional time at Lahore with the potter's daughter Matric' was Harry's retort even though he was mighty pleased by Matric's adulation. 'OK then, let us hope that our little excursion is a success and we are home and dry, at the end of it all.' Briefing over, the three exited the information room and headed back towards the barracks.

After lunch the trio divided the duties for the following day, got their uniforms ironed from the unit launderer, polished their boots and were ready for the out take parade scheduled for next morning. They happily went to sleep on this their last night in Madras at lights out.

They were ready in their Number 1 uniforms after breakfast and marched off towards the CO's office when the time by

Harry's wrist watch, wound up a moment ago, was 0845 hours. The out-take schedule was no different from the in-take routine which had been followed four days ago on their arrival except that this time the CO also thanked them for their *Bhangra* dance entertainment during the *Barakhana* and wished them a safe return journey. The formalities completed Harry sent Lachu and Matric to pack up and he himself went to the quarter-guard where the guard commander confirmed having received orders to hand over the prisoner any time after lunch. Accordingly Harry informed the prisoner to pack up and be ready to move after lunch.

He then positioned himself outside the information room, on a bench, under a tree, from where he could observe the activities of the unit HQ. Outwardly he appeared to be browsing through a newspaper he had lifted from the information room, so as not to draw attention to him-self, whereas, all the while he was keeping a watch on the HQ building from this observation post. He saw the CO leave the building at 1200 hours and his departure was soon followed by the Adjutant and the Second-in-Command and then there was a sudden exodus by all the remaining staff. The weekend had obviously commenced. All and sundry were taking off for recuperation and relaxation on this Saturday and would resurface on Monday refreshed, by when, Harry and his party too would be enjoying happy hours in Punjab with their families. Harry was satisfied that his clerk friend had not walked out of his office so far. He waited a little while longer and when he was sure that the coast was clear, he unhurriedly sauntered over to the HQ building where his clerk friend was waiting with all the relevant papers. He perused the all important movement order which now also included the name of the prisoner, Pioneer Neville Devar. Harry was satisfied to note that the date of commencement of journey in the order was 26 January 1942. The movement order also had an endorsement to the quarter-guard to hand over the prisoner to the escort on production of this movement order. Harry was also given a letter addressed to Station HQ, Jullundur giving a brief explanation of the circumstances under which the prisoner was apprehended by the police at Madras. There was also a sealed envelope containing the prisoner's personal papers. The clerk from the

Doaba region of Punjab had kept his promise and given him the documents on this Saturday the 24th of January 1942 and everything seemed to be in order. A final thank-you, a bear hug and Harry was off to join his team in the dining hall for lunch.

They collected cooked meal packages from the cookhouse and then moved their baggage to the unit out-gate. Harry took Lachu to collect the prisoner from his cell in the quarter guard where he showed the guard commander the endorsement in their movement order to hand over the prisoner to him. He then put his signature on the Prisoner Register confirming receipt of the prisoner. Lachu hand cuffed the prisoner on his left hand leaving his right one unfettered to enable him to carry his own baggage. And they then joined Matric at the unit out-gate. A unit vehicle took them to the railway station at 1700 hours by when they had done a re-check of their baggage, their documents, their return journey railway tickets and their cash umpteen times.

At the station Harry and Matric headed for the inquiry counter leaving Lachu to guard their baggage and the fettered prisoner. The inquiry clerk told them that they had just missed a direct train to Lahore and now there was no straight train to Punjab till the next morning. He suggested that they board a passenger train going to Bhopal at 0800 pm and from there they could catch any train coming from Bombay and going towards Delhi. This proposal appealed to them. Why waste a whole night at Madras when they could cover a fair amount of distance during the night in another train? So as soon as the rake of the Madras-Bhopal Passenger was shunted onto the platform at 1900 Hours Harry located a inter class compartment but a reservation slip was pasted on it meaning it was already reserved and its forcible occupation would create a palaver and draw the attention of the MCO as well as the Military Police. Harry wisely left the notion of occupying it. After a quick reconnaissance Harry homed on to a general category second class compartment which was still unoccupied and the quartet boarded it. Harry quickly took out the piece of chalk and wrote "Reserved for Military Prisoner Escort", in bold letters on either side of the compartment. He put the hefty Lachu on guard duty at the door on the platform side of the compartment while latching the other door, on the opposite side of the cabin.

Harry took stock of the compartment. It was a six berth cabin having three lower and that many upper berths with an attached toilet. He allocated the lower berths to the escort and earmarked one upper berth for the prisoner and then he sent Matric out to fill up the canvas *chagals* with water. He was satisfied to note that their prisoner had so far behaved like pet puppy. On Matric's return Harry took a stroll up to the railway engine. This engine was of the XB variety, meaning that it was used on long haul but slower passenger trains even though it had a six large traction wheels. Its Anglo-Indian driver was busy peering at various steam gauges wiping away the mist clouding their glass screens, while the fireman shoveled more coal into the furnace. Harry gave a mental salute to this mighty machine which pulled such heavy loads over long distances at high speeds. His tryst with the locomotive over, he returned to his compartment. Soon the train steamed out into the night and Harry took the proffered mug from Matric's hand and poured a drink for himself.

It was after the first swig that Harry started the conversation with *thambi*, their prisoner. 'So *thambi*, tell us why is everyone referred to as *thambi* in Madras? What does it mean?'

'Well saar *thambi* in Tamil language means brother, younger brother, but in its generic usage every male is a *thambi*.'

'And what would an elder one be named.'

'The elder ones are respectfully called *Anna*. So you are my *Annas* and when you call me *thambi*, I feel elated that such high ranking officers one of whom has two stripes on his shirt sleeve, refers to me as a younger brother.'

'I see.'

'Yes saar and it now becomes my duty as a younger brother to obey you and do nothing which degrades you in the eyes of the society.'

'Well *thambi*, tell us why did you run away while en-route to join your unit?'

'Saar it was this girl who I loved very much. I was worried that she may marry someone else in my absence. This insecurity in me made me to abscond, to enable me to be near her. But alas I could not stay with her because she went away to Ceylon with her parents leaving me for good. I now hate her for ruining my life. Saar one can't do without a woman but I tell you these women are poison.'

'All women can't be bad,' said Harry. 'Tell me, this wench of yours did she love you as much as you loved her?'

'Yes saar. She used to tell me of her love for me was great, but when it was time to migrate she did not tell her father of her love for me and went away to another country with her family.'

'Hey, you seem to have been truly in love with her. But were you ever intimate with her?'

'Yes saar, I have intimated her many times.'

'Where?' asked Matric.

'The place God made for the purpose, where else?' replied thambi. Matric doubled up in laughter at this reply and the other two also let off guffaws. It was some time and with some effort that Matric came out his fit of laughter.

'No, no, no. That's not what I meant. I wanted to know the place where you, in your words, "intimated" her; was it in a hotel room or was it in your or her house?'

'None of those, her father is a tyrant, doing it at their hut was far too dangerous and I don't have any permanent lodgings. As you can see, I am neither an Aga Khan nor a King Farouk, to have been able to afford a hotel room. So we did it where ever we could; in the fields outside her village, in the coconut groves and many other places.'

'What other places?'

'Well once I intimated her on the beach at a place called the Frenchman's Alcove, so called because a French noble had discovered it and used it for fornicating with a young local lass, whom he later took as wife, one hundred years ago. Sometimes we also used barns and on a few occasions we did it under culverts, to name a few.

'Boss, just hear this fellow, he is truly blessed,' said Matric

'Yeah, I am listening. But I won't be surprised if he is pulling a yarn on us,' said Harry.

'No yarn saar, no yarn. My story not invented, I tell you whole truth.'

The *thambi* kept on enthralling the trio with his sex-escapades and soon the escort removed his hand cuff since there was no likely hood of this honest lovelorn *thambi* attempting an escape especially when their train was racing at speed through the night. In any case all three of the escort, were wide awake and alert.

During a halt at Ponneri, a way side station, *thambi* suggested to them to taste the *mukuru*, deep fried spiced rice and chickpea flour crisp noodle, snack. Harry agreed to try them out and *thambi* summoned a vendor on the platform, who quickly dispensed three handfuls in a cone shaped paper container to *thambi* through the open window in exchange for one paisa. *Thambi* held the snack paper cone in his hand and went around serving it to his three bosses starting from Harry and all of them savoured it. Listening to *thambi's* unabashed love story and munching delightful South Indian snacks proffered by him, the escort was literally eating out of his hands.

Since their railway train was classified as a Passenger and not an Express, it halted at all small stations for short durations of a couple of minutes disgorging, passengers. *Thambi* explained to them that the detraining passengers were daily commuters working in the docks or at the famous Binny Cloth Mills at Madras, who were returning home after their day's work shift or on week-end leave. At the next halt, Kavaraippetta, *thambi* made them to try out mini *idli,* rice and lentil steamed cakes. He along with Lachu and Matric detrained went to a stall purchased the *idlis* and returned to their cabin just as the train started to move. Harry noted with satisfaction that Lachu had held on to the left wrist of *thambi* throughout and he and Matric had pushed *thambi* into the train ahead of them and entrained only after him.

You know *Thambi*, you were one lucky guy to have had a dame, to yourself, until she ran away' said Lachu mockingly.

'I think his girl deserted him for somebody better in Ceylon,' said Matric mischievously, as soon as he sat down and commenced munching on an *idli.*

'Saar, you call me lucky and yet you poke fun at me!' continued *thambi* while serving the *idlis* with spicy mint relish. 'But I do not mind you mocking me because I consider myself damned.'

'Hey it wasn't Matric's idea to be sarcastic. He was just trying to make a harmless joke. So don't take offence of a flippant comment,' said Harry. 'Nevertheless, how do you consider yourself to be damned?

'Firstly my houri has been snatched away from me by her oppressor father. Secondly, punishment and gaol await me at Jullundur. As you can see I am one unlucky fellow. So what else can I call myself other than ill-fated?' replied *thambi.*

'Hey cut out that sad sack story. Look at it another way, you still have a good job and that too under the crown. You are still young and will surely find another girl for yourself sooner than later. Who knows she may turn out to be prettier and even more loving than your past love,' preached Harry as he felt the train slowing down for another short halt. This time *thambi,* Matric and Lachu bought *wara,* lentil dough-nuts and Lachu had held on to *thambi's* wrist all the while and they had to be helped up into the compartment by Harry because the train had started to move when they were still on the Elavur station platform and again it was *thambi* who was the first one in, followed by the other two.

Devar continued to regale his audience with stories. The laughter that emanated from their compartment following each of his narratives would have been heard in adjoining carriages but for the noise of the running train. All three listeners nearly fell about laughing, at every hilarious joke bringing tears into their own eyes. If *Thambi* had wanted to escape, he could have easily done so when his escort was laughing their guts out, but he made no such attempt. This did not go unnoticed by Harry, who saw a totally guile-less *thambi* staring vacantly at them with wide innocent eyes.

As he continued his account, some more snacks were brought on board by *thambi* and his two chaperons at the next two halts taking the same security measures. The only change being that *thambi* himself gave his arm into Lachu's grasp before detraining for marketing of snacks. Just when a relaxed and bemused Harry decided to have dinner laid-out, the train slowed down yet again indicating another inevitable halt. *Thambi* suggested procuring of some *sambar,* spiced pigeon peas and vegetable gravy, to go with the dried chapatti and boiled rice packed dinner. The three took an empty mess tin and *thambi* extended his left arm into the hand-vice of Lachu and got down as soon as the train screeched to a noisy halt at Doravari to pick up the *sambar*.

They got the mess tin filled with ladles of *sambar* from the stall and started walking back towards their compartment carefully, ensuring that the gravy did not spill over; that's when the train started to move forcing them to quicken their pace. *Thambi* who was in the lead handed over the gravy filled mess tin to Harry and caught hold of the climbing handles located on either side of the entry but his foot slipped from the climbing board when he attempted to come aboard. Lachu who was behind him half lifted and half pushed him into the cubicle, with Harry pitching in, with a one handed pull and he was soon safely aboard. Once on the train, *thambi* took the gravy filled container from Harry and moved away from the entrance, further into the cabin, making space for the other two who were still trying to scramble aboard. Harry continued to assist the remaining two to entrain, by heaving them in since the train was gathering speed by the second. He helped Lachu climb up and then they both yanked Matric up and heaved a collective sigh of relief. It took them a moment to catch their breath. They then hurriedly retrieved their packed army food packets from their haversacks since the inviting aroma of the asafetida and spices emanating from the mess tin brimming with *sambar* lying on the lower berth had given them an appetite. Life was great, hot appetizing food laid out and a trip to their villages around the corner. What more could they ask for! They, hurriedly sat down opened their food parcels and dipped the first morsel into the inviting *sambar.*

———◄o►———

THE ROTTEN TIMES OF HARRY

They were on their second morsel when Matric said, 'where is *thambi*?' *Thambi* was nowhere to be seen. Harry quickly peeped into the toilet and found it empty. And then all hell broke loose. The ajar, door on the other side of the cabin swaying silently, in harmony with the movement of the train told a sad but true story. Their talkative parrot had flown. In an angry undertone Harry murmured a profanity pertaining to the pubic anatomy of his erstwhile prisoner's mother and pulled the emergency chain to halt the train as he thundered the codeword "Khatam" aborting their clandestine exercise "Visit Home". It was obvious that the rascal *thambi*, after entraining with the gravy bowl from the platform side of the moving train had detrained from the other side. He had apparently walked through their six berth compartment, unlatched the door diagonally opposite to his entry point; when two of his escort were busy giving each other a leg up for clambering aboard, actively assisted by the third and faded into the night. He had left behind his baggage, his dinner, the piping hot *sambar* gravy dangerously oscillating in its brimming open container and a very angry escort, in the train.

Despite pulling of the emergency chain, the momentum of the train and the pull of the powerful, XB, 4-6-2 configuration, locomotive took the train another fifty yards before it came to a braking halt. The suddenness of the halt threw all the three off balance, their baggage slid forward and of course as a consequence the *sambar* gravy undulating in its open gravy boat due to the motion of the train spilt over, resulting in one clean railway berth being messed up. Harry ordered Lachu to unload all their baggage and guard it. He took Matric and the torch and they both ran backwards along the platform and soon reached the end of the train where they nearly collided with the train conductor, who had detrained from the brake van to ascertain the cause of the emergency halt. Harry flashed his torch in the darkness and saw a coal freight train moving out of the siding and proceeding towards Madras. They both tried to get near it but going over the railway tracks filled with uneven stone ballast between its wooden sleepers in darkness was not only difficult but also very slow and the coal filled rake continued to pull away from them. They discerned silhouette of a moving figure against the night sky on top of one of the rear open wagons. Harry focused the beam of the torch light on the apparition and there he was looking straight into the torch.

'Come back you bastard', shouted Matric. In response *thambi* opened the fly of his trousers took out his penis and flashed it towards them with a pelvic thrust. His vulgar gesture was louder than a shouted profanity. The two could do nothing but stand there gawking as the coal freight train, now also laden with an additional unlisted live stowaway, continued to slowly but surely, enhance the distance between them, its rear red tail light fast receding into the night towards Madras. They continued to stand transfixed on the track gazing into the darkness long after the red tail light of the train had been swallowed up by the blackness of the night. The outlaw riding an iron horse had escaped. The VCO who had selected the escort with a firm belief that he had placed the right persons to cover unforeseen events surely had not catered for this one contingency.

Their trance was broken by the whistle of their own train as it recommenced its journey in the opposite direction, its red rear light also slowly dimming as it distanced away from them. Harry peered at his watch, the time was 9.35. How destiny had changed in these last five minutes? It didn't require a doctorate to analyze their future prospects. Harry's self prediction of the future was depressing; he could foresee obscurity and darkness, as gloomy and sinister as this night. How the hell was he to live down this episode? Two mighty soldiers with shoulders drooping marched with the help of the torch light towards the station-master's office to inquire about the next train to Madras. Harry was hopeful of catching the bastard if they could reach Madras quickly. In such adverse circumstances it is considered wise not to be either seen or heard, but Matric took a risk and made an effort to lift the spirits of his boss. '*Ustad* you have been teaching us during "field craft" that things are seen due to shape, shine, shadow, silhouette and movement. This teaching is indeed true because tonight we were able to locate that son-of-a-bitch on top of the train due to his silhouette and his movement.' No response from the sombre Harry. Indication enough for Matric to keep his trap shut.

Way side or rural railway stations in India are more in name than form. There is a ground level platform defined by markings than anything else. The name of the station is prominently displayed on either side of the platform in English, Hindi, Urdu and the local language, in this case Tamil. There is a boundary fence on the entry side of the platform and a small building in the middle of the platform which serves as an office for the station master and his staff and contains all the communication and other railway traffic wherewithal. Work during the night is done under light of kerosene hurricane lanterns. The signalling and track changing levers are generally located on the platform adjacent to this building. The signal poles have a recess on top where a kerosene lamp is lighted for the night and its light passes through the red or green glass of the signal arm depending on its position and which is visible to the drivers of the plying trains. There is a hand water-pump on one side and adjoining which are toilets without any roof.

When Harry and Matric reached the office building, the station-master and all other staff were off duty. The snack vend wherefrom the *sambar* had been procured was closed for the night and the vendor already gone. There was only a junior grade rotund assistant manning the station who informed them that there was no train towards Madras till four in the morning. An express train to Madras was scheduled to pass through without halting in the next half hour but this did not serve their purpose. Harry requested the railway official to stop the train for a minute to enable them to board it but his request was vehemently rejected by the high and mighty of the railways.

The party then ferried their baggage from the far end of the station, where it had been unloaded from their coach by Lachu and brought it to the middle of the platform. They took a bite of their unpacked dinner to keep up their strength and it was during dinner that Harry briefed them on the next plan of action and took a vow 'to hunt down the bastard to the end of the Earth.' He then deputed Matric to watch the railway track in the direction of Bhopal and inform him as soon as he saw the headlight of the approaching train to put their plan of action into play. In a little while Matric reported seeing the headlight. Soon thereafter they heard the whistle of the train and the Doppler's Effect, in its shrillness, indicated that the train was approaching at high speed.

On hearing the whistle, the plump hoity-toity, hard-hearted railway man emerged from his room with a bunch of large keys and two lamps, one green and the other red and moved towards the bank of signalling levers. He inserted one large key into a slot and turned it. He then moved towards the lever to heave it, so as to change the signal from red to green thus showing a clear line to the approaching express which could accordingly continue its journey to Madras without halting at this station. It was at that moment that Lachu and Harry emerged from the shadows and Lachu caught the unwary fatty in a crushing bear hug and Harry picked up the red and green lamps. He placed the green lamp in a defiladed position behind their baggage and started to wave the red lamp in the direction of the approaching train. In response the incoming locomotive let out one long shrieking whistle attempting to draw the attention of the signal man to change the line to green. It then let out a spurt of short piercing whistles like the snorting and neighing of an infuriated Derby Race Horse in gallop, who has been reigned-in, much before the finishing post. With the signal light and the platform light remaining red the train came to a screeching halt in the middle of the platform. Harry placed the red lamp behind a pile of stones and started to help Matric throw all their baggage into the nearest carriage. Meanwhile Lachu physically persuaded his humbled railroad lone ranger to yank the signal lever to green. He then caught him by the scruff of his neck, shook him violently and whispered menacingly in his ear to forget that this incident ever happened, if he valued his life. He then ran towards his partners where Harry had already retrieved the green lamp from its concealed position and was waving it over his head towards the engine; green all around, the locomotive gave one gentle whistle and resumed its journey to Madras with a jerk, as the three elegantly boarded the slow moving train having left the green signal lamp on a stone pile on the platform. Entering the train in motion came easily to them this time, because of their repeated practice in this art, all that evening. The chase was on, Harry checked his watch; it was 10 pm. The outlaw had a head-start of thirty minutes over the posse trailing him.

Harry had wanted to take a leak since commencement of the crises, but had successfully suppressed his urge and remained outwardly sangfroid during this half hour, of the greatest crises in his life. He now headed for the toilet leaving the other two to manage sitting space in the crowded compartment. Once inside, he hastily unbuttoned his fly but was unable to locate his pissing apparatus. His prick seemed to have shrunk and retracted into a hidden recess just like the neck of the tortoise which retracts inside its shell on sensing danger. He had to hurriedly unbuckle his belt, pull down his trouser and underwear and only then, was he able to locate the shrivelled fellow hiding within the thick mat of his tangled pubic hair. He had to tug at its foreskin, to pull out the cowering fellow, to be able to urinate properly. He took a good aim and let go a steady torrent straight into the drain hole. And not a moment too soon, because his muscles were on the verge of involuntarily releasing the overwhelming pressure built up in his bladder. Pleasurable relief overwhelmed him as he held his penis at its hairy root with his left hand while he held his unsecured belt, trousers and underwear, at the hip with his right hand. He must have looked much like an adult adaptation of the famous Manikin Piss, the child statue, spouting in Brussels in Netherland. He spurted and spurted and was engulfed with a feeling of delightful gratification, unique only to a satisfying piss, with each passing moment. He took a long time to empty his bursting bladder. Lachu and Matric saw a relaxed Harry emerge out of the toilet and knew that the boss had had a most enjoyable spill. Then it was Matric's turn to use the toilet. Lachu did not however use it; he had done his thing in the bushes when the other two were patrolling the railway tracks for the elusive enemy.

They overtook the stationary coal freight train thirty five minutes in to the journey. The speed of their express train was so much that the complete coal rake was just a blur in the fleeting lights of their windows and had been passed in a jiffy. By the time it crossed Harry's mind to halt their express train and go for the scoundrel they were already a mile beyond the stationary freight. In any case, searching sixty coal filled high wagons in darkness would have been unrealistic and they could again be stranded in the wilderness if their quarry gave them the slip. Better to reach Madras and ambush him on arrival. The express reached its destination at 11 pm and they de-trained at the same station platform where they had arrived for the first time five days previously. It was the same platform from where they had caught an out-going train just three hours back. No wonder then, that Madras Central seemed quite familiar to them, this time. Harry decided to go to the sprawling railway yard because freight trains are generally stabled there. But the large amount of baggage they had could not be lugged around in a yard. Leaving one person to guard it depleted the strength of the party. So he decided to park the baggage in the cloak room. It took them ten minutes to complete the formalities at the cloak room and then they headed for the yard armed with the torch and the hand cuffs.

The trio reached the yard and Harry did a quick reconnaissance to decide the deployment. There were three sets of railway tracks leading into the yard and there-after the number of pairs increased to ten with off shoots branching out from the three incoming tracks. The yard was dimly lit and that too only at a few points, the bulk of the area was in darkness. On the far side was a siding and a road ran parallel to it. There was also a small parcel office building ahead of the siding and an approach road lead to it. Beyond this infrastructure, across the road was a cluster of shanties with narrow lanes. Harry did not know which track would be allotted to the coal freight to come in and where it would be halted. He reasoned that the most likely parking track would be the farthest, so that it facilitated unloading of the coal. He decided to cover all the three incoming tracks and the tracks on the far side of the yard. He disposed off his troops accordingly. He himself took up a position on the flight of stairs of the signal cabin where-from he had an unencumbered view of the incoming tracks and to a large extent of the Northern end of the yard. He positioned Matric on the ladder of the huge water dispenser from where the coal locomotives quenched, the voracious thirst, of their steam boilers and from where he could easily look, onto the trains on the Southern side of the track. Lachu was installed on the far side, on the roof of the parcel office building in line of sight of Matric. Hand field signals were to be used when the quarry had been located and voice signals were to be brought into play once surprise had been lost. They took up their positions and waited.

They did not have to wait long, a few minutes later the freight passed below the signal cabin its headlight illuminating the railway yard as it made slow progress into it. Harry was satisfied to note that his troops had merged with the surroundings and remained obscure even in the glare of the engine's powerful headlight. Harry minutely surveyed each passing coal filled gondola shaped open high sided box wagon but did not see any body. He was about infer that his quarry had detrained somewhere else en-route when he saw the bastard in the second last wagon. He quickly raised his right hand and waved it towards the others and then pointed the hand in the direction of the carriage carrying the son-of-a-bitch. He then alighted from his post and followed the slow moving train as it snaked its way through the yard. Matric saw the hand signal of his boss and in turn signalled Lachu and they both descended from their places and converged towards the rear of the moving train. The time by Harry's radium dial watch was 1135 pm, when the train finally came to a halt on the fourth track from the far side but unfortunately, all its tail end wagons, by a quirk of fate, were in darkness, giving an advantage to their adversary. This however did not faze the hunters who had now surrounded their game in the last but one carriage from both sides; Harry and Matric on one side and Lachu on the other. Netting their game was now just moments away. While they waited for their prize to get down, they saw the powerful light of an incoming locomotive and all three ducked down and quickly scurried under the belly of the gondola carrying the bandit lest they be bathed in its light and be caught with their pants down by their quarry. In no time the intruding locomotive crossed them and a long line of freight wagons which it was pulling, rolled by. This meddling goods train finally came to a halt on the adjoining track on Lachu's side and the party re-emerged from its temporary cramped stations and took up their earlier positions on either side of the target wagon.

In-spite of all this additional activity, surprise element still seemed to be in-tact. They waited for the troublemaker to get off, but when the scallywag failed to dismount, Harry became uneasy. Maybe the destination of coal freight was further up, at some Power Generating Plant. In that case the rake was likely to get moving again. If that happened then they would lose the blighter once again. So Harry decided to take the initiative to seek him out. He crawled under the wagon and joined Lachu on the other side and signalled him to lift him up. Lachu sat down on his haunches and Harry climbed onto his shoulders and signalled Lachu to stand up. The powerful Lachu then stood up, carefully, lifting a perched Harry on his shoulders, without unbalancing him. Harry cautiously groped the side of the open box wagon as he was lifted by Lachu and soon his hand was over the top of the brim of the wagon. He gripped the edge, deftly with his left hand and stabilized himself. He peered into the coal laden large container when his face was above the lip of the ten foot high wagon but he could not see anything in the darkness. So he decided to flash his torch and locate the villain. As soon as he flashed his torch onto the pile of coal he heard an exclamation sound emanating from a corner of the large coal carriage and in a jiffy his startled quarry jumped off the carriage on their side of the train. He scurried under the recently arrived train on the adjoining track, like a fox darting out of a fox-hole and bolted towards the shanties. The bastard had been taken by surprise alright but was quick to recover and take off, upsetting the capture plan of the trio. Harry also leaped down from his wobbling place of duty and he along with Lachu scampered under the adjoining rake and followed in pursuit. Matric too joined the chase after scrambling under the railway cars to come to their side of the trains.

Their foxy prey darted across the railway tracks, crossed the road on the far end and entered one of the narrow lanes of the shanty slum, with hunter Harry and his two hounds in hot pursuit. When the hunting party entered the slum lane a moment later their game was nowhere to be seen in the dark alley. It was like playing blind man's bluff except for the torch light which Harry flashed occasionally. They bumped into a bloke in the darkness and caught him thinking it was their man but the catch turned out to be a pimp who offered them the best possible wares at the least possible rates and with a flourish pushed open a shanty door to expose a couple of highly made up young girls chewing betel leaf and nut. If they didn't have important detection work at hand, maybe, just maybe, they could have taken his offer and Matric would have lost his virginity this night in one of the dimly lit shanty parlours. They searched the labyrinth of alleys and combed each one thoroughly but that bastard eluded them. They peeped through loose slats, junctions and joints, some of which were more of embrasures than seams, into the shanties and saw some grunting males on the job but none was their *thambi*. It was nearly an hour after midnight when a morose Harry, whose belly and intestinal tract felt as if it was loaded with an overdose of Epsom salts, called off the search.

The scoundrel had just vanished. He could be anywhere in Madras. Should the search be aborted or should it be continued? These were some of the questions popping up in Harry's mind. The villain slipping away, yet again, had given collywobbles to Harry but he remained outwardly calm and decided to take a look at the Diamond Bar which had been the rascal's regular haunt in the past. They reached the Diamond half an hour later and were stunned to see its condition. It seemed a hurricane had hit the bar. All or most of its furniture was topsy-turvy and some bottles of hooch lay broken on the ground. There were a few customers nursing their bruised bodies but Devar was not amongst them. It was obvious that a major fracas had taken place recently and the owner was sitting on a bench holding his head with his hands. Harry took in the scene of devastation and then slowly approached the proprietor.

On seeing Harry, the owner started crying out, a-loud and narrated his tale of woe, between sobs and whimpers. Devar had come to the bar at midnight and ordered a drink. He was edgy and had seemed to be in a hurry. Devar had told him that he had escaped and was now on the run, heading for Ceylon where the long arm of law could not catch him and where he would be re-united with his girl. He had said that all his travel documents were ready and lying with an uncle living nearby from where he was going to get them as soon as he left the bar and then he was going straight to Panbam also called Rameshwaram Island to board a ferry to Ceylon from the Dhanushkodi Ferry Station. It so transpired that while he and Devar were engrossed in conversation the local hoodlum who had been let off by the police just that day had arrived at the bar with half a dozen of his tough necks and sight of Devar had sent them into a rage. They had gone after him, hammer and tongs. Devar had just about managed to save himself by the skin of his teeth, by crawling under the tables and through the spread legs of one of his assailants and speedily scooting away, even when blows were raining down on him by seven pairs of hands, wielding bamboo sticks and hooch glass bottles and that many kicking pairs of legs. They had given him a chase but had returned empty handed a short while later and then spent their ire on the customers who were enjoying their weekend Saturday night at the Diamond. They had also wrecked the bar as a parting gift and carried away the unbroken booze bottles.

The bastard was a tough nut, thought Matric. He had literally slipped out of the hands of over half a dozen armed toughs. Therefore his breakout from an empty handed escort of three, in comparison must have been a piece of cake for the son-of-a-gun, even if it was pulled off twice. While Matric was mentally taking small comfort from his argument that a stronger and more ruthless armed force than them had been unable to hold on to the bastard, Harry was in deep thought plotting his next step. Lachu was without any thought.

Devar must be on a train by now, heading out to Rameshwaram to catch a ferry to Ceylon, assessed Harry. But he did not have much of a head-start, an hour at the most. There was still a chance of catching him if they could get a train to Dhanushkodi on Rameshwaram Island quickly. They hitched a ride back to the station on a civil truck. While Harry went to the inquiry window the others quickly withdrew their baggage from the cloakroom. Harry had learnt that trains to Rameshwaram plied from the meter gauge station called the Madras Egmore Railway Station. So they quickly made their way to Egmore in a *tonga,* the two wheeled horse carriage.

They reached Egmore at 4.00 am but a direct train to Rameshwaram was not available till the afternoon however the inquiry clerk told them to take the train going to Madurai but get down before Madurai at Tiruchirapalli or Trichy. A train going to Madurai was running behind schedule and was expected to arrive from Cuttack at 5 am and if they boarded it, they would be in Trichy by 10 am and could catch any train from that busy junction proceeding to Rameshwaram Island. They boarded the train on its arrival without a proper ticket but no railway staff ever checked the ticket of soldiers of the British Indian Army. So while there was no problem from the railways, Harry was plagued by the same problem in the train toilet which he had encountered the previous night in the hijacked express train lavatory. His stately member had again retracted itself into a recess and had to be cajoled out to perform its primary role of emptying the bladder. Tension and fear of the unknown always did this to him. They were in Trichy by 1030 am and a listless Harry had wound up his watch and Matric had updated his account ledger. On the way during halts Harry had not detrained and taken his customary walk to view the train engine, this break in his habitual routine was a clear indication of the poor state of his morale to the other two. Getting a train from Trichy to Rameshwaram was easy because a number of trains carrying pilgrims on a pilgrimage to the conch shaped Rameshwaram or Panbam Island passed through Trichy. Lord Rama had halted and prayed on Panbam Island on his way to Lanka to rescue his wife Sita who had been abducted and gaoled there by Ravana the demon king of Lanka. In the battle that ensued, Lord Rama had to slay the evil Ravana thereby ridding the world of a demonic ruler.

If their mental tension, a result of the prisoner's escape, had not existed, their journey to Rameshwaram would have been memorable. Their train travelled over the one mile and three furlong stretch of the Panbam Bridge spanning the Palk Straits, connecting the Indian main land with Panbam Island. The bridge was considered an engineering marvel and opened in 1914. In the middle of this viaduct, was a segment having a draw bridge which could be mechanically hauled up to facilitate passage of ships below or lowered down to enable trains to ply over it, by manual cranking of its machinery.

At the entrance of this draw bridge was a strange picture of a man holding a corpse of an adolescent. The folk-lore behind this pictorial depiction was that one day, when the draw bridge was in the up position allowing a ship to pass below it, an unscheduled train was seen approaching the bridge. As soon as the ship had passed safely, the man in-charge of the draw bridge quickly started to crank the machinery to bring down the upright bridge spans to the horizontal plane to enable the fast approaching train to pass over the bridge. He knew if he failed to bring the bridge down in time then the whole train was likely to fall into the sea with hundreds of its passengers and this thought made him to redouble his efforts in lowering the bridge. Just then his young son came to deliver lunch to him and he ordered his son to assist him in getting the bridge down. The novice son's hand got struck in the machinery as he assisted his father and the boy was sucked into the giant mechanism. The man now had to make a choice; should he abort the cranking and save his son thus putting lives of hundreds of passengers in peril; or should he continue to bring the bridge down and save lives of all the passengers aboard the train and sacrifice the life of his only son? He decided to do his duty and kept on cranking the machinery and brought the bridge to its horizontal position in time making possible the crossing of the train over the bridge safely; its occupants unaware of the human sacrifice just made by a doting father of his beloved son to save their lives. The unusual picture at the entrance of the bridge was a pictorial depiction of this poignant tale of sacrifice.

The train continued its journey over Panbam Island for another twenty miles, leaving Rameshwaram town on a flank and it reached Dhanushkodi, Railway Station. Dhanushkodi their final destination was a small hamlet of huts, pilgrim *sarais*, guest houses, and temples which existed alongside the ferry station. The Southern tip of the island was also the land's end because ahead was the sea and beyond that lay Ceylon, referred to as Lanka in the Holy Epic Ramayana. Beyond the promontory, there exists an under-sea structure connecting Panbam Island with Ceylon referred to Adam's Bridge by the

Western Civilization and which Indians call *Ram Setu*, Rama's Bridge. Lord Rama had constructed this bridge up to Lanka on his outward journey to Lanka to rescue his wife Sita. On his return journey from Lanka after his victory over Ravana and successful rescue of Sita, he was requested by his ally Vibhishana, brother of Ravana to destroy the bridge since it had served its purpose. Lord Rama had then destroyed the bridge at this spot by hitting it with one end of his *Dhanush*, bow. Since *Dhanush* means bow and *kodi* means destroy, the place is accordingly named Dhanushkodi. Geologists have scientifically dated this under water structure and its age matches the Indian *Treta Yug*, the aeon of the Ramayana.

They arrived at their destination at 5.30 pm and rushed straight to the ferry station which was milling with jostling crowds who had come to see off their near ones embarking on the 20 mile journey on that day's last ferry to Ceylon. They reached a high vantage point and looked out for *thambi*. They scanned a sea of faces on the shore and on the ferry looking and waving at each other. But their *thambi* was nowhere to be seen.

'Boss how in hell can-we locate the guy in this vast crowd?' said Matric.

'Yeah, and they all look alike to me,' observed Lachu.

'This is the second time you have made this observation, the first was when you found all Gurkhas to be similar looking and now all *thambis* also look the same to you', said Harry. 'I endorse your observation Lachu. Nevertheless, you chaps keep on looking because this is the only escape route available to that fellow. We are bound to find him here.'

'We are looking, we are looking. The search has brought us to this location and if he is here we will find him. And you know what?'

'What.'

'Your vow to hunt him down to the End of the Earth does seem to be literally coming true, Boss because this place indeed looks like the End of the Earth.'

'My vow to hunt him down to the end of the Earth will fructify only when we catch the bastard. So keep on looking.'

'Yes Boss,' replied Lachu as all three continued to scan the sea of humanity.

As a matter of fact Harry's view was that in all probability they had arrived ahead of the runaway. During his last calculation Harry had put him just an hour ahead of them but given the fact that he had to collect his travel documents from an uncle in Madras meant that he would have needed some time to do so. Therefore, their start time from Madras should be more or less the same. They had not seen him en-route and there had been no train plying to Rameshwaram ahead of them. Even if he took an alternative mode of travel, he could not have reached ahead of them. The bastard was surely somewhere behind them.

Before long a bell sounded and the ferry gave its departure hoot. The boarding plank was soon lifted as the last passenger boarded the ferry. It pulled away from the dock for its twenty mile journey to Talaimanar, Ceylon across the sea channel, called the Straits of Mannar, which was now shimmering in the evening Sun in a deep pink hue. They waited till the crowd had made its way out of the area and then headed back to the railway station to spend the night and keep an eye on the arriving passengers. The returning passengers boarded the out-going train and soon the crowds depleted. They occupied two empty benches on the railway platform and made themselves comfortable. Matric arranged for dinner from the railway caterers and they had dinner, no drinks this night for them, in deference to the religiousness of this place. They took turns performing sentry duties during the night and kept watch on new arrivals but there was no sign of *thambi* during that night.

They were up and ready by 8.00 am with Harry's watch wound up and in position at their observation post before 10.00 am. They arranged themselves in such a manner that they were able observe the track leading to the ferry-station building and beyond up to the ferry departure berth. Presently they saw the ferry in the distance coming in to dock. The in-coming ferry from Ceylon seemed to be travelling on a visually discernible line on the surface of the sea. This distinguishable line on the surface of the sea was created by the confluence of the calm waves of the Bay of Bengal on one side and the agitated waves of the Indian Ocean on the other. The trio, were spellbound by this ethereal phenomenon resulting from the union of two mighty sea systems and their spell was broken only when the ferry noisily docked at its wharf and commenced disembarking its commuters from Ceylon. The three however had no interest in them.

They had to focus on outgoing passengers. Harry was quite certain that their deserter would make his appearance on the quay that day. At 12.00 noon the gates to the ferry building were opened and outward bound passengers started to enter the structure. These out bound travellers passed through the shed and emerged on its sea side and boarded the ferry, whose scheduled departure was at 0100 pm. The three observers kept a hawk like watch and saw each boarding individual and family group but there was no Devar. As the time for departure drew closer the passengers arriving at the last-minute jostled with each other creating a bottle neck at the entrance of the building as well as at the ferry access point. One of the last groups to board was a Muslim family with the male member in the lead followed by his *burka* clad wives and other family ladies. However there was still no sign of their man. Harry assessed that the chap had either changed his programme or some-how beaten them to this place and had already gone across. Or had been delayed and would now take the evening boat.

Soon the scene on the waterfront was similar to the one witnessed yesterday by Harry and his boys, with a swarm of hand waving people, bidding bon voyage to their departing relatives or friends. Just after 01.00 pm the ferry gave a hoot, the plank was pulled up and the commuter boat was on its way to Ceylon. The boat was about twenty to thirty yards out at sea when Matric shouted, 'there he is boss, over there on the first landing in stern of the ship.'

'Where, damn it, where?'

'Reference flag mast of the Ferry, down 6 O'clock *burka* clad passenger,' cried Matric making use of the army indication of targets technique.

They all looked open jawed as the bastard removed his *burka* disguise which had been adorned by him to get past them. He threw the *burka* on the deck, stood up erect and waved at them. He then coiled the fingers of his right hand into a fist, caught the elbow of this fisted arm with his left hand and simultaneously jabbed the fisted fore-arm in their direction, in the internationally understood mocking gesture of profanity, while he silently albeit elaborately mouthed the words, 'fu . . . u'. They could do nothing but gaze open mouthed while their *thambi* escaped right in front of their eyes aboard a ferry. The boat was distancing itself from its berth by the second, as it continued to sail towards Ceylon and all they could do was to watch helplessly. The powerful propeller of the vessel churned up the sea and its frothy wake obliterated the optically visible stripe on the surface of the deep, which had mesmerized them when the ferry came in, three hours ago. The trio considered erasure of the seascape wonder vein created by the confluence of two mighty water systems, by the foamy wake of the outgoing boat, ominous. To make matters worse, they were caught in a sudden rain squall and got completely drenched. Being down in the dumps they did not even bother to open their rain-capes. "Land's End" had become end of the road for the careers of the trio. Well so it seemed on this Monday, 26th of January 1942.

The three wet figures sloshed back to the railway station, head down and shoulders drooping, each immersed in his thoughts. On the way, while Matric grudgingly revised, rascal *thambi*'s, statistics of escape from their clutches to three, he was also heartbroken at the escape of the prisoner. He was hurting even more due to the profane gesticulations made by the son of a bitch after two of his getaways. His mocking them thus, was an insult to injury. Lachu's mind was blank as he carried the baggage of the escapee in addition to his own. A gloomy Harry was trying to weigh his options. There seemed to be only one option available to him, which was to head home and face the music.

On reaching the railway station they changed into dry clothing and draped their wet apparel on the boundary fence, of the station, to dry out.

Harry left the other two at the railway platform and went to inquire for a train out of the island. It would be another two hours for an out ward bound train. As he stood outside the small railway station next to the Inquiry Window contemplating his next line of action he observed dark clouds gathering over head. Normally a collection of clouds meant more rain could be expected before long but on this day these rain clouds also had a different connotation for a burdened Harry, to him they seemed portentous. That's when he observed a sage attired in a saffron coloured robe squatting cross legged on a mat under a nearby banyan tree, his long white beard flowing in the breeze and hair of his head tied in a neat bun on top of his head. The wise one was in meditation, his eyes shut. It was evident even from a distance that there was radiance in the aura of the pundit. A lad and a middle aged lady were sitting close-by, waiting for the wise one to complete his meditation.

When faced with a crisis or a complex situation Easterners run to consult astrologers, fortune-tellers, palm-readers and the like. These soothsayers are the equivalent of the Western Tarot Card Readers and Crystal Ball Gazers. Harry an Easterner was like all others and wanted to consult the meditating guru. On the other hand he was also worried of getting drenched again if it started to rain. However the critical situation in which he found himself at the moment, made him overcome his trepidation of getting wet again and he walked up briskly and joined the already waiting duo for consultations with the learned sage. The young lad who seemed to be about ten years of age appeared to be fascinated by Harry's uniform and smilingly gave Harry a mock salute. Harry returned the salute jovially at which the lad walked up and shook hands with Harry and introduced himself, 'I am Abdul Kalam, I live with my family here in Dhanushkodi and I study in Rameshwaram Elementary School.'

'Hello, I am Harinder Singh from far away Punjab. I have come to Dhanushkodi on some official work,' responded Harry. The lad is confident and self assured was Harry's appraisal.

'You have a smart uniform. I too want to join the forces when I grow up and get myself a uniform and fly aero-planes.'

'I am in the army and I can tell you that there are no aircraft in the army. But if you have a strong desire to fly aero-planes then you will have to join the air force.'

'Then I will join the air force.'

Their tête-à-tête, interspersed with flashes of lightening shooting in the sky followed by sounds of thunder, was cut short by the resonant voice of the sage, who had completed his meditation. 'Well, well. We seem to have our brightest star Abdul the genius of Dhanushkodi here today and we also have a traveller. Welcome all,' said the wise man and called Abdul Kalam and his escort near to him.

'Abdul will shortly be going to a mainland school for further studies. I have brought him to you for your guidance wise one.' said the chaperon of the intentioned pilot.

'Child, the boy will continue to excel in his studies where-ever he goes. Abdul has a great future. Good wishes of all the people of Rameshwaram are with him,' intoned the wise man.

After that he told her that the lad would become a great scientist and make *agni-bans,* fire bearing arrows which could be fired without bows to great distances across the seas. The sage also predicted that the boy would one day become a King, ruling over a vast empire. The lady then light heartedly mentioned that the eleven year old was fond of flaunting long hair on his head while the family preferred a more sedate crew cut. The seer told her to let the young man decide his hair style because hair sometimes plays a positive role in life. He cited the example of one Samson whose physical strength lay in his long hair. Similarly, it was possible that Abdul's mental prowess was somehow connected with his long hair. Soon the lady and young Abdul were gone and the wise one called up Harry.

'Come my son, come. First of all let me welcome you to Island of the Lord. This is where the Lord prayed and this is where He walked. You have come looking for the Lord to this far away land and the Lord will not disappoint you, He does not disappoint those who seek Him,' began the Guru. Harry wanted to correct the serene mystic and tell him that he had come to Rameshwaram looking for a Satan and not to seek the Lord but kept his council in the matter for the time being.

'Your countenance tells me that you are disturbed and you are under tremendous stress,' continued the perceptive one. 'Let me calm you by draining the negative energy and turbulence inside you.' He took Harry's right hand in his and massaged it with his palms like a faith healer. The palm rub-down and the soothing lilt in the voice of the seer indeed had a calming effect on the disturbed Harry and he began to relax for the first time since the escape of the Devil from the coal freight two days ago. He then commenced studying the complex lines in Harry's palm.

'The stripes on the right sleeve of your uniform shirt tell me you are a high ranking officer in the army and the lines in palm of your hand tell me that a greater future awaits you. Your fate line is prominent and it suggests that even your failures will turn into triumphs. Your good fortune will rub on those associated with you and they too will remain in happiness due to their link with you,' predicted the visionary. The learned one was perhaps right to some extent, reflected Harry, after all that rascal *thambi* had been associated with him for a short spell and there he was, about to be reunited in happiness with his girl in Ceylon. 'You will be a wealthy man, a happily married man and your lineage will be carried forward by your children. Your life line is long and you will live up to a ripe old age of over eighty years,' continued the sage.

'O learned one, how can your predictions be true?' said Harry. 'I have already failed in the duty assigned to me and I see only darkness ahead just like the black clouds over head.'

The savant took some time studying Harry's palm. He took out a magnifying glass from under his bolster and with its help he minutely scrutinized the lines on Harry's hand. Finally he declared, 'the dark clouds you see over head will soon release their water content and vanish and the umbra will be replaced by the bright rays of the Sun. When one door closes, the Lord opens another. Remember when the Sun rises it dispels darkness and hence there is always light after darkness. That is the rule of nature. I have examined the fate lines in your hand minutely and did not find anything to suggest failure. I say with confidence that the Lord has placed his benevolent hand on you and you will ultimately succeed in you mission. Where-ever you go and what-ever you do, His hand will guide you, always. So go in peace with a prayer of the Almighty on your lips and success will be yours son.' Harry did not know if any of the rosy predictions of the mystic would come true for the young Abdul or for him but he certainly did feel a lot better after the consultations with the sage.

On return to the railway station he sauntered up to the meter-gauge locomotive which was to power their train and found it to be of 4-4-2 configuration, which he believed was adequate for pulling the small train, the visit to the steam engine by Harry was a good omen because it indicated to his sidekicks that his morale was now improving. Their train soon steamed out of Dhanushkodi and this time he had no difficulty in ferreting out his appendage when he used the urinal in the train and the collywobbles too had vanished. The sage had certainly given him confidence.

———◄o►———

ONLY TIME WILL TELL

They were in Madurai by dinner time. They identified a direct train to Delhi boarded its inter class compartment and Harry's chalk reserved it for the "Military Escort". It was during dinner that a vagrant came to them begging for alms. The guy was in tatters, unkempt and dirty. He could do with a bath, a shave and a clothing change. Seeing his pitiable condition, Lachu wanted to give him a one pice coin as alms but was stopped by Matric under the contention that the chap had an uncanny resemblance to their hated deserter.

'You guys always take off at a tangent,' said Harry, 'first Lachu finds all Madrasis similar looking and now this poor bugger appears as a look-alike of our foe to Matric.'

'Yes *Ustad*. Take a look for yourself. Doesn't he resemble the forked tongued reptile who slithered out of our grasp?' said Matric.

'The snake must be in Ceylon by now,' muttered Lachu under his breath.

Harry looked the hobo up and down. Matric's observation was not quite accurate. This tramp was certainly not an out-and-out imitation of their nemesis. While his physique more or less matched the escaped *thambi*'s, give-or-take an inch here and there but otherwise he did not remind Harry of the runaway in any way what-so-ever. He therefore refuted Matric's point of view.

'Don't view all *thambis* with a jaundiced eye Matric. This guy in no way resembles that bastard. On the contrary I think we should view his wretched condition with compassion. I feel we should give a bite or two from our serving of food, like good human beings,' said Harry. He then called the hobo near to him and the trio pooled one item each from their recently purchased dinner and offered it to him. The tramp grabbed the proffered banana leaf platter with both hands and gobbled it down even when his benefactors were still not even half way through their serving of food.

They finished their meal and Harry detrained for his customary visit to the locomotive. He was happy to note that the engine was the long haul XC variety with the same 4-6-2 wheel configuration and the engine driver and the fireman were both busy doing their last minute chores. On return to the cabin he found the vagrant still there, looking at his colleagues like a hungry pup begging for more food, only this hungry pup was without a wagging tail. Harry ordered a platter of *idlis* for their uninvited guest and as the chap dug into his second course Harry shut his eyes in thought for a few moments and a notion took shape in his head. When he opened them, he had a plan ready.

Harry waited for the waif to finish his *idli* platter and he then beckoned him towards his compartment window. He was about to explore if the idea in his mind could be spawned. The poor blighter first licked the banana leaf platter clean, disposed it in a litter box, he then went to the water fountain washed his hands drank some water wiped his hands dry on his tattered clothing and then strode to the compartment window in response to Harry's summons.

'Hey fella, you are a well built guy and don't seem to be having any affliction and yet you are leading the life of a beggar. Why don't you work and earn a legitimate wage?' were Harry's opening remarks directed to the character through the compartment window.

'I am a vagrant by force of circumstances and not by choice Guv. I had a steady job and was earning an honest living but I had to give up the job because of bad luck and adverse circumstances. Given the opportunity I can work harder and better than others.'

'You are just spinning a yarn. It is more likely that you like drifting around instead of making a serious effort in landing a job because bumming comes easy to you.'

'No. That insinuation is wrong. I have tried my level best to get a job. I have tried at many places but everyone wants me to establish my credentials before they even consider me for a place.'

'So where is the problem in furnishing some kind of identity proof?'

'There is a problem Chief. I have no documentary proof of my birth. I don't know who my parents were. I don't know my place or date of birth. This is just a sample of my many problems.'

'Is that so? Surely you must be having a name. What's your name?'

'Thambi,' said the vagrant.

'Hey that's not what I meant. I mean your real name.'

'That is my real and only name.'

'How come you don't have a proper name?'

'It's like this. I was left outside an orphanage at birth. The nuns took me into their care and brought me up in the orphanage. Every one called me Thambi over there and so that is my only known name.'

'You do have one hell of a sad tale.'

'Yes your Lordship. I can see that you are high ranking officers of the army. You can easily get me employment in the army. Please get me a job and I will work day and night and make you proud of me and then I will not have to lead life of a tramp.'

'Whoa. Hold your horses. We are not from the army recruitment branch, which is the only authorised body to carry out recruitment for the army. In any case, even if we wanted to help you, how would you establish your bona-fides?'

'There is no other way?'

'No. However, tell me more.'

'Well, I was left on the second step of the four step flight at the entrance of the Charity Orphanage run by the Catholic Church at Madras in the middle of the night twenty one years ago in the cold month of January.' Harry quickly calculated that the chap was born in January 1921. Mr Thambi continued 'No one saw the person who left me there bundled in a light wrap. I was discovered the next morning by a nun when she opened the front door on hearing loud cries of a new born baby. I grew up at the orphanage along with fifty others, imbibing catholic values. Since no one knew the religion professed by my parents, I was brought up as a Christian at the orphanage.'

'Go on.'

'I studied in the local Christian School till the sixth standard and then I was chucked out of the orphanage and the school.'

'Why?'

'Just bad luck, that's all.'

'Not understood. How can bad luck get you thrown out? You must have done something wrong. Seriously wrong. These organizations don't toss out orphans just like that.'

'Maybe I did break a rule or two but those nuns are unforgiving and there I was on the mean streets of Madras at the age of about fifteen. I had no alternative but to drift and do odd jobs to sustain myself.'

'Hold on. What rule did you break to be kicked out of the orphanage?'

'That is a personal matter which I don't share with anyone.'

'Hey, if you want me to help you to land a job, I will have to know everything about you. Isn't it?

'Well to cut a long story short I was caught in the girls' dormitory at night by the Mother in charge and that's why I got thrown out.'

'Deliberately straying into an out of bounds area and that too at night and then getting caught, is not bad luck, its' bad planning. What happened next?'

'I drifted for a year or so but then fortunately, I landed a steady job with a canteen inside the fort in Madras and all was hunky dory for about five years. I was a delivery boy and delivered groceries and fresh meat, poultry and vegetables to the families of British army men and army officers' messes inside the fort area. It was a cushy job and paid adequately to enable me to stave off starvation. Then a couple of months ago bad luck struck me again. A British *Mem Sahib* called me inside her bed room when I went to deliver pork sausages and poultry at her bungalow. She made me do many things to her and we lost track of time. Suddenly her sergeant husband arrived home and I grabbed my clothing and ran for my life through the window semi-naked and have been on the run ever since. There was no way that I could continue living in Madras with a British Sergeant tailing me, so here I am, in Madurai begging for a living. That sir is my bad luck story.'

'Well we will try to help you find employment but no promises.'

'Right Sir Bruce, if you try you will succeed and this slave will remain eternally grateful to you for your kindness in getting me a job.'

Harry told Thambi to wait at a distance to enable him to consult his other colleagues and when he was out of ear-shot, Harry called the other two of his party for a war council.

'Guys I don't have to spell it out for you, but we are in shit creek,' he began, 'our prisoner has run away and will never be caught or make his appearance again because he is already in a foreign land across the ocean.' They nodded in agreement since they too were aware of the mess they were in. 'If we return to the unit empty handed we will be punished under the Indian Army Act for dereliction to duty but even worse is the shame and ignominy which we will have to bear in the unit for the rest of our service in the army. And within the community for the rest of our lives; even after retirement.' More nods.

'When I was taking a stroll by myself at Rameshwaram a wise man had called out to me,' why disclose that it was he who had approached the saint and not vice-versa. A little half truth was not going to hurt anyone. 'Even without my mentioning anything the wise one already knew of my problem as a result of some mystical power which such spiritualists possess. This diviner told me that when all doors are seemingly closed, when there is darkness and fear, when the position is hopeless and defeat stares you in the face; one should not despair. He also told me that one should continue to have faith in the Almighty because the Lord always opens a new door, a gateway to hope and triumph for those who have been purposely wronged by the devil,' intoned Harry. His audience listened with rapt attention as he continued, 'Wahe Guru knows our predicament and has sent this fellow, Mr. Thambi to us out of no-where and it is now for us to figure out the Will of Guru Maharaj ji. Should we consider this divine offer as His *Hukam,* Order, and grasp it and take this *thambi* in lieu of the other and give our-selves a chance to make amends and there-by retain our honour? Or should we let this God given opportunity pass and return to the unit empty handed and be discredited for the rest of our lives? Chaps I want your views on the matter before I take a final call.'

Honour is cherished in armies around the world. It is honour which makes soldiers face bullets and lay down their lives in battle. Success of a given mission is honourable its failure is considered dishonourable. Harry and his party felt that they had failed in their mission, not-with-standing the herculean effort made by them to catch the run away by chasing him all over South India. They had a deep sense of guilt and therefore blamed themselves for their failure to re-apprehend the deserter. They did not want to lean on mitigating circumstances of the case and termed the mission as a failure in their hearts. The notion of honour in the services will seem complex to a civilian; if you have a brawl—not dishonourable but hitting a downed opponent is dishonourable, gambling—not dishonourable but cheating during gaming is not honourable, killing enemy during war—honourable but wanton killing or killing after ceasefire is dishonourable. On top of the dishonourable list is obviously— cowardice in the face of the enemy. One has to serve in the forces to really comprehend the meaning and value of "Honour". It was this sense of honour which was pushing Harry to take a reckless decision.

'Boss your poser is a conundrum and not simple to answer. There is inherent danger in taking this fellow in lieu. We already have experience of one *thambi* and see what he has done. Now you want to take another *thambi* on board for a repeat performance? In any case, how can we make him pass off as the real *thambi*? The English sahibs are no fools. They will cotton-on to the phony in no time. I think the whole idea is ridiculous and fraught with danger. I am against it,' said Matric.

'Nobody has seen the original *thambi*. So we are safe there, right? In-so-far as documents are concerned, we retain the same name, the same address etc but replace the photograph of the runaway original *thambi* with photograph of our new volunteer rookie,' lobbied Harry.

'*Ustad*, I am a wrestler and hate being defeated. My honour is restored when I pin down my opponent in the ring. The applause of the audience at my victory is what keeps me going. I know that the English sahibs are clever and difficult to befool but I never shy away from challenges or dangers. I am for taking a chance with the new *thambi, jo hoega so hoega,* whatever will be will be, and damn the consequences. Even if something does go wrong, so what? They can't hang a man twice, can they?' the intrepid Lachu had spoken.

'Boss the thing does not end there. He may not be a known figure in our unit but what happens when he rejoins his original unit. The conducting NCO from whose party the original *thambi* had runaway and the other members of the party will immediately get to know that they have an imposter in their midst. What happens then?' questioned the cautious Matric.

'You are right. He will be recognised. But only if he goes to his original unit.'

'Where else will he be sent if not to his original unit?'

'He will apply for a re-muster into an infantry unit "because his calling is a fighting arm and not a pioneer service." He wants to be a soldier in the teeth arm and detests remaining a pioneer in a non fighting corps. This perhaps could be the reason for his running away in the first place, while he was en-route to his pioneer unit,' was Harry's riposte.

'Supposing the English sahibs see through the game and reject his request for re-muster into a new unit? Then he perforce will have to go to his pioneer unit won't he? So therefore the fraud will be exposed, right?

'If his request for a re-muster is declined and he is ordered to proceed to his original pioneer unit, then he simply runs away again, at the first possible opportunity. Needless to say, that his getaway this time would be with a lot of help from us.'

'Boss your argument is sound but there is always danger that some acquaintance of the runaway *thambi* stumbles upon the truth and then we are in thick soup.'

'Even if this happens and a doubt is created that the present fellow is a phony and not the real chap, no blame can be apportioned on us. You know why?'

'Why?'

'Simple, we will just say that this guy was handed over to us by station HQ Madras. How in hell were we to know if he was legitimate or not? We will say that the gaffe has been created by either Station HQ Madras or by the Civil Police or even the

Military Police in Madras. We just escorted the person given to us up to Jullundur. That's all.'

'While I understand that the plan made by you is good, it is not unassailable. The English sahibs can't be fooled so easily. I still say that doing this is wrong.' Matric was still obdurate.

'Don't take a myopic view young man. Look at it his way. We are helping a poor orphan. Yes, an orphan, to, not only get an identity but also honourable means of livelihood. In the bargain we are redeeming our honour. What's wrong with that? I say it's a gamble worth taking. There will be many challenges to face and hurdles to cross but if we are determined we will overcome these problems. The appearance of this man at this crucial juncture at our door is providential. I say it is a message from Guru Maharaj ji that His benevolent hand is on our heads in blessing. And you know what? Two of us are for taking this guy along as replacement you are the only one who is hesitating. Show some spine and let us see some espirit-de-corps Matric.' Come on withdraw your Veto man, withdraw it, yearned Harry silently from the bottom of his heart.

'Though I have serious reservations on the righteousness of the planned scheme, I will tag along with the two of you with a prayer to Wahe Guru ji Maharaj. Count me in. Let us go ahead with it *Ustad*,' authorized Matric. 'Only time will tell, if we have made a right decision or a wrong one.'

'One day, time will indeed tell us that Matric. And take it from me that the decision we made at Madurai would turn out to be correct,' said Harry. His prayer had been answered.

Thus the resolution adopted at the conference was unanimous and Harry declared "The Madurai Convention" as concluded. The three musketeers had decided to throw the dice one last time in a gamble of gambles.

'This is all very well *Ustad* but our whole idea hinges on one fact! Will Mr. Thambi acquiesce to go along with our audacious plot?' observed Lachu.

'We will find that out in a jiffy,' replied Harry. He then signalled Mr. Thambi to come over and carried forward his conversation through the open window of the compartment with him.

'*Thambi* I can try and get you a service in army.'

'The same army in which you gents are serving?'

'Yes, same army.'

'You must be joking. I don't have any authenticated personal bona-fides. As a matter of fact I don't even have a name and you had mentioned that identification proof is mandatory for getting into the army. How are you going to resolve this basic question?'

'We will arrange a name and all other things for you but we too expect something from you, after all we are arranging a job for you.'

'I am a homeless, penny-less beggar. What can I give you for your munificence? I have nothing to give except good wishes and blessings. But one thing I promise, I will remain your slave for the rest of my life and I also promise to share my emoluments with you gents.'

'Hey you misunderstood me. We don't want any money from you. All we want is that you do our bidding without questioning it, so that we don't land in trouble for helping you.'

'Will do so, but I have no clue about the army I would require training as well.'

'We will put you through training also and by the time the training ends you will be as good a soldier as any other. We will take care of every aspect but it is you who have to decide if you have it in you to become a disciplined soldier.'

'Yes, yes, I have it in me. I will work hard and be obedient, just get me the job.'

'OK then. Hop aboard and come with us.'

'But I don't have a railway ticket.'

'Don't worry we already have one for you.'

'Where to'?

'No questions Thambi, no questions. You will get to know everything, all in good time. Get on board if you desire the job.'

No point in giving a chance to these gentlemen to change their minds contemplated the vagrant. Thus a grimy, stinking, barefooted Mr. Thambi, clothed in filthy tatters quickly stepped in to the train at Madurai Railway Station on this night of Monday the 26th of January 1942, without any further questions to become a soldier.

Matric handed over the original *thambi's* baggage to Mr. Thambi and told him to open it. With their prompting the unsure hobo pulled out a towel, a set of under clothing, a shirt and a *lungi* from the neatly packed luggage. Lachu helped him locate the small toilet bag from within the folds of the blanket. He opened it to expose a soap case with a used soap cake nestled inside, a razor and blades, shaving soap and brush, a tooth powder tin. Lachu indicated the toilet and the vagrant entered it armed with the toiletries, towel and clothing. They heard the sound of the shower coming to life. The train pulled out with a whistle and a jerk, on its 1600 mile journey to Delhi.

Harry took out his note book and made out an outline training programme for their new recruit for the duration of the journey. He devoted 30% of the time on adaption of new identity, 30% was allocated to Drill, 5% to army organizations, 10% to Motivational Training, 15% to Dress and Turn out, 5% to PT and kept the remainder in reserve. He allotted the responsibility of Drill to Lachu, kept the ID Mutation of Mr. Thambi to the original run away Devar, under himself and the remainder subjects went to Matric. He gave out the training responsibilities accordingly.

He tore the page from the note book and had just finished inserting it into a recess behind the mirror screwed in the wall of the compartment for easy access of the instructors, when Mr. Thambi emerged from the toilet. For a moment they didn't recognize him. Shaved and bathed, he was a physically transformed person in clean clothes. He was truly, a handsome guy. He seemed to be having some white blood coursing through his veins speculated Harry. His tattered clothing was bundled under his arm and the first thing he did was to chuck the bundle out of the window of the fast moving train into the night. His action seemed a deliberate act. He turned around and faced them, open arms thrown upwards producing an effect of finality—past jettisoned and future embraced. And then he smiled exposing a perfect set of gleaming white teeth. Jesus this fellow could be a debonair hero in the film industry in Lahore if not Bombay, the Indian equivalent of the American Hollywood.

Harry told Mr. Thambi that from now on his new identity would come into force. His new name was to be Neville Devar and the army rank he held was Pioneer. Hereafter he would be addressed as Pioneer Devar. He was also told that his training phase had commenced. He was allocated an upper berth and told to spread the bedding, dispensed to him, on it.

Harry had already been robbed of his reputation by *Thambi-I* and he certainly did not want *Thambi-II* to clean-out their worldly possessions as well, during the night, when they were fast asleep. He was rightly worried that a clean-up of all their belongings by *Thambi-II* at this stage would further plunge their status from the proverbial frying pan into the fire. Harry had, therefore, decided to take the precaution of assigning guard duties for the remaining part of the night by rotation and accordingly announced the sentry duty roster. The new recruit was to perform the duty as an under-study to Lachu during his tenure. Everyone and everything at their appropriate places and in order, Harry declared lights out and took the first guard duty. He looked at his wristwatch when he suddenly remembered that it had been exposed to rain at Dhanushkodi. He was now not sure if the contraption was still working and therefore quickly put the watch to his ear for verification. He was relieved when he heard its reassuring ticking sound. It dawned on Harry that his shock proof, radium dial watch was also water proof. The English sahibs indeed provision their soldiers with the best gear which can take a beating and yet continue to operate successfully under all weather conditions too. Great guys these Brits. He peered at the radium dial of the watch in the darkness time was 0001 hours.

As soon as others had gone to sleep Harry removed the sealed envelope handed over to him in Madras containing Pioneer Devar's documents. He studied it minutely. There were three red sealing wax seals at its upper flap. These seals had the pressed imprint of the British Crown. The envelope's other flap was glue sealed. If he fingered the wax seals they were bound to get damaged. Re-sealing could be done but to emboss the crown imprint on the wax seal was not possible. He took out a blade and made an attempt to gently pry open the opposite side glued flap but soon realized that prying open the other flap would damage the envelope. What should he do? He had to access the papers inside to study and modify them if required.

Then he remembered that as a child he had a philately hobby and used to successfully remove glued foreign postage stamps from envelopes by applying a water film on and around the postage stamps which made the envelope and postage stamp soggy. The damp stamps could then be removed without difficulty and added to his collection after drying up. He decided to use the same technique tonight to pry open the envelope. He wet his hanky and carefully placed the same on the glued flap of the envelope. He set the cover with its wetted flap gently aside and waited for it to get moist, inspecting it from time to time. When he was certain that critical level of dampness had been achieved he picked up the envelope and got to work, attempting to open it with the help of a blade. Cautiously, very cautiously he started to pry it open. It was a slow and painstaking process and the moving train and the low illumination of the compartment didn't help but about twenty minutes later, presto, the flap had been un-glued.

Harry carefully took out the contents from the envelope. There was an original copy of their Movement Order, the Military Police Report, an inventory of kit and belongings of Devar, a carbon copy of the enrolment letter of the South Zone Recruitment Office containing six names including that of Pioneer (Recruit) Neville Devar addressed to Recruitment Branch Army Headquarters, New Delhi, a certified true copy of the original letter from South Zone Recruitment Office addressed to the Pioneer Centre, Bangalore, the original letter from Pioneer Centre addressed to 244 Pioneer Company having the photograph of Devar, a police verification cum character report of Devar issued by the police at the time of his enrolment, a medical certificate pertaining to Devar and Devar's pay book, IAB-64. The British Indian Army had numerous forms which were catalogued and numbered by the Army Stationary Depots and used for day to day work. One of the more important pieces of the army stationary was the Indian Army Book Numbered 64 or IAB-64 for short. It was a pocket sized booklet containing a number of formatted pages where accounts of salary payments disbursed to its holder were recorded. In addition, the annual training targets achieved by the individual were profiled there-in. It also contained the medical status, annual leave records and personal & family particulars of the soldier. The IAB-64 was referred to, by the men as the "paybook" since it contained the salary records and had to be produced at the time of receiving pay each month. Harry identified the IAB-64 and the original Pioneer Centre letter as the two important documents and kept them aside separately. He then re-inserted the remainder back into the envelope.

He sat down and commenced to study the two short-listed documents. Both had Devar's photograph affixed on them and each photograph had been partially imprinted with a round rubber seal stamp of the issuing office of the document in such a way that about 70% of the seal mark was on the face of the document and the remainder was on the photograph. In addition the photograph on the Pay Book had a half inch wide and about two inch long red graph paper strip glued below it. This narrow piece of graph paper carried the specimen signature of deserter Devar and it was pasted in such a manner that half of it lay over and along, the bottom edge of the photograph and the other half on the page of the Pay Book on which it was fastened. Harry assessed the amount of work and expertise required to replace the existing photographs with those of the new incumbent. He then commenced removing the photograph and the signature band of Devar from the pay book and the photo from original letter in the same slow and tedious manner. In this case he had to be even more circumspect because the reverse side of the page carrying the photo in the pay book also had some written material which had to remain untouched during the process. While the picture on the letter came away easily the pay book job was more challenging. Removal job done, he stored both the photo-less documents and the detached photos in a separate cover. After that he woke up Lachu and Mr. Thambi for their turn to take on the watch duty, handed over the wrist watch to Lachu to time his duty and went to sleep.

He woke up and looked outside. The train was stationary and Matric and Mr. Thambi were de-trained and breaking *datuns* from a nearby *Neem* tree and Lachu was doing his morning sit-ups. Seeing the boss awaken Lachu stopped his work out and returned the wrist watch to him. Matric and Mr. Tambi entrained and handed a *datun* each to him and Lachu. All four were brushing their teeth with *datuns* when the train recommenced its journey after the unscheduled halt. After completing their ablutions they commenced training of Mr. Thambi in earnest.

He was first made to adorn the army uniform. The shirt was a size small. Nonetheless its' tight fit was passable. The trouser was also tight at the waist but with the tummy tucked in, its fit too was tolerable. However the length of the trouser was clearly short by about an inch and could not pass scrutiny. Mr. Thambi a k a Pioneer Devar bent down and fingered the cuff of the trouser leg. He was able to discern that there was adequate additional cloth folded underneath the cuff crease to enable an increase in length of the trouser. The lower fold of the cuff of the trouser leg therefore would have to be opened and redone after increasing its length by an inch. He borrowed a housewife from Matric and took out a needle there from. He took off the trouser and inserted the needle into the stitching of the cuff of the trouser leg and broke its thread strands with its help. He then pulled out the broken thread thereby opening up the sewing. He was satisfied to observe that there was indeed adequate cloth in the fold of the trouser leg to make possible a length increase. The new soldier then increased the length of the trouser by an inch and darned it again with the Olive Green thread taken from the borrowed housewife. He repeated the process on the other trouser leg and got back into the trousers again. The three judges seem to be satisfied except that a tell-tale crease mark had now appeared one inch above the lower end of the mended trouser legs, where the previous fold of the trouser had been. This would have to be ironed out.

Matric demonstrated to *thambi* how to lace the boots without any twist in the laces. He, however, did not have to teach him how to polish the boots. The fellow had more experience in that field than all the three of them put together. He had learned and practiced that trade during his bumming days. The comfort of socks in his polished boots seemed heavenly for the new recruit. He was taught how to buff the brass components of the web belt. He then adjusted the belt as per his waist measurement. This was followed by donning of the headgear—a dark blue beret. Matric helped the green-horn in adjusting the band of the beret, horizontally one inch above and parallel to the eye brows, while keeping the cap badge above his left eye brow. The puffed beret looked like a chef's headgear at this stage. Matric then pulled the beret down on the right side so that it touched the top of *thambi's* right ear while it fitted snugly on top of his head, just the way its French creator had wanted it to be worn. Perfect declared the three judge bench. They then encouraged the new soldier to repeat the process independently.

'I have already given you, your new identity,' said Harry, 'we will now address you accordingly. Is that understood, Pioneer Neville Devar?'

'Yes understood.'

'In-correct reply. You must say "Yes Sir". Now reply once again. Is that understood?

'Yes sir, understood sir.'

The recruit was learning fast, thought Harry as he continued, 'Name of your father was Patrick Devar and you were born on . . . 'And so it went on and on, as the *thambi* took in his new identity. By the end of the briefing the nameless orphan had a name, he knew names of his late parents, was aware where and when he was born. They took a break at the next station and Harry ordered Matric, their accounts in-charge to give Pioneer Devar four annas and deputed him to fetch breakfast for the party from a vendor on the station. His other colleagues were aghast when they saw the phony Devar get down and walk away all alone, without any escort towards a kiosk selling eatables with a small monetary fortune in the pocket of his uniform. While Matric and Lachu worried that the fellow may vanish like the previous *thambi*, Harry remained unperturbed. He had purposely sent the recruit alone. If the guy wanted to spurn their offer of a new life he might as well do it now and be done with. Devar disappeared into the crowd surrounding the stall and two thirds of the party in the compartment were ill at ease and believed that his disappearance was for good. However Harry continued to remain, as cool as a cucumber, with a couldn't care less attitude, even when the shrill sound of two consecutive whistles, first from the locomotive followed by that of the train conducting guard fell on their keen ears. Just then Matric saw *Thambi II* surfacing out of the crowd, hands fully weighed down with food laden leaf platters and leaf bowls and heading for their cabin. On coming aboard he placed the breakfast laden leaf dishes on one of the lower berths with Matric's help. Devar then returned three annas, the monetary balance left with him after clearing the bill at the cash and carry outlet, back to Matric their accountant cum bursar.

After breakfast, they carefully disposed off the platters through the open windows of the speeding train and washed their hands in the toilet wash basin by turns and commenced their respective work schedule. Lachu took over the training of the new entrant while Matric updated his account book and Harry concentrated on studying the various existing entries in the Pay Book of Devar which was now sans a photograph of its owner. Lachu was aiming to teach the new Devar only a limited number of Drill movements within the short time available. He knew that the first major test for Devar would be during the orderly room when he would be marched up to the Commanding Officer on an offence report under an appropriate Indian Army Act Section for running away. Accordingly, he had shortlisted the drill movements which would have to be performed during this ordeal by Pioneer Devar. He thus gave priority to saluting, quick march, halting on the march, turning at the halt with special attention to about turn because Devar would have to accomplish this difficult turn at the end of the orderly room when he was marched out of the CO's presence.

Harry was careful to change training subjects at the end of every forty minutes. He knew that human interest wanes and boredom sets in, if one subject is flogged for long durations. So after Lachu's one period at quick march halt and saluting, he took over and carried out revision of the personal particulars assigned to him that morning by an inter-active question and answer session. He then tutored him on a simple story which he was to mug up and lay in front of the white Sahibs. The straightforward story being he wanted to become a fighting soldier in the Infantry but had by mistake got recruited into the Pioneer Corps. Since he did not want to remain an unarmed pioneer he had absconded. 'Whatever may happen, Thambi don't change this story line,' had been Harry's firm advice.

After this cramming lesson, Matric took over and tutored him on the rank structure and organization of an infantry battalion. Then it was back to Lachu for drill again. By lunch time Pioneer Devar had not made any improvement in the drill. All his movements were sill sloppy. Lachu impressed upon Pioneer Devar that getting the halt, salute and about turn were of utmost importance because these movements had to be carried out during the orderly room procedure which he would have to face as soon as they arrived in the unit at Jullundur. He also became aware that after the orderly room he would have to undergo some minor punishment for which he may be put behind bars for some duration. This information had put him off but he had bounced back when Harry assured him that the detention centre would be the unit quarter guard where he would continue to enjoy all soldierly rights and be served the same food as them and he would have a daily routine including study and training periods. The cell would be only for sleeping purposes at night.

Harry again sent Pioneer Devar all by himself to fetch lunch for all of them at a way side station and this time one whole rupee was given to him for the, purchase. Devar returned overloaded with eatables and gave back the balance money to Matric. Harry was indeed showing brinkmanship by giving a long rope to Devar. So far, Devar had not hanged himself and in the bargain also the three of them by scooting. Amen.

While the broad gauge tracks of the Indian Railways are 5 feet and 6 inch wide, the coaches plying on this ample track are even wider. The internal width of a carriage of the Indian Railways is nearly 10 feet but still this seemed to be in-adequate for the recruit's drill training especially in-so-far as saluting movement was concerned. In British Indian Army salute drill, the right arm with an open palm is fully extended to the right side in a swinging movement, the hand with fingers joined together, is then brought to the forehead with the index finger touching the forehead an inch above the right eye brow. Harry had noticed that the hand swing of Devar was inhibited because at every salute, his extended hand seemed to be brushing the upper berth, during its upward swing. Harry also observed that the carriage floor was getting damaged by the thirteen regulation metal studs nailed to the soles of the army boots due to the obligatory stomping of feet while executing the "halt". Accordingly, after lunch Harry had Devar's boots replaced with canvas shoes and he ordered Lachu to fold the upper bunks so that Devar got more space for his hand swing during saluting practice. The training of the volunteer conscript went on, far into the night by when he could give a rudimentary salute, halt clumsily but still could not do an about turn without unbalancing himself. Before turning in for the night, the recruit was told to increase the length of the other trouser as well.

Harry woke up at about 3 am and took out his note book and then the pay book of the runaway from the document envelope. He went through the entries recorded in the pay book twice and then jotted down four points in his note book. One was "height", the second was "colour of eyes", third was "weight" and the fourth was "identification marks". He put a "?" notation in front of each of these entries. It was obvious to Harry that something would have to be done to these features because they were not matching their new recruit.

Harry mulled over each of the four aspects. *Thambi-II* was certainly taller than that swine, *Thambi-I*. The height entry in the pay book read the height as "5 feet 8 inches". So the figure 8 would have to be obliterated and the new figure inserted in its place. The colour of eyes written in the pay book was "Brown" whereas the present chap's eyes were lighter, a result of perhaps, some unknown white ancestor in his lineage. This too had to be modified. There were two identification marks listed in the document. One was a "tattoo mark of a cross on the left fore-arm" and the other "a birth mark on the upper back of the left shoulder blade". Weight entry read as "1 Maund, 32 Seers" but the present fellow seemed heavier. Harry however reasoned that a person could always gain weight within limits, of course. So the first thing to do was to get the exact height and weight of *Thambi-II* and then decide further line of action. Having identified the crucial aspects which needed to be attended to, he completed his ablutions. He then woke up the others so that they too could do the same before reaching Delhi.

The train reached Delhi at 0400 hours nearly six hours behind schedule. Since this was the final destination of the train, all passengers got down and rushed towards the exit gates. Soon only they were left on the platform and Harry ordered Lachu to show him a full rehearsal of the orderly room procedure with Mr. Thambi now rechristened Pioneer Neville Devar wearing leather boots. Harry himself sat down on a bench which was to be taken as the CO's desk and an outline was made around it depicting the office of the CO. Commencing the phony orderly room procedure, Lachu gave the various words of command as Pioneer Devar was marched up to the CO as an accused. He was made to halt in front of the CO and as soon as he finished saluting, Harry took over the role of the CO.

'No XXXXXXX Pioneer Devar, is that you?' said Harry pretending to be CO.

Devar gave no response. He just stood there like a statue. 'Hey don't stand there like a statue Devar. You have to reply to the CO's questions. OK? Let's do it again,' said Harry.

'No XXXXXXX Pioneer Devar, is that you?'

'Yes Sir it's me.'

'Pioneer Neville Devar you are charged under section mumble . . . mumble and . . . more mumble, in that you ran away from the train while you were being escorted to 244 Pioneer Company on 5 February 1941 till apprehended . . . mumble . . . mumble. Are you guilty of this offence?' Again there was no response from the accused. 'Devar don't dope. You must reply to the questions posed to you. Understood? We will do it again.' Harry then repeated, 'Are you Devar, guilty of the offence?'

'Guilty Sir'

'That's the way to respond. Good'

'What's so good about a plea of guilty Boss?'

'Stop getting cheeky *thambi* or I'll kick your arse,' reprimanded Harry as he continued in a gruff voice, 'Do you want to say anything in your defence before I pronounce your punishment Pioneer?'

'Yes Sir. I joined the Pioneer Corps by mistake. I actually wanted to join the Infantry and fight the enemy from the front but due to inadequate knowledge I signed up for the Pioneer Corps. I am ready to face any punishment which may be awarded to me but I request that I be transferred to an infantry regiment.' He had learned his lines well thought Harry.

They went through the entire procedure at the end of which Harry had mumbled out an incoherent punishment followed by removal of Devar's belt by Lachu signifying that he had been formally put under arrest and his punishment commenced.

'March him out,' said Harry.

'March the prisoner out,' echoed Matric, now playing the role of adjutant.

Pioneer Devar who had been marched up as "Accused" by Lachu was now identified as "Prisoner" in the word of command by Lachu after removal of his belt. They went through the process half a dozen times before Harry called off the practice. He was not entirely satisfied with the theatrical piece but under the circumstances and constraints of time, performance of *Thambi-II* was passable even though he continued to unbalance himself and nearly toppled each time he executed the about turn. This one act play was to open for its' only performance at Jullundur to an exclusive VIP audience in a couple of days and it certainly required more rehearsals to avoid the dramatic piece turning into a tragedy or a comedy depending on the mood of the Commanding Officer. However, Devar and the party were, for the time being, more than saturated with the continuous dummy runs and hence a break was called for. Harry was winding up his watch when he heard the muezzin calling the faithful to the first of five prayers from the mosques in Chandni Chowk, followed by the *Shabads* emanating from Gurdwara Sis Ganj and the Temple Bells ringing from the temples in Chandni Chowk. Delhi was coming to life on this Wednesday morning of 28th January 1942.

They had a lot of work at hand. They ordered and consumed their morning tea and tidied up themselves. Harry permitted Lachu to visit Gurdwara Sis Ganj to pay obeisance since he had not visited the shrine on the way out but ordered him to be back by seven o'clock and take over guard duty of the baggage at the station. Lachu accordingly proceeded towards the station exit just as the first rays of the rising Sun were filtering out of the thick foliage of trees adjoining the station. They then had breakfast of *Poories* and curried potatoes downed with *Lassi.* After that Harry got hold of the document envelope which he had pried open in the train in one hand and took Devar's recently elongated and darned trouser in the other and went out. He planned to give the trouser to a *dhobi* for ironing out the crease which had appeared in the trouser cuff and to survey the flea market and identify the specialists whose services he would have to requisition for fabricating and converting the documents in favour of the newcomer. He directed Matric to teach Devar assembling and fitting of web equipment during his absence.

He returned just after seven o'clock by when Lachu too had arrived and was distributing *krah parsad* to the other two. He handed over the neatly steam pressed trouser back to Devar and then received a dollop of *krah parsad* in his cupped hands from Lachu and ate the same. He then ordered Devar to remove his web equipment and asked him to change into the pressed trouser. The dhobi launderer had done his job well. The wrinkles in the trouser had been removed and the crease at the cuff end of the trouser leg had been obliterated. He then asked Devar and Matric to accompany him. He told Devar to take one civil shirt and the second uniform trouser with him and the three went out leaving Lachu behind to guard the baggage.

They crossed the same road they had traversed ten days back while proceeding to Gurdwara Sis Ganj in Chandni Chowk, during their short halt at Delhi, on their out-ward journey. The tidy park on the far side of the road was slowly coming to life with traders setting up their make shift stalls and Harry knew that within the hour the souk would be full of milling humanity. They first went to the *dhobi* and gave him the second trouser for ironing and then went to a photographer who had already kept two small buckets containing photo developing chemicals at his make shift studio and was setting up his large box pinhole Kodak Camera, on its tripod. Harry carried out cost negotiations with the photographer for passport size bust photographs and insisted on getting the negative prints of the photographs as well. After a lot of haggling the deal was successfully concluded at one anna for four prints of the photograph. Harry then made Devar to remove his uniform shirt and don the civil one for the first photograph and simultaneously sent Matric to buy a black slate of 12" X 9" size, one chalk, a red coloured graph paper, a foot-ruler and one small bottle of glue from a stationary shop situated in Nai Sarak Road radiating from the Clock Tower Square of Chandni Chowk.

Devar was made to sit on a stool facing the capped pinhole aperture of the large box camera dressed in a civil shirt. The photographer uncovered the camera's pinhole by removing its lid. An upside down and laterally inverted picture of the sitting Devar appeared on the translucent, ground glass, screen on the rear side of the box, opposite to the pinhole as soon as light entered into the camera through the pinhole aperture. He then focused and centered the image on the ground glass by adjusting the height and distance of the camera till he was satisfied with the result. He then placed the cap back to obscure the aperture. Next, he removed the ground glass face by sliding it out and inserted a photographic plate into the same recess. The photographic plate was actually an opaque sleeve containing a photographic paper. He now draped the camera in a black cloth shroud to shield it from light. He then ducked his head under the shroud and carefully slid out the pinhole side opaque sleeve. The photographic paper inside the case would now receive light through the pinhole of the camera as soon as the aperture cap was removed. He then cautiously emerged out from under the black shroud. He stood to the side of the camera, told Devar to remain steady and gently removed the pinhole cap for a second and then put the cover back in place to mask the aperture again, in one flowing and graceful movement. He informed Harry that the photo graph had been taken and would be developed in the next ten minutes or so and again ducked under the black shroud and pushed back into place the opaque shield of the sleeve to cover the now exposed photo paper.

Leaving the photographer to do the developing work, Harry moved on to the next stand with Devar. The next stand was barber's make-shift salon named "Mehmood Hajam" under a banyan tree. A cracked mirror in a decrepit wooden frame was nailed to the tree trunk and adjoining it was nailed a leather strip for sharpening and burnishing his razors, both nails were rusty. Next to that, suspended from large spikes, doubling up as pegs, impaled into the aged tree trunk, were an apron and a towel, both dirty. Below the nailed mirror was an improvised stone and brick platform where tools of the barber's trade were laid out. Facing the mirror was a ramshackle chair. As soon as Devar sat down on the rickety chair the barber tied the dirty apron around his neck, irrigated his hair with water spray, ran a dirty comb through his hair like a plough and then got to work. He simultaneously commenced chatting. Barbers all over the globe have this compulsive habit to gossip while plying their trade and Mehmood was no different.

'You have the personality of a Tommy soldier, boss but it seems you have been getting your hair cut from *malis*, gardeners, in the past. They seem to have been trimming your hair with hedge clippers. I don't think a professional *hajam*, barber, like myself has ever attended to your hairdo with a proper barber's kit,' was his opening remark. After the preamble, Mehmood had continued his monologue non-stop. Devar saw his own face in the cracked mirror being transformed from a shoddy hippy into a groomed soldier, with every clip of the barber's scissors, while his ears took in Mehmood's anecdotes. Hair make-over took nearly half an hour, by when Devar had got to know that Mehmood had four wives, the eldest was an excellent cook, the next two were cousin sisters. The senior wife was able to keep the cousins in line but the youngest was a shrew and required taming by him every other night and sometimes he was forced to use the leather strip in the process. He had already sired seven children, 'thanks to the benevolence of Allah' and was still in fine fettle and would continue till he doubled that number; Inshallah. While his entire four-some would contribute in the creation of the planned second string, its major endowment was likely to be from the womb of the young shrew because of her youth and her compulsive nightly taming routine by Mahmood, was Devar's guess. So it could be safely said that the Lion's share or rather the Lioness' share towards the planned addition would be contributed by the young spitfire. This thought brought a wry smile on Devar's face. 'It pleases me to notice a smile on your face Guv'nor. What you like more? My hair cutting prowess or my story telling?' was the barber's take.

'Both' replied the customer. 'You are proficient in both subjects'. And also in your sexual performance, thought a bemused Devar.

'I work to satisfy my customers. If I have brought happiness to your exalted self then I am indeed blessed.'

Hair cutting was a family vocation which had been practiced for centuries by his ancestors. His family had been the official barbers to the Mughal Court, an honour bestowed on the family on account of their proficiency in this line of work. *Hajam* had ruefully stated that one of his illustrious ancestors had been born with-out genitals, either male or female, by a quirk of fate. He had however then stated with professional pride that even that *hijra,* eunuch, had been employed as a barber in the Royal household, in the Harem, because of his proficiency in the craft.

'Guv', you may well ask what the hell would a barber, be doing in a harem full of women? You know what? The mighty mughals wanted only freshly shaved pussy, for their nightly sexual escapades. Yes sir, shaved and then scrubbed with alum and then massaged with almond oil. My eunuch ancestor Allahditta Hijra was an exceedingly busy barber seeing the size of the harem and sexual appetite of the emperors,' concluded Mehmood.

Listening to his tale, his captive audience darted his eyes to the *hajam's* tools of trade displayed, on the stone and brick table, below the cracked mirror. He observed a lone razor and only a single shaving brush, which was rendered poor in bristles due to age and use, sandwiching a piece of alum and a over-used cake of shaving soap. He therefore inferred that if Mehmood had been inspired by the mighty Mughal Emperors then he possibly was using these very tools, on his female quartet for depilatory purposes. He therefore, not only declined the offer of a shave but also of getting the complimentary offer of his armpits sheared. He however, accepted a manicure and a pedicure from the barber. Harry paid one taka or two pice to the barber for his services.

The two returned to the photo studio where four prints and one negative of *thambi's* photo were received by Harry. This instant photo service perhaps was the precursor to Polaroid instant photography of the future. And when Matric returned from his marketing spree, he found Harry admiring Mr. Thambi's new photograph.

Harry sat down on a bench and extracted the photograph of runaway Devar which he had dislodged from the pay book during the wee hours in the moving train, from the envelope. He concentrated on the slate held by the runaway in the photograph where his personal particulars were written. Harry spelt out the Army No, Rank and name of the original Devar as it appeared on the photograph and made the new Devar write the same on the slate just brought by Matric with chalk in his own hand writing. He satisfied himself by checking and rechecking the same with the slate in the photograph and the written particulars on page one of the pay-book; he then tore up the photograph of the original Devar. Harry now ordered the new Devar to remove his civilian shirt and get back into his uniform. They checked the uniform and got Devar generally smartened up for his photograph in uniform. Devar again sat down in front of the camera and Harry made him hold the slate with the side having his chalk written particulars facing the camera, in his lap below his chest in front of him. Now Harry painstakingly explained to the photographer that the slate with its written matter should not only be part of the photograph but also clearly readable. When the photographer handed the four prints and the negative of Devar's photo in uniform, Harry read out the contents of the slate from the photograph loudly to confirm its legibility. It was evident that the photographer had not only understood Harry's briefing but he was also a good camera man. A satisfied Harry cleared the payment of two annas to the photographer.

The three collected the crisply ironed trouser from the *dhobi* and then returned to the station. Harry led them to an Avery weighing machine placed next to the station entrance. He asked Devar to stand on the weighing bench of the vending type weighing machine and inserted a one pice coin into its slot. The machine started to whirr, its coloured psychedelic lights came on, rotated and it soon vended out a ticket with Devar's weight printed on it and then went silent. Devar's weight appearing on the obverse side of the ticket was 1 Maund, 39 Seers and his printed fate on the reverse side read "A great future full of riches and love awaits you". These guys print only soothing future forecasts to ensnare more customers, "riches and love", for a penny-less orphan, my foot, thought Matric.

Harry was satisfied. He now knew the actual weight of *thambi II*. He however still had to take the new incumbent's height. And this posed a problem since there was no gadget available to measure heights of individuals at the railway station. On reaching their platform, Harry was contemplating how to overcome this difficulty when he suddenly got an idea which could resolve the problem. He would use one of the pillars, supporting the corrugated cement sheet ceiling covering the platform, as a prop to calculate the height of the fresher. He asked Matric to remove his shoes and turban. He flattened and parted the hair on Matric's head with his hand so that his scalp became visible. After that he made him to stand erect, bare feet joined together at the heels and the toes, next to the nearest iron pillar on the platform with his back touching the upright post. Harry then made certain that Matric's posture was correct by ensuring that his heels, buttocks and back of the head were touching the column. He then put the foot ruler flat on his head at the hair parting carefully in a horizontal position so that one end of the ruler touched the iron pillar. He then cautiously put a pencil mark on the pillar at the meeting point of the ruler and the pillar and made a triangular annotation next to it. This was the benchmark symbol he had assimilated during map reading classes and then he wrote "B-Mk" adjoining it. On the other side of the pencil mark he wrote 5'-7" since that was Matric's recorded height in his pay book. This point became the height benchmark for further calculations.

He then had a bare foot Devar replace Matric and marked his height in a similar fashion. He then made two decussating strokes on one side of the height line and the letters ND, depicting initials of his name, on the other. He then put the foot ruler vertically on the iron pillar with its "0" mark coinciding with the height bench mark determined in the past few minutes and found that Devar's height coincided with the "2" division of the scale. So Devar's height was two inches more than Matric's. Since Matric's height was 5'-7" Devar's height was now confirmed as 5'-9". Eureka. Harry may not be an Archimedes but he had created a rough and ready height, callipers to arrive at the new incumbent's correct height. Since mentioned height of *thambi*-I in his original documents was 5'-8", Harry computed that *thambi*-II was an inch taller than the run-away. Harry took out his note book from his pocket and made a note of this against the question marked entry "Height" and simultaneously ticked the "Weight" entry because the marginal weight difference was not a cause for worry. He was about to tear the weight ticket when Devar stopped him and requested permission to keep the ticket.

'Hey why you want to hang on to the weight ticket? Can't you remember that you weigh seventy nine seers?' queried Harry.

'It's not for the weight, boss. I want to retain it for my fate and fortune printed on its reverse face,' replied Devar as he accepted ticket from Harry. Bastard really believes in the printed forecast thought a cynic Matric.

Harry then got hold of Devar's left arm and marked a rough cross on his fore arm with a pen. He then had Devar remove his shirt and put a haphazard mark on his left shoulder blade with the same pen. He told Matric to take Devar to a tattoo artist and get a Catholic Cross tattooed on Devars left fore-arm and a light smudge tattoo mark depicting a birth mark on his back on his shoulder blade at the marked places. He reiterated that the smudgy tattoo on the shoulder blade was to depict a birth mark and therefore should be in black ink and only faintly visible. He then got up clutching, the all important document containing envelope and went to the park to look for "paper and ink experts", a handle used for document fabricators. It took him more than an hour and a four anna tip to a letter writer, before he was introduced to a bloke doing such artistic work. The bugger was a small skinny character with shifty eyes with betel nut stained teeth and henna dyed hair, who would not even divulge his name. So Harry, after taking one look at this disgusting character, christened him Mr. Shady. Shady said he would do the job but asked for five rupees to do it. Harry had no choice but to accede to this preposterous demand and Shady took him through a narrow lane to his place of work. There was one work table in a dingy room on which were laid out holder pens, assorted nibs, fountain pens, reed pens, erasers, ink removers, a number of ink pots, ink pads, precision measuring instruments etc. The shelves on the walls were overflowing with blank school and college certificates, passports, blank visa forms, blank ID covers, blank birth and death certificates and the like. Shady took the pay book and the letter from Harry and got to work.

Harry returned to the railway station in the evening when the time by his watch was five. He sat down on the bench and Matric and Devar gushingly showed him the tattoo on Devar's forearm and on his back. Satisfied with the tattoos, Harry exhibited to them the final documents. They were amazed at the result. The new Devar's photograph on the Pay-book as well the letter bore the original rubber seals and the signatures of the officers. Harry asked Devar to put his signature on the graph paper strip pasted so genuinely below his photograph which Devar did with a confident flourish. Everything seems to be in order. Colour of eyes entry now read "Lt Brown" instead of the original "Brown". Shady had been unable to prefix the full word "Light" due to constraints of available space before the existing "Brown" entry. He had therefore adroitly written "Lt" instead, which was generally accepted as the abbreviated form of "Light". Only the Height entry did not read 5'-9" because Shady had refused to modify the original entry of digit "8" to "9" because using an acidic ink remover, 'leaves behind tell tale marks', he had said. Instead he had cleverly inserted the figure 7/8 in the small space between the existing number "8" and the word "inches" and hence the height column now read 5 feet 8-7/8 inches, 'which was nearly 9 inches anyway,' had been his argument. Harry's insistence to make it more nearer "9" by inserting "9/10" had been brushed aside with derision by the expert, 'sardar sahib we are dealing in the British measurement unit and not the French metric unit. Ok? In this system the inch has eight subdivisions and not ten and hence I can only go up to the figure 7/8 and not beyond. Understood Sire?' The disdainful response from the expert had forced Harry to remain a mute spectator thereafter.

All said and done they were now ready to make their entry into the unit and hoped to pull off this incredible heist with some divine benevolence. He took out his notebook and was satisfied to note that all the four points requiring change in the documents had been taken care of. He had tick marked the weight point already and he now ticked the remainder three entries pertaining to height, identification marks and colour of eyes as well. As he was closing diary, he noticed that the page had become unglued from the diary. He tried to push the errant page back into the planner's covers but failed to do so. On examination he realized that the loose page had become separated because its other half had been removed by him earlier in the train to write out the recruit's training schedule. He pulled out and discarded this loose leaf as well, since matters listed thereon had been taken care of. He then popped the diary in to his breast pocket. After that he inserted the professionally modified documents into the original envelope and glued its flap.

They boarded a train being hauled by a 4-6-2 wheel configured X series locomotive for Jullundur in an inter class compartment and Harry ordered Matric to write the "Reserved for Army" on the outside of the compartment with chalk. The train pulled out of the station at 8 pm and as it gathered speed Harry cradled his army issue water bottle and uncorked it. The unplugging produced a resonant deep plonk which is exclusive to champagne bottles or half empty army issue tin water bottles at uncorking time. He poured himself a peg or rather a Patiala peg of rum cached in his water bottle, for the first time after the escape of the knave. It seemed an aeon since he had had a drink, though it was only his fourth night of forced abstinence. He gave out generous dollops of the dark fiery liquid to the others as well. Lachu was quick to pour cold *chagal* water into their rum filled enamelled mugs and a spontaneous clanking of their mugs followed by loud 'cheers' as they commenced downing their drinks. Matric produced a paper bag of *pakoras* from no-where which they munched making small talk mostly concerning the runaway *thambi* 'who could go and fuck himself for all they cared'. Morale was indeed on the ascension.

The new Pioneer Devar was really on top of the world. His past indulgence in alcohol had been locally brewed moonshine. The only time he had imbibed legit liquor was when the British sergeant's wife had given him a shot of gin laced with bitters and lime cordial in her bed room at Madras to get him going prior to making him do things to her. He was sure of being indulged by her with more gin and lime if her husband had not made a sudden and untimely appearance on that fateful day three months ago. But that was history. What mattered now was the reality of his drinking legitimate army issue XXX Rum and not hooch. After a few large gulps he considered himself to be the luckiest bloke in the world and couldn't thank his benefactors enough. They ate their dinner of *chapattis* and potatoes in gravy, purchased by Matric and Devar during a halt at Panipat Station. They disposed off the leaf crockery out of the windows into the night and rinsed their mouths, shooting into the night through the same windows, of their speeding train. While the full blown blasts of the experienced Sikh trio drew expletives, from the recipients of their returning rinse spray, from the trailing compartment, the weak spout of, green horn, *thambi* was received by him, squarely in his own face, bringing all round laughter to the merry men. Harry used the toilet after dinner and had no difficulty in locating his member for the pee. Things had certainly become normal. Lachu shuttered all the windows and latched the doors lest the thieving *sansi* strike them again on their return journey. Lights out and they were snoring when the time by Harry's radium dial watch was 11 pm.

They were up by 4 am and had completed their ablutions by the time the train halted at Ludhiana at 5 am. Matric and Devar dismounted with four mugs and brought them back filled, with hot tea and four bread-rusk biscuits from a vendor. They dunked the rusks into their hot tea and ate them while sipping tea. Harry then ordered Matric to collect the "EX VISIT HOME" papers and had all three copies torn to shreds and thrown out of the window. No point in carrying explosive stuff to the unit. If only the knave had not runaway and put a spanner in his plans, Harry would have visited his home at Machiwara by now and done what he had planned to do over there. His home and warmth of his wife were, just a stone's throw away from Ludhiana Railway Station but she might well be a thousand miles away since Harry could not visit her. To take his mind off his musing he shot off a question, 'Hey Lachu, tell me the location of RV-1, where you were to relieve me in "Exercise Visit Home"?'

Though busy doing his morning sit-ups, Lachu took a pause from his exercise routine, looked out of the window and correctly pointed to a bench on the opposite platform adjoining the Railway Police Post and said, 'there Boss.'

'Correct wrestler,' replied Harry and Lachu took up a prone position on the floor and commenced doing push-ups as part of his morning exercise schedule.

'Anyone for more tea?' inquired Devar. Harry and Matric answered in the affirmative, giving Devar their empty mugs and a one rupee coin having the profiled head of the British Monarch embossed on its obverse side. He and Matric then commenced to update and total up the expense account. Soon Devar passed two mugs of hot tea to them through the open window. They sipped the tea mechanically as they worked on the accounts adding another three pice to the total for the tea which they were now sipping, so focused was their concentration that the recommencement of the train journey went unnoticed by them. They continued to be absorbed in their accounting work oblivious of Lachu's work-out generated grunts or the loud clacking of the moving train as it sped on its way to Jullundur. Harry had Matric divide the common expenses incurred in three parts and gave his one third share of the total to Matric and told the exercising Lachu to do like-wise. Harry did not burden the others to share the expenses incurred by him on Devar's make over and documentation. It was at this point that Matric called out to Devar without lifting his head to return fifteen annas and one pice, the balance from the one rupee given to him for the second round of tea at Ludhiana. When they received no response from Devar, he and Harry looked up. But there was no Devar in the cabin. The two accountants and the physical fitness freak gaped at each other open mouthed, stunned by the magical disappearance of *Thambi-II.* The loud monotonous metronome like clatter made by the thundering train's wheels as they traversed the joints in the rail track, which had not disturbed them so far, now seemed louder than even the deafening clap of their bolt action .303 Enfield Rifles during firing practice at the range.

Matric was the first to react, 'the bastard has run away just like the other polecat boss. I always had misgivings about the fellow but nobody listened to me. Everything is back to square one.'

The escape by the second *thambi* had kick-started painful cramps in Harry's stomach and an uncontrollable desire to take a leak. How the hell had he got himself into such a mess he thought and headed for the toilet to take a piss. As he closed the toilet door behind him, he heard Lachu say, 'if I get my hands on the fucker, I will crush him to death.'

His organ which had a stately profile last night and which had stirred when he had reminisced about the warmth of his wife at the train halt at Ludhiana a few moments ago was now smaller than a newly hatched humming bird chick. He had difficulty in pulling it out of its thick nest. He broke wind loudly as he aimed his weak urine trickle into the toilet pot. He rued the day he had been assigned this escort duty. If the first escape engineered by *thambi-I* had enfeebled him *thambi-II*'s absconding while buying tea at Ludhiana had practically emasculated him, thought Harry as he jiggled his pathetic pissing apparatus to shake off the last drops still struck in its capillary. It occurred to Harry that the size and condition of his penis was directly proportional to the state of his morale. While outwardly he always managed to look positive, the degree of uncertainty and self doubt tormenting his mind was silently indicated to him, in private by his cock. He, therefore, might as well call it his own "Meter-o-Morale".

A dejected Harry came out of the toilet and listened to Matric's verbal onslaught on *thambi-II*. Matric was livid. He was convinced that he would never trust a *thambi* again. What's more, he was in no doubt that the scoundrel was now on a train chugging South-wards towards Madras or Madurai. Matric was additionally lamenting the fact that the bastard was worse than the *sansi*. While the *sansi* had just taken away a turban, this thug had not only taken away a reasonably good uniform and a pair of boots but also his pure silver, one rupee coin, weighing one *tola*, 1/3 of an ounce, which was over ten grams on the metric scale. The same questions which had haunted them when *thambi-I* had escaped came back to haunt them again. Harry could however not fathom a couple of things. Till last night *thambi-II* was considering him-self to be the luckiest man on the planet and was profusely thanking them for having hoisted him from a tramp to a respectable soldier and yet he had run away. If he wanted to abscond then why did he not do so during the night when they were asleep and dead to the world? Why did he wait for day break to flee? It did not make any sense. Be that as it may, *thambi-II* was gone and along with him was gone their hope of redeeming their honour. His morale as substantiated by his "meter-o-morale" was dismally low.

It was Lachu who tried to still remain positive. 'Boss it's quite possible that the fellow was doping when the train steamed out of the station and thus got left behind at Ludhiana. He may catch the next train and fetch up at Jullundur later.'

'Balls, I tell you it was all planned. Firstly the bugger manufactures an excuse to detrain by volunteering to buy a second round of tea. He then delivers two mugs of tea to me and *Ustad* through the window but does not entrain. Why?'

'Why?'

'Because, he never wanted to do so; he had come up to the compartment ostensibly to serve tea to us but his hidden aim was to see if we were indeed engrossed in other work and to assess his chances of an escape without our realizing it.'

'Well I agree with you that he should have climbed back into the cabin after giving you the tea mugs. But then it is also quite possible that he remained on the platform to loiter and missed the train due to absence of mind. This could be a possibility.'

'You are living in a dreamland, Lachu. I tell you it was all planned. When he was sure that we were all busy in other chores and there was no likely hood of a reaction from our side, he silently faded into the crowd on the station and made good his escape,' said a sceptic Matric.

'I still say that we should not jump the gun. If my conjecture comes true then we may yet see *thambi-II* reaching Jullundur by the following train,' said Lachu.

'You are being naïve, wrestler. The scoundrel disappears at Ludhiana and re-appears 40 miles away at Jullundur! These things happen only in Allah-din movies and not in real life. Come on Lachu wake up. The man has runaway; period.'

Getting no reaction from his captive listeners, Matric continued his tirade, 'You know guys, it just occurred to me that this escort duty has, willy-nilly, made us a part and parcel of a catalogue of escapes, which, sadly have been repeating themselves, like history. And let me tell you, we too are going to be history on reaching the unit.'

Harry did not speak. He kept his council. Both could be right but he did see merit in Lachu's argument. So, it was advisable to wait at Jullundur Railway Station after detraining and check out the next train arriving from Ludhiana. Maybe *thambi-II* would indeed re-appear at Jullundur and that would end this heartbreaking interlude on a positive note.

They would be at their destination in less than an hour. What was he going to tell the powers that be in the unit? How was he to explain the fiasco? In all his Annual Confidential Reports his British Commanders had assessed him "Above Average," and his reports were spangled with laudable observations like "full of initiative, dynamic, able to convert an adverse situation into a favourable one, smilingly accepts additional responsibility, an excellent section commander" and many other similar praiseworthy comments. These admirable remarks had been ascribed to him by his white masters, year after year in his reports and now this disaster. The same Brits were likely to annotate him as "despicable" in his coming ACR; reprehensible. He had not only let the real prisoner escape but had detached his photographs from the original documents and destroyed the same. The photographs pasted in the documents carefully ensconced in the perfectly sealed envelope held by him were of an imposter, an ersatz *Thambi*. The whole gamut was unpardonable. If the secret of fabrication of documents ever leaked out he was sure to get a ticket back home via a military gaol, where his stay was likely to be quite extended. He closed his eyes and prayed to Guruji Maharaj to show him the way forward.

He was still in prayer when the train stopped at way side Phillaur for its scheduled two minute halt but the pause did not mean anything to the three listless soldiers who were nervous from the fear of being derided by their colleagues on reaching the unit in less than an hour. God, how they wished they did not have to go back to the unit. Scarcely had the train jerked into motion when the entry door into their compartment was pushed open and a white enamel mug came clattering in, followed by a human hand clawing at their compartment floor to get purchase. As soon as the hand was able to grip the upright support of the lower berth, another hand, this one with a clenched fist, came into view and following these two appendages was a disheveled man who half crawled and half pulled him-self into the compartment and stood up swaying with the movement of the train. It was fucking *thambi-II*, Devar.

'Why you *behan-chod,* sister fucker, you went missing at Ludhiana and nearly gave us a heart attack,' thundered Lachu as he moved menacingly towards the swaying and huffing Devar.

'You *mother-chod*, where the hell did you disappear to?' yelled Matric as he caught him by the scruff of his neck gave a resounding kick on his fanny.

'You uncouth nitwits stop this bullying,' said a panting and perplexed Devar. 'What the hell have I done to deserve such a hostile reception?'

'Hey guys hold your anger. Look at his physical condition. He is not only in a messy condition but even his shirt buttons are missing. He seems to have come out of a fracas followed by a grueling marathon. He deserves our empathy and we should refrain from chastising him in this manner. I think we should make him comfortable and let him catch his breath first.' said Harry and made Devar sit down and ordered Lachu to give him a drink of cold water.

'Now Devar, tell us what happened. We are listening.'

'Hey why are you fellows so uptight?' said Devar after he had composed himself.

'These guys are worked-up because you went missing at Ludhiana and were immensely worried about you,' said Harry soothingly. 'Their anger was only momentary. Tell us what happened?'

'Well it's like this. I had given the tea vendor one rupee and he was to retain three pice for the three cups of tea and return fifteen annas and one pice back to me. After giving you the tea through the cabin window I went back to the vendor to ask for the balance. However the scoundrel purposely delayed returning the balance money to me. I realized that the bastard had a mala-fide intention of keeping the whole rupee by forcing me to entrain without my residual change. He knew that being a disciplined soldier I must continue my journey and was unlikely to miss the train for a small amount of cash.' Devar halted in his narrative to take a sip of water.

The heavy breathing of the three Sikhs was palpable as they listened to Devar. But no one interrupted him even when he halted his narrative to drink water, lest they break his line of thought.

'The train had started to move. I realized that I would miss the train if I extended my stay at the vendor. Just imagine my predicament. If he delayed returning the balance even a moment longer, I would, definitely, be unable to board the train. On the other hand if I was to board the train then I perforce had to leave the fifteen and a quarter annas with the crooked tea vendor. So there I was, torn between the Devil and the Deep Sea. Right?' recounted Devar.

'Understood, carry on.'

'The train meanwhile was gathering speed. So without losing any more time I threw the hot tea in my mug into the vendor's face blinding him temporarily. I then kicked him in the balls and as he folded up in pain I grabbed the one rupee coin lying on the tea counter and ran.'

'Why didn't you call out to us for help Neville?' asked Harry using his recently given first name soothingly.

'Call out? I yelled and I yelled, you deaf buggers. I shouted but you fellows were so engrossed in other matters that you failed to respond to my distress call'

'Ok, go on.'

'I ran towards our coach but the vendor's assistant followed me and caught hold of my shirt at the collar from behind. I elbowed him a couple of times but the bastard wouldn't let go.'

'Shit. What happened then?'

'Well I dragged him along losing two of my shirt buttons on the way. You can well understand that all this drag was slowing me down and also tiring me, and all the time the train was gathering speed.'

'We can well imagine your plight.'

'Well I was able to drag the bugger up to the edge of the platform and with one last Herculean lunge I managed to get hold of the boarding hand rails of the last coach of the moving train, the limpet still attached onto the collar of my shirt. Holding on to the boarding rails I anchored my left foot on the boarding plank and gave him a back kick which landed on his shin. He yelped in pain but the blighter didn't relent and continued to run along the platform still holding on to my shirt trying to pull me down. Suddenly the platform sloped down and ended, unbalancing, by now, a very tired assistant, who tripped. He had no option but to let-go of me to enable him to use his hands to cushion his fall and thus save himself from getting seriously hurt or even fatally landing under the wheels of the speeding train.'

'The brave always win and I commend you for showing guts against those crooks Devar,' said Harry.

'But if you chaps think that this was the end of my woes then you are mistaken?'

'What further misery befell you Mr. Thambi?' said Matric.

'Well there I was hanging onto the handrails of an overcrowded coach and my entreaties to the passengers inside to open the door to let me in fell on deaf ears. So I have travelled this far from Ludhiana standing on the boarding plank, clutching the hand rails of this fast express train.'

'That's not such a big deal for a tough soldier like you Devar,' said Matric.

'Try standing on a boarding slat of a speeding express, with soot carrying cold wind plummeting you at 60 miles an hour, while its coal particles are getting into your eyes and nostrils at that meteoric speed. Combine this with the prospect of getting a vertigo attack when the train traversed ravines and the swirling waters of a mighty river; and then you won't have the gumption to call it a small deal Matric.'

'The river which gave you vertigo while crossing was the mighty Sutlej. The British rulers have a plan to build a mighty dam upstream in the hills at Bhakra village. This river is one of the five rivers of Punjab. And by the way, the literal meaning of Punjab means five rivers? *Punj* means five and *Ab* means, river. Simple isn't it? The other four are Beas, Ravi, Chenab and Jhelum and they are further up North. All five are mighty rivers and for your information, I have criss-crossed the Ravi which flows next to my home town, Lahore umpteen times standing on the slats and holding on to the hand rails. I do so because it seems so very adventurous. I think you are making too much of your travel standing on a slat when you had the hand rails to hold on to.' It was Matric again, trying to needle *thambi*.

'You think holding on to the hand rails is adventurous travel. Then try holding on to the hand rails of a speeding express train while your one hand is simultaneously clutching a mug and your other hand is clasping a silver coin, next time you make a crossing over the Ravi. If you survive this perilous journey come back and show me the hand held items. If you still feel that the travel was adventurous, I suggest you leave soldiering and instead join a circus, Mr. Smart Aleck Matric?' said Devar in riposte.

'You son-of-a-bitch, you could have killed yourself by falling down if you had lost grip on the hand rails. Why didn't you throw away the mug or for that matter the rupee coin?' queried a puzzled Harry.

'And get court-martialled for losing government property on my charge or misappropriation of funds. I don't want to be court-martialled and that too at the very beginning of my army career. No way. I am here for good. However, it is the nature of reception given to me by you fellows which has upset me.'

'I, as the senior most in the party ask of you to forgive Lachu and Matric for the unsavoury treatment meted out to you. Their reaction was a result of a preconceived notion when you failed to entrain at Ludhiana. I can say with confidence that they had no mala-fide intention towards you,' said Harry applying salve on Devar's bruised ego.

The train halted again at way side Phagwara and Matric picked up Devar's Mug from the floor. He washed it clean in the sink, detrained and brought back hot tea in the mug for Devar. 'This is to compensate you for the tea you threw into the face of the crooked tea vendor at Ludhiana,' said Matric as he placed the tea mug near Devar. In return Devar smiled and opened his left hand exposing a shining one rupee silver coin which he transferred on to the curled index finger of his right hand and flipped it with his thumb to Matric who captured the somersaulting coin deftly in the palm of his hand. He looked at the exposed side of the coin, minted at the British India Mint at Devlali, fifty miles East of Bombay and saw the profiled head of the handsome British Monarch wearing a crown. 'It's heads boss,' he announced.

'A good sign', adjudicated Harry. Every one applauded. The train started with a jerk and they were on the final lap of their odyssey.

Just as a relaxed Devar started to sip his tea, Matric said, 'you know Devar you can still be charged legally for having committed an offence.'

'Which offence have I committed now?'

'Well, you can be blamed even now for losing property of the British Crown on your charge,' replied Matric.

'Pray tell me, loss of which property of the Crown would be apportioned to me, Mr. Smart Pants?'

'Well you could be arraigned for losing, "Two Buttons Shirt, Olive Green, four-holed (Mark-I), the property of the British Crown entrusted to you",' said Matric. And all four erupted into loud guffaws of laughter. Spirits were high again. Harry, discreetly, inserted his left hand into the pocket of his trousers to ascertain if his morale gauge was working. His probing fingers immediately encountered not only a working meter but this time the meter clearly pointed towards an upward swing of his morale.

'Ok fellows enough. Assist Devar to stitch the two four holed buttons back on his shirt and help him tidy up. The next and final halt Jullundur is a few moments away and we should present a picture of a well turned out disciplined outfit when we disembark,' directed Harry.

'Boss we have yet to attend to one more job,' said Lachu.

'Now what is that?' asked Harry.

'Well, I think we should pay a visit to the last coach whose occupants had refused to open the door to our perilously hanging *thambi* and teach them a few lessons in civic sense.'

'Agreed,' chorused Matric and Devar.

'Chaps I am as keen as you fellows to let Lachu loose in that coach for a few minutes. But this can only be done at the next station which is Jullundur Cantonment, our destination. When people see we soldiers bashing up civilian passengers they are likely to raise an alarm and the military police and the RTO staff is likely to descend on the scene, pronto and we will be blamed for ill discipline. If the matter gets out of hand then unforeseen complexities could surface. I feel we should not draw attention to ourselves unnecessarily by taking the law into our hands. My considered view is that we should over look the issue. Therefore I over-rule this proposal.'

Whilst a 5 foot 9 inch tall, dirty, half starved waif in tatters calling himself Mr. Thambi had boarded the train at Madurai on the night of Monday the 26th of January 1942, a well-groomed, 5 feet 8-7/8 inch tall, elegantly turned out in an army uniform, Pioneer Neville Devar, dismounted from the train along with an escort of three Sikh soldiers on the morning of Thursday the 29th of January 1942 at Jullundur Cantonment. This morning Harry had not wound up his wrist watch. No point in winding it up because it would soon be resting in its "West End Watch Company" velvet case, in the "Controlled Stores" steel cupboard of the battalion store room. Harry was now more inclined to buy a watch which would not only be radium dialed but which would also be shock and water proof, after seeing the performance of his army issue watch in rough conditions.

Harry marched the party up to the RTO's office and reported arrival. An hour later a truck 15 cwt 4X4 belonging to the Dogra Regimental Centre arrived and took them to their unit, 1 M and R Sikh where they were ordered to dismount by the Battalion Regimental Police at the battalion "IN" Gate. They waited for the duty NCO to make his appearance and do their arrival formalities.

Whilst their formalities were in progress the BHM, equivalent to RSM of a British unit, arrived and ordered that first of all, the prisoner be taken to the quarter guard by Harry and his remainder party could simultaneously take their baggage to the company barracks. After depositing the prisoner Harry was told to deposit documents pertaining to the prisoner with the adjutant's office and then he was to return the items drawn on loan at the time of proceeding on duty to the Quarter Master Store.

Soon Pioneer Devar was lodged in a cell in the unit quarter guard his, removed fetters were deposited with the guard commander. A suitable endorsement was made in the Prisoner

Register by the guard commander from whom Harry obtained a receipt for the prisoner.

Harry had deposited the sealed envelope at the adjutant's office by lunch time. After lunch he took Matric along to deposit the loan stores in the QM stores. En-route they paid a visit to the incarcerated Devar who gave them a thumbs up sign. All stores and equipment had been deposited by the afternoon. Harry then returned the thirty rupees he had been provided at the time of setting out to cover any unforeseen eventuality during their assignment, saying that there had been no additional monetary outflow during the duty. No point in getting into an explanation mode for a few coins was Harry's argument. The three were given the remainder day off for personal administration.

They were interviewed by their company commander Subedar Mit Singh, the following morning who patted them for the good work done while welcoming them back. He was satisfied that they had performed such a long arduous journey in a disciplined manner and brought a good name to D Company, their sub-unit and he expected them to always execute future assignments in a similar manner. They felt a pang of guilt on hearing this undeserved eulogy. A day later at their intake parade the CO Lt Col Price too showed satisfaction at their work. God if the *sahibs* only knew the truth.

The orderly room was held on each Monday in the unit. On this Monday, the 2nd of February 1942 there were four cases which were to be disposed of by Lt Col Price. God how, he detested punishing his own men for minor transgressions. But it had to be done to maintain high level discipline in the unit. Like most Mondays, today also the cases pertained to over-staying of leave. Price could not understand why the men came in late by a day or two. His company commanders and staff officers too could not assign any specific reason for the same. The reasons for overstaying leave, given by the men on rejoining the unit, were connected to agriculture related work. Price thought that there was more to it than just assisting old patriarchs in ploughing the fields or cropping them because some simpletons in the past had admitted to over staying because of other reasons. Of these, the raison d'être for overstay was due to a demand, from a *sali,* younger sister of wife, to prolong the stay. Now why would a wife's younger sister compel her *jija*, brother-in-law, to put off departure by a couple of days? Because a couple of, extra, days had that many additional nights as well. And these appropriated nights could be fruitfully spent gamboling by the young *sali* with her *jija*. Price's lips curled up in a smile as his mind produced the obvious answer.

Today, while three cases pertained to unit personnel, one case was of an outsider attached with the unit for discipline. This idiot from the Pioneer Corps had runaway and absented himself from duty en-route to his unit. He should have been charged with desertion but when Price had been briefed on the case, he had decided to apply a lesser charge of being absent without leave or AWL on him as well. There was a war going on and his majesty required as many soldiers as possible. No point in applying a desertion charge and as a consequence shunting out a trained soldier who actually wanted to continue serving the Emperor.

Pioneer Devar was slotted to be marched up after the three M and R Sikh boys had been dealt with. Devar observed three British officers lounging outside the CO's Office where a bugler in liveries stood next to the CO's stick orderly. Soon he saw the adjutant enter the CO's Office with a bunch of files. He soon came out and announced start of the Orderly Room procedure. On cue the bugler blew a note on his bugle signalling commencement of the process. The adjutant re-entered the office followed by the Subedar-Major and called in OC "Able" Company. One of the three Brits lounging outside the CO's office went in and there after Sepoy Jassa Singh of "Able" Company was marched in. After his punishment was pronounced he was marched out and OC "A" Company also exited. Next was the turn of "Baker" Company which had two cases. Devar had been minutely observing the action preceding his turn and knew the procedure to be followed. He was thankful to his friends to have put him through the process in Delhi a number of times and the motivation they had been providing to him for the last three days during their visits to him in his cell. All in all he was being taken good care of so far. Only God knows what awaited him inside the haloed precincts of the CO, *sahib's* office.

Suddenly it was his turn to be marched up. He was positioned in front of the CO's office and OC of HQ Company

Major Brown was called inside by the adjutant. Soon he heard the voice of the adjutant ordering Subedar Major to have Pioneer Devar marched in. The Subedar Major repeated the order loudly and the BHM sprang into action.

'Accused Pioneer Devar, atte . . . ntion', he bellowed. As soon as Devar came to attention he barked out, 'quick march.' Hiding behind a tree not far away, Harry crossed his fingers and his lips started to move in a silent prayer.

Expertly judging when Devar was four steps away from the desk of the CO, the BHM gave the 'halt' word of command and Pioneer Neville Devar came to a halt two paces in front of the CO's desk. Devar was then ordered to salute and there he waited standing at attention for the proceedings to begin. He observed the sitting Lt Col Price wearing his peak cap and a tan coloured cross belt, perusing some papers in the file placed in front of him. Standing at attention like a rod Devar took in the scene. The office was plush with trappings of the army. On the wall behind the sitting CO was a succession board with the heading "COMMANDING OFFICERS" and below this were five sub headings, "Serial No", "Rank", "Name", "From", "To". The board had just one name on it, that of Lt Col Price at Serial No 1 and the "from" column had a date, 1 Oct 1941 written, the "To" column was vacant because the incumbent was still in harness. Above the board was the photo graph of the British Monarch and on either side of the board were photo graphs of the Viceroy of India and Commander-in-Chief of the British Indian Army, all three seemed to be staring directly at Devar making him even more nervous. Devar could see the photograph of Colonel of the Regiment on the wall at his left side and the opposite wall had an array of photographs of Sikh Pioneer Soldiers in their liveries. The HQ Company Commander, Major Brown was standing on his left and the Adjutant and Subedar Major were standing on the right, all at attention like him. In a corner behind the CO on a stand was the tri-coloured regimental flag ceremonially unfurled, to expose the regimental-crest. The CO's desk had a green flannel table cover on which was kept a pen holder stand with two ink pots, one blue and one red. Adjacent to it was a blotting paper holder and a couple of paper weights, an ash tray and a pin cushion. Adjoining the ashtray was a call bell and a stack of coasters. In the right corner was a table calendar and next to it was a family photograph. Must be the CO's family photograph thought Devar. On the left side of the CO was a small table on which stood a telephone and a clock by which the time was ten minutes past nine. On the right side of the CO were three file trays. The tray marked "OUT" contained three files stacked on one another, the trays marked "PENDING" and "IN" were empty.

At last Lt Col Price looked up and his piercing blue eyes looked him up and down a couple of times appraising him. Handsome chap may be with some European blood coursing through his veins, due to an encounter of some European soldier with a local hussy in the Madras region in the past, was Price's evaluation. On the other hand Devar was sure that the CO Sahib had cottoned on to their heist. Suddenly he heard the baritone voice of the CO as he commenced reading the offence report in front of him.

'No XXXXXXXX Pioneer Neville Devar is that you?'

'Yes, Sir,' mumbled Devar. Bless you Harry *ustad* for the in depth briefing and repeated rehearsals.

'You are charged under Section 39 of the Indian Army Act for absenting yourself without leave, in that on 5 February 1941 you absented yourself from Jullundur Railway Station and remained absent till apprehended by Madras Police on 20 December 1941.' The CO paused and looked up and asked 'do you plead guilty or not guilty to the offence?'

'Guilty, Sire.'

The CO picked up a red ink pen from the desk and entered the plea "Guilty" in the appropriate column of the offence report. 'Do you want to say anything in your defence which may mitigate the gravity of your offence?'

'Yes Sir. I actually wanted to join the Infantry and fight the enemy right from the front but due to inadequate knowledge I signed up for the Pioneer Corps. My joining the Pioneer Corps was a mistake. I am ready to face any punishment which may be awarded to me for the offence committed by me but I request that I be transferred to an infantry regiment.' Accused Pioneer Neville Devar, looking straight ahead, parroted out the lines he had mugged up so well with the guidance of the triumvirate who were now ruling over his destiny.

'Why the hell should I believe you. You are a confirmed runaway and could be a liar as well.'

Bloody hell this was not in the script. What should he do? He was bound to be caught and then sent to *Kalapani,* the Indian name given to the cellular jail on Andaman Island in the Indian Ocean used by the British rulers to incarcerate incorrigible and dangerous prisoners. Pull yourself together he urged himself. Then came to fore the art of winning over the others he had acquired during his begging days and he heard himself say, 'sir I am not a liar. I do not want to dig saps for the rest of my life in the Pioneer Corps. I want to remain in the army and do some real soldiering. I want to defend the Empire against evil enemies.'

These Indians can make tall promises to get out of an adverse situation. Let me probe this rascal further. 'You don't look much of a soldier to me. Firstly you run away. And secondly you look like a fat pig having added so much weight during your absence that even your own uniform is now one size too tight for you. You must be weighing over two maunds,' said the CO. This remark made Devar pull his stomach in and throw his chest out.

'I am actually, less than two maunds sir,' blurted out Neville Devar without thought.

'Really, that's interesting but how are you so cocksure that you are under two maunds?'

Fucks, the play was going beyond the script and there was no prompter to assist him. Has the *sahib* got to know that he was an imposter and not the real fellow? Devar was confused. He knew that it was better to remain silent but the *sahib* was egging him on, forcing a response.

'I had taken my weight recently sire. That's why I am sure. I can prove it as well,' blurted out Devar. He had felt the reassuring presence of his weight ticket, with his radiant future printed on it, in his left breast pocket when he had thrust his chest outward at the *sahib's* over-weight tell off.

'We will check this out. But what prompted you to measure your weight soldier?'

What the hell should he say? Should he tell him he had taken the weight so that entry in his IAB-64 could be suitably fudged? Should he tell the *sahib* that the uniform he was wearing was not his? Should he spill the beans and tell the *sahib* the whole truth? But owning up the heist meant a straight passage to *Kalapani.* Better to remain clamped up instead of blurting out something which may compromise them all.

'C'mon don't stand there like a statue. Say something,' it was the CO once again. What should he do? Just remain calm, don't panic, Devar told himself again and again. He wanted to play the dumb mute but the shrewd *sahib* want let him be. Let me reply and see what happens.

'Sire, I wanted to know the Fore-cast of my future. That's why I took my weight.'

'I don't understand. What possibly could be a connection between astrology and weight?'

'Sir when one takes ones weight, by inserting one pice coin in the niche of the weighing machine at the railway station, it automatically vends out a ticket. While the weight of the individual is found imprinted on one side of this ticket, one's future is notified in print on the other facet. Since I was to face punishment on arrival at Jullundur, I spent one pice to ascertain what the future held for me. The weight information was merely incidental. The ticket is still in my possession.'

'Show it to me.'

As soon as *thambi* tried to open his pocket a thundering 'don't move' voice of the Subedar-Major stopped him. Shit these guys are mad. The *sahib* wants me to show him the ticket and the other fellow orders me not to move. How in hell can I retrieve the ticket from the pocket and show it to the *sahib* without moving? The riddle was solved soon when he felt the hands of the BHM pat his pockets. Having located the ticket in his breast pocket he removed it and handed it over to the CO. The *sahib* read the 1 Maund and 39 Seers weight printed on it. On impulse he turned over the ticket and read out loudly, 'A great future full of riches and love awaits you'. He then burst out laughing and tossed the ticket back to the BHM who quickly reinserted it into the pocket of the accused and exited.

'You know Pioneer notwithstanding the prediction on the weight-ticket, your immediate future is not going to be so rosy. Your ill fitting uniform is bursting at the seams and your saluting and drill movements are sloppy to say the least. This shows to me that you did not take adequate interest in your training after recruitment. If your crew cut mug was not staring out of the documents lying in front of me, I would have thought that you were a civilian in a stolen or borrowed uniform.' No response came forth from the accused this time. 'Well I will give you one last chance to mend your ways. I will let you continue in the service and try to get you re-mustered in the Infantry. But if you break discipline one more time then you are finished with the army forever. Understood?'

Devar had intended to answer the CO in a full throated voice but the 'understood sir' reply came out as a dry throated croaking whisper. The sahib had correctly analyzed that he was a civilian in army uniform. Only his photo, snapped by the photographer after the army style hair make-over by the, quartet fucking, barber in Delhi; which now embellished his documents duly authenticated with official rubber seals had saved him. Whew, it had been a close call.

Price picked up the red pen holder, dipped it in the red ink pot, shook off the additional ink from the nib and wrote down in the "Punishment" Column of the offence report "Awarded 28 days Rigorous Imprisonment & 14 days Detention, both punishments to run concurrently in the unit quarter guard." In the "Remarks" Column he then wrote "Take up a case with Army HQ to re-muster the individual into the Madras Regiment". He then put down his signature to authenticate his endorsements and dated the same as on 02 February 1942 (FN). The FN, forenoon, signified that the count of his incarceration would commence with effect from that day. He then picked up the half moon shaped blotting paper holder and rolled it over his writing, in a see-saw motion to dry up the ink so that it did not smudge. After that he pronounced the punishment awarded and ordered the prisoner to be marched out.

'March the prisoner out,' echoed the Adjutant.

'28 days Rigorous Imprisonment and 14 days Detention awarded. March the prisoner out,' repeated the Subedar-Major more loudly.

The BHM came into the office and removed Devar's belt deftly, saluted and then walked out. After that he gave a word of command, 'Prisoner Devar about turn'. Devar executed the turn awkwardly unbalancing him-self and almost falling down. The clumsily performed movement brought a wry smile on Price's face. The solo act had not been a hilarious comedy but it had managed to elicit a sardonic smile from the lips of the *sahib*, hence the act certainly could not be termed as a tragedy. A 'quick march' order took him out of the office premises and he joined three other beltless soldiers who had preceded him into and then out of, the CO's Office. Harry saw *thambi* sans a belt joining the others from his defiladed position and uncrossed his fingers and faded away towards the unit training area.

Soon Major Brown exited from the office and his exit was followed by the Adjutants voice seeking permission to end the orderly room proceedings for the day. The CO gave his approval and the bugler on cue, played the "Orderly Room Termination Note" on his bugle, signifying end of the orderly room proceedings for the day. While the Subedar-Major came out of the CO's office thereafter, the adjutant stayed back inside.

'I say, John, get the blubber sweated out from this pioneer fellow. He seems to be a good find. You know how hard it is to come by such a fine specimen. Except for the weight problem the man has a good soldierly bearing which could be further improved by training. If he trims down by a few pounds he will certainly fit into his uniform elegantly,' said Price removing his peak cap and handing it over to the stick orderly who then hung the peak cap on the hat rack placed adjacent to the door, saluted and went out.

'Right sir,' replied Captain JD Maling, MC, the adjutant.

Un-known to Price or Maling the thought of fitting into his uniform more smartly was also on the mind of the subject himself. However the means of accomplishing their identical goal, in their respective minds were different. In the opinion of the CO the overweight had to be administered a concentrated dose of a grinding physical regime, to trim him down, to enable him to properly fit into his uniform. While in the thoughts of the beltless, *thambi* prisoner, being marched towards the Quarter-guard, on the first day of his 28 days Rigorous Imprisonment, by the duty NCO, this goal could be conveniently achieved, overnight, by arranging a one size larger uniform for him. As it turned out both means would come into play. As per the ruling of the Commanding Officer the prisoner would be put through a toiling physical regime and this strenuous routine would result in wearing out the tight fitting uniform at the seams in a couple of days compelling the unit authorities to substitute it with a one size larger replacement from the Quartermaster store.

'And John also tell, someone to give him additional drill training as well. Did you notice that the blighter nearly fell down while executing the "About-turn"? These guys at the Pioneer Training Centre seem to be taking it easy, as otherwise the bloke's movements wouldn't be so shoddy.'

'Ok sir. I will put the Jemadar Adjutant on this job straight away,' replied Captain Maling.

Outside, the duty NCO who was walking the prisoner with three others, in single file formation to their cells, too had already assessed that the *thambi* required additional training to help him improve his drill movements. The clumsy oaf was giving him a harrowing time. The lout just could not keep in step with the other three, despite his continuous chant, 'left right left right left . . . hup two hup two . . . left right . . .', while marching them for their incarceration. The nincompoop had got his foot entangled with that of the prisoner in front of him, who in turn fell on the fellow ahead of him, triggering a domino effect resulting in a pile up of four soldiers. If it wasn't day time, Devar would have surely received a resounding kick on his butt from the vexed NCO. As it turned out, he only heard the word '*chootia,* stupid block-head,' being hissed into his ears, which was considered a mild rebuke in the regiment, which boasted of a rich and varied vocabulary in expletives. After the pile up the duty NCO had made him to march independently up to his cell to avoid any further mishap.

'And obtain a written request from this Devar fellow for change of arm from the Pioneer Corps to the Infantry and then put up a DO from me to Dick, that's Lt Col Charles Dickson.

He is AAG, Assistant Adjutant General in the Recruitment Directorate at Army HQ who deals in such matters,' continued Price.

Charlie Dickson's name brought a glint in the eyes and a faint smile of reminiscence on Price's lips. They had been cadets together during training. Charles had been addressed as Charlie by his family and friends all his life. However he had been assigned a fresh nick name by his army colleagues during training; when it was revealed in the showers, during the daily bathing ritual that Charlie's member was disproportionally large for his short and skinny physique. The cadets' self appointed working group, led by the six foot tall, Big Pete Tytler, which met each Saturday night, after lights out for the forbidden cigarette smoke or a glass of beer and ribald gossip, mostly concerning past sexual escapades and planned future ones had decided to assign an additional and suggestive nick-name to him after his mismatching revelation. This group by tradition had arrogated upon itself, ragging and vigilante duties and its' decisions were always final. Many names were suggested and rejected by this self appointed band. Only four names finally remained in contention; they were—Bazook, Big Dick, Hung Joe and Dick. After a heated and articulate debate the first two names were dropped since these could not be used in presence of families or ladies due to the very obvious connotation. The third was dropped since it sounded more Chinese than English. Therefore "Dick" was adopted by a voice vote. This name would convey its association to the prominent size of Charlie's member to his army friends while it would just be an extraction of the first four letters from his "Dickson" surname for others. So while he continued to be called Charlie by his family and civilian friends, he was known as Dick to the army fraternity after that point.

'Yes sir,' replied Maling to a smiling CO.

It was in 1938 that half a dozen of Dickson's batch mates had met again during the Staff College Course, at Quetta. This half dozen included Big Pete and Dick. Each had been married by then and was accompanied by his wife. They had commented on how small the world was to have brought them together once again. Their reunion made them recall old times and exchange notes as they back slapped one another. The zealous six wanted to know about each other and their six dirty minds wanted to be acquainted with each others' conjugal gossip. They therefore decided to hold a party so that they could meet each other's wives and also update one another on personal tidbits. It was at this party that Big Pete's wife Betty had met all his friends and their wives, including Dick's wife Jane. Big Pete and his buxom wife Betty had dominated the party in all manners of speaking while Dick and his shy introvert wife Jane were at the other end of the spectrum. By the end of the first month of the course, all the, college faculty, as well as the students had learnt why gregarious Betty had been labelled as Wild Betty in army circles. And the quiet, inward looking Jane had been conversely branded as Plain Jane.

The curriculum at Quetta was academic in nature without any burden of responsibility. The college like atmosphere in a salubrious climate made the students let down their hair. War clouds were on the horizon and everyone wanted to make much of the peace time environment of Quetta. There was much partying and socializing. It was rumoured that a wife and husband swapping club called the "Key Club" had come into existence by the efforts of Big Pete and Wild Betty and active participation of like minded people. Membership to this secret guild was only for married couples and that too by introduction. It was whispered that this band would assemble every other night at the residence of one of its members, where the female constituents would toss their residential keys into a bowl. The keys would then be juggled after switching off the lights. The men would then be asked to pick up one key each at random. He would then spend the night with the female member whose key had come into his possession. What a carefree environment that had been at Quetta.

Price brought himself back to the present when Maling discreetly cleared his throat to indicate, to his bemused, day dreaming boss, that he was still around awaiting further instructions.

'We could forward the request to him with my strong recommendation. I am sure old Dick will do the needful.'

'Roger, sir.'

'That will be all, John.'

Captain Maling picked up the four case files from the "Out" tray and exited after a smart salute as Price picked up a news paper and scanned its headlines while waiting for the *Dak*, daily official mail, to be placed before him.

Devar's punishment started in earnest. He was made to wear Field Service Marching Order or FSMO weighing 30 seers and slogged for four hours on the first day along with the other three prisoners by the Regimental Police Havildar. This was followed by a filling lunch. While the others rested after lunch, his afternoon rest period was used for additional drill lessons and practice, by when his whole body ached. This was hell and he wanted to run away. He was quite certain that he couldn't take such physical punishment. After a hearty dinner of one *nafri* of *chapatis* eaten with meat and a mess tin full of rice and lentils followed by a generous dollop of *halwa,* sweet, he was ready for running away. He decided to escape some time during the night. It never occurred to his tired mind that his cell had a big padlock on its barred door whose key was hanging on the key board in the main room of the quarter guard building under the constant watch of a sentry. It also did not come to his mind that there was another sentry assigned to keep a watch on the cells and this guard carried a rifle slung over his left shoulder and a whistle strung on his lanyard to raise an alarm in the event of an escape attempt. He decided to get two winks before his clandestine departure and dozed off with the thoughts of flight on his mind.

He woke up to a rough shake of his shoulder and a cheerful *Sat Sri Akal*, good morning greeting. He opened his eyes to a new dawn and a proffered hot mug of tea. He had been so tired that he had slept through the night like a baby and the plans of running away had been thwarted by the most beautiful dreamless sleep he had ever had, inside a draped mosquito net without the menacing mosquito bites under the warmth of two army blankets.

A visit by Harry when he was getting into FSMO to start the day was a welcome change. He was able to tell Harry frankly that he was done-for and army was not a place for him. He wanted to quit. However Harry over-ruled his plan to give up.

'*Thambi,*' he said, 'you have a name and an identity now. You have successfully crossed a major hurdle by convincing the CO S*ahib* of your bona-fides. You are at this moment Neville Devar holding a respectable job in the Indian Army as a Pioneer. Don't ruin everything because of one day of physical effort. Mind you, after a few days when you become leaner and fitter, your body will get accustomed to take the exertion in its stride, after that you will feel exhilarated and would not want any other way of life.'

This pepped him up a bit and Harry sensed his hesitation and went on to say 'C'mon, *thambi* don't tell me that I picked a sissy, that evening at Madurai and staked my life on a wrong one. Don't eat the hand that fed you *thambi*. Do you want to go back to a life of bumming and begging? The fate printed on your weight ticket, which you cherish so much, is only possible in a well paying job and not as a tramp. And you want to throw away all that just because of a few drops of sweat. Wake up man wake up.' The pep talk seemed to have the desired effect and prisoner Devar tightened his web FSMO and buckled his belt purposefully to commence the second day of his imprisonment. He then requested Harry to try and arrange for a larger size uniform because the present one was a tight fit. The shirt hurt him at the arm pits while the tight girth of his pants made breathing difficult during the excruciating punishment. Harry promised to look into it and doubled away to attend the PT period with his company. In the event Harry did not have to make any effort because *thambi's* uniform was automatically replaced after a couple of days since the one he was wearing had worn out "due to fair wear and tear".

The prisoners were given a breather for breakfast. During the time out, an office runner brought a request letter for change of arm for Devar's signature. The runner handed a fountain pen to Devar and asked him to sign it at the pencil "X" mark which he did with a confident flair. After a substantial breakfast of *poories* and tea, they were ordered back into FSMO and the heart-less RP Havildar, whom he now saw as his nemesis, commenced to put the prisoners through the grind again.

It was a tradition in the army that the CO took a round of the unit every few days. During the round he was always accompanied by the Subedar-Major and the head sweeper. This morning too Lt Col Price was accompanied by the Subedar Major, with the head sweeper in tow at a discreet distance when he made the round. The inclusion of the head sweeper in the party ensured attendance of any cleanliness related point in the unit instantly. Price noted with satisfaction that the unit was odourless and looked clean and tidy this morning. This meant that the men's latrines had been properly cleaned by the scavengers and the unit area had been swept well by the sweepers. He also noted with satisfaction that the RP NCO had the four prisoners, incarcerated by him yesterday, being trudged in FSMO. He was confident that the over-weight Pioneer would discard a few pounds by the end of his imprisonment if the RP NCO did his job properly. The head sweeper broke off as they neared the office area. The CO was received and briefed by the adjutant and he then met all the men lined outside his office for the intake/out take parade for that day. After that he entered the office and his stick orderly took his beret cap and hung it on the hat rack. He was mopping his brow when the Subedar-Major entered the office to render the unit status report which included any ill discipline related activities of the previous day and night.

As soon as the Subedar-Major departed Price's eyes darted to the stack of files in the "In" tray and he picked up the top most folder marked *"Dak"*, today's mail, and went through each letter thoroughly and wrote down his directions where ever necessary in red ink and initialed and dated each letter. Having done so, he tossed the folder into the "Out" tray. He then continued to meticulously peruse and clear all the files disposing them in the "Out" tray. The office runner brought in a fresh pile of files and placed them in the "In" tray and on his way out cleared the "Out" tray.

He picked up the top file marked "Priority" with a neatly typed letter flagged "For Signature please" and opened it. It was a DO, Demi-Official, letter from him to Lt Col Charles Dickson, AAG, Recruitment Directorate, AG's Branch, Army HQ, New Delhi. The letter was typed on official issue stationary with the emblem of the British Crown printed in red on the top middle, of the letter head. The Heading superstructure of the letter contained his own name and appointment typed on the upper left side of the page just below the letter number while the address of the unit and the date was typed on the right of the page, all as per the DO format laid down in the minor staff duties pamphlet of the British Indian Army. Below the heading superstructure, the subject of the letter "CHANGE OF ARM IN RESPECT OF NO XXXXXXXX PIONEER NEVILLE DEVAR" had been typed in capital letters and under lined. Whereas normal official letters only required ink signatures of the originator, the DO letter format called for the "Date", "Greeting" and the "Close" of the letter to be hand written by the originator of the DO. Therefore the typist had left adequate space for this purpose in the letter.

He picked up the blue nib holder dipped it in the blue ink well, jerked the holder to rid the nib of surplus ink and neatly endorsed the date and scribbled the greeting. He then perused the letter. The first paragraph had a summary of the case and the main text was contained in the paragraphs that followed. Maling had drafted the letter well and he was satisfied with its contents. He dipped the nib again in the pot jerked it again and wrote a complimentary close at the end of the letter and signed it with his first name. On impulse he wrote down a post script concerning a common friend and initialed it. He blotted the ink written portions with the blotting paper to rid the letter of any unwanted ink, perused the address on the attached envelope and found it to be in order. As an afterthought he wrote the words "By Hand" one space above the unit address in the letter and initialed it. He then closed the file and placed it in the out tray.

After that he picked up the phone and cranked the phone handle, removed its dangling ear-piece from its hook and placed it to his ear. He simultaneously brought the mouth piece of the upright phone closer to his mouth by tilting the instrument towards him and asked the exchange to be put through to the adjutant. As soon as John's static voice came through the ear piece into his ear, Price directed his voice into the mouth piece of the vertical phone and said, 'John, I have signed the DO to old Dick. I think we should send it to him by hand through an NCO. You know that the DO has a number of enclosures, some of which are original. The NCO will ensure security of the documents and his presence in New Delhi will also expedite matters.' As soon as

Captain Maling acknowledged his directions, the colonel put the ear piece back on its hook severing the phone connection.

Two days later Naik, equivalent to a Corporal in the British Army, Jarnail Singh of Able Company 1 M and R Sikh Regiment, alighted from the train at Delhi and promptly ran into Harinder alias Harry at the railway station. Jarnail was a fair skinned individual from the Ramdasia Community and hailed from village Kala Khurd in district Karnal about ninety miles North of Delhi. He was of medium built and obedient like a pup. He was however slow on the uptake and he had never visited Delhi earlier. He had heard that Delhi was a big place, a formidable place, where one could get lost and remain lost forever. He had therefore tried to wriggle out of the assignment of performing this courier duty of carrying some very important documents to Army Headquarters but his plea had gone unheard and here he was, standing on the railway platform at Delhi overwhelmed by the bigness of the railway station and the largeness of the milling crowd. His bumping into worldly wise Harry had been a stroke of luck. It turned out that Harry was on ten days casual leave and he was spending it in Delhi to take care of an un-named uncle's pension related work in Army Headquarters. Jarnail, whose name was the Indian equivalent of the word "General", saw Harry's chance appearance at the railway station a mana from the heavens. Little did he know that running into Harry at Delhi was not an accident but a well planned manoeuvre on Harry's part!

Thambi had informed Harry that his signature had been obtained on a document that day during the breakfast break when he visited the incarcerated fellow during his lunch break. Harry had rightly concluded there and then that the "change of arm process" had been initiated by the unit for *Thambi* and a suitable request letter would now be sent by the unit authorities to Army HQ. He therefore had to, somehow, intercept the letter and carry it to the addressee himself to enable him to overcome any unforeseen pitfalls in the process. He knew that Matric was friendly with the clerical staff in the adjutant's office since he, being a high school graduate, had on many occasions done clerical duties in that office in the past. He directed Matric to manipulate the dak dispatcher and somehow obtain the letter from him. Matric had accordingly met his dispatcher friend and volunteered to post that day's letters from the Post Office on his behalf since he was going to the Post Office for a personal work. Having managed to obtain the outgoing mail from the dispatcher he and Harry had rummaged through the stack but they had not found the said communication to Army HQ. Matric after posting the letters went back to the dispatch clerk to give him the postal registration receipts. That's when he had seen the bulky envelope addressed to Army HQ still lying on the dispatcher's table. Matric learnt that the letter being important was being sent by a special courier to Delhi. On return to the barracks Matric had accordingly shared this piece of information with Harry. That evening Harry had expected to be deputed to perform the said courier duty but during roll call no such announcement had been made by the company CHM. He had then sent Matric and Lachu as undercover agents to the dining halls of other companies to ferret out who had been earmarked for the duty to Delhi. He was having his pudding when Lachu on return had whispered in his ear that the duty had been given to "Able" Company. Next morning Harry had obtained sanction for ten days leave on compassionate grounds and by lunch he had learnt through the grapevine that Naik Jarnail Singh had been deputed by "A" Company as a courier to carry a letter regarding a prisoner to Army HQ. He had caught the first available train to Delhi and commenced his wait for Jarnail at the railway station. He had been checking all in coming trains from Jullundur ever since his arrival in Delhi and was relieved when he sighted Jarnail getting off the train this morning and hurried to "accidently" collide with him. The expression of relief instead of annoyance on the face of Jarnail at the collision appeared to be heavenly to Harry; and the relieved Jarnail immediately shared his predicament with Harry.

'Don't worry about a thing,' was Harry's reassuring response. 'Leave everything to me. I know Delhi like the back of my hand and I also know my way around Army HQ. You know the corridors of South Block where Army HQ is located are wider than the lanes of our villages and their extent is longer than the combined length of streets of a score of villages of Punjab. The worst part is that they are a labyrinth in the true sense of the word. So you just stay close to me lest you get lost and I will help you in your assignment.'

Harry was a great guy. No wonder the CO Sahib had so much faith in him, thought Jarnail as Harry led him to General Auckinleck *Fauji Sarai,* Military Guest House named after the Auck, at the railway station where they both registered for stay.

———————◄○►———————

An hour after entering his office at South Block in Army HQ, Lt Col Charles Dickson opened the DO letter and spread it out on his desk and the two Sikh soldier couriers stood at shun in front of him. Dickson told the soldiers to wait outside. As soon as they saluted and marched out, he commenced reading the DO dated 03 Feb 1942.

Cp   <u>*By Hand*</u>

No 3340/A
Lt Col C H Price,
Commanding Officer

1 M and R SIKH,
JULLUNDUR CANTT.
3 February 1942.

SUBJECT—CHANGE OF ARM IN RESPECT OF NO
<u>XXXXXXXX PIONEER NEVILLE DEVAR</u>

My dear Dick,

I am writing to you for a change of arm related work pertaining to an Other Rank who is on attachment with my unit.

It so happens that a *thambi* got erroneously enrolled in the Pioneer Corps whereas his bent of mind was to serve in the Infantry. The expected happened and the blighter ran away while on his way to his pioneer unit on completion of basic training. Since he had absconded from Jullundur Railway Station, he was brought here after being nabbed and was attached to my unit for discipline.

I could have done a Summary Court Martial and chucked him out of the army for running away but instead I decided to retain him. My reasons for so doing were that he is a good specimen who wants to see action on the front lines and not stay behind in the rear in a supporting role. You would know better than me that we require such motivated men for the war effort. Therefore, why kick out a fellow when we are looking for good men. In any case, the Crown must have paid a handsome commission to some well oiled, pot bellied Madrasi recruiting agent for this guy and I won't be surprised if the agent also squeezed some money out of the man as well. Combine this with the effort and expense invested by the Empire in training this bloke and it would add up to a tidy amount. For these reasons, I have dealt with him softly to enable him to continue serving in the army by switching his parent arm to Infantry.

After due deliberation, I have concluded that he is likely to make a good infantry soldier. We have a volunteer who wants to serve the crown on the front lines fighting the Japs or the Jerries. Our Army requires such motivated men who are ever ready to lay down their lives for the Empire. He hails from Madras and we could easily re-muster him into the Madras Regiment so that he could get a chance to fulfil his desire to be in an eye-ball to eye-ball contact with the enemy.

Since the matter comes directly under your control I am approaching you to kindly do the needful by shifting him into the Madras Regiment and simultaneously allocating an additional recruit vacancy to the Pioneer Corps to cover their shortfall resulting from this re-mustering. Accordingly, I am forwarding an application for change of arm from Pioneer Corps to Infantry duly signed by him, along with connected documents to you for necessary action. I am sure you will do the needful expeditiously.

Please do remember us to Jane. With best wishes.

Lt Col Charles Dickson,   *Yours sincerely,*
Assistant Adjutant General (Recruiting),
Adjutant General's Branch,   *Prix*
Army HQ,
New Delhi

Enclosures: Application from individual along with all original documents held by the other rank. Details listed at Appendix attached.

PS—Big Pete and his charming wife Betty had dropped in a few days ago. They were on their way to Rawalpindi. We reminisced of our times together and when I mentioned that you were now stationed in Delhi, Betty remembered you straight away from the staff college days at Quetta and her eyes lit up as she harked back in time. She even recalled Jane's incarceration in the military hospital in Quetta due to a bout of flu. She was articulate in her praise for you as a husband and considered your wife a lucky Jane. The snob that he is, Big Pete did not seem to share her enthusiasm though. They may be stopping in Delhi next month on their return journey to Jhansi and may look you up. Prix

Pete was called Big Pete because of his six foot frame. He was handsome and considered himself to be a ladies' man. He was vain and a show off, claiming many conquests in bed. His wife, Betty had been a nursing officer in the Army Medical Corps and complimented him in built and beauty and his tempestuous ways. As a matter of fact she had met Big Pete while he was admitted to the Army Base Hospital as a patient. As Big Pete's health improved, so did their affair. Soon their relationship developed beyond that of patient and nurse. She had volunteered for night duty in his ward and after her mandatory nightly round of patients Betty would rush to his bed side and spend her remaining nightly duty hours in his cabin. Thus by the time of Big Pete's discharge from hospital they had got to know each other quite intimately. They had continued to date and cavort and had finally married. She was aware of Big Pete's pre as well as post matrimony dalliances. She did not mind his flirting since she too had been a wild one and had bedded many male friends during her stint with the Medical Corps and had accordingly been given the soubriquet Wild Betty by her acquaintances.

It was a belief amongst men, especially those with under sized members, that women had a yen for big penises therefore none of the cronies had ever shared Charlie Dickson's size related nickname with their better halves, perhaps due to their own insecurity; you never could tell when a woman may indulge in an extra marital experiment with a man possessing a bigger apparatus. However it was at Quetta, during a bout of love making, that an inebriated Big Pete had let the cat out of the bag. He had divulged to Betty that it was he and his friends who had given the moniker "Dick" to Charles during their training days. As soon as Big Pete disclosed the reason behind this given code name, a supine Betty was all ears. A smashed Pete had laughingly told her the four considered options for the name. Betty had decided, there and then, to check out this information personally. It wasn't for nothing, that she was called Wild Betty.

An opportunity had presented itself when Jane was hospitalized for a few days on account of influenza at Quetta during the staff college course. During a birthday party of one of their colleagues, Betty had moseyed on to Charles Dickson. After a third drink she had wanted to show him her collection of postage stamps and maneuvered him out of the party to her house. Big Pete as usual was busy charming an unsuspecting female and took no notice of their quiet departure.

Once inside her house she forced a drink into his hand and brought out her philately collection and sat down close to him. She opened the stamp album at the Argentina page and leaned closely towards him, while pointing out the rare stamp pieces and first day covers in her collection, her upper blouse button having opened as if by magic, giving old Dick an unfettered view of her large pieces. Old-fashioned Dickson however was a one woman man and conservatively kept to himself. She then deliberately bent over and brushed her largeness on his face while pointing towards her collection of "Wheat Harvest" postage stamps printed in 1922 by Hungary but could not elicit any response from Dickson. Wild Betty was not making any progress and they had already passed the Magyar Posta page of her collection. By the time they reached Switzerland, Betty had moved and sat down on the coffee table in front of him and moved the hem of her skirt above her knees but he seemed preoccupied by an 1881 vintage, 25 Centime postage stamp of Helvetia, the female national personification of Switzerland. Shit, here she was in flesh and blood and in physical contact with the dope and he preferred to stare at a robed female allegory, in an old postage stamp. This way she would soon be at the Zanzibar page without having achieved anything.

She didn't have the whole night to complete her self-assigned mission. She was already behind schedule. She had to change tack if she wanted to accomplish her task before Zanzibar. She abruptly closed the album, took hold of unadventurous Dickson's hand and led him into her bedroom. As soon as they were there, she pushed him on to her bed and had removed his belt even before old Charlie Dickson realized what was happening. It was futile to resist this athletic wild, primed female Tarzan. Five minutes later, Betty had not only viewed the subject matter which had inspired his colleagues to allot a suggestive moniker to him during their training but had also verified it by touch, smell and taste. She had also arrived at a verdict that all the names considered by the cadet huddle at the academy were remarkably suitable but "Bazook" would have been her choice. Ten minutes later she had proved to herself that size did matter. Oh, how she wished that hubby Big Pete had a bigger endowment down there than in his life insurance. Plain Jane was, in point of fact a "Lucky Jane" and Big Pete was relatively speaking "Tiny Pete" were her thoughts when she felt Dick's convulsions. Dick too had smirked in the darkness because he too had reinvented the spelling of her surname when he felt her ever increasing tightness during the final moments, from Tytler to Tightler. The nymphomaniac had really kept her muscles well toned, obviously with regular muscular exercises and practice. He wondered why Big Pete was always on the lookout for fresh conquests when he had such stuff in his own back yard. Some guys just aren't satisfied with home stuff, to them grass is always greener on the other side of the fence. Big Pete belonged to that category.

Conservative Dickson had never divulged this encounter with Wild Betty Tytler beg your pardon that should read Wild Betty Tightler, to any of the coterie or to his wife Jane. His bout with Betty was the only time he had ventured into extra marital sex. Her mention in the letter by old Prix, had rekindled memories of that night in Quetta. Maybe, just maybe, he might get another chance to be caught in her strong grip once again when she happened to be in Delhi next month. He reluctantly put Betty Tightler out of his mind an re-commenced reading the DO once again and simultaneously pressed the call bell to summon the *chaprasi,* peon.

Harry and Jarnail had been waiting outside the office of the AAG for nearly twenty minutes after delivering the DO letter to the sahib. They however could not relax even for a moment. They remained fairly busy, saluting officers who moved up and down the corridor carrying files and papers. They had just finished saluting yet another officer when they heard the ring of the AAG sahib's call bell. The *chaprasi* who had been slouching on a stool next to the office door under the identification board of Lt Col Charles Dickson, AAG had suddenly come to life at the summons of the bell and briskly entered the office only to exit a moment later and hurry towards a nearby room. He was back in a jiffy and in his wake followed a middle aged man in civvies with a note pad in his left hand and pencil tucked in between the side of his head and the upper part of the helix cartilage of his right ear. He knocked at the AAG's door and sought his permission to enter and then went in. A little while later the courier duo, too were called in.

'I have given suitable directions to Mr. Misra, my civil staff officer who will do the needful,' said the AAG. He turned towards the civilian officer, who stood deferentially on one side of the desk and who now also held the opened DO letter they had brought from Jullundur in addition to his note pad in his left hand while his right hand held the pencil which till now had been securely stuck behind his ear and said, 'Mr. Misra you can use these fellows to do the leg work between various offices so that the work is done expeditiously.' Looking back at them again he continued, 'Go with him and he will explain everything to you.' The two saluted and followed Mr. Misra out of the room. Misra reinserted the pencil back into his auricle pencil holder whilst leading them to his office.

Mr. Misra's office was a big hall in which there were at least a dozen clerks. The walls were lined with wooden cupboards and shelves where files had been neatly stacked. Only half of the dozen clerks seemed busy at their desks because they were clacking away on their typewriters. The other half seemed to be whiling away their time consuming tea or exchanging gossip. Misra summoned two clerks who were gossiping away at the far corner of the room. The clerks left their chitchat and came towards Mr. Misra who handed over the DO letter to them. While they got busy perusing the letter, Misra turned towards Harry and Jarnail and told them to go sightseeing and return after lunch by when he would have had the appropriate letters ready for them.

The two decided to utilize the opportunity to pay obeisance at Gurdwara Rakabganj which was walking distance from where they were. Mr. Misra whole heartedly endorsed their itinerary and told them to bring back the holy *krah parsad* for him and his staff. Mr. Misra then deputed a *chaprasi* to guide them out of this outsized building called South Block through an exit facing North Block. The *chaprasi* took them through what seemed miles of corridors which had inestimable number of offices on both sides. It indeed took a lot of staff to manage the British Empire. They were both quite convinced that without a guide they would have got lost in this maze. They remained adjacent to their guide throughout their march through this never ending labyrinth lest they go astray.

They emerged on a wide stately road aptly called Kingsway. On their left about a furlong or two away was the domed Viceroy's house which was rumoured to have over 300 rooms. On the right, Kingsway sloped downwards and one mile down this straight avenue, they could see the India Gate War Memorial and through its arch, a bit further down, they could faintly discern the statue of the British Monarch in his Coronation Gown facing in their direction under an umbrella shaped dome held up by four columns. In front of them stood North Block, a mirror image of the building they had just exited. The fountains in front of both, the South Block and its mirrored image the North Block were playing, their sprays making mini rainbows in the morning Sun. The vista was really awe inspiring. These English sahibs really did things in a grand way. They thanked the peon guide and were on their way. They crossed the majestic boulevard and entered the North Block and out through the back side and headed towards Gurdwara Rakab Ganj.

Gurdwara Rakab Ganj Sahib is a historic gurdwara connected with the martyrdom of Guru Teg Bahadur. While Gurdwara Sis Ganj Sahib, visited by Harry and his party during their sojourn to Madras stands at the site where the revered Guru was beheaded, Gurdwara Rakabganj is built at the site where the guru's headless body was cremated by his disciples. History has it that his body had been spirited away during the night by his disciples Lakhi Shah Banjara and his son Bhai Naghaiya from Chandni Chowk police station where he had been beheaded and brought to their hut in Village Raisina. The two burnt down their own hut, so as to cremate the body of the headless Guru. The Guru's severed head was taken to Anandpur Sahib in Punjab, by another disciple and was cremated by his son, Gobind Rai, who later became Guru Gobind Singh, the tenth and last Guru of the Sikhs. Just as Gurdwara Sis Ganj, had been initially built by the Sikh military leader Bhagel Singh in 1783, Gurdwara Rakabganj too had been constructed by him at the same time.

The two reached the Gurdwara some thirty minutes later. What a serene and beautiful marble structure it was. Village Raisina where the Guru had been cremated was long gone its residents shifted to alternative areas when British Architect Lutyen carved out New Delhi. After paying obeisance the two spent some time in the sanctum listening to the *Gurbani,* hymns of the Guru recited by the priest. They requested for additional dollops of *krah parsad,* from the dispensing assistant priest, for Misra and his staff which was given to them in a generous measure in leaf, *dona,* bowls. After re-emerging from the gurdwara they joined the congregation at the *langar,* community meal. While Jarnail was keen to return to Misra's office after the meal to get the work done early, Harry didn't seem to be in any hurry to do so. He had told Jarnail that work at higher HQ moved at a snail's pace and instead of returning to the HQ they partook in *karseva,* voluntary community service by washing utensils and assisting in making *chapatis* at the Gurdwara *langar*.

On their way back Harry had told Jarnail that work at higher HQ moves rather slowly and it may take a few days before his work was done. 'But you know this sluggish pace has its advantages,' said Harry.

'Yes! Having free time on your hands enables one to do sightseeing or take in a movie?' replied Jarnail.

'Not only that. One can undertake a more productive venture.'

'Like what?'

'Well one could always pay a visit home while the work is being done. Of course the home should be nearby, say, within 3 to 4 hours distance from Delhi.' An idea had been planted in Jarnail's mind as they continued back towards Mr. Misra's office. It took a lot of time reaching Mr. Misra's office since they had to repeatedly ask for directions once they were inside the Army HQ building. Jarnail had an uncanny feeling that Harry had got disoriented and lost sense of direction as soon as they entered the Army HQ building. He had taken many wrong turns on their way back and in the bargain had drifted off course thus losing a lot of time on their backward journey. At last they were back at Mr. Misra's room by 4 pm, after having lost their way umpteen times in the corridors of South Block.

An empathetic Misra and his staff were dished out the holy *krah parsad* by the two and each member received it reverentially, with two cupped hands and head bowed. Misra then took out two neatly stacked envelopes from a drawer and handed them over to them. He explained to them that one of the envelopes was to be handed over to The Infantry Directorate and one to the Engineer Corps Directorate which had a Pioneer Corps Record section and dealt with all matters pertaining to the Pioneer Corps. He told them that the Pioneer Office in return would give them a sealed envelope which they should bring back to him. He laboriously explained to them the location of these two directorates and gave them suitable directions to reach there. Jarnail signed for the letters and they were on their way.

They were able to locate the Infantry Directorate and delivered the letter to them. However, locating the Pioneer Corps office turned out to be an exceedingly difficult proposition. At last they reached the place which was located in a hutment type of accommodation away from the main office complex. The office was just shutting down for the day but the kindly civilian took the sealed letter from them and read it before consigning it into his pending tray and weighing it down with a paper weight.

He called them the next morning when he promised to attend to their work.

'Now you have the whole night up to 10 am tomorrow at your disposal,' said Harry.

'That's nearly eighteen hours of spare time,' said Jarnail as they hitchhiked to the railway station in an army truck.

'Right, pal.'

'And you think I could nip across to my village in Karnal and be back by that time.'

'Sure. As a matter of fact since I have to attend to my work which is also in South Block, I could pick up this letter from the Pioneer people and deliver it to Misra tomorrow and you could be back day after tomorrow to pick up the reply from Mr. Misra and head back to the unit.'

Harry put an eager Jarnail into a Northward bound train to Karnal and turned around and rushed towards the park outside the railway station as soon as Jarnail's train had moved out of the station. It didn't take long to locate the henna dyed hair and betel chewing paper and ink expert. He fixed an appointment for some urgent work for the next day with the expert. He had time on his hand and could do some sightseeing or take in a movie or just relax. He decided to remain at the *fauji sarai* and relax and do some thinking and planning. On the way back to his place of stay he spent a few moments with Mehmood the barber who was closing down for the day and would soon be en-route home to his brood of kids and his four wives.

He was outside the hutment office of the Pioneers when the peon was opening the lock of the office. Within the next few minutes he witnessed a deluge of humanity as the staff of the British Government arrived on buses and cycles to attend their offices. By mid day Jarnail had received a large sealed envelope addressed to the Adjutant General's Branch (Recruiting). An hour later he and the hennaed paper and ink expert were bent over the opened envelope examining its contents. There were two documents in which the original *thambi's* photograph stared at them, one in civvies and one in uniform. Harry produced the new *thambi's* photographs from his pocket and the paper specialist expertly removed the old photos and replaced them with the new ones. Harry shredded the old ones and put the pieces in to his pocket while the professional worked on restoring the seals on the documents. They were now confronted with another problem—signatures. There existed signatures of the old *thambi* on one of the two documents, his recruitment application. Harry produced a blank paper on which he had obtained the new *thambi's* signature but the expert was unable to change the whole existing page since it had endorsements, signature and seals of a number of other officials on it. So he copied the first few and the last couple of alphabets of the new *thambi's* signatures on the open space in front and behind the old *thambi's* signatures partially over writing on the existing signatures. This action brought an immediate angry retort from Harry, 'what the fucking hell? You have ruined the whole original document idiot.'

'Keep cool *sardar*. I know what I am doing,' replied the professional.

He then took a drop of water in an eye dropper and carefully smudged the existing signature of the old thambi in such a way that the additions of new *thambi's* signature made by him now remained untouched. He then expertly pulled the water smear to a nearby endorsement and signature of an official on the document. 'Rain drops don't know rank or place,' he commented as he did so.

When dried, the document showed that a rain drop splodge had stained an endorsement and two signatures on the document. However the endorsement could still be read and luckily the smear had not obliterated the new *thambi's* signatures totally. The signature, especially the beginning and the end could be easily recognized even now. Harry paid Rupees ten, a fortune for the work to the slimy expert for his services and was at Mr. Misra's office by 4 p.m. and handed over the sealed envelope to him. Misra broke open the seal, went through the papers and again summoned the two clerks and assigned them the task of doing the needful. He told Harry to be back the next day by when he would have done the work.

Harry was waiting on the platform when Jarnail alighted from the train from Karnal the next morning. Harry updated him suitably and told him to meet Mr. Misra any time, to collect the reply letter to our CO Sahib. Profusely regretting his inability to accompany him because he himself was tied up with his own work that day, he put an indebted Jarnail Singh into an army truck going to Army HQ. As soon as the truck was out of sight Harry turned around, entered the railway station and caught the first train to Ludhiana. Sacrificing a couple of days leave and some money had been worth the resultant outcome. He had prayed for success of his mission at Gurdwara Rakabganj and was hopeful that everything would go off smoothly, as planned.

He was in the evening of the fifth day of his leave in his village when a telegram recalling him from leave arrived from the unit. It took the wind out of him. Something had gone wrong. As in the past, such a situation always brought about collywobbles in his stomach and an urge to urinate. Since there were no toilets in village dwellings, he rushed to the *deori,* the small foyer at the threshold entrance to the house, where an open drain exited from his small house. Harry sat down on his haunches, pulled out his member and pissed into the drain. Men in the Indian sub continent by tradition have always squatted while passing water. The standing piss was brought into India by the Europeans. The native men who took to wearing trousers like their British masters were the first ones to switch to a standing piss since sitting down on their heels wearing trousers and unbuttoning their flies and pulling out their penes was practically difficult. However even these converts preferred to squat to urinate when in their native dress.

Harry racked his brains as he sat pissing into the open drain in the *deori* of his house. Had Devar squealed? Had Matric or Lachu let the cat out of the bag? Or had the real Pioneer *Thambi* somehow returned from Ceylon and reappeared in the unit and exposed Harry and party's lie? These thoughts were still racing in his head as he completed his urination in the *deori,* and flushed it with a *lota* of water, as per practice of the family. A *lota* is a small squat vase shaped handle-less jug, voluptuous at the lower end with a short neck and a flared top. Although the house remained relatively odour free due to this water flow, the *gali,* lane, stank to high heaven.

————◄○►————

There were no toilets or bathrooms in Indian village dwellings. Only a few well to do land lords had hand operated water pumps and small cubicle bathrooms which also doubled up as urinals, in their residences. All others drew water from community wells in buckets and carried it to their homes where they bathed in a waist high walled area in the courtyard or in the *deori* which was also used as a urinal by the entire household, since it was the only place having a brick lined floor and a brick lined drain in their mud abode houses. The bathwater emptied out from the house through the open drain via the *deori,* into a common open gutter running in the middle of the narrow *gali,* lane. The gush of the bathing water streaming out cleansed the gutter somewhat thereby slightly ameliorating the stink in the *gali.*

Harry had inherited this house from his father. It was like most village abodes, constructed from mud, straw and dung adobes. Its flat roof was made of elephant grass thatch which had been plastered by a mixture of earth, straw and cow dung and kept in place by wooden members running between opposite walls. Harry's house consisted of two rooms astride the *deori.* Beyond the *deori* was a court-yard and further inside was the *kothri*, a window-less store-room. The small court yard could be used for a multiple purposes. One of its flanks was used as a kitchen and the other as an open byre, to tether milch animals and its central portion was used for outdoor sleeping during summers. The *kothri* was used as a mini granary cum warehouse, for harvested food grains like wheat, rice, pulses and fodder for the animals. Farming implements too were stored here.

Latrines were nonexistent. The whole village used adjoining fields for defecating, their excrement providing free manure for farming. The defecating was done every morning before day break even before the village cocks gave their morning crow. Women traditionally went earlier than the men, their fields demarcated separately from those of the males. They carried a *lota* of water while going for this daily custom. On reaching the ladies' latrine field, they made a small hollow in the field with the heel of their foot and pulled down their *salwar,* baggy trousers and sat down on their heels ensuring that the indentation just created was vertically below their arse holes while they parked the *lota* near at hand. They then commenced the inescapable daily routine of easing themselves. The early morning darkness provided adequate privacy, as they sat gossiping with each other while relieving themselves, while the early morning breeze played with their exposed front and back sides. The dames remained unfazed if a delay occurred in the schedule and the Sun broke over the horizon. In such an event they just covered their faces with a veil and made no other effort to cover their exposed South ends. They were not embarrassed, even if a Peeping-Tom came their way, after all, with their recognizable appearances masked, their features down below looked all the same any way. Defecating over, they would tilt the *lota* and take the water into their cupped left hands and splash it over their holes, front one first. Their washed and cleaned pissing holes and arses may well be sparkling enough to be kissed but their left hands could not be even touched though. They would then kick some mud over their excreta and exit the field.

They would next throng a nearby well, preferring the one where a Persian water wheel was in operation to avoid manual drawing of water with roped buckets. The Persian water wheel is a simple water-lifting device in which a circular horizontal movement powered by a yoked draft animal e. g. Ox, donkey etcetera, is converted in to a movement in the vertical plane by a system of gears and shafts. The vertical movement rotates a wheel drum placed over the well with a garland of a bucket chain suspended over it. As the wheel rotates, the buckets on the suspended chain, scoop water from the well and get lifted upwards to the surface. At its high point these filled buckets riding the wheel, tilt as they commence arching downwards in a circular motion of the rotating wheel, pouring out water into a suitably placed water receptacle. The empty buckets recommence their downward journey with their open ends facing down to scoop up more water all over again. This cyclic process lifts large quantities of water from the water well, which is ultimately transferred into a channel for irrigation via a cistern.

Our bevy from the farting fields would fill their *lotas* with water as it gushed out from the cistern into the irrigation channel. They would next pick up a handful of mud and wet it in their hands and use this mud as a powder detergent to sterilize their hands by scrubbing them clean. They would then break twigs from a *Neem* tree and use them as *datun* toothbrushes, scrub the *lota* with the mud detergent and sluice it with water, till it sparkled. After that the *datuns,* were discarded, mouths rinsed and the gaggle headed homewards; with clear insides, laundered pubis and rectums, sparkling teeth and gleaming *lotas* to commence the day. It was then the turn of the men folk to venture out for the same ritual.

◄o►

A morose Harry was deep in thought as he emerged from the *deori* and commenced packing his gear to return to the unit. Had Mr. Misra and the AAG Sahib in Army HQ realized that the documents of *thambi* had been tampered with and fudged? Did the letter brought by Jarnail from Army HQ contain bad tidings?

Women can sense when there is something wrong. Jagtar Kaur was no different. She had been through numerous re-call and leave cancellation notices in the past but she had never seen Harry as tense and nervous as he was at this recall. She had heard rumours that a war was ongoing and a large number of Indian soldiers were being thrown into battle by the white *sahibs*. Maybe the present leave cancellation was due to the unit being moved to the front and this perhaps was the reason for Harry's being overwrought. It was her duty as wife to provide him support and solace in such situations. In this direction she had successfully persuaded Harry to postpone his departure for the unit till the next morning when she observed him packing to proceed to the unit straight away. 'The Sun is about to set and it will soon be twilight. By the time you finish packing it will be nightfall. I don't want you to venture out of the village at night. In any case what will you do in the unit at night when everyone would be asleep. Heavens are not going to fall if you reach the unit tomorrow,' Jagtar Kaur had reasoned. You couldn't argue with her logic and Harry was swayed to put off his departure to the next day.

She then went to the village water well and brought him a bucket of water for bathing and went out again. In winter the well water seems warm and during summer the same water

175

appears cold to the touch. In this cold month the water drawn by her from the well seemed warm to Harry as he quickly took a bath mouthing the name of the Almighty which seemed to help in keeping the cold at bay. When Jagtar Kaur returned with two radishes and that many carrots plucked out from the fields of some farmer, one *pao*, half pound, of pork purchased from the butcher and a *paua*, quarter bottle, of country brewed moonshine liquor, procured from the village bootlegger, Harry had bathed and was sitting on a string cot under the thatched canopy in the courtyard of their dwelling under which a buffalo used to be tethered during his father's time. She placed the small size quarter bottle of hooch and metal tumbler on a stool near him. She then fetched him a *surahi*, a thin necked lightly porous terracotta water pitcher and placed it on the ground adjacent to him. Then she went to the kitchen to cook the evening meal.

The two side open kitchen was located on one flank of the courtyard in the corner made by the common partition wall with the neighbouring house and the wall of the living room, under the mud and straw staircase, leading up to the roof of the house. Its two covered sides were obviously the dividing wall with the adjoining house and the wall it shared with one of the living rooms of the abode. The top covering of the kitchen was provided by the flight of stairs leading to the roof of the house. The remaining two sides were open. These exposed sides had a two foot high parapet wall with a small opening to facilitate entry and exit. Along this low enclosure were lined water buckets and pitchers, a flour urn, a *chakki,* stone hand grinding mill, mortar and pestle and a *jali,* a small wire mesh cabinet shaped meat-safe, to store milk, poultry, meat, *ghee,* clarified butter, oils and other left over eatables etcetera. While the *chuhla,* the wood and cow dung cake fired U shaped clay-plastered stove, was located in the segment under the higher side of the stairway, the lumber and cow dung cakes used as fuel were neatly stored below its lower end. The common walls, with the neighbour and the living room, had a number of large wooden spikes called *killis* embedded into them. Small vessels containing yogurt and other milk products and wire mesh baskets containing eggs, potatoes, onions and other fresh vegetables were suspended from these *killis* thus keeping them out of reach of the stray cats foraging for food, during the night. The walls also had numerous *ala*, cubbyhole recesses, and two shelves. The larger recesses and one shelf were used for storing the utensils. The other shelf and the smaller cubby holes were used to keep lentil containers and the spice box and the *diya,* oil lamp. Larger cook-ware was stored in a wicker basket and kept next to the parapet near the *chuhla.*

She commenced lighting the *chuhla.* Since the wood fuel did not fire up easily, Jagtar Kaur peeled off small shavings from the log and used it as kindling and lighted it. She then took a *phookna*, hollow bamboo wind pipe, and blew into it, aiming the *phookna* wind at the kindled ambers in the *chuhla.* Though the smoke emanating from the slow burning wood in the stove irritated and brought tears into her eyes, yet she continued in her attempt to flare the ambers. Her persistent puffing into the *phookna* got the fire going, at last. She wiped her eyes with the hem of her shirt, broke a dung cake in two and inserted it into the stove to ensure the fire kept going. She then placed a pot on the stove and commenced cooking the pork she had just bought from the butcher. She added *ghee,* to the pot and spiced it with one whole black cardamom, a couple of cloves, a bay leaf, an inch piece of cinnamon, followed by finely cut onions, garlic and ginger, turmeric, red chilies and coriander powder. After sautéing the spices, she added the pork and fried it, swirling it around in the pot with the ladle. She then added water and salt to the potion and covered the pot and let it simmer on the *chuhla.*

After that she flattened a couple of onions with her fist and washed clean a radish and a carrot, sprinkled them with salt, put them in a plate, squeezed a lemon and took this salad to Harry. He relished a salad with his drink. She was concerned when she found that he had not even opened the bottle of booze. Harry who liked a daily evening shot had not poured a drink for himself this evening. She sat down next to Harry and took his face in her hands and could discern lines of worry even in the dim light of the *diya,* lamp. Her soothing touch brought a little twinkle in his eyes.

'The telegram has brought some bad tidings for my lord. But worry not my husband. You are a good man, a loving and faithful husband, a good provider, a God fearing man. I know in my heart that no harm will befall you,' she said.

God if she only knew the shit he was in. Nevertheless such words coming from his unlettered wife brought a faint smile on his lips. She trusted him totally. She seized the moment when his lips curled up in a grin and in one flowing movement perfected by repeated practice, opened the booze bottle and poured a drink and handed the tumbler to him. And then she poured cold water from the *surahi* into the drink. Harry took a swig and followed it by a bite of the salted onion and radish from the salad platter.

They had been married for a decade and she knew him like the back of her hand. She knew of his fondness for two things. The first was making love to her and the second was having his evening drink. She had got him going on his second favourite pastime and would indulge him in his favourite sport after dinner and perhaps next morning as well before his departure to his battalion. She hurried back to the kitchen to complete the cooking. She considered herself to be really lucky. She had so far failed to bear him a child even though they were married now for over ten years. Though his relatives, especially his *chachi,* paternal aunt, had branded her barren, a most degrading insult for a woman in Punjab, he had never berated her at her failure to fulfill this major conjugal duty. She really loved him. And she knew that he too loved her. She knew that he had never been unfaithful to her. While many of his army colleagues had caught sex related VD disease from prostitutes, he had remained free from the clap. After dinner she will coddle him and pander to his wishes during love making thus demonstrating her love in a more practical way.

An hour later they had finished their dinner of chapattis and pork gravy and onion salad. She did the utensils, using the warm ash from the *chuhla* as detergent while he went out to the house of his *chacha,* paternal uncle, for fixing a ride up to Ludhiana for next morning. His *chacha* was in the business of hides and skins, who took consignments of hides to the tannery or leather merchants in the town on his bullock cart every few days. He was quite close to his *chacha* having been an assistant to him in treating and drying the hides of animals before he joined the army. Once upon a time he had also been close to his *chachi,* wife of his *chacha*. He had been intimate with her. It was she who had initiated him into the wonderful world of sex one afternoon, when he was still a strapping young lad of fifteen, during *chacha's* absence on a business trip to town to sell hides to a leather merchant. The *chachi* and the young nephew had continued their affair clandestinely for a number of years and it had ended when he had got married. Despite the *chachi's* entreaties he had remained faithful to his wife Jagtar Kaur after wedlock. No wonder then that she was the one who had spread the canard of Jagtar Kaur being barren amongst the relatives. He avoided eye contact with the *chachi* on reaching their dwelling. He was happy to learn that a consignment of pelts was being taken to Ludhiana the next day and he would be able to take a lift on the bullock cart sitting on top of the stacked buffalo hides.

Jagtar Kaur had done her work in the kitchen and then reserved one full glass of cream laced milk which had been left to simmer over low fire for a long time, sweetened it with *gur*, dried molasses, in the *jali*. She gave him this milk every night before he turned in for the night during his leave. She also put heated milk in another container and added a spoon of yogurt to it and wrapped this container in warm woollen cloth and kept it in their room. This would ferment during the night and set to a thick creamy consistency to become yogurt by next morning in the warmth of their room and would be used by her for breakfast. This was also her last chore of the day, in the kitchen.

She took her nightly piss in the drain, flushed it with water and was lying under the quilt on the string cot, waiting and ready for him to come and indulge in his favourite past time with her. The scraping and squeaking noise of their front door announced his return as he pushed it open and then shut it close. The jingle of the hasp and staple latch of the door being secured came into her ears next. She readied herself by undoing the knot of her *salwar nara* string belt, and her brassier at the sound of approaching footfalls. Then she heard the sound of a creaking cot. Not her cot but the empty one lying adjacent to hers. He had not approached her but instead gone and lay down on the other empty cot. This had never happened before. He always came to her especially on his last night at home and made love to her on the spindly string cot. She was always uneasy that the bamboo cot groaning under their combined weight would give way during his humping and land them both on the mud floor. However the bamboo frame of the cot had continued to show a lot of resilience and her apprehension had remained unfounded so far in these ten years. The worse that had happened was that the strings of the cot got loosened prematurely and had to be pulled tight every time after his visit.

Avoiding her, on this cold last night, when she could keep him warm in her arms, seemed wrong. The evil telegram from the unit was responsible for his adverse mood. Well if the Lord does not come to her mounts, she would carry the mounts and vale to the Lord and perform her wifely duty. She got out of her bed and went to him, dropping her *salwar* on the floor on the way. She crept under his quilt and took him in her mouth. Slowly but surely, he came to life. And then she mounted him and brought him to a climax. Afterwards she recovered her *salwar* from the mud floor and put it on. She then retrieved and served him the tumbler of milk cached in the *jali* by her a little while earlier. In Punjab, wives traditionally serve this thick milk laced with *malai*, cream, to their husbands each night to replenish the energy they squirt out into them at sex time. Wives in rural India believe that it takes one hundred drops of blood to create one drop of semen. The nightly milk routine is thus essential to keep the husband's juices flowing. Up even before the cock's crow, Harry repeated the night performance but in this bout, it was Harry who dominated the show. He had so far not sired a child but it was certainly not due to lack of effort on his part, it was just the Will of the Almighty.

They did their morning field rituals and by the time Harry got ready his loving wife had prepared four *parathas* stuffed with spiced boiled potatoes and a tumbler of sweetened *lassi,* churned-yogurt, with a sprinkling of water. Harry downed *lassi* but did not eat his breakfast, he would eat it in the train to Jullundur since it was still dark and far too early to eat. He picked up his gear hugged his wife who touched his feet as per tradition and bade him farewell with a Sat Sri Akal. Harry took a lift in the, hide laden, bullock cart of his *chacha* up to Ludhiana, from where he found his way to the railway station and boarded an early morning train for his short journey to Jullundur.

It was still dark when he reached Jullundur Railway Station. He did not wait for any army transport but instead hired a horse drawn *ekka,* cart and dismounted a short distance from the unit area. He then took a long detour, cross country and parked himself in the broken ground behind the unit lines. It was important that he meet Lachu or Matric before entering the unit. He did not have to wait long. He saw Lachu emerging from the barrack to do his morning push-ups even before reveille had been sounded by the bugler. He waved at him from his hiding place but realized that the wrestler was unable to see him in the inadequate light of dawn. He therefore gave a loud enough "psst" to get Lachu's attention. That did the trick Lachu looked up and saw the frantically waving Harry. The wrestler looked over his shoulders at the barrack and then ducked and came to him in a stooping lope, much like a bear.

Harry took one look at Lachu and knew that they were in trouble even before the wrestler had opened his mouth and whispered, 'we are in deep trouble *ustad.*'

Harry went for his meter-o-morale and its condition was pathetic. The collywobbles had started yet again. The way Lachu was whispering and furtively looking over his shoulder meant that they were marked men. What had gone wrong? Had *thambi's* cover been blown? But how was that possible without one of them spilling the beans; or had Army HQ cottoned on to the fabrication done in the documents? Aloud he said, 'tell me what happened?'

The wrestler said, 'the news we have will cause considerable distress to you, boss. Matric is aware of the matter in detail so I will go and fetch him because he will be able to explain clearly the gravity of our problem.' Without waiting for an answer he flitted back, again in a crouched position, towards the barrack and was back in a jiffy with Matric in tow.

Matric updated him on the developments resulting in his recall. He told him that a complaint had been received from the railways that three Sikh soldiers had forced two trains to halt at a suburban station in Madras on 24 January. In this act they had even manhandled a railway officer and compelled him, forcibly, to halt an express train. Army HQ was trying to ascertain who were the culprits of this illegal commotion? Since our unit had sent a party into that area both Matric and Lachu had been grilled repeatedly by the company VCOs as well as the JA. So far both had with-stood the interrogation successfully. Harry had been recalled from leave for questioning in that regard. Harry heaved a sigh of relief. *Thambi*'s cover had not been blown. He was also satisfied that his cronies had not broken down during the investigation. He took the same detour to egress from the broken ground area, a semblance of a smile flitting across his face because *Thambi's* identity was still intact. An hour later he presented himself at the "IN" gate of the unit and formally reported for duty on being recalled from leave. Having been fore-warned by his cronies, Harry was now, fore-armed to face the grilling. He knew that his fate would be decided before Sun-set that day; contingent, of course, to his performance at the probe.

On conclusion of his arrival formalities he was taken to Subedar Major Jiwan Singh. 'Well, well so you are here Harinder. So why don't you tell me what happened down South, at Madras?' The old goat did not waste time in getting to the point.

'Nothing sahib, nothing at all, I and the escort brought back the prisoner without any major hassle sahib.'

'Don't give me that crap Naik,' said Jiwan and picked up the cane lying on top his table and pointed it towards Harry while he continued, 'I know you from the Sikh Pioneer days Harinder. You are a good lad but you also have a devilish streak in you. So don't try my patience. Just tell me what happened.'

'Sahib I don't know what you are talking about.'

'I am referring to a forced stoppage of two trains by you in suburban Madras on,' Jiwan paused and referred to a letter kept on the table in front of him, 'on . . . mm..mm..m on 24th of January. Yeah here it is on the evening of 24th January 1942 at about 9 pm.'

'There seems to be some mix up sahib. We commenced our return journey on 26th of January from Madras. You can check this out from our movement order. The date which you mention is two days prior to our date of departure from Madras. On that date we were in the Gurkha unit, in the fort area of Madras garrison. Someone is trying to blame us for nothing.'

'Well a train proceeding to Bhopal was stopped by chain pulling at Doravari. Shortly thereafter an express train coming from the opposite side was stopped forcibly and boarded. In both cases up to three Sikh soldiers were involved. I am going to find out if you guys were mixed up in that misdemeanour.'

'I wish the Sahib's indulgence for a couple of moments. If, a Madras bound train was stopped and boarded, the culprits must have wanted to go to Madras. And sir we were already in Madras.'

'Don't try to be clever Harinder Singh. You were involved in some hanky-panky. So out with the truth,' said old Jeevan menacingly.

'Sahib seems to have even made a directional mistake. Sahib is saying that the errant soldiers hitched a ride towards Madras on a train coming from Bhopal side. Now why would Punjabi soldiers halt a train to proceed to Madras? One can understand Punjabi soldiers forcing an unscheduled train halt to proceed North wards towards their villages in Punjab but doing so, to proceed in the opposite direction is incomprehensible.'

'What do you mean? It's all here in the letter.' He referred to the document once again and said, 'the train which was forced to halt and boarded by you was proceeding to Madras. I have made no directional error while interpreting the letter. The described physical portrayal in the letter of two of the *khalsas* matches you and that of that wrestler, Laxman Singh of your party. How would you explain the uncanny resemblance of the culprits with the two of you Naik Harinder Singh?'

'Sire, I don't know how a person can be recognised at 2100 hours in the darkness and then described lucidly by any one. Sir, all Sikhs look similar to Madrasis just as all Madrasis look the same to us,' replied Harry, plagiarizing Lachu's observation, on the spur of the moment. Silently blessing Lachu for the idea, he continued, 'so the description in the letter at best could be of a general nature. What would I and Sepoy Laxman Singh be doing in a suburban station in Madras? What possibly could be the urgency which compelled us to halt a train to reach Madras from that station, when we were not even there? We have come under suspicion without any fault of ours just because we are

Sikhs who were in that general area at the time the misdeed was committed by someone else.'

'Don't try to confuse me with your arguments. I think you went to that place to visit whores. I know that Madras especially the sea front is notorious for its red-light areas. You stopped the outward train from Madras to dismount at this out of bound red light district for sex. And you lost track of time playing sex games and got delayed in the bargain. I think when you fellows were unable to get return transportation to Madras you panicked. You realized that you would be unable to make it back to the unit before the nightly head count. Absence at the night muster meant drawing the ire of the CO of the unit lodging you. You therefore had to find a way to get back. Since no conveyance was available, you had no option but to force the train to halt and take a lift thereon.'

Bloody hell, the Subedar Major was known for never failing to crack a case. Today his imagination was running riot. It was a cold February day but he could feel sweat breaking out on his face and under arms. He could tell, even without laying a hand on his meter-o-morale, that it was displaying an abysmally low level of his morale. Luckily, he had finished his workout with Jagtar Kaur this morning prior to this interrogation, as otherwise it would have been surely a no-go for him.

Harry knew that there was always danger of blurting out something which would expose them if such grilling continued by the Subedar Major for long. He must try to change tack. 'Sir, if we were Jat Sikhs your hypothesis may well have been bang-on. These Jats have this flamboyance to lay dames, even of ill repute, without batting an eye lid. The episode in suburban Madras has the hallmark of boys from the Sikh Regiment. I therefore humbly submit that the culprits are most likely to be Jat Sikhs. Sahib is aware that the Jats consider themselves superior to us and they scoff and ridicule us at every possible opportunity and yet get away with it.' The British Indian army had two regiments based on the Sikh Religion; while the M and R Sikh Regiment drew its stock from lower caste, Mazhabi and Ramdasia Sikhs, the upper caste Jat Sikhs comprised the Sikh Regiment. And it was not uncommon for the Jats to ridicule their brothers who were on lower rungs of the Indian caste system ladder. No reaction from the old coot.

'Sahib I have worked under you in the Sikh Pioneers. You may have observed many of my weak points but bedding a woman of ill repute could never have been one of my shortcomings.'

Subedar Major Jiwan Singh was familiar with Harinder's character from Sikh Pioneer days and knew that Harinder was truly faithful to his wife. He had on many occasions visited his village Machiwara in Ludhiana which was about a two hour journey from his own village Shahzadpur in Ambala and the elders of the Mazhabi and Ramdasia community of his village had always praised Harinder's unblemished reputation. So much so that when his wife had failed to give birth to a child, Harinder had spurned efforts of the community elders to persuade him to take another wife. Therefore he could not have possibly gone to suburban Madras for sex. Maybe our boys were truly innocent and the palaver was indeed created by some other Sikh soldiers.

'You may have a point or two there Harinder. But I am not finished with you. You know I can see through you and I have a gut feeling that you are hiding something. If you have done a wrong I will unearth it for sure and then come down heavily on you.'

It was during this interrogation that the CO summoned Subedar Major Jiwan Singh. The hawk dismissed Harry with a wave of his hand and hastily walked away towards the CO's office carrying the complaint letter with him. Whew that had been close. Harry knew that he wasn't out of the woods yet but he had veered the needle of suspicion towards his superior brothers of the Sikh Regiment. Now old Jiwan had an opportunity to put forward this theory to the CO and Harry hoped that he didn't let this chance slip by. Meanwhile all he could do was pray and hope for some divine intervention.

Jiwan was in CO's office along with the 2IC and the adjutant for a long time. Their emergence from the office of the CO triggered a hectic activity in the battalion. Buglers commenced summoning the CHMs, the VCO second-in-command of the companies and office orderlies were doubling around with typed messages for CO's conference for officers that afternoon.

Harry however, had to wait till the evening to learn what had transpired in the CO's office that day creating this unprecedented bustle in the battalion, when their CHM read out the Battalion Routine Order to the assembled company at the roll-call. The unit had been ordered to move out from Jullundur to Multan. All leave had been suspended and those already away on leave were being recalled. All the prisoners incarcerated in the unit quarter guard were to be released a week before move of the unit and their pending punishment remitted. The three friends standing in the ranks listening to the CHM nudged each other with their elbows in happiness because this meant that Devar too would be out of the kink before doing his time.

This occurrence seemed favourable to Harry since everyone who mattered got busy with the move planning, packing and other activities related to the location change. He could observe Subedar Major Jiwan Singh dart from company to company, from barrack to barrack, armoury to ammo dump, quarter guard to battalion stores; supervising and guiding the VCOs and the men in sorting out their stores, weapons, equipment and so on. He seemed to be everywhere, omnipresent. It was on the fourth or fifth day after receipt of the move orders to Multan that Harry sensed old hawk eye's absence. He came to know through the unit grapevine that Jiwan had proceeded on one week's leave. It got Harry momentarily thinking that while leave for all personnel had been stopped old Jiwan being given leave must be for some very compassionate reasons. He was happy at this development though, because it willy-nilly kept the hawk off his back. In the event Harry was never called for further grilling by Jiwan even after he rejoined from leave or by anyone else again. His luck seemed to have held.

Accordingly a suitable reply was sent by the Battalion back to Army HQ that a unit investigation had confirmed that no personnel of 1 M and R SIKH were involved in any way in the stoppages of trains of the Indian Railways in the Southern Railway Region of Madras on 24 January 1942. Harry and party were out of the woods.

The three had continued to meet Devar regularly and his morale seemed to be high. His posting order to the Madras Regiment had been brought by Jarnail Singh by hand. As soon as his pending punishment was remitted and he was released from his incarceration, the three took him to Sadar Bazaar, main market, of Jullundur Cantonment and purchased and presented to him a Madras Regiment cap badge, a green coloured beret cap and Madras Regiment shoulder titles and a pocket diary in which they wrote down their village addresses.

His documentation and other out-take formalities were done and Lt Col Price was satisfied to see a trimmer and smarter fighting fit *thambi* or rather Sepoy Neville Devar all decked up in a properly fitting, well ironed, neat Madras Regiment uniform at the out-take parade. The CO perhaps was not aware that the *thambi's* aye-one turnout stemmed from the fact that he was wearing one of the two pairs of, one size large, new uniforms issued to him as replacement, for his old ones which had been rendered unserviceable due to strenuous wear and tear. He also gave full marks to the adjutant and his subordinate staff, at having utilised the time of the chap's internment fruitfully in imparting training when he noticed the fellow's flawless salute. And just to see if his other drill movements had improved, the CO with a mischievous glint in his eyes asked Devar to demonstrate an about turn and his playful grin turned into a happy smile when Devar executed a perfect about turn. The confinement in the unit quarter guard had indeed done the man a lot of good. He would, now be able to find his place amongst his peers in 1 Madras, his new infantry unit, with confidence.

That evening the four friends had a quiet party, clandestinely, behind the ten foot high wall of the obstacle course on Devar's last night in the unit. They had chosen the venue for the party skillfully. While the high wall kept them out of view, the low-wire-entanglement or LWE on the other edge ensured that they could not be taken by surprise by any meddler from that flank. Even if someone was foolhardy enough to cross the LWE, wrestler Lachu was positioned tactically to push him into one of the ditches of the double-ditch obstacle. The party started on a happy note and they toasted each other on the successful conclusion of their secret exercise. By the end of the party the quartet however became emotional, especially Devar who dreaded the thought of parting from them the next day. Harry as always came up with suitable advice when he told Devar that this was not the end of the road. As a matter of fact his joining his Madras Battalion was a beginning of a new life for him. In any case they were friends for life and would continue to remain in touch with one another through letters and meet each other whenever there was opportunity to do so. The emotive trio told him to change his permanent home address in his army records to any one of their addresses which were available in the diary given to him, if he so desired.

Next day Devar boarded a train for Aurangabad to join 1st Battalion the Madras Regiment and he was seen off at the railway station by his three friends who wished him bon voyage and success in his future endeavours. Overcome by emotion Harry, the locomotive buff, passed the opportunity on this day to visit the steam engine and just stood there trying to suppress his tears as the others bear hugged each other till the train rolled out taking *thambi* towards far away Aurangabad but surely not out of their lives.

They kept in touch with one another through mail. Devar learnt of the move of the unit to Multan and then on to Peshawar and about transfers of Matric and Lachu to newly raised 2nd and 3rd Battalions of the M and R Sikhs through such correspondence. While Matric had been sent the 2nd battalion being raised at Multan in July, Lachu had been packed off to Rawalpindi to join the third battalion a month later. Harry had mentioned in his letters that he suspected the hand of Subedar Major Jiwan Singh, the hawk in breaking up their troika for good. He was despondent to receive this news because it meant that their meeting each other collectively was now improbable since all four were now posted in different units and were not likely to be stationed at one place ever. Devar knew that all of them would be very unhappy for having been deliberately torn apart. No doubt they would remember the friendship and comradeship they had developed but at that time each must have thought that that their association was now finished forever. Not so! Unknown to them fate would bring the four together again, in the future.

In mid November of 1942, Jagtar Kaur gave birth to a bonny boy. On hearing the good news, Harry had wired all his three friends of the happy information and him-self rushed home to Machiwara to be at his wife's side. Harry could tell that the baby was conceived during his spot of leave in February when he had been suddenly recalled to the unit to answer some difficult questions pertaining to his Madras trip. However, when exactly was the baby seeded during that leave was a brainteaser he wanted to solve? He had come home after his successful visit to Army HQ Delhi and spent five days there in February. In the first four days he had been in a state of exhilaration because of the success of his Delhi trip. It was on the fifth day that the recall telegram arrived from the unit plummeting, his upbeat mood. The baby could have been conceived on any of these five days but he had a gut feeling, it was at the fag-end of his leave that the miracle had happened. Was it on the last night of his leave when he was listless and Jagtar Kaur had laboriously brought him to life and humped him till he had poured himself into her? Or was it due to his-own effort on that last morning of his leave before day break, even before the village cocks' crow ushered in a new dawn? Though he couldn't crack the brainteaser he had set for himself, he was more inclined towards the "woman-on-top" occasion where-in his loving Jagtaro had played the dominant role. His argument being that he had always adopted the dominant position during their cohabitation all these ten years of their conjugal life but without any result and Jagtaro had done the trick in just one go. It actually didn't matter thought Harry as he lovingly cradled the baby in his arms. Their hard work in bed had paid off, at last. Or rather Jagtar Kaur's one-time toil had borne fruit. And in the bargain it had also automatically removed the disparaging "barren" adjunct given to her by invidious relatives, once and for all.

Matric and Lachu could not get leave to join him on this happy occasion due to exigencies of service. They had nonetheless sent congratulatory telegrams to him. On the other hand, Devar had descended on Machiwara on a short leave from his unit in early December of that year. Getting leave of absence was not easy in these troubled times. Though Devar's unit was under orders to move to the Eastern Front but because he had not taken any leave since joining the battalion and given that he was in the good books of his seniors due to the hard work and dedication, he was granted leave for a week as a special case. This meant that he would get to spend three days at Machiwara after discounting his train journey period. He arrived in Machiwara in a *tonga* laden with gifts for the child and performed all rituals which were traditionally the responsibility of a maternal uncle of a new born as per Indian customs. He showered cash gifts on the new born, hand-outs to the eunuchs, who always appeared at the house of a new born in India, monetary contribution to the midwife who had assisted at childbirth and donations to many others who appeared out of nowhere at the news of disbursement of cash gifts by an army crony of Harry. Needless to say that he and Harry celebrated by emptying a bottle of Jamaica Rum, procured by Harry from the officers' mess cellar by bribing the mess NCO before coming on leave, each night of his three night stay at Machiwara.

While the first day of his arrival was devoted entirely to gaiety and distribution of largesse, the second day was spent by, Devar in ordering and paying for, a hand-pump which would be installed in the court yard of the house. On the third day he purchased a cow from a cattle dealer at the cattle fair. However, when the cow refused to budge from the fair in-spite of goading and use of a stick; he had picked up her new born calf in his arms and started walking towards their house and the recalcitrant bovine had followed him with alacrity, mooing all the way, into the house; where cow and calf were tethered in the court yard at a little distance from each other ensuring that the teats of the mother cow were not accessible to the calf. Jagtaro's sister who had come to assist during Jagtaro's confinement and was now carrying out and supervising all household work, took charge of the cow and its milking duties. The hand pump installers were still sinking the three inch pipe into the courtyard floor when Devar left for his unit before daybreak on the fourth day. Thus Naik Harinder's residence would become one of the handful households, boasting of a hand pump and its own dedicated dairy in the village. And Neville Devar would change his permanent residential address in his personal army records to Harry's house in Machiwara. He would be the only *thambi* in the

Madras Regiment to have a permanent address in Northern India in Punjab. His recorded "next of kin", NOK, in his documents would also now become Jagtar Kaur and relationship with NOK would be recorded as "Sister" and he would spend his future leave, thereafter at Machiwara with Harry and his family in Punjab eating yoghurt, fermented milk, from their own cow and bathing in fresh water pumped out by the hand pump and playing with Harry Junior.

The war ended. Hitler was defeated and committed suicide. On the other front, the atom bomb was used to subdue the Japanese. The British Indian Army had played an active role on both fronts and valour of Indian troops was acknowledged by the British. Many Indians were given awards for bravery beyond the call of duty in the face of the enemy. One such bravery award was going to be awarded to Neville Devar, who was now a Havildar and part of the parade reviewed by Lieutenant General Hodson and being witnessed by his three Sikh friends and Sophie at Wellington Barracks.

◄○►

THE PARADE

A lectern and the Public Address system had been put in place in front of Hodson and height of the microphone adjusted at his mouth level. An aide had then placed the typed script of Hodson's address and his reading glasses on the lectern, saluted and faded away. Hodson took a step forward perched his reading glasses on his nose and commenced his address.

'Brave thambis of the Madras Regiment, ladies and gentlemen,' said Hodson, paused and looked towards the translator.

'Madras Regiment Veer Tamil Sagodar sagodrigale thaymaargale matrum peryavergale,' translated Doraiswami, the moment he saw the sahib gazing at him. As soon as he had completed the vernacular version he looked back at the sahib indicating that his part was over.

'Yours is the oldest regiment of the British Indian Army. Your bravery in battle has been acclaimed far and wide. The parade being held today is significant since it was on this day a hundred and forty seven years ago that your ancestors had won the Battle of Srirangapatnam overcoming a most formidable foe.' He paused again to enable the translator to articulate the version in the vernacular but Doraiswamy's translation was interrupted even before it had started with a round of clapping by the English savvy spectators.

Doraiswamy waited for the applause to die down before recommencing the Tamil version, 'oonglodiya Madras Regiment Indian paadgaap padaiyail migvum paladaanad. Parthaldil onnglodiya veeran oolagil pervayunada . . . ' Needless to say that the natives interrupted Doraiswamy's translated version a number of times, with their resounding applause.

'Your finest hour was in 1803 when your regiment won the battle of Assaye under Lord Wellesley. The crown had instituted three medals exclusively for the Madras Regiment to show its

deep appreciation for your bravery. It is thus a singular honour for me to have been deputed to review your parade this morning and bestow upon the bravest of the brave amongst you with their well deserved gallantry medals on behalf of His Majesty the Emperor.'

Pause—applause—pause—Tamil rendition—and again a booming applause and that's how, it progressed. Hodson would pause every few sentences and Doraiswamy would natter out the speech in its' Tamil version and all the time their speeches were interspersed by loud spells of clapping. Hodson traced the heroic deeds of the regiment in his speech and the resultant gift by the Empire of billeting the regimental centre in the Wellington Barracks which had so far been the exclusively reserve of British Troops.

'Your turn-out and parade this morning has been excellent which speaks volumes of your training. Your nation's Independence from the British is around the corner. So I extend my good wishes to all of you and your families and hope you will continue to excel in battle and all other fields in Independent India as you have done under the British Crown,' said Hodson as he read out the last line in the script placed before him. Doraiswamy read out the Tamil version as soon as the weak applause of the English spectators had died down. To his astonishment, his Tamil rendition was received by a thundering ovation from the native spectators and continued for a long time. The difference in the decibel level between the two applauses, one by the British spectators and the other by the natives, was not lost on Hodson. It was obvious from the applause levels that the British were sad to be leaving their colony while the natives, who had remained faithful to the British Crown these two centuries, were now passionate about their Independence. Since his job was over Doraiswamy folded his papers and inserted them into his coat pocket and looked up towards the sahib to do namaskar. To his astonishment he saw the sahib lean towards the microphone and speak into it—in Tamil.

'Veer Madrassi, Adi Kollu, Adi Kollu,' said the sahib. It took a moment for the non-plussed native spectators to comprehend that the sahib was speaking from the dais in their language but once it had sunk in, the natives in the spectator

stands stood up all together and gave a standing ovation to the sahib's Tamil elocution.

Hell this was not part of the written address given to him. The sahib's sudden switch into Tamil from English had taken the translator by surprise but old Doraiswamy was quick to recover, he wasn't called the best in his trade for nothing.

'Brave Madrassi, Hit and Kill, Hit and Kill and always win' said Doraiswamy, echoing sahib's Tamil phrase in English, into the microphone.

As soon as the English version oozed out of the overhead loudspeakers the English spectators who had been flummoxed by Hodson's unexpected switch to Tamil, also stood up and gave a standing ovation just like their native counterparts. For the first time since the commencement of the address all the spectators were in applause at the same time, irrespective of the colour of their skin or their spoken language. Hodson had articulated the catchphrase after ending his address on the spur of the moment. This valedictory slogan coined by Hodson on impulse and off the cuff seemed most appropriate even to him especially after tracing out the gallant history of the Madras Regiment in his address. He however, could not have ever imagined at that time that the refrain would be adopted by the Madras Regiment as its war-cry after Indian Independence.

His aide appeared at his side and removed the script and the reading glasses from the lectern and as it was being removed from the dais, Hodson unobtrusively looked over his shoulder at the still clapping spectators. The three Sikhs were clapping enthusiastically and Sophie's applause seemed to be equally passionate. Hodson hoped that she did not bruise her delicate hands in her fervour since sore hands would take away half the fun when they fooled around in bed after the parade. He heard the parade commander order the awardees to advance to their predetermined places near the dais to receive their medals.

He watched four men step out from the parade array and march in step smartly towards the saluting base. Hodson looked back at the spectators again while the four award winners were advancing towards him. Sophie was now seated and flushed due to the applauding exertion and looked even more desirable. Patience Eric patience, she will be soon in your arms, Hodson *told himself. Better concentrate on the investiture and hope it finishes soon.*

As soon as the four recipients were lined up in-front of the saluting base the voice of the master of ceremony came over the PA equipment as he read out the citation of the first recipient.

'No XXXXXXX Havildar Neville Devar was part of 1st Battalion Madras Regiment during the Burma Campaign. As a section commander he had led the men under his command as part of the attacking company in the capture of Mount Popa providing the initial break-through and there after he bravely led his men in pursuit of the Japanese up to Rangoon. His finest hour came in November 1945 in an assault landing in Java. When the assaulting troops of his battalion were pinned down on the beach due to effective automatic fire of the enemy Havildar Devar crawled nearly one hundred yards up to the enemy nest under direct and effective enemy fire in utter disregard to his own life. He was hit by enemy fire and seriously injured but he continued to progress toward the enemy bunker and lobbed two grenades into the bunker killing all its occupants thus silencing the enemy fire successfully. This enabled the remainder of the battalion to move inland and capture their objective. Thus Neville Devar showed bravery beyond the call of duty in the face of the enemy. For his act of valour Havildar Devar is awarded the Military Medal.'

Deafening applause as Hodson stepped down from the dais and picked up the star shaped medal which was suspended from a one inch red and blue ribbon from the velvet covered tray proffered by an NCO. He hooked the decoration into the small loop provided above the left breast pocket of the recipient. He returned the beneficiary's salute and then shook hands with him. It was obvious that he had been impressed by the act of bravery of this handsome thambi.

The applause subsided as the loudspeakers came to life with narration of the next citation. The entire process was repeated three more times till all four gallantry award winners had been anointed with their decorations. Hodson turned about and climbed back the single step to the podium to take his place at the saluting base. Before turning around to face the parade he took a quick look at Sophie's enclosure. Hell, she wasn't there, her chair was empty. She had left. Hodson's forehead creased with unease. What the hell was going on? Why had she left? She had come to the parade to see him review it and yet scooted before the parade came to an end. He did an about turn and faced the parade for that last salute and suddenly it dawned on him that she had left early to be in his room before his arrival. If she had waited till the end of the parade she was likely to lose a lot of time in the jostling crowd. This way she would save time and be ready for him when he arrived. He decided to use the extra time by asking her to rub him down to drain the stiffness acquired by his body from standing erect at the parade for the past one hour. She had learnt the art of kneading dough in the bakery from her grand-parents and he knew, from personal experience, that she used this knack with finesse during massage. The furrows on his forehead vanished at this thought and he braced himself to return the final salute.

————◄○►————

SOPHIE

Hodson dressed in his blue patrol mess dress called Dress No 2 in the Dress Regulations for the British Indian Army gulped down his second scotch and soda and a waiter, in white liveries silently appeared at his side, gliding in with a tray laden with whiskey glasses, soda water bottles and an ice bucket. Each shining glass on the tray had one shot of scotch whiskey measuring two fluid ounces, which in army jargon was a peg. Hodson transferred the remnants of the drink in his glass into, one of the freshly arrived array of scotch glasses and kept his just emptied tumbler on the tray. He picked up this fresh glass and the waiter deftly topped the new tumbler with ice and soda and moved smoothly away to refuel more, empty or emptying whiskey glasses. It was a convention in army messes that a fresh drink was always to be taken in a fresh glass. The new drink was never to be poured into the residual drink, into the in-use tumbler. However the old drink leftovers, if any, could be tipped into a fresh one. Hodson had correctly maintained that practice while taking his third drink of the evening.

Hodson, escorted by a Liaison Officer detailed by the Madras Regimental Centre, had arrived at the officers' mess at exactly 2000 hours as the bugler's "call to dinner-note" came drifting through the open window of his car into his ears. He had been received at the entrance by Tweed. The band had struck the first tune of the evening as soon as he stepped into the ante room of the mess which was already full of regimental officers, both serving and retired. Serving officers were in their blue patrol mess dress like Hodson while retired ones were in dark lounge suits and regimental neckties, their miniature medals pinned on the left side of their suits above the jacket pocket. The dinner night had progressed as per army tradition with scotch flowing freely during the pre-dinner drink session but Hodson seemed far-away and preoccupied as he sipped his scotch and

197

soda and made small conversation with the regimental officers who jostled with each other to come forward to shake hands and converse with him.

The subject of his pre-occupation was Sophie. He knew that it was taboo to discuss women and politics, in messes but there was no embargo on having women in ones thoughts. Sophie's sight at the parade ground had made adrenaline secretions run riot in his loins. Especially from the time he had observed her seductively uncrossing and opening her legs when he had stolen a glance in her direction while waiting for the installation of the microphone on the dais. Ever since, Hodson had expected Sophie to join him at his place of stay at the planter's club after the parade. He had been looking forward to a glass of bubbly with her over a private lunch at his quarters, followed by an afternoon of languorous love making before the formal dinner night at the Madras Regiment Officers' mess, where he was slated to be the guest of honour. But she had not turned up for the whole day while a horny Hodson had waited and waited. The bitch had made him horny and then stood him up. Hodson, the expert on Indians, knew that the native Indians had a perfect phrase to describe his pickled condition; they called it—"*KLPD*" or "*Kha... . . . Pe Dhokha*", an approximate translation of which would be "defrauding or cheating or double-crossing a horny male". A *KLPD* had been done to Lieutenant General Eric Hodson by his reliable Sophie. She had never failed him in the past but today she had tantalized him, provoked him, titillated him and then double-crossed him. A tormented Hodson recalled that she had been generous and giving in the past, ever-ready to experiment in bed and her non-appearance today was a big blow to his ego. The rumours about her wild ways with young men could perhaps be true and that possibly was the reason for her absence from the chamber of the elderly Hodson on this day; the two-timing bitch.

The diners, chit chatted as the band played favourite classics. Each of the diners had gone up to the seating plan chart displayed outside the dining hall to locate his sitting place at the table during dinner. The seating plan had been made with a lot of deliberation to ensure old acquaintances and cronies sat in adjoining chairs within conversation making distance of each other. Talking sideways during dinner was permissible but talking across the table was considered bad etiquette.

At exactly 2100 hours the mess havildar, a smart NCO wearing a red sash and displaying the gallantry medal he had received that morning at the parade over his left breast pocket, marched up to Colonel Tweed, saluted smartly and announced, 'dinner is served, Sir.'

'Thank you Devar,' replied Tweed. While Hodson was senior to Tweed both in rank and service, the mess NCO had given the dinner readiness report to Tweed and not to Hodson. This was not a faux pas but a normal custom in the British Indian Army wherein the report of readiness of the meal was given to the commandant of the regiment in the mess and not to an outsider even if he happened to be senior in rank.

Havildar Devar saluted again, did a perfect about turn and marched away into the dining hall and parked himself behind the chair of the chief guest. He would stay there during the entire dinner and ensure smooth service to the diners. The diners quickly drained their whiskey glasses and hurried into the dining and hall and stood behind their allotted black mahogany chairs and waited for the chief guest to appear and take his place at the table. In front of each chair was a white cloth table mat which stood out in contrast to the mahogany black table top. Each individual mat had one Regimental Crested quarter plate on its left side with the Crest in the 12 o'clock position, on which lay a white napkin folded in the "bishop's cap" configuration. On the inner side of the plate lay two forks. The outer fish fork slightly smaller than the other. On the right end of the mat lay one soup spoon and two knives; the soup spoon was outer most piece of cutlery, next to which was a fish knife and the inner most item was the second knife. One spoon lay on the far side of the mat for the pudding. On the right upper corner of the mat were placed three glasses, one was a normal tumbler for water and two were tulip shaped stemmed wine glasses which would be used for the white and red wines. A name card lay in the vacant space in between the cutlery arrangement with the name of the diner prominently written there-on. There were bread baskets full of dinner bread rolls and butter dishes, with butter knives, interspersed along the length of each table. The upper table which was to seat Hodson also had a number of shining silver trophies on it.

Soon Tweed escorted Hodson to his chair on the upper table. The moment Hodson pulled back his chair to sit down he heard the rasping sound of 240 wooden legs of the dining chairs being dragged on the cemented floor as they were collectively pulled out by the 60 diners to get seated. Once the, diners had plonked their bottoms on the dining chair seats, some more inward heaving took place to adjust the position of the chairs. As soon as the shuffling ended, the band struck a tune and a battery of waiters in liveries emerged from the pantry, laden with soup plates and the diners removed the napkins from the side plates and spread them out on their laps. Chief guest Hodson's last supper in Wellington had commenced.

The waiters started to serve from the two ends of each table and moved clock wise. In no time all the guests had been served but no one commenced eating. They started to eat only after Hodson picked up his soup spoon and took his first swallow. It was a well prepared chicken almond soup deduced Hodson as he wiped his lips with the white damask napkin. He then eyed the displayed menu card, held upright in the card holder, on the table in front of him. He had indeed correctly inferred the soup's nomenclature by taste. He could see on the menu card that a course of fish fillet in mayonnaise with mashed potatoes-in-cream accompaniment would follow this soup. The second course was going to be a meat pie with garlic-onion sauce, Chicken-a-la-Kiev and boiled vegetables in white sauce. And then, there was trifle pudding laced with brandy.

The three course dinner took an hour to finish by when Hodson had convinced himself that Sophie was balling someone else, someone young. His eyes had darted from one youthful face to another as he surveyed each young officer sitting in the dining hall trying to figure out who was the lucky scoundrel laying her. They had all looked a little flushed but that was due to the wine intake and surely not due to any pre-dinner strenuous humping. He could not arrive at any conclusion. It could be any one of these innocent looking, dozen fresh fellows sitting here demolishing their three course dinner. He was hit by pangs of jealousy; the unknown fellow perhaps would be bedding her even this night after dinner. However, many questions remained unanswered. She came up to the hills only for a few months during summer, how the hell did she get acquainted with her lover in this short spell? For whom had she come at the parade that morning? It certainly wasn't for him? He must try and find out.

The decibel level of the conversation had been increasing in direct proportion to the number of wine bottles consumed. But by the closing stages of the dinner the conversation died down. The tables were cleared of the post dinner debris and one fresh tulip wine glass was placed in front of each diner for the concluding part of the dinner night, a toast to His Majesty the King. Two wine decanters were simultaneously placed at extremity of each table, one at the head of the table and the other at the foot of the table, signalling commencement of the last but sombre part of the dinner. The plugs of the decanters were removed and set aside at both ends of the tables by the officers sitting there and the decanters were slid on the table to their left side in a clockwise direction. The first diner picked up the decanter, decanted a little wine into his wine glass, placed the decanter back on the table and slid it to his left where the next diner got into action and did likewise. It went so on, till both decanters reached the opposite sides of their starting point. The officers sitting at the two ends of the table then poured wine into their wine glasses and plugged the decanters with the stoppers lying at hand. Waiters then hurriedly removed the decanters from the tables. A head waiter then brought a small wooden mallet and a mallet pad to the head of the upper table and placed it beside the officer presiding over the meal, who, picked up the mallet and struck it on the pad with a thud bringing complete silence in the hall. He then stood up with the wine glass in his hand and said, 'Mister vice, His Majesty the King'.

In response the officer nominated as the Vice president for the meal, seated at the foot of the table, directly opposite to the president stood up with the wine glass held in his hand and said, 'Gentlemen His Majesty the King'. On cue all diners pushed back their chairs and stood up at attention holding their wine glasses to toast the king's health while the band struck "God Save the King", the British National Anthem. At the end of the anthem every one said, 'the King' and drank the wine toast to the emperor's health. Just as the diners sat down again, a bag piper bandsman trilling his bag pipe compulsively entered the dining hall from a side door and the shrill music from his bag pipe reverberated in the enclosed space. He went around the diners in a clockwise direction swaying his shoulders from side to side, in time to the beat of the music, in a swagger, special to bagpipers. After completing a circle once he halted behind the Commandant's chair and stopped playing the pipe. A waiter appeared by his side carrying a very large shot of rum in an oversized tumbler on a tray. Tweed got up and handed over the fiery liquid to the musician who threw it down his gullet, in one large gulp, to an appreciative applause from the diners. He kept the emptied flute back on the tray and swaggered out of the hall playing the bagpipe. A battery of waiters now appeared with goblets and cognac bottles and served the diners with the amber liquid. The diners warmed the goblets with their hands swirling the amber liquid in the goblets and sniffed at it to enjoy its wafting headiness as they took small sips there-from. Coffee and cigars also appeared after that and the waiters brought in ash trays and placed them in front of the smokers and in next to no time the room was filled with cigar and cigarette smoke. In a little while Hodson pushed back his chair and got up. This was a signal for others to follow suit.

He carried his cognac snifter to the ante-room where light hearted conversation continued. It was here that he commenced his conversation with a group of young officers on the social life at Wellington. Within a span of the ensuing fifteen minutes he had got to know that there were four dance parties every month, one each at the Madras Regimental Centre Officers' Mess, the Planter's Club and two at the Railway Institute where the railways', six piece combo band was in attendance. If the band was unavailable, 78 rpm records were played on a hand cranked, large horned, His Master's Voice Gramophone and couples danced to the golden tunes of the day. These parties drew a large number of British and Anglo-Indian couples and unattached young girls and boys. So there it was; a perfect setting for flings. Lonesome Sophie would have been swept off her feet most likely during one such party. After all, as a young 19 year old, Sophie had met John Blair her late husband also in one such assemblage at the Railway Institute in Madras a dozen and a half years back in 1929. She most likely must have had a repeat encounter here in the Nilgiris.

Young people were having a ball these days not only in the Nilgiris but also in New Delhi. While a middle aged Sophie was rumoured to be giving it away to young men in Madras, another middle aged woman or rather a lady was similarly having a good time with young officers in New Delhi. Yes, New Delhi where it was common talk that young aides to the Viceroy, Count Mountbatten were frolicking with Countess Mountbatten. It was rumoured that the youngsters on the Vice Regal staff had even twisted her title from Countess Mountbatten to Mountess Count-baton. He however had not believed in such gossip but then he had also not believed rumours about Sophie who turned out to be nothing more than a floozy. Hodson was confused. He just wanted this trip to end and get back to his work in New Delhi. And perhaps try his luck with the Mountess!

On his way out he was conducted to the table kept in the foyer where he signed the visitors' book under the watchful eyes of the photograph of General Nye, Colonel of the Regiment. Soon he was seen off by Tweed at the foyer and driven off to his living quarters in the planters' club with the liaison officer accompanying him. Within moments all the guests departed. Tweed then went to the band accompanied by his regimental officers and gave them a *shabash*, a well done, and presented them with two bottles of neatly packaged rum. He then complimented Havildar Devar, the mess havildar on a job well done. Bidding good night to all he too went towards his quarters and the remaining officers followed suit. Within minutes of their having left the mess building, the mess staff had cleared the premises and locked up the place and turned in for the night.

One hour after departure of Hodson, a Triumph Motor Cycle belonging to the Madras Regimental Centre came to life and its lone rider slowly eased the beast out of the Officers' Mess complex towards the road to Ooty. Once on the open road, the night rider gunned the Triumph into speed and was at his destination in Ooty, within thirty minutes flat. She had kept the gate of her villa ajar and he thus had no problem in entering the villa's compound. He parked the bike next to her red coloured

Buick Coupe. After dismounting he first closed the gate and then hurried up to the main building and pushed open the door. She was waiting there in her negligee and came into his arms as if she had been doing so, all her life. They kissed standing there for a long time. Both did not want the moment to end. They moved inwards, towards the bedroom, their lips still glued to each other, stopping at each step to continue exploring one another orally. It took them a long time to reach the double bed and then their slow march changed to a frenzied double as she let her negligee fall to the floor and then helped her lover to get undressed. Once out of their encumbered clothing they made love—slowly, very slowly. An hour later, a sated Sophie lay on her side in a fetal position, legs curled, looking out of the window into a moonlit night as her lover slept behind her also on his side facing her back. She could feel his breath on the back of her head, his chest intimately touching her back, his groin was joined with her buttocks and his hairy legs were coiled with her smooth ones. His upper arm was thrown across her nude body and his hand was cupping her breast. She considered her-self to be a most fortunate person to have found love two times in one life time. The first time had been with the Railway man in Madras and now it was in the Nilgiris with this wonderful Army man whom she would be marrying, soon. She had lost one love to an accident and she would ensure that she did not lose this one. She shut her eyes and went to sleep, her lips arched upwards in a smile of satisfaction. That's how they slept every night after coitus, she curled up in the hollow of his hunch, her back snuggled up against his chest; like two spoons.

She awoke at six and found the bed vacant. He had apparently left during the night without disturbing her. Her negligee which she had dropped on the carpeted floor last night was now carefully draped on the back of the reclining chair which she quickly donned and went out. His motor cycle was not there and the gate was closed. He was always meticulous.

She had met him about two months ago at the army mess where she had been invited by 2/Lt Moriarty a thin lanky Brit on the rolls of the Indian Army. She had met Moriarty a couple of times at the dance at the Railway Institute and he had invited her over to the army mess dance. During the dance, Moriarty had been plying Sophie with Bloody Marys and had started to paw her when she was on her fourth drink. Though inebriated, Sophie had successfully parried his advances and staggered out of the dance party. The slimy Moriarty mouthed an obscenity at her but did not bother to follow her out. She had wobbled up to and then leaned against her parked car, to control her swaying and unsuccessfully fumbled in her hand bag for the car key. It did not occur to her befuddled brain that she would be unable to even reverse the car out of the car park leave alone drive it on the hill roads in her drunk condition and that too at night. Cursing loudly she just stood there swaying back and forth but held on to the car lest she fall. She could sense the bile rising in her throat and knew that she was going to be sick. Suddenly she doubled up and vomited. The retching forced her away from the car and she was unable to keep her balance she swerved dangerously and then she passed out.

Her fall was cushioned by two strong hands of a stranger who appeared beside her out of nowhere in the darkness like a phantom. He had been silently monitoring the goings on at the dance and had observed her stumbling out of the party. He had followed her out from the back door of the mess and reached the parked Buick Coupe just when Sophie had thrown up and fainted.

She woke up many hours later with a start. She was having a nightmare. A horned devil had tied her to a bed and was prying her legs open. When she resisted with all her might he moved up and sat down on her breasts. He held his enormous curled up organ in his hand and used it as a whip and lashed her on both her cheeks, repeatedly with it, and then he tried to shove it into her mouth. That's when she awoke with a start, her forehead swathed in sweat. It took a moment for her bleary eyes to orientate herself to the real world and saw him sitting in an arm chair near her with his left hand carelessly thrown over his left leg and the right elbow resting on the chair's right arm and the fist of his right arm glued to his right cheek supporting the weight of his head intently watching her. This wasn't the fiend who was in her nightmare. His physique, his highly tanned handsome face and his sitting posture immediately brought Auguste Rodin's famous Bronze Sculpture, "The Thinker" to her mind. Only this sculpture moved as soon as he saw her awaken.

'Good Morning ma'am,' said the stranger. There was warmth in his clear voice. 'You have been stirring and mumbling for the past half hour. I reckoned you were in a bad dream and knew that the disturbing dream would soon awaken you,' he got up and tried to wipe the sweat from her brow but she stopped him and took the hand towel from his hand and mopped herself.

'I had readied some coffee for you. Black coffee is helpful in killing a hangover,' saying so he poured out steaming black coffee from a vacuum flask into a cup kept at her bed side table. The refreshing aroma of strong coffee was most welcoming for Sophie and she found herself staring at the tanned attractive stranger, who was totally engrossed in the decanting process. She accepted the coffee, from his proffered hand and took a sip. The hot black concoction scalded its way down her throat. By the end of the second cup her head had commenced to clear. He appeared to be courteous and mannered. He had softened the impact of her terrifying nightmare by terming it as a bad dream. Last night's horrendous events were like a kaleidoscope still spinning in her brain. She vaguely remembered having retched before passing out but nothing else. She would never forgive that snake Moriarty.

'Where am I?' she said looking at the handsome stranger warily. Gosh he looks like a Greek God, with a tan, was her first take.

'Ma'am you are in the Army Guest Room of the Madras Regimental Centre,' replied the stranger as he handed over another cup of coffee with a buttered bread toast to her. She declined the toast but the stranger said, 'some solid food will do you a world of good ma'am' and the order like timbre in his voice made her accept the toast. He was addressing her as "ma'am", just like the cowboys in Hollywood movies, and well brought-up Indians and British in junior positions did here. A bright smile lit up the urbane stranger's face when she hesitatingly bit into the de rigueur food. He was correct, the solid grub immediately gave a faded out Sophie some strength. She had been pumped with copious amounts of alcohol camouflaged in tomato juice by that scoundrel, Moriarty at the dance and all on an empty stomach which perhaps was the reason of her blacking out. She thanked the Lord that despite Moriarty's black designs, she had been able to get away from him unharmed. But what had transpired after she collapsed? Did she continue to remain unscathed or was advantage taken of her during her unconsciousness?

She looked down at her clothing and realized that she was wearing a large gent's shirt and not her own clothing.

'Who brought me here? Why am I in this male clothing? What has happened to my dress? Who removed my dress and changed my clothes?' were rapidly fired queries from Sophie.

'The shirt you are wearing is mine, ma'am. I am a bachelor and could not have got hold of female apparel in the middle of the night from anywhere. Your party dress had been completely soiled because you heaved onto it when you retched and fell unconscious. I carried you from the car park into this room, fetched a shirt from my room, removed your mucky clothes and replaced them with the clean shirt you are now wearing,' said the urbane cowboy. Sophie's hand quickly went to her breasts and then her groin and she heaved a sigh of relief when she found her brassier and panty still in place. The cowboy continued laconically, 'and I also removed your jewellery, ear tops and neck chain and have placed them in the small pocket containing your make up things, in your leather hand bag.' She was touched by the honest deeds of her savior. This handsome stranger was chivalrous in the true sense of the word. He had gallantly saved a damsel in distress, carried her into his castle and then stood guard over her. Like a true gentleman he had not taken advantage of her condition. Chivalry wasn't dead thought Sophie as she looked at him with admiration in her eyes. In contrast Moriarty had been a scoundrel forcing her with laced drinks, to wrong her against her wishes. It was paradoxical that she had come across two army men under the same roof of an army mess, on the same evening, one of whom, her host, had turned out to be a villain and the other, a total stranger, a gallant gentleman.

The stranger got up and went to a cupboard and returned holding her dress draped on a clothes' hanger in one hand and her leather bag, from which she had been unable to locate her car keys in her drunken state last night, in the other. The dress had been laundered and ironed to perfection. The leather of her closed hand bag seemed to be shining from a good buffing of wax and the brass lining on its access opening as well as its fastener, too was glowing from a rub of brass polish. He draped the dress on the back of a chair and put the handbag on her bed side table. He put a pair of large sized slippers on the floor next to her bed and pointed to a door and said, 'ma'am that is the bathroom. You may use it to freshen up and change back into your clothes again.' He had remained silent and taken no credit for wiping her clean of her vomit, laundering her soiled dress and remaining awake through the night, keeping a vigil over her.

The stranger left the room closing the door softly behind him as Sophie dismounted from the bed, slipped her dainty feet into those giant sized slippers and headed for the bath room carrying her dress and hand bag. She appeared quite clean wearing a washed shirt, all due to the efforts of the stranger. However the fact remained that she had puked last night and this thought made her feel grubby. The coffee and toast had helped but her head was still groggy with a dull headache. Maybe a bath would help to alleviate her mood. She closed the door of the bathroom behind her and then she hung her dress on the clothes hook and placed the hand bag on a shelf and looked around. It was a large bathroom with a bathtub, a wash basin and a water closet. On a shelf next to the wash basin rested fresh towels, a fresh cake of soap in a soap case, a new tooth brush and a tube of toothpaste. She removed the tooth brush from its cover, covered its bristles with toothpaste and commenced brushing her teeth. Moving around the spacious bathroom she plugged the bathtub drainage hole and opened its water taps, the hot as well as the cold one, to draw up a bath. She then lowered her panty and sat down on the WC and urinated.

She knew from past experience that men were uncouth in sexual matters, especially vain handsome men. Was she right in giving a clean chit to the handsome bloke who claimed to be her savior? Had she developed a weak spot for him?

STORY OF HARRY SINGH & SOPHIE KAUR

Was her perfunctory examination of her under clothing
adequate to signify that she had not been sullied during her
unconsciousness? Was her coming closer to the stranger,
infatuation or had she fallen head over heels for the guy? The
events were moving far too fast, she must remain pragmatic
in the matter. She wasn't too sure if she had been sexually
violated during her stupor. She therefore decided to put herself
through an acid test, which would put her mind to rest once
and for all. She inserted the middle and index fingers of her
left hand into her vagina and carried out an exploration while
continuing to brush her teeth with her right hand. She did not
encounter any tell tale signs of semen. She considered this two
finger examination a litmus test; proof enough to exonerate the
handsome stranger from any sexual wrong doing during the
night, when she was most vulnerable. Her savior was indeed a
remarkably good man and losing her heart to him did not seem
to be a mistake. Still brushing her teeth she removed her panty,
got up from the WC, tossed her panty in to the open space on
the shelf and yanked the cistern chain and saw water cascading
from the cistern into the WC, flushing it clean. She then moved
to the wash basin, soaped and washed her left hand, completed
her brushing and rinsed her mouth.

She then looked into the bathroom mirror and saw her
reflection. The over sized gent's apparel which went down to her
dimpled knees, hid her vital statistics of 34-30-34 but it revealed
hell of a lot more of her upper torso. Though all her shirt buttons
less the upper most had been fastened by the stranger, the large
girth of the neck collar of the shirt exposed the inner side of her
elevated white breasts and the décolleté between them. She lifted
the hem of her large sized wear till she could view the pubic-hair
triangle around her pussy in the mirror. Hell, she looked damn
sexy in this oversized male shirt. She inserted her hands under
the shirt and cupped her mammary. They were firm to her touch.
Taking off the stranger's shirt she was dressed in, she bundled
it up and then put this wrap to her nostrils, inhaling deeply.
The stranger's male pheromones came through her olfactory
senses and made her horny. Still holding the bundled shirt to her
nose with one hand, she unbuckled her bra with the other and
out popped two white beauties. She fingered the teats of these

209

two lovelies with her index finger and thumb and saw them becoming pea size and erect. She would have lost complete control over herself but for her persistent alcohol induced headache.

She removed the bundled shirt from her muzzle and hung it on the hook next to her dress, removed her loose bra and tossed it on to the shelf where it landed atop her panty and then she picked up the soap case and moved to the bath tub. She placed the soap in the soap niche, tested the temperature with her hand, finding it just right she turned off the faucets and climbed into the water. She soaped her firm breasts and her body and then scrubbed herself, thoroughly, especially down below. She had half a mind of setting aside the process of soaping and instead inserting her index finger into herself for manipulating her clitoris in the warmness of the water bath. In the event her unrelenting head ache forced her to discard her adventurous inclination and she just luxuriated in the warm water and let the pain in her head ebb away.

Twenty minutes later she stepped out of the bath and pulled the plug from the water outlet of the bath-tub to let the water out. She picked up a fresh towel and commenced drying herself as the water spiraled out through the small outlet of the bathtub making a deep guttural sound. She had towelled and practically made dry, her upper body and was giving one final rub with the large towel to her back when the dying whirlpool collapsed in the bathing fixture with a loud gurgling noise and the last drops of water dripped out through its outlet. And then it was suddenly all quiet. While mopping up her crotch in the silence of the bathroom, she suddenly pined to be near her bronze knight. So she hurriedly gave the final rubdown to her crotch and legs and cleansed her toes, picked up her bra and panty and pushed them into her hand bag and got into her dress sans the under clothing. She put on her jewellery, and a touch of make-up brought back colour to her cheeks and lips.

A nicely washed and freshened Sophie with a smiling visage, emerged from the bathroom, fully dressed in her own clothing holding the shirt of the stranger draped on a hanger in one hand and her hand bag in the other. She took one last whiff of his shirt while handing it over to the waiting gentleman.

Her nicely polished sandals lay next to a chair. She sat down on the chair, removed the large size bathroom slippers and slipped on her sandals, stood up and thanked him profusely and moved towards the door, she was about to exit the room when she slowly turned around and faced the stranger and gave him a good bye peck on the cheek and he reciprocated likewise. Then suddenly she took a step closer to him, stood on her toes and sought his lips with hers but he backed away. This was a problem with gentleman types, they don't even accept a thanks giving wet kiss with good grace. Nevertheless she was not put off by his retreat and continued in pursuit till his back was against the wall of the room and he could go back no further. She then managed to kiss him squarely on the lips. The gentleman stranger did not respond initially but her probing tongue in his mouth and her unrestrained bra-less breasts pinning against his torso and her panty-less groin pinioned against his crotch would have been too much even for a saint leave alone a soldier. She was successful in eliciting a response from him after a short while and they locked themselves in each others' arms, their lips glued. And that's how they remained for a long time, a very long time.

Later, much later he saw her off at the car. Both were careful not to step on the, dried up bile strewn in the car park. This time she had no problem in locating her car keys from her hand bag. She inserted the key into the car door, and opened it. He assisted her to get in behind the steering wheel and then carefully shut the car door. She pulled out her personal visiting card from her hand bag, cranked down the window glass of the door and gestured him to come nearer. She handed over the visiting card to him through the open window and then caught him by the shirt, pulled him down and kissed him yet again and then she extracted a promise from him, to visit her that evening. In no time she had started the car, reversed it out of the car park and after a quick wave of the hand she was on her way, the morning wind rushing in through the open window of her Buick Coupe tousling her hair, making her appearance even more desirable. A love affair had begun.

Some would later say that the expression of love was demonstrated by Sophie first. Others would argue that love was initially expressed by him when he had tailed her out of the mess and carried back an unconscious Sophie in his arms even though she was oblivious of his love due to her condition at that time. However, it would be fair to say that both of them had fallen in love at first sight. They were fifteen days into their affair when they decided to get married. She insisted on his chucking the army and he acquiesced. She considered the army service as a high risk profession. Her apprehension was that she may lose him the way she had lost her first husband, who had been killed while on duty because his' too had been a high risk occupation. She told him of her grand plans for the future. Her desire to settle down in Europe, now that the war was over; where he would be able to help her look after her estates and other businesses; which certainly was a more sedate line of work than the army. She divulged to him her yearning to raise a family, her desire to take him on long cruises and sightseeing and so on. He agreed to her every wish. He was truly in love with her and did not want to be separated from her, even for an instant.

—◀o▶—

She came back inside and went to the kitchen and filled the tea kettle with three cups of water and plugged it into the electric socket. She always boiled three cups of water before appearance of the maid, two for herself and one for the maid. The maid came in before breakfast and took care of all the work at the villa for the whole day and went away only at night after preparation of the dinner. Sophie had observed that the maid on arrival would not commence work before imbibing a cup of tea to shake away her early morning blues. Since the yawning maid wasted a lot of time, brewing her cup of tea Sophie found it expedient to keep a cup of tea ready for her to get her going as soon as she came in. So she commenced adding some additional water in her morning tea quota resulting in a cup of tea being readily available for the maid each morning and that got her going with her household chores immediately on arrival. And it also kept the maid's yawns at bay.

She added three spoons of tea leaves into a tea pot and then poured the steaming water from the kettle into the pot and covered the pot with a woollen tea-cozy to keep it hot. She placed a cup and saucer, a tea spoon, a strainer, a milk pot and a sugar pot on the dining table and brought the covered teapot on a tray from the kitchen. She poured its dark amber coloured contents into the tea cup through the strainer and swathed the tea pot with the woollen wrap again. She then added milk and sugar, to the tea cup, gave it a stir with the tea spoon and a purr of satisfaction escaped from her lips as she took her first sip of the day. Carrying the cup she went back into the bed room and saw the neatly folded white paper lying under the base of the table lamp beside the bed. She unfolded it and immediately recognised his child like hand writing on the paper. She read it.

Good Morning, honey,

I went away before first light when you were still soundly asleep.
You did not even stir when I pecked your lips. Keep the bed warm lover, the soldier will be back in the evening.

Your loving slave

You won't be soldiering for long lover, she thought, as she proceeded to the dining room to replenish her tea cup, taking his note along. She placed the epistle on the dining table and re-read it. His handwriting wasn't the only thing child like about him, she mused. He was child like in other ways as well. He loved to fondle and suckle her breasts like a child and she loved to let him do so. She had realized that he not only wanted a lover but a lover who could mother him as well perhaps due to some short coming in his upbringing as a child. Oh, how she loved playing both roles. With his army service getting out of the way soon, they could now sit down and decide on the wedding date and their future plans. Then she could continue to play both roles for the rest of her life. She had emptied her second cup of tea by the time the maid arrived for duty.

ADIEU

Wellington Railway Station, Madras
5 May 1947 (Morning)

While Sophie was sedately sipping her second cuppa of the morning at her villa in Ooty, twelve miles down the road, Wellington Railway Station, was a hub of activity this morning. The guests who had come to witness yesterday's parade were assembled at the station to catch the morning outgoing train for their return journey. There were numerous LOs and other staff in uniform to ensure a smooth departure of the invitees. In the middle of the platform stood Colonel Tweed and his staff officer and just behind them stood personnel of the mess detachment with their wherewithal. To one side of the mess detachment stood a guard of one NCO and three soldiers from the Madras Regiment. They had all positioned themselves in the middle of the platform since General Hodson's saloon was expected to be coupled to the middle of train rake. The mess detachment and the guard would accompany Lt General Hodson and travel in two of the cabins of the saloon. The guard was for security as well as ceremonial purposes, the mess staff had more practical use. They would cook his meals in the saloon kitchenette and serve it to him in his cabin during the journey.

At the far end of the platform stood the three Sikh soldiers along with their *thambi* friend, who had come to see them off.

A sound of the siren of the approaching pilot vehicle implied that Hodson's cavalcade was about to arrive and every one immediately became alert. The VIP's vehicles drove onto the ground level platform and Hodson dismounted from his car and was received by Tweed. The accompanying LO got the VIP's baggage placed on the platform. Soon the small narrow gauge toy like train, powered by a Compound "X" Class Locomotive made by the Swiss Locomotives Machine Works

214

located at Winterthur, Switzerland having two high pressure and two low pressure cylinders, chugged onto the platform. The low pressure cylinders were used for powering the rack wheels and were mounted above the main high pressure cylinders which drove the main wheels. Such compound engines were a necessity, since the gradient of the narrow track in the Nilgiris was very steep. One of the Sikh soldiers, the older one, who was the locomotive buff, did not move ahead to check out the engine in pursuit of his hobby today. The zealot had completed his appraisal of this engine during their inward journey to Wellington a couple of days back.

A railway attendant dismounted from the saloon carrying two red coloured star plates and inserted one of them into the recess made for the purpose on the side of the carriage. Its three, five pointed, brass stars shining in the morning Sun left no doubt to any one of the high rank and status of the VIP travelling in that carriage. The attendant proceeded to do likewise on the far side of the coach as well. Soon the conducting guard of the train, an Anglo Indian appeared and after checking if the star plate had been properly embedded in its niche, he joined Hodson and Tweed on the platform and got into a conversation with them. As soon as the LO informed Hodson that baggage, the army guard and the mess detachment were in place, a round of handshakes and saluting followed and Hodson entrained into the plush cabin of his saloon. The train guard gave the traditional 'all aboard' call, waved the green flag and mounted his cabin. Devar shook hands with his Sikh cronies through the open window of their compartment and Tweed and others waved a good bye in the direction of Hodson's three star embellished compartment. The compound engine gave a shrill whistle and the train commenced its journey.

As soon as the train negotiated the first bend on its down-hill journey, a waiter appeared in front of a pensive Hodson through a small door vestibuled to the kitchenette, with a hot cup of coffee and a couple of chocolate wafer biscuit and that morning's neatly folded "South India Herald". He placed the coffee bearing tray and the folded newspaper on the low table in front of the VIP and retreated back into the adjoining kitchenette. Hodson opened the newspaper dated 5

May 1947 and saw a large, nine inch tall photograph, spread over four columns, of him in salute on the front page. The Headlines in large bold capital letters proclaimed "GLORY AT WELLINGTON—HODSON DECORATES BRAVE TAMILS AT INVESTITURE PARADE". The story below the picture was date-lined Wellington dated 4 May 1947. He concentrated on the photograph where some spectator stands were visible in the background. He could vaguely make out Sophie in one of the stands. Looking at her blurred snap, Hodson took a sip of the espresso and pondered if Sophie would have had her two cups of morning tea by now. He got pangs of envy just visualizing the tea ceremony being performed by the floozy in her negligee, with active participation of her, semi-nude, new lover. Suddenly the espresso didn't taste too well and the shrill whistle of the engine sounded most annoying to the General. The magnificent scenery of the tea gardens, rising and falling on the rolling Nilgiri hill-sides, passing by his compartment windows, too did not look so gorgeous to him anymore. The words spoken by his illustrious name-sake William Hodson at Lucknow in the last century and recorded in History had been "I hope I have done my duty". The words which hissed out from the Hodson travelling in the toy like train today were, "the fucking bitch". Luckily there was no historian around to record his words.

◄○►

Three coaches to the rear, the three Sikhs looked out of their compartment windows, their eyes resting upon the picturesque sloping landscape of the Nilgiri Hills as the train meandered, down-hill, towards the plains. They could see the broad leafed jackfruit trees, their trunks heavy with large fruits, green tea-bushes on the undulating slopes interspersed with white huts with red tiled roofs. The sight of young girls in colourful dresses, deftly plucking the tea leaves and buds and storing them in the wicker baskets strapped to their backs brought a chuckle from Matric. 'You know boss, seeing these young lassies harvesting tea, brings to my mind that the *asli*, real, Devar's girl must also be similarly picking tea leaves in a tea garden somewhere in

Ceylon and the scoundrel could be helping her carry the heavy tea laden basket to the tea processing factory.'

'Hey why the hell did you have to bring in the name of that *behan chod,* and spoil this beautiful morning,' replied Lachu. 'You can take it from me that the offending, cock flashing and groin thrusting, bastard must be rewarding himself by "cocking her nook", behind a tea bush in Ceylon, than giving the poor girl a helping hand.'

'Agreed, the bastard indeed had a one track mind,' said Matric. 'It really hurt when the bastard had flashed his organ at us from the coal freight and made that profane gesticulation from the ferry boat.'

'Yeah I have often wished that I come across the mother *chod* somehow, somewhere and then I would render his apparatus unserviceable for good,' said a fuming Lachu.

Harry could not blame Lachu for his angry outburst, time to butt in and cool the wrestler. 'Relax boys, relax. Let us change the subject. That so-and-so may have got the better of us but we are no less. Look at Lachu, he has just coined a new phrase, off the cuff, which succinctly defines the vulgar mocking antics of that devil,' said Harry.

'Kudos to you wrestler, your "cocking a nook" creation may find a place in the English lexicon one day,' said Matric in support.

'That one unpleasant incident which happened five years ago was like a bad dream, that's all. Let us try and forget that occurrence. You know, time is a great healer. Look at the positives. Our replacement of that bandicoot, the new Devar, has made us proud. He has been awarded a medal for bravery at the parade yesterday,' said Jemadar Harinder Singh. 'As far as we are concerned he is the only Devar; period. So put that incident of the *asli thambi* behind you. We all have moved on in life. You are both NCOs now and are happily married to girls you love; and God willing, you will sooner than later become VCOs and also proud fathers like me. So relax and enjoy life.'

'Right boss, let us forget about that Ceylonese scoundrel,' said Lachu, 'and talk about our *thambi*.'

'Right, Sahib.' said Matric. "*Ustad*" had been upgraded to "Sahib" in the forms of address because on being promoted a VCO, Jemadar Harinder was now entitled the prefix "Sahib".

'Did our *thambi* disclose if he has any marriage plans in the offing?' asked Lachu.

'He wasn't specific but he did hint that he may soon tie the knot,' replied Harry.

'Any idea who the lucky, girl might be?' enquired Matric.

'Nope, he was mighty secretive there.'

'Well, I hope she adapts to the army environment.'

'More importantly she should be able to adjust with us and not come in the way of our friendship,' commented Lachu.

'Well said wrestler.'

———◄○►———

In the event *thambi* suddenly became incognito and vanished from their lives. Letters written to him by the trio were returned undelivered by the postal authorities. The three were apprehensive about his well being. Lachu was sure that he had married and it was his wife who had told him to sever ties with them and that was the reason behind his sudden disappearance from their lives.

Harry however took a more pragmatic view. He wrote to Madras Regiment Record Office inquiring about his whereabouts. A few days later he received a reply to his query— the concerned individual had taken premature discharge from the Army on compassionate grounds in July 1947. His address in his papers continued to be Village & PO Machiwara, District Ludhiana, Punjab; this piece of news only increased their anxiety. Now, where the hell had he vanished to? Not to Ceylon like the *asli* one, they hoped. They could do nothing but wait. And perhaps forget him with passage of time.

———◄○►———

THE FINAL ENCOUNTER

Arrivals

28 August 1957 (Afternoon)
Safdarjung Airport, New Delhi

The sleepy atmosphere around the modest terminal building at Safdarjung Airport was slowly coming to life with a surge in vehicular activity, on this sultry afternoon of Wednesday the 28 August 1957. This airport was called Wellington Airports during the British Raj and had been rechristened to its present name in 1947 when India attained independence. It serviced independent India's capital, New Delhi but plans were afoot to move all operations to Palam Airport in West Delhi. Presently only the Indian Air Force operated out of Palam Airport. The shift to Palam was necessary since Safdarjung, located on the periphery of Lutyen's Delhi would soon be unable to handle bigger jet engine aircraft or increased volume of air traffic because it did not have scope of further expansion. The plan envisaged that the Delhi Flying Club would continue to operate from Safdarjung while all other operations would be shifted out to Palam.

While Safdarjung aerodrome took its name from nearby mausoleum of Safdarjung who had served his Mughal masters faithfully, first, as *Nawab* or Governor of Oudh, in present day state of UP and later, as *Wazir or* Chief Minister of India; Palam airport took its name from a nearby village of the same name. The proliferation in the bustle around the terminal at Safdarjung meant that a flight was either coming in to land shortly or a flight was scheduled to depart soon or perhaps both.

Two dark blue coaches and that many station wagons with the letters BOAC emblazoned in white on their flanks came to a halt, one behind the other in front of the unpretentious airport terminal. About two score passengers, majority of them foreign nationals poured out from the coaches, collected their baggage from the hold at the rear of the coaches and made their way into the terminal building through the "DEPARTURES" entrance. A BOAC crew comprising three men and five young women, all in their blue uniforms ambled out of the two station wagons leisurely. Two of the male members in trousers and tunics with peak caps were the pilots and the third was either its navigator or onboard engineer. Their pretty female compatriots wearing blouses and tight skirts with caps worn tilted on their heads were surely the airhostesses. They all carried small overnight attaché cases and sauntered behind the passengers into the terminal through the same gate. Having disgorged their commuters, the two coaches and the two station wagons parked themselves in the area reserved for them in the vehicle park.

This meant that there was a BOAC flight arriving soon whose tired crew would be replaced by a fresh one. The crew getting off duty and disembarking passengers would be ferried to the city by the waiting empty BOAC vehicles and the taxis. The same BOAC aircraft was likely to be used for a departing flight most probably to an international destination with the fresh crew which had entered the terminal building just now. The passengers of this outgoing flight were probably completing their embarkation formalities inside the departure hall of the terminal at this very moment. Some more private cars and taxis came and emptied their passenger loads and either went away or parked themselves in the car park situated just beyond the huddle of taxis standing under a couple of large and shady *neem* trees, their Sikh drivers either lounging or snoozing on the seats inside their black and yellow cabs.

In the midst of all this activity, three cars, all American sedans, came rolling into the airport area. The first two cars went straight to the parking lot and parked in two slots, nearer to the airport terminal. A five foot seven tall, slim, man and his partner, a slender young woman, a couple of inches shorter than him, emerged from the, double tone blue, Chevrolet Bel Air. The man was dressed in a brown lounge suit, a striped tie and a sky blue turban. Beard trimmed and his brown brogue shoes shining. Expensive links kept the cuffs of his white silk shirt together. His partner adorned an expensive light blue *Banarsi* silk *saree,* the popular and yet graceful ladies' wear of India. It took its prefix from the town of Banaras which specializes in the manufacture of this six yard long wrap-around sarong for rich Indian women. Her *saree* had a broad golden thread brocade border and she wore a matching blouse with her dress. Her dainty feet were clad in heeled sandals, her hair was dressed in an elegant bob, a powdered nose with rouge on her cheeks, a dark red lipstick on her lips and kohl in her eyes completed her make-up. She had long well manicured fingers which one would associate with an artist but a closer look showed that her hands were coarse indicating that they had performed rough and tough jobs in the past. She was decked up in a diamond studded necklace with matching bracelets and a gold Rolex watch embellished her wrist. The two strolled side by side towards the modest airport terminal building and their appearance would have drawn the word "becoming" or "fetching" from any one observing them walking together.

The second car was a whale backed black Ford Mercury from which had alighted another Sikh couple. The man must have been around five feet eight inches tall but his stocky built gave the impression of his being shorter than his real height. His bulging muscles could be discerned through his tight fitting grey flannel lounge suite and his light blue cotton shirt clung to his chest. The shirt was certainly a size too small for the gent; so-much-so that the top of his shirt collar had remained unbuttoned. As a result the front of his thick neck was visible over the knot of the triple coloured striped necktie which noosed around his neck. Dark blue and golden yellow stripes of his necktie were interspersed with light red pin stripes and it was identical to the one adorned by the first Sikh. His head was crowned by a red turban tied in a perfect Patiala style with its six neat folds clearly visible and parallel to each other. His well groomed beard had surely seen the service of a scissors quite regularly. He wore officer pattern shining black shoes. He had the right kind of clothes which one would associate with rich people but yet he seemed ill at ease in his formal wear and would have been more at ease in a tee shirt performing duties of a bouncer in a joint. His wife too adorned a *Banarsi saree,* a green one, having a black border and a matching blouse. Her hair was combed back and done up in a bun which rested on the nape of her neck. She appeared to have a flat chest and only the rubber padded cones in her bra gave her a semblance of a bosom. Her make-up was gaudy, as was her expensive jewellery and wrist watch, which embellished her neck and arms. She was a wee bit taller than her hubby hence her preferred foot wear should have been heel-less but instead she was sporting stiletto high heeled sandals. As a result their height difference appeared to be exacerbated. The illusion, of his being shorter than he really was and she being taller than she actually was, seemed exaggerated as the two walked towards the airport terminal. From a distance they might have given the impression of a tall Laurel and short Hardy and that in a way, had been the long and the short of their story, all through their one decade of conjugal life.

These two young Sikh couples had no baggage with them which implied, they were not passengers but had come to see off or receive someone. Both couples greeted each other effusively near the terminal building. They did not enter the building but stood outside, chatting and waiting.

Soon a third car, an ivory coloured Buick Road-master, chauffer driven, came to halt in-front of the two waiting couples and the two waiting men opened the rear doors of the sedan with alacrity and from it alighted a middle aged Sikh couple. The man was in a cream gabardine suite, his thick salt and pepper beard neatly tied and kept in place under a beard net. Brown shoes shining, links on his Arrow shirt sleeve cuffs were strikingly ornate and he too sported the same striped necktie as the other two. He greeted the others in a booming *Sat Sri Akal*, the Sikh greeting with folded hands as he stepped out of the sedan. He then shook hands with the waiting men. The hand shake exposed the heavy golden *karas*, Sikh bangles, one of the five *"Ks"*, the symbols of their religion, worn on their right wrists. He took out a gold *killi* from his pocket and tried to insert any unruly hair back into his beard net and under the turban with it, more out of habit than necessity. His matronly wife emerged from the other door helped by the trim Sikh. She wore an expensive yet simple Punjabi dress, her dyed hair was worn down her back in a, three strand interwoven *guth* or braid. But that's where the simplicity ended. She wore an expensive diamond studded gold necklace with matching ear rings. Her forearms were heavy with a dozen matching gold bangles and a diamond and ruby studded bracelet. A gold Rolex watch strapped to her left wrist with a twin black silken cord strap, held together by gold loops and secured by a gold buckle, peeped out between these trappings. The accoutrements jingled when she took the bouquet of roses from the proffered hand of the chauffer.

A couple of commonalities which stood out in the three men, apart from their shared religious calling, were their alliance to each other through the common striped necktie and their being well heeled, probably neo rich. As it will soon emerge, both these observations were indeed true. Before they made their entry into the building through the "ARRIVALS" door, the elder, thick bearded Sikh checked the time on his radium dial Rolex automatic wrist watch and commented that they were well in time. He, holding the hand of his bouquet bearing wife then led the way into the terminus through the "ARRIVALS" entrance. The other two couples followed in their trail. Once inside, they occupied a chair array and commenced waiting for arrival of the BOAC flight carrying their guest, who too was surely, linked to them via the striped necktie.

When the three Sikh couples had just about sat down inside the terminal and commenced chatting, a maroon coloured Rolls Royce with the erstwhile Jaipur state, coat of arms painted on its flanks came to a silent halt in front of the building. A Rajput sporting a streamer trailing, Rajputana style turban, attired in a white Jodhpur tunic over his *khaki* riding breeches and wearing riding boots, dismounted from the co-driver's seat of the Rolls and also entered through the "ARRIVALS" entrance. The Rolls meanwhile proceeded to the car park.

On entering the terminal the Rajput surveyed the scene inside and in a moment focused on the three Sikh couples. By the deference shown to the Sikh with the grey beard by the others, he rightly assessed that he was their boss in some sort of a way. Accordingly he walked up and tapped the honcho on the shoulder.

―◄○►―

Palam Airport

When the maroon Rolls, was reversing into a parking space in the Car Park, at Safdarjung, eight miles to its West, at Palam Airport, a cavalcade of half a dozen assorted, olive green army vehicles was entering the restricted zone of the airport. This section was the air force station of the Indian Air Force and was the hub of its flight, training and maintenance activities. It was also used by government guests, minister rank politicians and the like for arrival and departure by exclusive dedicated aircraft. The arriving motorcade consisted of a couple of Hindustan Land Master cars, built at Calcutta by Hindustan Motors on license from the parent Morris Motor Company of Oxford, England, two Land Rovers, one Willy's Jeep and an army truck 15 cwt, all of World War II vintage. Rulers of Independent India did not believe in upgrading Army equipment since they assessed no future conflicts were likely to take place. Hence the Indian army continued to flog WW-II equipment left behind by the British in August 1947, at the time of independence ten years ago.

One Colonel of the Indian Army wearing an arm band on the shirt sleeve of his olive green uniform on which were embroidered the letters "LO" in capitals dismounted from the leading vehicle and was received by an Air Force Squadron Leader who too had a similar arm band on the sleeve of his *khaki* bush shirt walking out uniform. The two LOs or Liaison Officers conferred with each other in hushed tones and then signalled the air force police to marshal the vehicles for the return journey. As the army vehicles were being lined up, an Austin Devon, bearing a diplomatic corps number, on a blue no plate, belonging to the British High Commission also appeared on the scene. The British Military Attaché, a major from the British Army disembarked from the pretty Austin and was welcomed by the two LOs with a handshake. The three entered the small but neat reception building of the air force. On the far side of the building facing the taxi runway, a neat banner had been suitably hung, which read, "A WARM WELCOME TO THE BRITISH DEFENCE DELEGATION".

They were soon joined by a betel nut chewing short statured official from the Ministry of External Affairs, who introduced himself as Mr. Harkesh Kumar, Under Secretary. He was dressed in a white bush shirt and grey trousers whose visit to the *dhobi* was long overdue. He was wearing loafer shoes of undeterminable colour which had definitely not seen the service of shoe polish or brush for a long time. In India one can generally pinpoint the area of birth of most individuals from their physical features or the pigment of their skin, or their accent, pronunciation, eating habits and so on. The reader has already sampled this in the case of Mr. Doraiswamy the Madrasi interpreter at the parade in Wellington Barracks ten years ago. The domicile of the civil servant could be roughly estimated from his *paan,* betel nut leaf, chewing past-time. He was undeniably from one of the Eastern states, Bengal or Assam or Jharkhand region of Bihar. The confirmatory evidence would spill forth only if the fellow had an accent or elocution special to a certain group.

It is said that one day a *paan* chewing Indian, visited the Marks & Spencer Store on Oxford Street, London. Luckily, the sales-man attending on him had spent some years on His Majesty's Service in British India and recognized that the red in the mouth of the Indian was not blood but just the effect of *paan* and hence did not panic. He however could not determine the exact demand of the gent who wanted to buy some *"Shaarts".* Since the slogan of M&S was : "The customer is always and completely right!", the salesman prudently placed two piles of merchandise on the counter in front of the customer; one pile had shirts and the other contained shorts and invited the client to make a choice.

'And pray my good man, why have you placed two types of garments before me when I only require *"Shaarts"*?' retorted the Indian, exposing the red cavernous mouth once again.

'Well it's like this sir,' replied the sales person civilly, 'though I consider myself conversant with the Indian milieu, I was unable to comprehend your exact requirement for merchandise. I could also not figure out your correct domicile which would have enabled me hazard a guess of your need. Since Punjabis pronounce "shorts" as "shaarts" and conversely, Bengalis call "shirts" as "shaarts", I have placed these two items of clothing before you. If you hail from the Punjab then a selection from the pile of shorts will most certainly meet your requirement. But in case you are from Bengal then you are definitely at the Marks & Spencer to procure the merchandise placed in the shirt stack.'

The shopper picked up two shirts, one white, whiter than snow and the other even more crimson than the colour of the saliva in his mouth and stomped to the payment counter. The petite girl cashier fainted as soon as she saw, what she believed, was a profusely haemorrhaging oral-cavity of the man. Whilst the alarmed, staff, got busy in reviving the teller, the Indian walked out, with the merchandise tucked under his arm, without clearing his bill or looking back. It is said that this was the only occasion when merchandise was pilfered during day light hours, in full view of the security and staff of the Marks & Spencer. No Prizes, Marks or Pence, to the reader for guessing the domicile of the buyer. They say that the London metropolitan police were pulling their hair out, in helplessness, since they could not apprehend the dishonest patron. The man had diplomatic immunity.

Here at Palam, one did not have to wait for long to establish the domicile of the *paan* relishing, untidy civil servant prancing about in the waiting hall of the Air Force area. He spewed forth the clinching evidence along with a spray of red saliva when he expansively suggested that they all "shit" down comfortably and enjoy a cup of tea while waiting for the arrival of the delegates. The British Military Attaché had audibly dittoed the jolly good idea of "Mr. 'arkesh" to sit down "to 'ave tea". Blimey he too had an accent. While in the inflection of Mr. Harkesh Kumar, the letter "S" had sounded as "Sh" in the word "Sit", which was special to the Eastern state of Bengal, the Brit had not aspirated which was a unique to the cockneys of East London. Mr. Harkesh Kumar was definitely from Bengal, no doubt about it and the English man most likely, a cockney from East end of London. However the place of residence of the two Indian LOs could not be determined by this rule of the thumb. They seemed to have mastered the art of keeping their burrs and annoying traits under wraps.

The reception party consisting of the Bengali, the Indian defense service officers and the East Londoner did not have to wait long for the plane. They had just finished their cuppa when a corporal announced that the RAF Dakota carrying the British delegation had been cleared for landing. The LOs were joined by the Air Force station commander as the twin engine Dakota taxied and was guided to its parking slot, a short distance from the reception building and cut its engines, which spluttered to a stop and its two propellers came to a halt.

The five-man British delegation alighted from the RAF Dakota and was received by the reception party, the civil-servant in the lead, as laid down in the protocol. They were not put off by the red mouth or shabby appearance of the civilian because each one of the delegates had served in British India. The delegation comprised retired officers who had served in India during the British Raj and was led by Lt Gen Eric Hodson and his deputy leader was Colonel Price. There was one naval officer and two air-force guys. They were in India to offer Vickers tanks to the Indian Army, Hunter aircraft to the IAF and an old aircraft carrier to the Navy. Service aircraft especially the size of a Dakota are designed for carriage of cargo rather than passengers and are hence sans toilets. For this reason, the first thing passengers do after deplaning from a service plane is to rush to the loo to take a leak. However the delegates on deplaning from the RAF Dakota had to agonizingly control their urge even though their bladders were bursting and go through the customary ritual of handshakes and introductions with contrived smiles on their faces. And then they rushed to the urinals at speed. Their smiles on exit from the toilets were certainly not synthetic.

The traditional cup of tea and spicy Indian snacks which followed, were genuinely relished by them. Their baggage was unloaded from the Dakota by a few airmen and an official from customs politely asked if the delegates wanted to declare any item debarred from entry into India. Getting a negative response from the delegates he cleared their baggage without much ado.

An official from immigration was at hand who stamped the delegates' passports with the "Arrival" rubber seal. The baggage was loaded onto the truck brought for the purpose. Arrival formalities completed the delegates moved out to their waiting vehicles which they identified from their names boldly written on paper slips pasted on the left side of their windscreens. The senior LO and the leader of the delegation got into the front vehicle and the motorcade pulled out of the restricted airport area and headed towards the Imperial Hotel, ten miles away, on Queensway. Everything had gone like clockwork precision so far.

———————◄o►———————

Safdarjung Airport

Just as the cavalcade of army vehicles carrying the delegation was departing from the Palam air force area, eight miles away, the terrace of the main airport terminal building of Safdarjung Airport was jam-packed with people, their eyes focussed on the runway. This motley crowd had come to receive, incoming guests, arriving by the inward bound BOAC flight. They were on the roof of the building to witness the landing of the aircraft and to see their near and dear ones from close proximity, when they emerged from the plane. Soon they saw a BOAC Super Constellation make a three point touch down on the main runway of the airport. Amongst the observers on the terrace were the three Sikh gentlemen with their spouses. The turbaned Rajput who had arrived by the Rolls stood a couple of steps behind them. Their guests would perhaps be unbuckling their seat belts in the first class section of the Super Connie at this very moment.

The three couples and the turbaned Rajput had been chatting in the terminal hall a moment ago awaiting the arrival of the flight. The Rajput who had tapped the elder Sikh on the shoulder was the *munshi,* secretary, to his Royal Highness the erstwhile Maharaja of Jaipur. The Maharaj had sent him with his personal

Rolls for conveyance of the arriving guests from Amsterdam during their stay in New Delhi. He had therefore married up with them at the terminal for this purpose. These past few moments the *munshi* had been regaling them with stories of travels of the Royals, their parties, their hunts and of their treasures. They soon learnt that the arriving guests were not only good friends of his Highness but were also his neighbours in France since both had adjoining villas on the French Riviera. They were all ears to the Rajput's account of the Riviera where he had accompanied the Royals a number of times. The ladies listened with rapt attention to the explicit erudition of the unparalleled beauty of their villa and the Riviera by the *munshi*.

Their tête-à-tête had been cut short when the tannoy in the reception area expectedly came to life with a husky voice of a female announcer, 'May I have your attention please. British Overseas Airways Corporation Flight BA-113 from London via Amsterdam, Paris, Beirut and Aden will be arriving shortly. Thank you.'

The announcement triggered an exodus of the waiting throng towards the flight of stairs leading to the terrace. The three couples had moved upstairs along with the crowd. The husky voice, repeating the arrival announcement over the tannoy, followed them while they ascended the stairs. Once on the terrace, they jockeyed for a vantage position nearer to the railing so that they could not only see the flight come in but more importantly, from where they would be able to wave at their guests as soon as they emerged from the aircraft door. They had seen the big airliner land through the simmering haze and then make its way towards the terminal building. The dolphin shaped aircraft with three tail fins taxied to its parking slot and cut its four large engines. Two sets of stair-cases were manually wheeled by the airport staff into position one at the front exit and the other at the rear door and chocks were positioned under their wheels. And passenger started to file out from the Super Connie.

They emerged from the front exit of the plane, side by side and halted for a moment at the top landing of the stairs. They looked towards the multitude on the terrace of the terminal and their attention was immediately drawn towards the waving six. Devar and his beautiful companion waved back enthusiastically at Harry, Matric and Lachu and their consorts before commencing their descent down the flight of steps, carefully, holding on to the banister on the flank of the, not so steady, stairs.

'She is as pretty as she was at our first acquaintance. She does not seem to have aged in these so many years,' said Jagtaro. 'How long has it been since that encounter in Machiwara?'

'Well, that meeting was on the day of our first Republic Day. That's 26 January 1950. That would put the meeting, a month over seven and a half years ago,' replied Matric's wife Sohni.

'You know that meeting is etched in all our minds like an engraving,' said Harry. All six smiled in reminiscence.

They had mused over that first engagement and the kaleidoscopic events that followed a number of times whenever they were together. They had all but written off *thambi* from their lives after he vanished from their horizon and became incommunicado. He had broken all communications with them ever since they had bid farewell to each other at Wellington Railway Station on the morning of the day following the investiture parade in May 1947.

He however had resurfaced suddenly, two years later through a letter to Harry, to their pleasant surprise. The letter had been originated from a European country, whose name was unknown to Harry at that point in time. The dispatch informed Harry that he was now settled abroad and was in fine fettle and would be visiting India in January of the following year. He had desired that all the three friends be present with their spouses at Machiwara on Thursday, the 26th of January 1950.

Harry had written to the other two accordingly. After taking leave of absence from their units, Lachu had picked up his wife Veena from Patiala. Matric had done like wise and accompanied his wife from Amritsar, where he was now settled, after having shifted from Lahore, at the time of the partition of the nation. They had all then travelled to Machiwara to keep appointment with Devar.

On 26 January 1950, whilst Dr Rajendra Prasad, the phlegmatic, first President of the Republic of India was taking a salute of an impressive army parade, on Kingsway, New Delhi on the occasion of first Republic day of the country; the congregation of three friends with their wives was patiently waiting at Harry's house, sitting on low *charpoys,* cots, in its sunny courtyard, not far from the two tethered cows and that many calves. The village bull had been performing his duty diligently and the single cow and calf gifted by Devar on that heady day seven years ago, had multiplied to double that number. While they had been imbibing sweetened milk and exchanging gossip, the women had remained busy putting together a meal of *sarson ka saag,* mustard leaf vegetable and *makki ki roti,* maize chapattis, a known favourite of *thambi.*

A knock on the door, with the link of the dangling chain latch, had announced *Thambi's* arrival. Harry had sprung up like a jack in the box and run to the door and held it open. And there he was, suited and booted like a *gora* sahib with a memsahib on the crook of his arm. The sight of a memsahib holding on to *thambi's* arm had rendered Harry speechless.

'Hello Harry sahib,' he had said. 'Aren't you going to call us in?' So saying he had brushed past a dumb-founded Harry, the amused memsahib still on the crook of his arm. If Harry had been dumbfounded the remainder congregation was thunderstruck. It took some time for them to become cognizant and that too only when Devar looking at Jagtaro had said, 'hello sis, I did surprise all of you this time, didn't I?'

A flabbergasted Jagtar Kaur had been the first to gather her wits, when she exclaimed! '*Ve veera ay kaur vargi gori tere naal kaun hai*, hey brother who is this princess-like foreign madam with you?'

'She is my wife Sophie,' Devar had announced.

And then there had been a tumultuous clamour, as each one introduced himself or herself to the new arrival. Appearance of the taxi driver, who had driven Devar and Sophie from New Delhi, on the scene, carrying two large bags full of gifts and a child's tricycle only added to the chaos. The insistence of six year old, Harry junior to commence pedalling his three wheeled gift further compounded matters. The turmoil and the noise had made the bovines to shy and fidget and choose that very moment to pass water and dung, adding to the mayhem. It had taken better part of an hour for things to settle down by when the foreign gifts had been distributed and admired. Everyone had got a wrist-watch, men had got shirts and trousers, neckties, cuff links and tie pins while the ladies had been given vanity boxes, containing perfumes, broaches, lace lingerie and other make up toiletries like lipsticks, nail polish and face-powders etcetera.

This was followed by lunch consisting of *sarson ka saag* and *makki ki roti* served with large dollops of home churned butter, chased by a glass of butter milk. They had all been surprised that Sophie had not only relished the meal, just like the others but had also given a loud, post meal burp, to show her appreciation of the food. She had washed her hands at the, hand cranked, water pump and had insisted taking her turn to pump the lever to enable others to also wash up. Lachu's apprehension that she may become a hurdle in their friendship was laid to rest. She had passed his scrutiny with flying colours. She had not only attuned with them but in a sense became a part of them in just one meeting. Jagtar Kaur had therefore christened her as Sophie Kaur. Kaur in Punjabi means "Princess" and is customarily used as a suffix to Sikh female fore-names. So, thereafter, Sophie was their, very own princess, Sophie Kaur.

It was during the post lunch banana eating session that Harry had turned towards Devar and asked, 'I say Neville why did you specifically ask us to congregate today the 26th of January 1950? What is the significance of this date to you?'

'Simple,' Matric had barged in, 'Devar knows that today is our Republic Day. He has selected this Historic day to meet us.'

'I think Matric is right unless it is your wife's birthday today.' Lachu had speculated.

'Both guesses are wrong,' a smiling Devar had said.

'Then what is the significance of this date to you?' Harry had enquired.

'You dopes this was the date on which we met each other for the first time at Madurai, exactly seven years ago. Now, that I consider to be more significant than anything else. Don't you think so?'

The three had stopped masticating on the banana for a moment. They had tossed the left over bananas into the fodder trough of the cows and had got up shouting, 'whoopee, *thambi*, you got us there.' And then the three friends had bear-hugged *thambi*, forcing him to fling his banana also into the animal fodder channel. As soon as things calmed down, Devar had made some serious conversation with them in hushed tones for the ensuing forty minutes while the ladies had remained busy with Sophie Kaur.

Devar and Sophie had left for Delhi the same evening and Harry and the other two had followed them two days later. They had spent a week in Delhi scouring out business premises and hiring professional staff. Lease deeds for selected properties were drawn and signed. Contractors were hired to do up the interiors and as they got to work sprucing up the sites, Sophie and Devar had flown back to Amsterdam. The three *khalsas,* or pure, had also left Delhi to return to their respective units where they had put in their papers and were back in Delhi a month later as civilians. The offices of "Amsterdam Diamonds" and "World Wide Tours and Travels" had opened a month later. And the rest, as they say, was history.

————◄o►————

From their vantage point on the terrace, they could see Devar and Sophie walking together towards the terminal and looking up every few steps and wave at them. Needless to say, that she received back a similar gesticulation from the enthusiastic half dozen on the terrace. 'You know guys I often wonder how fate threw us together and how *thambi* met his wealthy better half and how he never forgot us when he came into fame & fortune! He has indeed changed our kismet,' said Harry.

'It is all karma,' said Jagtar Kaur. 'You had performed noble deeds in the past life and the Almighty Guru has rewarded you with this friend.'

While the three Sikhs gave complete credit of their becoming rich to the benevolence of their friend and his wife, paradoxically, it was their friend who gave credit for his own good fortune to them. Mutual admiration! Perhaps!

'Well, I don't know about that. But Wahe Guru has certainly kept our past hanky-panky under wraps,' said Lachu.

'We surely were helped by some divine power. But Harry Sahib, it was your ingenuity, which enabled us to successfully cover our tracks. As a matter of fact no one even knows that something wrong ever happened on that trip. With the white sahibs having gone to their island nation, no one is going to go back into the past and dig up that story now. In any case Devar has not only resigned from the army, he now has a foreign nationality. I think our heist will continue to remain a secret forever,' said a glib Matric.

'Well let's hope it remains that way,' said Harry.

Unknown to him and the other two, the wheel of fate was destined to steer them shortly to an event where their so far concealed, misdemeanour, would be laid bare to the world.

The six turned around when their guests entered the terminal building and thus went out of view. They retraced their steps down stairs back to the waiting hall. In their wake at a discreet distance followed the Rajput.

The welcoming crowd was waiting in the hall by the time they emerged from immigration and customs. Sophie was received with *namaskars* and the bouquet of flowers, followed by some cheek kissing amongst the women, all quite subdued. On the other hand it was tumultuous bear hugging and back slapping reception accorded to *thambi* by the men. The striped necktie brought much laughter from Devar. Meetings of friends in the West are more restrained but this raucous welcome in no way fazed Sophie who seemed happy and a willing participant in the boisterous proceedings.

They all filed out of the building, a porter following them with their valises loaded on a trolley. Seeing the turbaned Rajput emerge, the Rolls moved up to the terminal gate and its chauffeur dismounted and got their baggage placed in the Rolls. The two arrivals were ushered into its back seat while the Rajput *munshi* took the co-driver's seat. The Rolls gracefully glided out of the car park and the three American sedans with their passengers followed.

———◄○►———

Rendezvous and Climax

Hotel Imperial, Queensway, New Delhi
28 August 1957 (Evening)

Hodson standing in the lobby of the Imperial Hotel saw the shining "Flying Lady" emblem, riding on top of the chrome radiator grille of the Rolls, glide under the spacious front porch of the hotel. He noticed the coat-of-arms of the erstwhile princely state of Jaipur painted on its flank, on the front door panel. Though the license plate of the limo was not visible to him, yet he was sure that its red coloured plate would have the word "JAIPUR", in capitals, followed by a single digit number, which was the registration code of the Royal Household, written on it, in white. A Rolls Royce belonging to the erstwhile Royal state of Jaipur meant arrival of royalty. Maybe it was the suave Maharaja Jai Singh himself with his pretty wife Maharani Gayatri Devi, arriving at the hotel. They were both known to him. Rulers of erstwhile Indian states were very close to British Army officers during the British Raj and both were an intrinsic part of the social life of each other. Hodson hoped that it was the Royal couple because an inter action with them would be a pleasant interlude from the expected drab negotiations with some accented upstart from the Indian bureaucracy.

The near side rear door of the Rolls was yanked open expertly by the hotel liveried gate keeper with his left hand as his right hand went up to his forehead in salute. Hodson craned his neck to glimpse the royal arrivals through the large glass doors. The moment he saw two pretty legs emerge from the car door and find purchase on terra firma, Hodson ruled out the Royal family angle. He knew ladies of the Indian Royal families remained conservatively attired in sarees, covered literally, from head to toe, even though this did not deter them from downing copious amount of Scotch Whiskey, camouflaged in sterling silver glasses, under cover of their veils during parties. And of-course the scotch was imbibed openly in French crystal glass tumblers, on the rocks, in the privacy of their palaces, every evening. But exposing legs in public, was another matter, it was taboo. Therefore the arriving passenger in the Rolls possibly would be a friend or associate of the Royal Household. Even so, Hodson observed a good looking dark man, dismount from the far side door of the car, skirt the automobile from the rear swiftly and hold out his hand to the passenger with the beautiful legs. The proffered appendage was clasped, unhurriedly, by a most beautiful hand, embellished with a solitaire ring from inside the car but before the passenger could emerge from the limo and come into view, Hodson's vista was masked by a lot of bell hops, valets and newly arriving guests who had crowded near the entrance. Hodson lost interest, yawned discreetly and turned his attention to the Indian LO and his own deputy, Colonel Price, who were engrossed in completing the check-in formalities at the hotel desk on behalf of the delegation.

His back was turned when she entered the large foyer through the main door, held open by a liveried hotel guard. She saw a number of tastefully done seating arrangements in the hall, some of which were occupied and some were vacant. She paused for a moment to decide on a seating place while their check-in formalities were attended to by the *munshi.* But before she could make a decision, her eyes noticed the familiar back profile of a man standing at the far end of the room near the check in counter. Just at that moment the familiar profiled character suppressed a yawn and then turned around in her direction ostensibly to survey the new arrivals. She could not believe her eyes when she found herself face to face with the gentleman. He wasn't any familiar acquaintance, he was more than a good friend; he was Eric Hodson, her intimate pal of yester years. He seemed to have aged since she last saw him on the dais at the parade in Wellington a decade ago. She had left him standing on the podium that day and had run into him, by chance, today ten years later and ironically he was still standing. She suppressed a smile at her own joke.

He was standing there, taking in the spectacle of multitude of guests coming into or exiting the reception area through the door. He had a vacant and seemingly bored look and while she had recognized him, he had not even noticed her even though he was looking in her direction. On impulse she waved at him. The waving drew his attention towards her and their eyes locked with each other's but it still took a moment for recognition to dawn on him. He was so nonplussed that he failed to wave back at her and remained motionless. She was at his side in a jiffy and following in her wake, was that handsome tanned man.

'Hello Eric, nice to see you,' she said. That broke the trance, enabling the stock-still Hodson to stir and gather his wits.

'Hello Sophie.' His reply sounded like a croak even to his own ears. God she didn't seem to have aged in these ten years. She must now be on the wrong side of forty but was still as captivating as ever. Her presence had brought about a feeble stirring in his loins. That was something which had not happened for a long time, in spite of efforts of a masseuse in Soho, with *Sande ka Tel,* Sand Lizard Oil which he had secretly carried from India. That failed trip was his only solitary visit to the Red Light District, in London. The stimulation he experienced, at her sight now, demonstrated the magic-spell this enchantress, still held over the nearly seventy year old Hodson.

'You know, I am married now Eric,' she said and the shine in her beautiful eyes shamed the sparkle of her Cartier diamond studded necklace. Turning around slightly she lovingly caught hold of the hand of the handsome bronze standing just behind her and pulled him forward and said, 'meet my husband Neville.' The beginning of the rousing in his loins came to an abrupt end at the introduction. Even the hand which he extended robotically towards the bronze for the introductory handshake was limp. Her partner on the other hand, grasped the paw firmly and shook it strongly.

'I am Hodson, Eric Hodson. Nice meeting you, sir.'

'I am Devar, Neville Devar. The pleasure is mine, General.' So this was the rascal she had chosen to spend her life with. He was at least ten years her younger, reckoned Hodson. His face was a bit familiar. I have seen him somewhere before but where? He had addressed me as "General", so the blighter also seems to know me. Hodson racked his brains but came up with a blank.

'Hey. Why in heaven am I introducing you to one another; it just occurred to me that you guys have already met, even if, that encounter was only momentary and *sans* a formal introduction. Do you remember the meeting, Neville darling?'

237

'Yes, I do dear. I am sure the General will be able to recall that encounter as well, even though it took place many years ago. I doubt if he would remember me, though.'

C'mon Eric think, who, where, when, how? No answer was forthcoming and all the while the cock-sure bugger had a broad smile on his face showing gleaming white, even teeth, straight out of a tooth paste advertisement.

'Don't exercise your grey cells Eric. I will give you the answer,' said Sophie through a bout of light laughter, 'you met at the investiture parade in Wellington in May 1947. It was you who pinned the medal for bravery on Neville's chest. I had been allotted a ring side seat at the parade being a guest of award winner Neville and witnessed that very formal, engagement between you two from the stands. Remember Eric?'

Hodson remembered all too well. The shock was so great that he simply stood there, transfixed, while peals of her light hearted laughter drifted into his ears, just as the intoxicating scent of her Chanel No 5 perfume came wafting into his nostrils. This Neville fellow was the *havildar* of the Madras Regiment whom he had decorated at the parade that day. She had been in the spectators' stand for this man while he, like a vain old fool, had erroneously titillated himself in the belief that she was there for him and conjured up scenes for an afternoon of ecstasy with her.

His mind had run riot when she had stood him up on that un-forgetful, day at Wellington. He had speculated at that time that she was fooling around with some young officer from the army or from the railways. He had even attempted to home-on to the philanderer by scrutinizing each young face in the mess that evening but all suspects had looked innocent to him. And all the while the real Judas, in the guise of the mess sergeant, was standing barely a step behind him during his last supper in the officers' mess hall. Christ. It could never have occurred to him that it would be a half breed pipsqueak who had trounced him. The scoundrel had not only taken a medal from his hands but also stolen his woman, from his arms. And what about her, the bitch had chosen a mixed strain NCO over him, not for a fling, but for keeps. He could never understand women. He shouldn't be saying so though. He knew this woman since many years and was acquainted with her fondness and dislikes. Such women are not impressed by rank or status when they fall for a man. They pine for raw love. Therefore, he should have understood why she had chosen another over him that day itself. Or even figured her out today, if only, he had, dispassionately, compared his adversary's firm handshake against his pathetic one. The handshake had said it all, louder than words.

'Sat Sri Akal, Prix Sahib *Bahadur*,' chorused three well dressed Sikhs. Their cheerful greeting was addressed to Colonel Price, the deputy of the delegation, as he broke away from the reception desk to join Hodson.

'I will be damned if it's not Harinder Singh Harry, Lachu the wrestler and the educated Ram Singh Matric,' said an astonished Colonel Price. 'Sat Sri Akal, Sat Sri Akal. This indeed is a pleasant surprise.'

'We are also happy to see the Sahib Bahadur again,' said Harry.

'I too am very happy to see you guys. But hey, you guys are dressed as *Gora,* white, Sahibs, whatever happened to your army uniforms?'

'We had resigned from the army about seven years ago sahib and since then we are working in a civilian vocation.'

'Well it's nice running into you after so many years. I am here as part of a delegation which is putting up at this hotel. But first tell me how did you get to know about my visit and place of stay to enable you to come here to meet me?'

'We did not know about your visit Sahib *Bahadur.*'

'If you were not in the knowledge of my visit or of my scheduled residence at the Imperial, then you couldn't possibly be here to meet me. Don't tell me that our encounter is just a coincidence.'

'Everything is ordained Sahib Bahadur, nothing is a coincidence. Wahe Guru is great. He has brought you here to this hotel in India and simultaneously He has directed us to this location to enable our meeting.'

'Well I don't know if our rendezvous was orchestrated by the Almighty Guru or it is simply a chance meeting? But it sure is nice meeting you men. But what brings you to this grand hotel this night?'

'Sahib *Bahadur* the Imperial is our regular haunt for booze and *tandoori* food. However we are here today for a celebratory purpose. Your honoured presence will give more glitter to our planned celebrations this evening.'

'What a piece of luck. You fellows are celebrating in the same hotel where I am slated to stay. If my presence adds more shine to your scheduled festivities then I am even happier,' replied Price. Looking over their shoulders the colonel continued 'And Harinder I can see three ladies standing demurely behind you. My guess is that they are your spouses. Correct?'

'Sahib Bahadur is correct,' answered Harry. Indian women especially those with a rural up-bringing were by habit shy and always remained a step or two behind their men, thus it was no surprise that the colonel had taken one look at their deportment and deduced accurately. Harry continued by way of introduction, 'the tall one in a green saree is Lachu's wife, the shorter one in blue is Matric's missus and the plump one in the Punjabi Dress is mine.' He then lovingly ordered the three ladies '*Kurio, Colonel Prix Sahib Bahadur nu fateh bulao*, girls greet Colonel Prix.' The three folded their hands in an Indian *namaskar* greeting and whispered a Sat Sri Akal in the direction of Colonel Price in unison. The chubby one quickly also added, '*jee aaya nu*', which would be equivalent to a respectful "Welcome" in English.

Colonel Price reciprocated with a Sat Sri Akal with folded hands and even bowed down, from the waist. '*Aagman da Sardarni ji nu mera dhanyavad hai*, I thank the elder lady for her welcome greetings,' responded Colonel Price. Old boots had not forgotten the Punjabi lingo he had picked up while serving with the *Khalsa* in India.

Turning towards the trio he took a hard look at Lachu's and Matric's trimmed beards and said, 'Harry I can see that your friends Lachu and Matric have added a personal sixth "K" to the five "K"s mandated by the Sikh faith.' The Sikh religion has mandated five *kakaas* or "K"s. These are *Kanga, Kesh, Kach, Kara,* and *Kirpan;* meaning comb, hair, underwear, bangle and sword. The British officers who had served with the gallant Sikhs in India had coined an acronym, "CHUBS" for ease of remembering the five "K".

'I know that the Sahib is alluding to their using *Kainchi,* scissors, as the sixth "K" which they seem to be using regularly to trim their beards. Sahib you were a strict CO and never permitted any man under you to cut his hair since it was against the Sikh religion. The practice is still followed in the army stringently. But these boys are now civilians and there is no check on them. Sahib, times are changing and these boys see no wrong in using a *kainchi* occasionally. However, we all have added a couple of more "K"s which would warm the cockles of the sahib's heart.'

'Don't take my opinion for granted Harry. Let me first hear you before I give a nod of endorsement.'

'What will the sahib say if I tell him that the two additional "K"s I mentioned stand for *kothis* and cars. Yes sir we now have our own bungalows and cars.'

'Well, these, two "K"s I approve. Waheguru has been indeed benevolent towards you in more ways than one. You are attired expensively like *Gora,* English sahibs and your wives are attired in most expensive Indian clothing and are weighed down in gold-jewellery like *maharanis,* queens. By my reckoning there is more gold on them than stocked by the Zhaveri Jewellers, of Chandni Chowk. So my guess is that the bungalows you own must be spacious and the cars you possess must be huge sedans or limousines.'

'The sahib *bahadur*, as always, is right again. Lachu's Ford, Matric's Chevrolet and my Buick are parked outside and our *Kothis* in South Delhi are roomy enough,' replied Harry pronouncing Chevrolet as "Sheverlett" like all neo rich Punjabis.

'Well that indeed is good news. If I am not mistaken one piece of jewellery adorned by the elder *Punjaban,* Punjabi lass, seems to have been modelled exactly like the jewellery of Cartier of Bond Street, London. I compliment you for having such an expert craftsman as your *sonar*, gold smith.'

'Sahib's eye sight has not dimmed with age,' said Harry. He then leaned towards the colonel to be out of earshot of the others and whispered confidentially, 'and we hope the power of his other faculties too remains in an equally good condition,' this with a suggestive wink of his twinkling eye.

The colonel caught hold of Harry's neck tie and pulled him even closer and replied in a mock menacing hiss, 'don't you worry about the health of my "below the belt faculties", you cheeky rascal. Because if you persist to pull my leg, I may convey, loud enough for your wife's ears, that like all rich *khalsas* you too have attached yet another, more intimate, "K" to yourself.'

'And what would that "K" denote?'

'The unambiguous, allusion of that "K" would be, to a tucked away "Keep", also known as "Concubine", Jemadar Harinder Singh.'

Harry turned white, white as a sheet, as blood drained out from his face. He only hoped Jagtaro had not heard the insinuation as he looked back at her furtively. 'Sahib that would be hitting below the belt, surely you would not create family crises for me by this unfair lie,' he managed to say.

Price burst out laughing on seeing the chalk white mug of his erstwhile subordinate. It was evident that the brave Harry, like most husbands, was mortally scared of his wife in the domestic arena. Price controlled his laughter and continued in a whisper 'Harry you hit me below the belt and you too get hit where it hurts most. Understood?' It was obvious that the camaraderie between the two soldiers had not diminished in all these years. Aloud he said, 'you must accept the fact that the craftsmanship of your *sonar* is indeed praiseworthy, Harinder. '

Heaving a sigh of relief Harry replied, 'Sahib *Bahadur* I can't accept the accolade on behalf of my goldsmith. The piece sahib refers to, is not a replica copied skillfully by my *sonar*. It is an original obtained from Cartier gold smiths of London.'

'Hallelujah! Partying and boozing at the Imperial Hotel, bungalows, limos and now Jewellery from Cartier, do you know that Cartier is, by appointment, the official jeweller to the British Royalty and referred to as "the jeweller of kings and king of jewellers"? Even Maharaja Bhupinder Singh of Patiala used to get his diamond jewellery from them? You guys must be financially loaded to buy a piece from such acclaimed jewellers. Tell me did you guys hit a jackpot or something? Or did you guys loot a bank to become so rich?'

'We did not win any sweepstake or hold up a bank sahib. We are now successful businessmen.'

'What line of business are you guys in?'

'Sahib we are in the Export & Import and Travel & Tours business.'

'Ah, you mean smuggling? The travel and tourist business must be providing an excellent cover for your unlawful activities. Right! Send out contraband along with tourists. Smuggle in forbidden imports with visitors. Your foreign partners must be across the border in Pakistan, possibly ex army soldiers and your pre-partition friends.'

'This time the sahib is wrong. We shudder to think of those dark days of partition. Matric's family and the family of his wife had to leave their homes and all worldly possessions and trudge on foot from Lahore as refugees, as part of a foot column up to Amritsar. They carried their infirm grandparents on their backs and barely escaped death in the rioting which had erupted at partition of the country ten years ago. Not only that sahib; our armies were shooting at each other in Kashmir shortly after independence. Our business is legit and we have no link or friends across the border.'

'Yes. I know that the partition in 1947 was a traumatic experience for Indians.' Price silently reproached himself for his cantankerous remark. How possibly could these simple Indians have a friendly disposition with Pakistan when the wounds of rioting, killing and raping had not yet healed? 'But tell me, how were you able to establish yourself in business so well and so quickly?'

'Sahib this has been possible with the blessings of the Almighty and a lot of help from our special friend,' said Harry.

'Hey guys, I too attend mass at the church each Sunday. I also have a lot of good friends and yet neither Jesus nor my friends have enhanced my financial capability. I continue to drive an old rickety Morris Minor jalopy and have to think twice to even visit my local pub leave alone a grand hotel bar. Your God is certainly more amenable to listening to prayers than mine is. And this friend who put you on the road to riches must indeed be extraordinary,' said Price.

'Yes this friend and his missus are indeed very special to us.'

'Well, you are lucky to have such friends. By the way, if our meeting today was purely incidental, then why-the-heck are you guys sporting regimental neck-ties?

'It is like this sahib, we always wear our regimental ties when this friend of ours is in India because he has a lien on our regiment, though his stay with regiment did not last long. He and his missus have come from abroad today. We received them at the airport, this afternoon and have accompanied them up to this hotel where they will be staying for the next few days.'

'I may be familiar with him if he was associated with our regiment,' said Price. 'Who might he be?'

'Sahib knows this friend of ours and I lay a wager that sahib will be able to recognize him without difficulty.'

'Is that so? Please show me where he is?'

'He is standing to your left in front of General Hodson sahib,' said Harry pointing towards Devar. 'Does the Sahib recognize him?'

'I will be damned if it isn't that renegade *thambi.*' An astonished Price had verbally cussed himself twice, within a span of fifteen minutes, while standing in the foyer of the Imperial. This second time was in a murmur of astonishment. 'Am I correct?'

'Bull's eye Colonel,' said the man.

'And who would be the pretty lady holding his hand be?'

'I am Sophie, Neville's or rather your *thambi*'s better half,' Sophie self introduced herself as she extended her pretty arm in his direction.

'And she is the heiress of two inheritances of Europe,' interjected a sulking Hodson, 'the De'Souza Empire and its Estates in Lisbon from her father's side and the van der Coot inheritance in Amsterdam from her maternal grandfather.'

Price took her pretty hand in his and raised it to his lips, 'I am Price. Colonel Price. It is a pleasure to make your acquaintance ma'am.'

'Thank you Colonel. The honour is all mine,' said Sophie.

He then turned around towards Hodson and said 'I think the check-in formalities are likely to take some time. So we might as well sit down.' He gestured towards an empty rectangular arrangement of settees and plunked in the corner seat of the

"L" shaped corner couch. Hodson shrugged and also sat down in line with him at the other end of the array without making a comment.

'Good idea sahib' said Harry as he occupied the other corner seat of the "L" shaped sofa. He was thus sitting closest and perpendicular to Colonel Price while his two sidekicks came and sat next to him. The others followed suit by finding suitable places to sit in the array, Sophie and *thambi* occupying a place near Hodson, directly opposite the Sikh trio.

'Prix sahib we had planned to celebrate the arrival of *thambi,* Devar and his missus with a bash here evening. I take this opportunity to request you and your other delegates to join us for the party,' invited Harry.

Price looked inquiringly at Hodson who gestured an approval before answering, 'Ok Harry, we will join in your celebrations provided our LO has no objections.'

'I will manage the LO.'

So saying Harry went to the check-in counter and informed the LO who not only endorsed the idea whole heartedly but also informed the delegates that he would have their baggage moved by the hotel staff to their respective rooms while they were partying.

Harry then signalled a waiter by waving his hand above his head. As soon as the waiter appeared on his side he expansively ordered a round of scotch and soda for all the men, champagne for Sophie and coffee for their three demure wives. 'And the party commences right now,' he announced expensively as the waiter hurried out to fulfill the order.

'I want to show you a personal memorabilia Colonel,' said Devar as he came across and shook hands with Colonel Price. 'I call it my exclusive visiting card,' He removed a pure leather Lious Vitton wallet from his coat pocket and removed a weathered visiting card sized, weight ticket, from it and gave it to Price.

Price took the worn out weight ticket from *thambi* and read it, first the obverse side and then the reverse. The date imprinted on the ticket was not legible but he could make out the month and year which were, "Jan 1942". The weight impressed on the ticket was 1 Maund, 39 Seers. On the reverse side was printed a fate forecast which said "A great future full of riches and love awaits you". Price burst out laughing since he had read this very ticket in the orderly room at Jullundur a decade and a half earlier. The only difference being that on that occasion, another NCO had fished it out from *thambi's* uniform pocket since he was standing at attention in an orderly room and thus not permitted to move; and of course this frayed ticket had then been in a pristine state.

'You kept this ticket with you for so long. Why?'

'It is my lucky charm. I kept it with me in my left breast pocket, next to my heart all through the Burma Campaign. It brought me out of the war in one piece. And Colonel, the fate forecast printed on it has come out to be true.'

'I sure can see that.'

'And Colonel Price, his weight continues to be 72 Kilograms equivalent to your 158 British Pounds. If you convert that into the Indian weight measuring units you will come to the figure printed on that weight ticket,' added Sophie.

A sullen Hodson was following the proceedings with hawk-like eyes. The fucking bimbo knows his weight by heart; and that too in different units of weight measurement. All because she supports his weight every night during humping, was his mental take. Price flipped the ticket around in his hand and read the weight printed on it once again. He then converted the 1 Maund 39 Seers printed on the ticket into English weight units in his mind. The answer did come to 158 Pounds the figure given by Sophie. She was right *thambi* had neither gained nor lost weight in over a decade and a half. He did not attempt to convert it into metric units because he abhorred the French system which he perceived as a threat, not only to the English units of weights and measures but also to its legal-tender. He had heard talk that the Royal Commission on Decimal Coinage had recommended that the Pound Sterling be divided into 1000 mills when Britain went the decimal way. He had also heard that some members of the commission had wanted to, even change, the name of the Pound to "Royal". He could not understand why some upstarts wanted to change the legal-tender, which had existed for ages. So far, right minded people, who could not imagine the English currency without its "pounds, shillings and pence" had resisted the change. However, Price knew that decimalization of the English currency was certain, ever since minting of the farthing had been stopped, last year; a clear sign, of the inevitability of change in the legal-tender. It did not matter what *thambi's* weight was in Kilograms and in any case, he was loath to convert it in to a unit he detested. He only hoped that Britain retained its existing weighing and measuring units.

Price smiled at Sophie and said, 'madam is indeed right.' He then returned the vintage memorabilia back to *thambi* who carefully cached it back into the recesses of his wallet.

'Harinder, you know, I was initially bothered to see you and your cronies in a plush grand hotel environment, flush with money. Frankly, I thought that you guys had done something illegal to come into such a large an amount of money.' His discourse was halted as a quartet of waiters with scotch and soda laden trays appeared in front of them and started to serve the amber liquid. Price signalled to his other delegates to come and join them. Coffee was served to the three Indian ladies and bubbly was poured into Sophie's stemmed glass straight from the bottle by a waiter. When everyone had been served, they raised and clinked, each others' glasses, to a disorderly, 'cheers' before taking their first sip. Price continued his discourse, 'that or you had hit a lottery jackpot or something.'

'In a manner of speaking we did hit a lottery jackpot sahib *bahadur*. The lottery ticket is our friend *thambi* and his foreign *mem*-sahib heiress wife. We now take care of their diamond and tourist and travels business in South Asia from here. Sahib *Bahadur* should banish any thought about our, ever, indulging in any illegal activity.'

'My concern has been laid to rest on learning that your road to riches was entirely above board. And Harry being a success in your new vocation in civilian life is a good achievement, especially in such a short time span, even if it was with the support of friends. I am really happy and proud at your accomplishment.'

'Thank you sahib *bahadur*. Rest assured, we are trying to follow the values inculcated in us during our army service and will not dilute them for the sake of making a quick buck.'

'Yes indeed. I know you guys quite well. You may pull an odd prank here and there but you would not resort to expediency to make a quick buck.'

Turning away from Harry and facing Devar Colonel Price said, 'Harry had mentioned that you have travelled from abroad to India today. Where are you now settled?'

Before Devar could reply Hodson volunteered the information. 'Well the heiress has properties and businesses in two countries,' said Hodson. 'My guess is that they possibly could be spending the summer in Amsterdam and journeying to Lisbon for the winters. Like migratory birds.'

'And what has brought you to India? Is it business or is it pleasure?' asked Price.

'A bit of both, Colonel,' replied Devar. 'Sophie has some property related matters to resolve in Madras and Ooty. We also have to visit Sophie's ancestral graves in Madras and attend to them in case they require maintenance. We will try to visit Goa if the Indian Government permits since we have a proposal lying with the Portuguese Government to set up a hotel there. And I am slated to attend a reunion at the Madras Centre at Wellington on 23 September which also happens to be a Battle Honour Day of the regiment.'

'That date, if I can recollect is the day when the Madrasis won the Battle of Assaye in 1803. Did you know that Major General Wellesley had termed this battle as the bloodiest battle of the campaign?' said Price.

'428 dead and 1602 wounded on our side and enemy casualties were estimated to be 6000,' interposed Hodson.

'Correct. The reunion has been scheduled to be held on this historic day by the regiment,' said Devar.

'Well have a fruitful reunion,' said Price and he then turned around towards the three Sikhs and continued, 'Hey, guys you know what? This meeting with you has rekindled old memories.'

'Yes indeed Prix Sahib. So many army incidents are etched in our minds as well. We reminisce on such memories all the time. I remember breaking the headlights of the Brigade Commander's car when it refused to halt at my check point one night in Jullundur. It was you, who saved us from the Brigade Commander's wrath for that incident.'

'I did not, in any way, save you from his anger. On the contrary it was the commander himself who took the incident sportingly and gave us a pat for being alert at night and performing our duty without fear or favour. As a matter of fact he became our fan and admirer after the incident.'

'Is that so?' Harry could not understand these British *sahibs*. He had gone and smashed the headlights of the big *sahib's* car and the fellow was happy about it. 'Which incident is your favourite *Sahib?'*

'I do not have any favourites but ever since I have just been shown an old memorabilia by *thambi*, an incident involving you four comes to mind,' said Price with a mischievous smile on his lips.

'Which of our indiscretions is Colonel *Sahib* going expose? We do not remember any worthwhile incident which included the four of us.'

'You will recall it better than even me, since you were lead actors in this episode. As far as I can remember this was the only incidence where you also crossed the line.'

'*Sahib* is mistaken. We have never, ever, crossed the line.'

'Harinder I know you a bit too well. I know you are a good man but you do have a predilection for trouble. Don't tell me you do not recollect the misdemeanour, you enacted out on the temporary duty to Madras in the winter of 1942! Remember?'

Hell! Of all the sack full of funny tales, indiscretions and anecdotes, *Sahib* had gone and pulled one out of the Pandora's Box, thought Harry. Aloud he said, 'I vaguely recollect having done the escort duty *Sahib* is alluding to. The hot and humid weather combined with spicy food of South India and difficulty in communicating in the local language Tamil, are a few difficulties etched on my mind about that trip.'

'Is that all?'

'Well we found a new friend for life in *thambi* during that trip. That's all. We had never carried out any misconduct in the past or on that trip which would have brought shame to the unit. We were always obedient and disciplined soldiers. You know us.' And he signalled to the maître d' for another round of drinks and snacks.

'I know that wrong did not shame the battalion but none the less it was a transgression. I am certain that you pulled off a major mischief on that trip,' said Price, simultaneously winking in his direction, 'and concealed it successfully from us. Since the shenanigan was carried out by you in connivance with each other I thought it prudent to order the three of you to be split up to keep you out of trouble in the future. That was the reason for posting two of you out to different battalions. So seeing you together now and with *thambi* also in tow, brought back that incident to my mind and hence a concern of the possibility of some more monkey business being enacted by you fellows.'

So, it was Prix *sahib* who was responsible for their forced separation and not that hawk, Jiwan Singh. Aloud he continued, 'I think the *sahib* is mistaking us for some other chaps. We have always remained within bounds of discipline while in the army. We did not team up for any waywardness.'

'Well I don't think so.'

'Sahib *Bahadur* we did nothing to bring dishonour to the regiment,' said Harry, he wasn't letting the sahib ride rough shod over them. 'As a matter of fact we collected the prisoner from Madras and delivered him to the unit under very trying circumstances.' Turning towards Lachu and Matric for support he said, 'Isn't that right guys?'

'Right **boss**,' replied the two side kicks in unison. Seeing the amused face of their erstwhile commanding officer, Harry realized that Prix *sahib* wasn't convinced of their innocence. He seemed to be in the know of more details of the trip than was good for them. How the fucking hell has he got wind of that incident?

'*Sahib* will recall that he had deputed Subedar Major Jiwan Singh to carry out an investigation. I was grilled by the old fox regarding our conduct during the tenure of duty to Madras and he seemed satisfied with the explanation given by me. Therefore *sahib* is surely mistaken.'

'Harinder, old Jiwan Singh had the kit of all three of you searched after we received the complaint from the railway authorities of a forced halt of two trains by Sikh soldiers. In your kit, Harinder, he found your personal notebook and came across a page with the heading "EX VH".'

'Sahib *Bahadur* that notebook was used by me as a diary cum scrap book. The letters "VH" can mean anything. You know that Madras is hot and humid. I may have hinted to the "Very Hot" or "Very Humid" conditions over there by writing "VH" in short form in that note pad, just for the heck of it.'

'Harinder I think "VH" entry prefixed by Ex in your diary was not for the heck of it. I believe it was an acronym for "Exercise Visit Home" because below that title were paragraph-headings and jottings for a planned clandestine visit to your homes. Translated copy of which was shown to me by the adjutant. You want me to go on?' said Price.

Receiving no response from his moustache twirling musketeers, Price continued, 'The search also revealed that you had made a schematic diagram of the briefing for the clandestine visit to your villages.'

Sahib is surely fibbing thought Harry since he had, himself seen one of his side-kicks tearing up, the only three copies of the diagram in existence, into shreds and throwing them out of the train at Ludhiana. He was confident there was no sketch in existent, as was being made out by Prix Sahib. Being sure and thus on firmer ground he confidently rebutted Price's claim, '*Sahib* is surely mistaken. Jiwan Singh could not have possibly found a sketch in our belongings since I did not make one.'

'C'mon Harry, have some respect for old Jiwan. I know what you chaps called him behind his back especially with reference to his penetrating and telescopic eyesight. It is the presence of ladies which inhibits me from elaborating more in the matter.'

Mention of Jiwan Singh's trait brought a flicker in Harry's eyes. The old buzzard was truly a hard task master. The men, especially the wayward ones were mortally scared of him. That, however, did not prevent them from jokingly voicing an anecdote, behind his back, pertaining to his ability to count the pubic feathers of a bird in flight; little realizing that their jest, in a sense, was praising his competence. Aloud Harry said, 'we know Jiwan was a sharp and efficient VCO. But surely he could not have found a sketch in my kit sahib.'

'How are you so sure Harinder? I think your confidence stems from the fact that you thought you had destroyed all the copies of the sketch. Am I right?' Harry just smiled. Let us see what the *sahib* is up to.

'But have you heard the adage that "there is no perfect murder"? Every culprit leaves behind some clue which ultimately does him in, Harry. Similarly you guys also left a glaring proof of your wrong.'

Harry kept smiling but the other two were now uneasy despite the whiskey intake. 'Old fogey Jiwan while rummaging in your kit found two carbon-papers, double folded and neatly, inserted between the last two pages of your pay book. Now, what would two, practically new, neatly double folded carbons be doing in your IAB-64, he asked himself?'

For the first time this evening Harry felt a little disconcerted but he kept the smile on his face intact. Matric's warning aired at Madurai so many years ago, that the English cannot be fooled, came rushing into his mind.

'So he opens up the carbon papers, holds them up, towards the sunlight, one at a time and looks skywards through them. And what does he see? He sees the handiwork of a sharp pencil having chiselled away a perfect diagrammatical rendition of a briefing of an exercise called "Visit Home",' said Price and by now he had the look of someone enjoying himself.

'He hands over the carbon papers to the intelligence boys who in no time produce a hard copy of the sketch on white drawing paper and it is on my table before lunch the same day.'

'*Sahib* I swear to God that we did not visit our homes during that visit.'

'I know that Harry. I know you did not visit your homes.' He paused again to let everyone replenish their drinks and to savour the fish finger snacks being circulated by the waiters.

'There you are. Then you do believe that we are telling you the truth,' replied Harry wiping off the remnants of fish batter coating from his hand on a serviette left at his side by a waiter.

'I believe you on this point. I believe you only because I had corroboration on this score. I had sent old Jiwan Singh ostensibly on leave but he was actually sent to visit your places of residence. On return he confirmed to me that none of you had visited your homes during that period. We, therefore, concluded that something had gone wrong for you to abandon a perfectly laid out plan. What could that be?'

Hell, he did remember Jiwan proceeding on leave which he figured, was for compassionate reasons whereas all the while the old guard was doing detective work in their villages. Gosh, *sahib* knows more, a lot more, than was good for them. In such circumstances they followed the old dictum of keeping their traps shut. The three sat there like statues much like the General, sitting on a couch across the carpet in front of them, near their relaxed Sophie Kaur and their friend *thambi*. They were all listening with rapt attention while sipping their drinks.

'We were reasonably sure that something had gone amiss at that way side station on the outskirts of Madras. The adjutant was of the view that you guys had broken journey to visit, ahem,' he looked in the direction of the seated Sophie and the other three ladies, 'ahem, begging the ladies' pardon, the red light district. But this theory was set aside by me since I knew that you would never indulge in such a past time and neither would you permit juniors under your command to do so.' He looked at Jagtaro and then in Sophie's direction once again and continued, 'ladies, our friend Harry, here, was not only a good soldier but also an out and out gentleman.' Hodson turned a shade pink at this comment, observed an amused Sophie. Price continued, 'and in any case you had a visit all laid out to your families in the next couple of days and hence the adjutant's hypothesis went kaput.

'Another theory was that the prisoner had escaped but this premise was set aside since you had brought the prisoner with you. The second-in-command then theorized that the prisoner you were escorting had scooted from your grasp and you spent a few days relocating him and when at last you got hold of him you rejoined the unit with the prisoner as if nothing had happened. This seemed plausible since the prisoner with all his documents was transported to the unit by you.

'The only hole in the second-in-command's thesis was that, it would have been nearly impossible for someone to successfully ferret out a runaway prisoner in the vastness of Madras State and that too in just a couple of days.'

'Maybe he had a change of heart and voluntarily gave himself up to the escort,' suggested Hodson. By now Harry was murmuring a silent prayer to the Wahe Guru.

'Possible but didn't happen in this case, General. If indeed he had a change of mind he would have returned to the suburban station looking for these dudes. However, the complaint letter from railways did not mention any one coming in search for them. In any case, even if he had returned, he could not have found them there, since they were steaming away in a commandeered train towards Madras Central. So the question surfacing again and again was how in hell did you guys ever relocate the runaway prisoner so quickly?'

'*Sahib* all this discussion is only academic. You have very correctly observed the near impossibility of locating the runaway, especially, without any leads and I endorse this view point. I would also like to say that finding a needle in a haystack and that too, blind folded and in pitch darkness, would have been easier than finding a runaway *thambi* at night in an alien environment,' said Harry in response. He had flinched while using the "haystack proverb" since it dredged up memory of the runaway *thambi* in his head. That bastard had cleverly used this very axiom while befooling them over fifteen years ago, in that train on the outskirts of Madras. The son of a gun must be still doing it in haystacks with his dame somewhere in Ceylon. He dismissed the scoundrel's thought from his mind and came to the present, took a large draught of the amber liquid from his tumbler and continued, 'Luckily, we did not have to play blind-man's-bluff in Madras to catch him because he never escaped from our custody. He was with us all the while.'

'Wrong there Harry. We were quite certain that the prisoner did slip away from your charge forcing you to halt the train in which you were travelling on the return journey and then doubling back to Madras in a hijacked train to re-apprehend him. We reckoned that this unexpected turn of events forced you to abandon your "visit home" exercise which you had so painstakingly planned.'

'*Sahib* if he had run away, how in Heaven could we have ever located him? And sahib is forgetting that we did bring the prisoner and handed him over to the unit, didn't we?

'Correct. You did bring a handcuffed *thambi* to the unit, claiming to be the prisoner handed over to you by Station HQ, Madras. Presence of the prisoner was not an illusion he was there in flesh and blood, doing his time in the unit lockup. No argument there. So, how did you pull off the re-apprehension of the runaway?'

'*Sahib* even at the cost of repetition, I say that there was no need to track him down since he never ran away in the first place. He was with us all the time,' defended Harry.

'Balderdash, we had proof that the detainee had escaped from your custody. You will naturally ask me, what proof did we possess? Right! I will tell you. Remember your gear was searched? We had located a diary in Matric's kit, where-in a couple of pages, contained the account of the expenses incurred during the duty to Madras. If one was not fussy about wrong spellings, then Matric's entries in this mini account ledger could be considered to have been made competently.

'We focussed on the return trip record. We observed a "payment entry" for a *Tonga* conveyance. Now why would you hire a *Tonga* when army transport would have been provided by the Station HQ to you? Someone suggested that you probably hired the conveyance to chase the runaway but another gave you the benefit of doubt. He suggested that maybe you did not have the patience to wait for army conveyance due to your hurry to reach the railway station and get on board the earliest train to Punjab and this compulsion forced you charter the horse carriage. This was quite plausible. So we did not pursue this point.'

'Sahib I remember vaguely that the *tonga* we hired was for sightseeing purposes.'

'C'mon Harry. You wouldn't be doing sightseeing on the last day of your stay in Madras. Would you? Especially when, you also had to commence your return journey on that very day. Leave that aside. Let us come to the food expense record.

'Following the *tonga* disbursement entry was the catering expenses record. The accounts of two days following the reported, forced, halt of two trains at the wayside suburban station were a revelation. On the first day and up to lunch of the second day, cost of meals for three persons was debited for

255

Breakfast, Lunch and Dinner. Similarly three cups of tea had been bought each time tea was purchased. This established that the dining strength on these two days was only three persons. However the expenses endorsed by Matric from dinner of the second day onwards clearly showed that payment was made for four diners. That was odd. You were four people travelling back from Madras therefore expenses in Matric's ledger should have shown constant ration strength of four, on all days, for all meals. So why was the outflow of money restricted to cost of meals for three people on those two days?' posed Price and then provided the answer himself. 'The expenses on food were less because only three people were eating on these two days because the fourth man had run away; why else? Surely one of you could not have starved himself for nearly two days, missing five major meals at a stretch?'

'Sahib *Bahadur*, one of us could have foregone a meal by rotation on these two days. That is possible isn't it?'

'The gluttons that you are, I doubt if any one of you would miss out on a meal voluntarily.'

'Sahib you are over estimating Matric's account keeping prowess. He could have made some mistake while writing down the accounts.'

'Cut out the excuses Harry. The fellow scooted from your charge on the return trip forcing you to go back to Madras to re-apprehend him. I think you got hold of him again after two days and perhaps also used a *tonga* in that chase. And we had Matric's account book to substantiate this premise.'

'Sahib we have gone over this argument and you yourself conceded that finding a runaway in such a big place was well neigh impossible. So how did we find him?'

'Some of the officers too were of the same view Harry. That is why the adjutant put forward another theory; which he argued was plausible. He said maybe the prisoner you brought was not the genuine one but a phoney. If I recall correctly, some company commanders supported this theory. They argued that since you were a resourceful character, they would not put it past you to bring in a fake replacement after the elusive runaway gave you the slip. I had said that I also knew you as well as anyone else. I, too, had always been impressed by your penchant to get things done but I doubted if you would take such a drastic step. I accordingly told them that their surmise was implausible.

'On the other hand some officers felt that the escape of the prisoner would be taken by you as a failure of a mission, which is considered dishonourable, for any soldier worth his salt. We all knew how difficult it was to live down such a *faux pas,* especially, by a soldier. Thus they contended that with limited or no option available, you were quite capable of doing something as outrageous as to bring in a counterfeit in lieu.

'I knew that you would hold yourself responsible for the embarrassment the battalion would have to face because of the escape of the prisoner from your custody and that you would leave no stone unturned to re-apprehend the runaway. But I also knew that you were brave enough to own up a mistake and face the music. I therefore felt that you would go as far as the search took you but no further.

'It was obvious that the officers were not entirely in consonance with my view. So, even though I did not agree with their conjecture, I acceded to give them time to test out the adjutant's hypothesis.'

Harry and his coterie remained silent. Everyone was listening with rapt attention, as if mesmerized, while Colonel Price unfolded the story. His unfolding of the mystery of *thambi* was so competently narrated that it would have given detective Hercule Poirot a run for his money. And he was recounting it without the advantage of a, setting or a script, from Dame Agatha Christie.

'The adjutant, ably assisted by his head clerk went through the documents of the prisoner with a tooth comb. They found that two pages of your personal note book had been removed. If something had been written on the missing pages then there was a likely hood of the impressions of the written matter appearing in the following pages. They found such faint marks on the adjoining pages confirming that some written work indeed existed in the discarded pages. However, try as they may they were unable to decipher the contents due to dimness of the indentations. The best the two, ahem, detectives, could do was to establish that there had been four tick marked entries on one of the pages while the other page had a number of jumbled up faint indentations. On this page they could faintly discern the letters LS &RS and these we believed were initials of your two assistants. They could not draw any inference despite their labour. The other papers seemed to be in order.

'The Adjutant however focused on the two identification marks recorded in the documents of the detainee. These should exist on the person of the prisoner but which had not been seen by him or noticed by his JA. The stated tattoo mark on the fore arm of the subject had remained obscured by the full sleeved jersey he was wearing as part of the winter uniform. Similarly existence of a birth mark on the left shoulder blade of the man had to be confirmed. Accordingly he ordered his Jemadar Adjutant to check if the prisoner had a birth mark on his shoulder blade and a tattoo on his fore arm. This was checked out without arousing any suspicion during bathing time by the quarter guard commander. The prisoner indeed had a discoloured mark on his shoulder blade and a cross was definitely tattooed on his left forearm. The adjutant nonetheless wanted to pursue his theory to a final conclusion. He wanted the documented record "height" and "weight" of the prisoner, to be substantiated by an actual check.

'So we told the Regimental Medical Officer to carefully determine the weight and height of the prisoner during the monthly medical check-up.

'The doctor's report said that the prisoner was nearly five seers more than his recorded weight. The report also confirmed that the incumbent was slightly taller than his registered height but the difference between his actual height and that registered on record was just a small fraction of an inch.'

Price paused to pick up a glass of whiskey and a mutton kebab which had appeared yet again. He waited till everyone had been served by a band of waiters and then picked up the thread of his story.

'We beckoned the doctor who confirmed that that gaining weight was ordinary at his age due to poor eating habits and inadequate physical activity. We too had observed that the recruit was podgy at the time of his orderly room hence we set the weight point aside. However can one gain height at his age? So, we grilled the doctor on this point. The medico said that height increment was perhaps not possible but contended that errors in taking height measurements were not rare. He explained that the height taking apparatus was not a precision instrument. It was just a wooden contraption having two major parts, a stationary wooden base plate having a rigid upright member and a movable head plate. While the fixed vertical upright component affixed on the base plate had measuring units, in feet and inches denoted on it, in ascending order, the movable head plate was slid up and down on this vertical appendage with the help of an attached cuff. When recording height, the head plate was slithered up and the incumbent was made to stand on the base plate, below it. The head plate was then dropped down till it rested flat on the head of the candidate. The measurement division on the vertical scale coinciding with the bottom edge of the head plate indicated the height of the individual. Thus an incorrect standing posture or an additional mop of hair on the scalp of the person could give an erroneous result. Also there could be a human error while interpreting the mark which corresponded with the head plate especially when their meeting point was between two fractions.

'So here we were without any firm out come. The doctor had put us in tight spot instead of offering a clear cut solution. The prisoner could be the original fellow or a hurriedly found replacement.'

'If the *Sahib* had even an iota of doubt on the bona-fides of the prisoner then surely he would have punished us?' cut in Harry.

'Hold your horses Harry. Something had gone wrong on that trip but cleverly covered up by you. We were sure of that. But I would be damned if I would even consider punishing you for a purported height difference of a whisker between the recorded height and actual height of the subject. But our fears had to be allayed. So to close the chapter once and for all I told the adjutant to send someone to Army HQ, New Delhi to compare our papers with their records.'

'You did that?'

'Yes, of course Harry. The head clerk carried your pay-book along with a DO letter from me. He spent two days and compared the photograph and signature of the subject on the pay-book with the signatures and photo pasted in the documents in Delhi.

They matched perfectly. The Head Clerk's report on return from Army HQ set aside the sceptics' perceived misgivings about the prisoner's veracity.

'I, therefore, posed a question to the officers who had touted this fanciful theory during a conference. I said if the real *thambi* had definitely slipped out of the grasp of the escort for good, how and from where was a volunteer replacement found in so short a time? How were his documents matching the papers in Army HQ? On the other hand, if the real fellow had actually been recaptured and brought back, then we were all barking up the wrong tree any way. I did not get any cogent response to my posers.'

'See, I had all along argued that Sahib *Bahadur* was misled by inexperienced junior officers who were in a manner of speaking just groping in the darkness, trying to solve a nonexistent problem. They were wrongly assuming that we had brought a phony to the unit. And I still maintain there was no crisis during our return journey out of Madras,' said Harry.

'I can't agree with you there Harry. I don't think the officers were misleading me,' said the colonel. 'They had their apprehensions and carried out a check on *thambi* to clear any, lingering, uncertainties, that's all. And frankly, when in doubt it's better to be sure than sorry.

'At that stage all aspects had to be considered. I therefore gave a lot of thought to the conundrum. The prisoner brought by you was good in all manners of speaking. He was by far the best young soldier I had seen. I don't know how the lackadaisical recruiting office had managed to find someone like him and that too for the Pioneer Corps. He seemed to be highly motivated to volunteer to serve in the front lines as an infantry man. The fellow had all the qualities one looks for in a soldier. I had a gut feeling that he would do well in war.'

'*Sahib* your hunch turned out to be correct. The man showed bravery in battle and won a gallantry award,' exclaimed Harry.

'Some times instinct can indeed be true Harry. So I asked myself, as to why in hell were we getting bogged down just because of an unfounded far-fetched theory questioning his bona fides had emerged?

'It was the second in command who stood by me. He said that it did not matter how or where the fellow was caught by you. What really mattered was that the prisoner had been brought to the unit. We had established the man's genuineness, the fellow was in the kink, doing his time and thus the matter stood closed. He reiterated that the unresolved question of how and from where the escort re-apprehended the escapee should not be flogged any further. I could see nods of approval from the remaining assembled company.

'We knew our men. They were simple and had childlike innocence. I doubted if you fellows who accepted life saying "*Jo hoega so hoega"*, would ever indulge in an act of ill discipline of this magnitude, deliberately. In any case we had more pressing work at hand than chase Quixotic Windmills. So I told my officers that the topic stood closed.

'And listeners with your acquiescence I wish to digress a bit, on a lighter note, pertaining to "*Jo hoega so hoega"*, at this juncture.'

'Go ahead Prix,' authorized Hodson while replenishing his drink from a waiter.

'Thank you General,' said Price as a waiter appeared infront of him. 'This "*Jo hoega so hoega"* quote has been playing havoc with me for the past one year,' he continued as he refreshed his whiskey.

'How is that Prix?' inquired Hodson.

'You all must have heard the number "Que Sera Sera, whatever will be will be" crooned by Doris Day.'

'Of course we have heard it and hummed it too. It is her latest and recorded only last year. What an endearing song.' said Sophie.

'I too have heard the exceptional rendition of the song by the gorgeous Doris Day, in her engaging voice. The juke boxes in the restaurants all over Delhi keep on playing the number day and night,' said Matric.

'The same is happening in England. The juke boxes, the televisions, the radio-receivers in homes and cars are all blaring, this number. This song is everywhere.'

'What else can one expect if the number is so popular? It is already a year old but continues to be a favourite of most of us

Colonel,' said another, while other delegates nodded their heads in consent.

'In my case it is the popularity of the number which is troubling me. Do you know the meaning of the lyrics "Que Sera Sera, whatever will be will be", Matric?'

'Sure, the lines are the English version of the Punjabi quote "*Jo hoega so hoega*".'

'You are spot on Mr. Matric, spot on. And that exactly is my problem. Whenever, wherever, I hear the song, the phrase "*Jo hoega so hoega*", comes rushing into my mind because of my past association with Mazhabi & Ramdasias Sikhs. And this expression continues to spin and echo in my head all the time. It is maddening. Do you guys also face this difficulty?'

'No sahib. The song only evokes the pretty freckled face of Doris Day in us,' answered a smiling Matric on behalf of all the three. The listeners including Price burst into laughter at this response.

'You are incorrigible Matric,' said Price, as soon as he was able to control his laughter; by when the waiters too had receded after completing their topping up round.

'Colonel we have been hearing the song quite regularly but this connection between the lines of the song and the vernacular quote of your ex soldiers is indeed new to us,' said one of the delegates. And all listeners nodded again.

'We will take leave of the rambling and get back to our discussion,' said Colonel Price. 'Harry, while I had closed the issue pertaining to the runaway but the fact remained that you guys had broken the law. You had left the Gurkha unit in Madras at least one day before your scheduled departure. You were lax on duty thereby permitting a prisoner in your charge to escape. And then there was this business of holding up a couple of trains in Madras. There may be countless other violation of the law which would surface if we ordered an inquiry.

'I was aware that you were an honourable man and any legal transgression done was forced on you by fear of being disgraced for failure. I certainly did not envy your predicament. I read and re-read your annual reports and did not come across a single negative point. All your reports had graded you above average and each one spoke of initiative, pluck, hard work resourcefulness and the like. When I looked at the other two, I realized that Lachu had just brought laurels to the unit by winning the wrestling finals and his performance in the tug of war had been excellent; Matric was a lead scorer at the inter unit firing championship and he was performing additional duties as officiating as clerk quite satisfactorily, if one overlooked his atrocious spelling. So what should I do? Should I overlook these infringements or should I take cognizance of your transgressions? If I took cognizance then I would have to sue you through a court martial. The least punishment a court martial would hand out was likely to be dismissal from service for you three and as well as for *thambi*. Correct?'

'Correct, sir.'

'I was aware that the Empire was raising new units for the ongoing war and finding it difficult to come across good men; I therefore said to myself, why the hell should I kick out trained manpower when we were having difficulty in recruiting fresh blood? And frankly, I didn't have the heart to lose four good men.

'Consequently I took the view that you had successfully performed your duty by escorting the prisoner from Madras. The only question which the second-in-command had termed as, inconsequential, but which still pricked me was; how and whereupon did you stumble on the slippery eel and in such a short time, at that? That's all.

'My assessment of *thambi* turned out to be correct. The soldier in him was valiant during the war bringing laurels to himself and his regiment. His being invited by the Madras Regiment for a reunion shows that he is not only remembered but also held in high esteem by the regiment.'

'I agree with you Colonel,' said Sophie, 'he is also a good human being and a great husband.'

'And an excellent friend,' chorused the three Sikhs.

'I am not too well conversant with English but I want to add that he is also a good brother to me even though it is by verbal adoption and not by blood,' said the matronly Jagtar Kaur. All this praise had brought a blush on *thambi's* face and he turned cherry red when Sophie turned around and pecked him on the cheek.

'Meanwhile I had your briefing notes for your planned home visit exercise extracted from your note book. We already had the associated schematic diagram for the planned clandestine visit to your villages. I had both these documents translated into English. The exercise was so well planned and equally well written that I had the English translation sent to the Army HQ in UK who, after evaluation, included the exercise in the platoon commander's course as a "Case Study" at the Infantry School.'

'See? I told you that the plan made by you was excellent boss. My observation stands substantiated by, none other than, our CO himself,' barged in Matric impulsively, without heed. Harry's glare of disapproval at Matric came a bit too late. Matric's ears reddened at receiving the angry stare and he sheepishly averted his eyes.

Colonel Price was quick to grasp the gaffe. He smilingly said, 'Well I must thank Matric for vindicating my point of view. I now know without a doubt that you guys had planned an un-authorised, excursion to your homes during the Madras trip. And Harry will you please stop glowering at the boy!'

'Prix *Sahib* it was just a plan. You are aware that it was never executed. You couldn't be regretting your decision to let us off the hook for making that plan at this belated stage?' said Harry.

'No, I am not. The only regret I have is in my not being able to fully solve the puzzle. How and from where did you re-apprehend *thambi* after his escape from the train?'

'I wish to add that successful re-apprehension of the escapee could have only been possible if the escort knew of his secret hideouts and haunts,' cut in the, Naval Member, in the delegation. 'So we should ask Harinder to share that information with us.'

Their tête-à-tête was interrupted by a shaggy haired guest who tapped Harry on the shoulder. Who the hell was now drumming him on the shoulder when he had already received enough drumming from the CO *Sahib* for one evening, thought Harry? He looked up at the intruder and came face to face with an unkempt hairy man who urbanely, said, 'Excuse me, are you Mr. Harinder?'

No one felt offended at the interruption. They utilized the interlude to add some more scotch to their tumblers from the trays, of the battery, of bearers waiting on them.

'Yes I am,' replied Harry and looking at the stranger he continued 'do we know each other?'

'Yes. We have met once in the past. I recognized you the moment I saw you. Don't you remember me?' said the long haired one.

'No. I do beg your pardon but I really don't remember you.'

'Ah, Mr. Harinder, I don't blame you. Its' been many years since that meeting and my physical appearance too has changed. I am Kalam, Abdul Kalam. We met at Panbam Island in January of 1942 when you were on some official business over there. I was a young school going lad then. Remember?'

Harry remembered all right. Meeting the lad and the sage on that island after their wild goose, or rather wild gander, chase had come to a painful end.

'Yes I do remember now,' blurted out Harry. 'Gosh! You have really grown up. I had seen you as a young boy and now you are a fully grown man. Did you join the Air Force as per you desire?'

'No. I couldn't due to medical reasons. I am a scientist just as predicted by the sage at Panbam. What about you? Did his predictions come true in your case?' said the man through his cascading hair.

'Yes, to a large measure. And before the end of this evening I will also get to know what the future holds for me,' replied the Sikh jovially.

'And how is that?' asked the scientist.

'Well we are in the midst of a conclave as you may have observed. My future will be decided before the end of this meeting. Why don't you join us?'

The hirsute scientist looked around the assemblage and observed, 'well this throng looks more like a drinking caucus having a binge rather than a serious conclave to me. I can't accept your invitation though. I am on my way to the airport to catch a flight to the USSR. It just happened that I spotted you while I was on my way out of the hotel and could not resist the temptation of meeting you. I will not keep you away from your conference. I bid you good bye Mr. Harinder. It was nice running into you after so many years. I hope this conclave decides your future favourably and you continue to have a secure life as predicted by the learned one at Panbam.'

'And I also reciprocate your wishes young man. I hope you continue to do well in life,' said Harry. He stood up and walked his young friend up to the exit of the hotel and bid him farewell.

'Harinder I can see that the cameo by this unkempt young man certainly wasn't in your script; just like Matric's impromptu offering,' said Price. He again had a smug look on his face. He was enjoying himself at Harry's discomfiture. 'Now what would you be doing at Panbam, a place nearly 200 miles away from your station of duty?'

'*Sahib* we had gone to Panbam, which as the *sahib* will know, is also called Rameshwaram, to visit the holy temple of Lord Rama. The whole island is considered holy since Lord Rama had crossed over to Lanka, now called Ceylon, from there. Rameshwaram being so near to Madras, I considered it a once in a life time opportunity to visit this holy site of pilgrimage.'

'C'mon Harinder, don't give me this cock and bull story. I think I may have the missing piece of the puzzle within my grasp now. I think you went to Rameshwaram to catch the runaway. But I do not want to make any more conjectures in the tale. Why don't you come out of the denial mode and tell us what happened on that trip. The incident happened a long time ago and has ended on a happy note for all concerned. Why are you carrying the lie on your subconscious mind? Unload everything and you will sleep better.'

'Yeah, tell us how you caught the scooting *thambi* at Rameshwaram,' persisted, the Naval Officer.

'Yes tell us,' chorused a couple of more members.

Harry refreshed his drink and then he looked at his wife who gave him an affirmative nod of her head, he then looked at *thambi* who too gave him a thumbs up and last of all he looked at Matric and Lachu. Matric shrugged but it was Lachu the wrestler who gave a clear green signal, '*Sahib* already knows quite a lot. There are just a few grey areas in Prix *Sahib's* narrative. I think we should fill up the blanks for him and for eternity. After all we did what we did for honour of the regiment.

We did nothing to shame anybody. Surely the *sahib* understands us. You know how tender his heart is. He did not harm us when he could have done so and I am sure he will not take any step to ever hurt us. We are soldiers at heart and like to remain closer to the truth. In any case telling the truth never harmed anyone. So tell all, without fear. *Jo-hoega-so-hoega.'* This perhaps was the longest speech Lachu had made in his entire life. But whatever the wrestling simpleton had said had been said from the bottom of his heart; Que Sera Sera.

'Right then,' said Harry and took a deep gulp of scotch and soda, 'Prix Sahib Bahadur you assessed very rightly. The prisoner did run away from our custody from the moving train when we were in the suburbs of Madras. I was devastated. How was I to return to the unit and show my face to you? How was I to face my own community at having failed on a mission and that too during peace time? How was I going to live this one down for the rest of my life? I vowed to hunt the snake down to the end of the earth, catch him and bring him to you. There was no way that I was going to return empty handed to the unit. Our pursuit of the scallywag took us to Rameshwaram. That is where I met Kalam, whom you just saw talking to me. He was just a lad then with a lot of dreams.'

Harry then commenced his narrative. It took nearly fifty minutes for him, to unload himself of the burden he had carried for so long. In these fifty minutes his audience remained spellbound as he unfolded the story. He left out nothing, no detail, how-so-ever minor, was overlooked. Even the waiters replenishing their drinks realized the meeting had reached a state of sombreness and moved on tip toe to recharge empty glasses. Towards the end of his narrative Harry paused to take a sip of the amber liquid and then closed his account by saying, 'that *sahib bahadur* is the unabridged story of our trip to Madras.'

So saying, he excused himself and headed for the loo. The squeak of his leather shoes was audible over the pin drop silence in the hall, as he walked to the wash room. When Harry unloads he really unloads, in all manners of speaking. The squelch amongst the listeners remained in place long after Harry's squeaking shoes had announced his return from the toilet.

It was Price who broke the ice, 'Harry are you saying that the man sitting across holding the hand of the fair lady and known to me as *Thambi* alias Neville Devar is in fact not him!'

'In the present context it is him. And yet in another sense it not him, Prix *sahib*,' said Harry.

'I will be damned,' cussed the colonel under his breath. His cussing count had climbed to three since his entry into the Imperial. 'You successfully fooled me a decade and a half earlier. Don't confuse me with your semantics now, Harry.'

'We never had the intention to be-fool you, Prix sahib. The Englsh cannot be fooled. They are far too intelligent. I just did what I did on the spur of the moment due to force of circumstances. I have laid bare the entire truth before you. Remember *sahibs* this man seated on the other side, near the general, was awarded a medal for exceptional bravery in battle by the British Empire. And kingdoms don't award phonies. They award only the genuinely brave ones. So which one is genuine, the one who deserted even before a shot was fired or the one who faced and trounced the enemy in war? And mind you, he did so voluntarily. It is up to you to decide which of the two you consider as genuine,' belted out Harry.

It was Hodson who came in to the conversation by saying, 'all things considered everything turned out splendidly on the face of it. But two wrongs were done. One by Harinder by introducing an imposter into the army and the second wrong was done by you Price for unwittingly accepting the phony into the army. And as we English say "two wrongs don't make a right".'

'Don't be a grouch Eric. Harinder brought back a lion heart who, fetched laurels for the British Empire on that beach in Indonesia. You yourself decorated him on behalf of your King Monarch and now you have the temerity to refer him as a phony? And Colonel Price dealt with the case with understanding and compassion. But how would you understand empathy with men when you have never served with troops. All you have done is to push files in the Headquarters all your life sitting on your back side. I propose a toast to Harry.' So saying Sophie stood up and all followed suit, even the recalcitrant Hodson. All joined in toasting Harry's good health and the waiters got busy replenishing the drinks as soon as the gathering sat down once again.

'Well the missing piece in the jigsaw puzzle has been inserted by Harinder. And we English say "all is well that ends well". There is however one point still irking me,' said Price, 'I observed a lacuna in your briefing notes pertaining to "ex visit home" Harinder.'

'What mistake did the *Sahib* observe?'

'You had forgotten to give the mandatory time signal at the end of the briefing. How did you overlook that?'

'I deliberately ignored that *Sahib*. It was pointless to give a time signal because these two imbeciles did not possess watches at that time.' The listening delegates broke into smiles at this response.

'We however have watches now Prix *Sahib*,' barged in Lachu and Matric in unison, exposing their watch strapped left wrists towards Price.

They may be rich tycoons now but they continue to remain child-like and simple just as he had known them in the battalion when he commanded them, thought Price. 'I say, the time by your gold plated watches is nearing 9 pm. Your audacious plan worked to the hilt. The *Thambi* conundrum now stands completely solved. I think we should end this meeting on this happy and piquant note.'

'I agree with the Colonel. I just want to add that the account makes one helluva story,' said Sophie, 'maybe someone will put this chronicle to pen someday.'

'And what do you think will be an appropriate title of the story, if it is ever written,' queried Harry.

'The title would be, "THE THAMBI CONUNDRUM", what else?' offered one of the tipsy delegates.

'Why not "TWO WRONGS MAKE A WRITE"?' said another, giggling at his cleverness.

'How does "A MADRASI FROM PUNJAB" sound?' exclaimed Jagtar Kaur.

'Well, I would go for a "FOUR GOOD MEN",' said Colonel Price.

'Poppy cock,' called out Hodson. 'I offer the most appropriate title, "OF SCOUNDRELS AND SCALLYWAGS" for the tale.'

'The title put forward by you is most inappropriate. I think Harry and Neville are gentlemen and brave. They both did a good job under the circumstances. You are just being a spoil sport by suggesting such an inapt label for the story Eric,' countered Sophie.

The Royal Air Force delegate joined in the naming game by saying, 'I have witnessed conjurers change cards. I have also heard of card-sharps and gamblers swapping cards with a sleight of hand but here.' At this juncture he paused for effect and then continued, 'here, our Harry has managed to substitute a larger than life, King of Hearts in place of a Black Knave and . . . .'

'And that King of Hearts was dealt out to me by Harry,' interjected a happy Sophie, completing the sentence on behalf of the pilot.

The interruption did not put off the aviator. He quickly came back into the conversation, on the rebound, and said, what he had intended to say, 'and therefore what is stopping the future storyteller from naming the novel "SLEIGHT OF MAN"?' He wasn't going to let someone, even if that someone was the beautiful Sophie, steal his thunder by changing substance of his line of thought by a mid-sentence intrusion. After all he had flown thundering jet planes during his flying days.

'Hey, that's another nice one,' said Sophie. Then winking at the grinning listeners, who by now were her confidants, thanks to the alcohol, she continued, 'and gentlemen, with that King of Hearts, dished out to me, I won the game of love. Am I right my King?'

Devar nodded in agreement and said, 'You are so very right, my Queen of Hearts.'

Sophie picked up the thread of the conversation again and said in conclusion, 'I say guys, all the names suggested for the title of the book barring one, are good, really good. So the unknown future raconteur indeed has many choices. He may choose one of these or carve out another, even more suitable for the tale. Meanwhile this story will pass around by word of mouth and remain in army folklore till that someone reduces it to prose.'

'Yes indeed,' cut in a flushed Colonel Price.

Everyone, except Hodson, let off guffaws, giggles and deep throated gurgles of happy laughter and booming ayes of approval. The style and decibel level of the mirthful response of each was in direct proportion to his or her alcohol intake. And then all the merry men, including the sullen Hodson, rushed, to the place where Harry had gone before.

On re-emerging from the wash room they recharged their drinks. Still jovial, they continued to engage in joyful banter with each other on the extraordinary tale they had just heard while waiting for dinner to be announced. A smiling Sophie mingled with the jovial gathering and then turning around she faced Neville, stood on her toes and kissed him, her very own King of Hearts, squarely on the lips, to a resounding applause from the partying company.

End